A CASE OF
TWO CITIES

ALSO BY THE AUTHOR

FICTION

Death of a Red Heroine

A Loyal Character Dancer

When Red Is Black

POETRY TRANSLATION

Treasury of Chinese Love Poems

POETRY

Lines Around China

A CASE OF TWO CITIES

QIU XIAOLONG

St. Martin's Minotaur New York

This is a work of fiction. All of the characters, organizations, and events portrayed in this novel are either products of the author's imagination or are used fictitiously.

www.minotaurbooks.com

Design by Maggie Goodman

Library of Congress Cataloging-in-Publication Data

Qiu, Xiaolong, 1953–
A case of two cities / Qiu Xiaolong.
p. cm.
ISBN-13: 978-0-312-37466-2
ISBN-10: 0-312-37466-6
1. Chen, Inspector (Fictitious character)—Fiction. 2. Police—China—Shanghai—Fiction. 3. Shanghai (China)—Fiction. 4. Corruption investigation—Fiction. I. Title.

PS3553.H537 C37 2006
813'.6—dc22

2006047447

10 9 8 7 6 5 4

*Journey**

IN MEMORY OF MONA VAN DUYN
1921–2004

Out of the train window,
the gaping windows of the buildings
are telling stories all along the line,
about the past, the present, and the future.
I am not the teller of the stories,
nor the audience,
simply passing through there,
then, full of ignorance,
so full of imagination.

The high tension cables
outline the score of the evening.

Simply passing there,
then—"Next stop is Halle."

* I wrote the poem during a trip in Germany, looking out of the train window, when I was seized by an inexplicable sadness, and upon my return to the States, I learned about the death of my friend, Mona Van Duyn.

ACKNOWLEDGMENTS

No book is an island, entire of itself, but is involved in others, among which, particularly, Keith Kahla, with his great editorial work; S. J. Rozan, with her generous friendship; and René Viénet, with his grand support.

A CASE OF
TWO CITIES

PROLOGUE

AN ANONYMOUS PHONE CALL came to the Fujian Police Bureau at 1:15 a.m. on that early May night.

"Come to Inebriating Money and Intoxicating Gold immediately. Room 135. You will find front page stuff for the *Fujian Star*."

Sergeant Lou Xiangdong, the cop who answered the phone, had heard of the place before. It was a so-called karaoke center, but really known for its karaoke-covered sexual service among the corrupt officials and businessmen. The *Fujian Star* was a local tabloid newspaper founded in the mid-nineties. The telephone call delivered an unmistakable message: there was something scandalous going on in that room.

But Lou felt sleepy and grumpy. He had chosen to work on this late shift for the night subsidy. A bachelor reaching his mid-thirties, he had just met a lovely girl, with whom he was going to have dim sum the next morning, and a week's subsidy would probably cover the expense. He had been dreaming of golden bamboo steamers of the mini shrimp buns and crab dumplings, her crispy laughter rippling in a tiny cup of Dragon Well tea, and her white fingers tearing the green lotus leaf off the sticky rice chicken for him . . .

The police bureau received this sort of anonymous call occasionally, but most of them were false alarms. With corruption spreading like an uncontrollable plague all over the country and the gap between the poor and the rich increasing, people reacted out of their frustration. Consequently, when cops hurried out to those notorious entertainment places, more often than not they found decent businesses there, the K girls—karaoke girls allegedly hired to sing along with companionless clients—dressed demurely, as if still buttoned up with the puritan codes of Mao's time. People knew too well, however, what they really performed, totally unbuttoned, behind the closed doors of private K rooms.

But Lou was not so sure about the calls being false alarms or practical jokes. Infamous resorts like Inebriating Money and Intoxicating Gold were known to be associated with high-ranking officials in the city government, with insider tips readily available to them. That was probably why the police raids had ended up fetching water with a bamboo basket—total failures.

Despite this, the sergeant made up his mind to go. The informer sounded urgent, with a specific room number too, and like other low-level cops, Lou was concerned about the corruption getting out of control in "China's brand of socialism." He did not mention anything to his colleagues, and he took an office cell phone and set out in a jeep.

Ten minutes later, he walked into the club. In the large entrance hall of Inebriating Money and Intoxicating Gold, he saw a stage at one side, with a bevy of girls strutting around in bikinis, and in the mist, a willowy girl in transparent gauze with cloudlike trails danced barefoot to lambent music, which floated out of the imitation Dunhuang murals behind. Off the stage, a line of K girls waited in their black mini slips and transparent slippers. One of them rose and flurried toward Lou, reaching out her skinny, pasty arms like clipped chicken wings. It reminded him of a brothel scene in an old movie. From the private rooms along the somberly lit corridor, he heard a chorus of moaning and groaning. Two or three clients in the hall were moving among the K girls like fish in the water, bargaining with a muscular night manager in a black Tang costume.

Lou turned to the night manager, who started an introduction, grinning though a ring of his cigarette smoke.

"My name is Pang. We are pleased to offer you our service. Puncturing the clock costs a hundred yuan. For a rich and successful man like you, you will definitely need more. Puncturing the clock three times, I would say. Not including the amount for puncturing the hole. For the whole night, you can enjoy a wholesale discount. You may discuss the details with the girl you choose. Take a look at Meimei. So beautiful, so talented. She can play your jade flute into a soul-ravishing song."

Pang must have taken Lou for a new client. Puncturing the clock probably meant half an hour or an hour, Lou supposed, but he did not have to guess about "puncturing the hole" or "playing the jade flute."

Lou took out his badge. "Take me to Room 135."

Startled like a wakened sleepwalker, Pang tried in vain to convince the cop that no one was there. When they arrived at the room in question, the door was locked, with no light coming out of it. At Lou's insistence, the night manager took out a key, opened the door, and turned on the light.

The light outlined a sordid scene. On a sofa bed lay two naked bodies, their legs still entwined like fried dough sticks. A middle-aged man with gray-streaked hair and long hairy limbs slept next to a young girl, thin, ill-developed, perhaps only seventeen or eighteen, with slack breasts and a broad patch of black hair over her groin. The room stank of sex and other suspicious odors. The glaring light failed to wake them up.

Walking over to the bed with a frown, Lou shoved the man on the shoulder. When the man showed no sign of response, Lou leaned down and was shocked to find him dead. The girl slept on, a luscious smile playing on her lips, her hand resting on his cold belly.

A more stunning discovery came to Lou. The dead man was none other than Detective Hua Ting, the head of the special case squad of the Fujian Police. Impulsively, Lou grabbed a blanket to cover the body before he pulled back the dead man's eyelid—a bloodshot eye stared back at him with an unfathomable message. The corneas were not exactly opaque, which suggested that the death was recent. He turned to pick up Hua's clothing, which was scattered on the ground, and felt something bulging in the pants pocket. It was a pack of cigarettes, Flying Horse.

Across the room, the girl finally stirred and awoke. Opening her eyes, she appeared terrified. She jumped up, fell down, and tossed her head from side to side, her naked body twitching like a rice-paddy eel. Lou then realized that he should take pictures of the crime scene.

"Don't move," he shouted, holding the camera while she broke into a hysterical fit of screaming and squirming. The pictures might truly be stuff for the *Fujian Star*. He would never do that, though. Hua had been one of his trainers upon his entrance into the police.

"The eighteenth level down in hell, rats and snakes," she sobbed, like she was still struggling in a nightmare, her eyes vacant. "Old Third, I want to cut your damned bird to a thousand pieces. A small sip, like a teardrop. Never seen him. Never known him."

Getting anything coherent from her was out of the question. Lou had to call the bureau. This was a scandalous case, and the bureau might be anxious to control the damage to its public image, especially since corrupt cops had started to appear on Chinese TV series. No one seemed to be immune, incorrigible, in the age of Inebriating Money and Intoxicating Gold, even a veteran officer like Hua. Lou decided to make a phone call to the bureau head, Ren Jiaye. It was a long call, and Lou came to an abrupt stop toward the end of his report.

"What's wrong?" Ren asked.

Something disturbed him. Lou recalled the case assigned to Hua—"China's number one corruption case," as described in the *People's Daily*. It was an investigation of Xing Xing, a high-ranking Fujian Party cadre and business tycoon with an empire of smuggling operations under him, run through his connections at all government levels. To be exact, it was an investigation of the corrupt officials connected with Xing since Xing had fled the country. But it was only a hunch at the moment, Lou thought, and he did not mention it to the bureau head.

Finishing his report, Lou hung up with the bureau and dug out Hua's home number. He hesitated. He started pacing about the room, the girl sobbing like a broken electronic flute, and Pang still standing like a terra cotta figure in a Tang tomb.

Lou tried to rehearse what he was going to say to Hua's widow, but it was a daunting task. He finally decided to wait until the next morning. To his surprise, a group from Internal Security, headed by Commander Zhu Longhua, arrived at the scene in less than twenty minutes. The appearance of Internal Security, trusted by the Party authorities in circumstances of "highly political sensitivity," made sense—the dead was a cop possibly involved in a sex scandal—but their speediness was amazing, especially since it was already after midnight. Internal Security lost no time taking over. Without even listening to his report about the crime scene, they ordered Lou out as they started searching, questioning, and shooting pictures in the room.

Shoved out of the room by Internal Security, Lou and Pang were left looking at each other like two clay images. Neither of them knew what to do. Lou was in no position to argue with Internal Security, however baffling their way of doing the job. They had not even questioned Pang.

Pang handed Lou a cigarette. It was a Camel, far more expensive than the Flying Horse in Hua's pant pocket.

"Have you seen Inspector Hua here before, Pang?"

"No. I have worked here about three years, and I have never seen him."

"What about the girl?"

"Oh, Nini. She's not a regular. A temporary girl without the K permit, and we follow the government regulations strictly."

It was absurd that K girls had to receive professional ethics training before obtaining a K license, Lou reflected, but it was not his business for the moment.

"When did you come to work tonight?"

"Around eight. I did not know there was anyone in that room, there was nothing in the record. It doesn't make sense, unless Nini sneaked Hua in before my shift."

Lou thought Pang was telling the truth. As they finished their second cigarettes, Commander Zhu came out, shaking his head. He too lit a cigarette, drew the smoke into his lungs, and turned to address Lou.

"According to the girl, Hua was a regular customer here. Though only in his early fifties, he had problems getting an erection. So he usually took Tiger and Dragon Power, a drug smuggled in from south Asia. Very expensive on the black market, and effective too. Early this evening, he finished half a bottle of liquor, and popped in a double dose of Power. She was not aware of any difference in him, she said, except that he came twice that night, and the second time in the back. Exhausted, they both fell asleep. She was totally unaware of the change in the man lying beside her."

Lou was stunned. Through the half open door, he caught a glimpse of the girl trembling hysterically at the foot of the sofa bed. How could Internal Security have obtained a confession from her so quickly? Zhu stepped back into the room and shut the door after him.

Lou thought of the earlier remarks made by Pang, who looked more puzzled than before. Lou accepted another cigarette from him. Doubts rose in the spiraling smoke. As the head of the special case squad, Hua was known to have been a capable cop and a good man. He had never heard of the detective engaging in indecent activities. Lou also recalled the blank, almost drugged expression on the girl's face. If things had happened the way Zhu had just described, she should have reacted differently when Sergeant Lou entered the room earlier.

"A hundred coffins. Perhaps the first one," Lou murmured in spite of himself, grinding out the cigarette.

"Coffin?" Pang repeated in utter confusion.

Lou did not explain. More suspicions barged into his mind. Hua's colleagues had worried about his latest assignment. Xing was reputed to be one with a long arm reaching into the skies. To investigate the high-ranking officials behind Xing was to bring a hornet's nest about one's ears.

In a recent press conference, the premier of the Chinese government had made a statement about the corruption eating up the system like cancer. "To fight against those corrupt Party officials, I have prepared one hundred coffins. Ninety-nine for them, one for myself." It was not a pompous speech to impress the audience. With those Party officials interwoven into "a gigantic net covering the heaven and earth," it was not inconceivable that the premier might fall as a victim.

"Have you seen the latest episode of Judge Bao on TV? The swarthy-faced judge who carries a coffin for himself all the way to the palace."

"Judge Bao?" Pang repeated. "You mean the legend of the incorruptible Judge Bao in the Song dynasty?"

The premier's coffin metaphor might have been an echo from the old legend. In his efforts to punish law-breaking officials, Judge Bao pulled a coffin all the way to the emperor, as a token of his determination to fight to the bitter end. Now, about a thousand years later, Hua had met an infamous end shortly after he had gotten a similar assignment.

Once again Zhu came out. "Lou, you don't have to stay here anymore. It has been a long night for you, we know. We are going to send Hua and Nini to the hospital for tests, and put him into the mortuary afterward. You may notify his family if you want to."

It was the last thing Lou wanted to. Hua had only a sick, old wife left behind. Their only son, an educated youth, had died in a tractor accident in the countryside during the Cultural Revolution. Lou wondered if the old woman could survive the blow of losing her husband too.

"I'll go to the hospital too. After all, Hua was my colleague for many years. It is up to me to accompany him, I think, for the last part of his journey."

Lou drove at the back of the convoy of vehicles that took Hua's body to a special army hospital. As before, Lou had to wait outside in the corridor, watching as the old cop under the white sheet was pulled in, followed by Internal Security. Again, he could do nothing but smoke, affixing a second cigarette to the butt of the first one. All these years, Lou recalled with a bitter taste in his mouth, Hua had smoked Flying Horse, one of the cheapest brands. It spelled a face loss in this gilded age, but Hua had had no choice. The medical bill for his wife was no longer covered by the state-run company on the edge of bankruptcy. How could Hua have had the money to be a regular customer in a karaoke club—with Flying Horse in his pocket? Lou added a third cigarette to the first two. It looked almost like an antenna, trembling in a pathetic effort to catch imperceptible information from the surrounding blank walls.

Initial test results came out. The medical examination proved that the girl had had sex earlier that night and the remaining semen detected in her vagina was from Hua. The autopsy had to wait until morning. According to the doctor, an overdose of the Tiger and Dragon Power could have led to a heart attack. Internal Security had found a package of the drug in Hua's pocket.

That was the last nail knocked into the coffin. Lou staggered. The cell phone started ringing like bells. Calls from people both in and out of the bureau. He was surprised at the speed the news spread around. It was still early. Everyone was shocked, and no one believed that Hua could have done something like that.

Lou even got a long-distance call from Yu Keji, nicknamed Old Hunter, who was a retired Shanghai cop with a national police information network. Perhaps people did not have to be too cautious talking to a retired man. Old Hunter seemed to know a lot about the Xing case assigned to Detective Hua.

"I don't believe a single word of it, Sergeant Lou. I've known Hua for twenty years. All that must have been a setup," Old Hunter said. "Have you found anything suspicious?"

Lou told the old man what suspicions he had for the night.

"Damned Internal Security must have been part of it. Today's China is like a rice barn ravaged by those red rats. A good man like Hua tried to do something about it, but what?"

"Yes, those corrupt Party officials, like fattened rats. But why call them red rats?" Lou asked.

"Those Party officials are of course politically red—before their corruptions are exposed. The so-called red spearhead of the proletariat marching along the road of the socialist construction. But they are really barn rats moving all around. The one-party system is like a specially designed barn, where they can run amok without getting caught. Why? Because the barn is theirs. Nothing independent of this system can challenge or question it. Think about the Xing case. To smuggle on such a large scale involves a long chain of numerous links—ministry, custom, police, border inspection, transportation, distribution, and whatnot. And this chain of connection and corruption worked all the way—"

"You are right, Old Hunter." Lou recalled another nickname for the retired cop—Suzhou Opera Singer, a reference to a popular southern dialect opera known for its singers' tactics of prolonging a narrative by adding digressions or ancient anecdotes. But it was too late to stop the old man.

"In the Qing dynasty," Old Hunter went on, "high-ranking Manchurian officials wore red-topped hats. If an official happened to do business on the side, people would call him a red-topped businessman. It was such a notorious term at the time that few liked to be called so. Nowadays it is taken for granted. And those officials are hardly businessmen. They simply steal or smuggle, like Xing, like rats in their own barn. So how could they let an honest cop get in there?"

"Yes, it's a warning to those who try to investigate the case in earnest." Lou had to cut the old man short. It was a long-distance call.

"Another cop wasted," Old Hunter said with a long sigh. "It's a damned profession. I made a huge mistake having my son succeed my job."

"But Detective Yu has been doing fine—together with his boss, Chief Inspector Chen," Lou said in sincerity. "The two are almost like a legend, you know, in the police force."

"People shoot at a bird reaching its head out. Lao Zi put it so well thousands of years ago. It's not easy to be a good cop these days, let alone a well-known good cop like Chen. I'm devastated, but I'm no Old Hunter unless I can kill some damned rats for Hua. Let me know if there's anything I can do for him. Also, buy a wreath for him on my behalf. I'll mail the money to you."

"I'll do that, and I'll call you too," Lou promised. "I, too, want to do something."

Looking at his watch, he realized that he had missed dim sum with his new girlfriend. He wondered if she would forgive him. He might try to explain everything to her, but then he thought the better of it. Nowadays, it was not considered too bad to be a cop, not as Old Hunter had declared. However, one had to be a clever cop. Hua was not. Nor was Lou, perhaps. If she learned that, their relationship would be tossed out like a dirty crumpled napkin in the dim sum restaurant.

1

CHIEF INSPECTOR CHEN CAO, of the Shanghai Police Bureau, was invited to a mega bathhouse, Birds Flying, Fishes Jumping, on a May afternoon.

According to Lei Zhenren, editor of *Shanghai Morning,* they would have all their worries luxuriously washed away there. "*How much concern do you have? / It is like spring flood / of a long river flowing east.* This ultramodern bathhouse is really unique. Characteristics of the Chinese brand of socialism. You won't see anything else like it in the world."

Lei knew how to persuade, having quoted for the poetry-liking chief inspector three lines from Li Yu, the Southern Tang emperor poet. "Characteristics of the Chinese brand of socialism" was a political catchphrase, which carried a discordant connotation, especially in the context of the unprecedented materialistic transformation sweeping over the city of Shanghai. As it happened, Chen had just read about the bathhouse in an English publication:

Every weekend night, about two thousand Chinese and several dozen foreigners gather together naked at Niaofei Yuyao—a gigantic bath-

house, where the masses soak in tubs of milk, sweat in the "fire jade heat room," watch movies, and swim in the pool. It's public and legal. After a round of miniature golf (clothing required), you can get a massage (clothing removed) and watch a Vegas-style show (the audience in pajamas, the performers in less than pajamas) . . .

It took Chen two or three minutes to figure out the exact wording from the Chinese phonetics *niaofei yuyao*—"birds flying and fishes jumping." The name of the bathhouse actually came from an ancient proverb: *The sea so wide for fishes to jump, the sky so high for birds to fly,* which meant figuratively "infinite possibilities." Perhaps too pompous a name for a bathhouse, yet a plausible allusion to its size and services. So he responded, "Such a bath may be too luxurious, Lei. I now have a hot shower in my own apartment, you know."

"Come on, Comrade Chief Inspector Chen. If you flash your business card, the owner of the bathhouse will come rushing over, barefoot, to welcome you in. A high-flying Party cadre, and a well-published poet to boot, you deserve a good break. Health is the capital for making socialist revolution, as Chairman Mao said long ago."

Chen had known Lei for years, first through the Writers' Association, to which both had belonged. Lei had majored in Chinese literature, and Chen in Western literature. But early on, they had both been state-assigned to their respective jobs, regardless of their own interests. Starting out as an entry-level business reporter, Lei had since enjoyed a steady rise. When *Shanghai Morning* was founded the previous year, he was appointed the editor-in-chief. Like other newspapers, *Shanghai Morning* was still under the ideological control of the government but responsible for its own financial welfare. So Lei made every effort to turn the newspaper into a more readable one, instead of one simply full of polished political clichés. The efforts had paid off, and the newspaper rapidly grew popular, almost catching up with the *Wenhui Daily* in its circulation.

Lei talked about treating Chen—in celebration of the newspaper's success. It was an invitation Chen found difficult to decline. For all these years, Lei had made a point of publishing Chen's poems in his newspapers.

But he could not be too cautious, Chen thought, in his position, in the days of *guanxi*—connections spreading all over the city like a gigantic web. "My treat, Lei," he said. "Last time you bought me a great lunch at Xinya. It should be my turn now."

"Tell you what, Chen. I'm writing about the latest Shanghai entertainments. No fun for me to go there alone. So you're doing me a favor. Business expense, of course."

"Well, no private room or private service, then."

"You don't have to tell me that. It's not a good idea for people like you or me to be seen in those private rooms. Particularly in the heat of another anticorruption campaign."

"Yes, it's the headlines again," Chen said, "in your newspaper."

Niaofei Yuyao turned out to be a six-story sprawling building on Jumen Road. The dazzling lobby, lit with crystal chandeliers, struck Chen more like a five-star American hotel. The entrance fee was two hundred yuan per person, with additional charges for services requested inside, a stolid manager explained, giving each of them a shining silver bracelet with a number attached to it.

"Like dim sum," Lei said, "you'll pay at the end of it, with all the services added to your number."

A reporterlike young man sidled over, carrying a camera with a long zoom sticking out like a gun. The manager rose to wave his hand in a flurry: "Pictures are not allowed here."

Chen was surprised. "If the picture is going to appear in a newspaper like yours," he said in a whisper, "it may bring in more business."

"Well, a large tree brings in a gusty wind against itself," Lei commented, changing into plastic slippers. "This bathhouse doesn't need any more free advertisement, or the city government may feel obliged to check into its incredible business."

The pool area was the size of three or four soccer fields, not including the area for women. The water of three large pools shimmered green in the soft light. Majestic marble statues and fountains stood in each of them, imitations of ancient Roman palaces, except for an impressive array of modern water massage appliances along the poolsides. There were also special tubs with signs such as BEER, GINSENG, MILK, and HERBS. The brownish froth in the beer tub formed a sharp contrast to the white ripples over the milk tub. Chen looked into a gauze bag floating in the ginseng tub—expensive if the thick roots it contained were genuine, though he was not so sure of their medical benefit in the hot bathwater.

"These tubs are supposed to be effective," Lei said with a grin.

"And very expensive too."

"The pools alone could have cost millions. A gamble on the boost the WTO accession will deliver to Shanghai—an economic restructuring with waves of overseas capital inflows. China is currently the second-largest destination for foreign investment after the U.S. Soon it will be the largest."

Lei was taking an MBA class in the evening. For the new newspaper, he had to know things beyond his major in Chinese literature years earlier.

"So you're writing an article about the bathhouse?"

"Not just about this place, but the latest entertainment trends in general. Eat, drink, bathe, sleep, and whatnot. A middle class is rising up fast in China. They have money, and they need to know how to spend money. As an editor, I have to write what they want to read."

"Indeed, pools of wine, woods of flesh," Chen said, echoing a classical description about the decaying Shang dynasty palace, as he stepped into a steaming hot pool.

"Oh, much, much more," Lei chuckled in high spirits, "like the Winter Palace in Russia, except it's so warm here, like the spring water. Or like in the late Roman empire."

Chen reclined against the poolside, the water massaging his back and purring as if with a collective contentment, including his. He tried to recall the name of the poet Lei had quoted, but without success.

"What are you thinking, Chen?"

"Nothing—my mind is relaxing in a total blank, as you suggested."

"Take it easy, Chen, with your new position in the city congress, and with your name as a best-selling poet."

To all appearances, Chen had been moving up steadily. His new membership in the Shanghai People's Congress was seen as another step toward his succeeding Party Secretary Li Guohua in the police bureau. But Chen was not so sure about it. The congress was known as a political rubber stamp, and thus city congressman was more of an honorary title. Possibly a compromise more than anything else, Chen knew, for quite a few hard-liners in the Party opposed his further promotion in the bureau, on the grounds of his being too liberal.

It was true, however, that his poetry collection had enjoyed unexpected success. Poetry makes no money and, in a money-oriented age, its publication was nothing short of a miracle. And it was actually selling well.

His thoughts were interrupted by two new bathers flopping down into the water, one short with gray hair and beady eyes, one tall with an aquiline nose and beer-bottle-thick glasses. Apparently, they were continuing an earlier argument.

"Socialism is going to the dogs. These greedy, unscrupulous dogs of the Party officials! They're crunching everything to pieces, and devouring all the bones," the short one declared in indignation. "Our state-run company is like a gigantic fat goose, and everyone must take a bite or pluck a feather or two from it. Did you know that the head of the City Export Office demands a five percent bonus in exchange for his export quota approval?"

"What can you do, man?" the tall one said sarcastically. "Communism echoes only in nostalgia songs. It's capitalism that's practiced here—with the Communist Party sitting on the top, sucking a red lollipop. So what can you expect of these Party cadres?"

"Corrupt throughout. They don't believe in anything except doing everything in their own interest—in the name of China's brand of socialism."

"What is capitalism? Everybody grabs for his or her money—in spite of all the communist propaganda in our newspapers. They're just like the beer froth in the tub."

"The cops should have bang-banged a few of those rotten eggs!"

"Cops?" the tall one said, splashing the water with his big feet. "They're jackals out of one and the same den as those wolves."

Chen frowned. Complaints about the widespread corruption were not surprising, but some of the specifics did not sound too pleasant to a naked cop, or to a naked editor either.

"Chinese is still an evolving language. Corruption—*fubai*—literally means 'rotten,'" Chen said in a quiet voice to Lei, "in reference to bad meat or fish. Now it refers exclusively to the abuse of power by the Party cadres."

"Yes, things go bad easily," Lei said. "You can put Yellow River carps into the refrigerator, but you can't put in the Party cadres."

It was intriguing to think about the linguistic evolution. In the sixties, corruption meant the rotten bourgeois way of life, in reference to something like extramarital sex. A young "corrupt" teacher in Chen's school was fired for engaging in prenuptial sex. In a more general sense, the word could also have referred to bourgeois extravagancy—even to such a bath, whose entrance fee alone cost more than the monthly income for an ordinary worker. In the last few years, however, the word took on an exclusive target—the Party officials.

"In Mao's time, corruption was hardly a serious issue in that sense," Lei said nodding. "In the stagnant state economy, everybody earned about the same, in accordance to the old Marxist principle: to each according to his need, from each according to his capability. But after the Cultural Revolution, people have become disillusioned with all the ideological propaganda."

"A spiritual vacuum. That worries me."

"Let's see things in a different perspective," Lei said, stepping out of the pool. "After all, China's been making great progress. Those two bigmouthed bathers, for instance, could have talked themselves into prison during the Cultural Revolution."

"You can say that again," Chen said, aware of something he and Lei had in common. They, too, could be cynical about or critical of the system, but in the last analysis, they were rather defensive of it.

Lei called his attention to the shower rooms lined along one side, each with an outlandish name: Pistol, Needle, Five-Element, Yin/Yang, Chain, Mist . . .

"I'm like Granny Liu walking into the Grand View Garden," Chen said. In the classic Chinese novel, *The Dream of the Red Chamber,* Granny

Liu was a country bumpkin, totally awestruck by the splendor of the garden. "Look at the Jade and Fire Sauna Room."

"Today you can do everything with money."

"We cops are really in trouble, then."

Lei did not answer, perhaps too busy experimenting with something called Zhou-Heaven-Circulation: he sat on a steel stool with an iron bar cage hanging overhead. The showerhead jerked out a spray of water, and he jumped out like a monkey in *The Pilgrim to the West.*

They then filed through a "dry up room," where they were wiped by attendants with large towels and invited to change into the special red-and-white-striped pajamas before taking the elevator.

"The fourth floor is the recreation area—billiards, Ping-Pong, basketball, and a fishing pool, too, with a lot of golden carps—"

"Let's skip that, Lei."

"Fine. I'm hungry today. Let's eat first."

The third floor entrance led into a marketlike place, where stood rows of large water tanks with swimming fishes and jumping shrimps. Large shelves displayed a variety of dishes and pots wrapped in plastic, vivid in color and shape. A sort of live menu. A waitress, also in red-and-white-striped pajamas, came over. At her recommendation, they ordered pork rib soup with tulips in a stainless-steel pot over a liquid gas stove, steamed live bass with ginger and green onion scattered over a blue and white platter, water-immersed beef covered with red pepper in a large bowl, tomato cups with peeled shrimp, and chunks of fried rice-paddy eel on bamboo sticks. They also requested two bottles of ice beer.

The waitress led them to a table, her wooden slippers clacking pleasant notes on the hardwood floor. The dining hall had a uniform atmosphere, probably the result of the identical red-and-white-striped pajamas worn by everyone there.

"We have realized communism here, or the appearance of it. Everybody looks the same—at least in clothing," Lei said, raising his chopsticks. "But look at that large table, the so-called Complete Manchurian and Han Banquet. The name, if you were wondering, originated from the need for a united front during the Qing dynasty. To demonstrate his solidarity, the Manchurian emperor had delicacies from various ethnic cuisines served on one table in the Forbidden City. Camel dome, bear paw, swallow's nest, monkey brains . . ."

"Every rare and expensive item imaginable under the sun," Chen said, glancing toward the impressive table. "Those upstarts show off like anything."

"Well, it's no longer an age of showing off just for the sake of doing so. It's a banquet for *guanxi*. Big bucks in the business for big bugs in the government," Lei said, putting a chunk of beef onto Chen's plate.

"As Old Master Du said," Chen replied, *"The meat and wine go bad behind the vermilion door; / by the roadside lie the bodies starved to death."*

"Life is short," Lei said. "Let's eat and drink."

Across the aisle, a young girl was putting her bare foot on an old man's thigh, her red toenails like rose petals blossoming out of his carrot-thick fingers.

After the meal, they moved down to the rest area on the second floor. It consisted of large halls and small private rooms. The halls were for common customers, where men and women kept coming and going in their striped pajamas. Private rooms came in different sizes, providing privacy and special service at varying prices.

"Look, it's Tong Tian, the head of Zhabei District," Lei whispered, casting a suggestive look toward a man stepping into the private room across the aisle.

"Yes, Secretary Tong. I recognize him too."

"He sent his wife and daughter abroad. Vancouver. His daughter studies in a private school. They have a mansion there."

"Well—" Chen understood the implication. Tong's government salary was perhaps about the same as Chen's. It took no brains to figure out Tong's means of supporting his family abroad.

"With the door closed, a couple of pretty young girls at your service, a few thousand yuan could go in a snap of fingers. The room fee alone costs five hundred yuan an hour." Lei concluded with an unexpected twist: "If our Party cadres were all like you, China would have realized communism."

The hall appeared cozy, comfortable. Each customer had a soft recliner and a side table for drinks and snacks, and two large projection TVs showed an American movie. In front of them, massage girls kept walking back and forth, like bats flitting in the dusk.

"We've talked enough corruption for an evening," Chen said. "Not a pleasant topic after a rich meal."

But it was not simply a matter of indigestion. The expense for the afternoon would be more than Lei's socialist monthly salary. As a Party cadre, Lei had a comfortable business expense allowance—supposedly in the interests of the newspaper. According to a Chinese proverb, Chen recalled in self-deprecating humor, those fleeing for fifty steps should not laugh at those fleeing for a hundred steps.

"Don't worry, Chen," Lei said, as if having read his thought. "When you are no longer shocked at the sight of a devil, the devil will go away."

That was also a Chinese proverb. The devil of unbridled corruption, however, might be a different story. Presently, two massage girls came over to them, both dressed in the red-and-white-striped pajamas, except that they were in short sleeves and short pants, their bare arms and legs glistening in the dark.

Lei had already given the order. "Back massage to start with."

The girl for Chen appeared to be only seventeen or eighteen. She helped him remove the pajama top and rubbed oil on his back. He looked back over his shoulder and glimpsed a slender and fragile-looking figure kneeling over him in the semidarkness, her arms moving in rhythm, and her fingers concentrating on the troubled spots. It was an exotic experience, which reminded him of a remark Lei had made: "In the late Roman empire."

The Roman empire fell, Chen thought, with his face pressed against a soft pillow, because of corruption and decadence. Lei probably had not meant it. For him, the newspaper empire had just started.

The girl was turning him over again. Perching herself on a low stool, she placed his feet on her lap, and his toes seemed to be touching her soft breasts through the thin pajama material. "Your feet make my heart jump," she said in a husky voice, her face flushed with exertion, her brow beaded with sweat. Then unexpectedly, she leaned down and put his big toe into her mouth. He was too flustered to stop her, his toe lollipop-like on her soft warm tongue.

Then his cell phone rang. He took it out from under the pillow. Not too many knew his number, which he had just changed.

"Comrade Chief Inspector Chen Cao?"

"Speaking."

"I'm Zhao Yan, of the Central Party Discipline Committee. I am speaking to you on behalf of the committee."

"Oh, Comrade Secretary Zhao Yan."

Chen immediately snapped to attention. Zhao was a legendary figure in Beijing. Having joined the Party in the forties and rising to a top government position early in his career, he spent a large part of the Cultural Revolution studying in jail, and he reemerged as one of the few self-made top Party intellectuals. It was said that Comrade Deng Xiaoping had adopted a number of suggestions made by Zhao in the beginning of the economic reform. Zhao was the Second Secretary of the Party Discipline Committee in the early eighties, founded as an inner-Party self-policing measure. Because of the cadre retirement policy, he then retired to an honorable position. But he remained a most influential man for the committee, which became increasingly powerful in the Party's effort to fight corruption.

"I'm retired, only an advisor now. Call me Comrade Zhao. Is this a good moment to talk to you?"

"Please go ahead, Comrade Zhao." There was no telling him that the chief inspector was luxuriating in a bathhouse, half-naked, with a half-naked girl sucking his toes. He waved his hand at her, jumped down, picked up a towel, and ran out to the corridor.

"You must be aware of our new anticorruption campaign?"

"I have been reading about it," Chen said, wiping the sweat from his forehead with the towel.

"Have you read about the case of Xing Xing?"

"Yes, I have been following its development."

Lei came out too, with concern on his face and a glass of wine in his hand. He might have overhead something in connection with the name of Zhao Yan, and he handed over the wine without speaking a word. Chen took it, and he raised the phone as a gesture of apology before Lei moved back in.

"Xing has caused a huge loss to our national economy, and great damage to our political image. Having fled to the United States, he continues making no end of trouble there."

Chen did not know anything about Xing's activities abroad. There seemed to be quite a lot about Xing in the newspapers. People could be cynical about believing what they read, but when it came to brazen corruption cases involving senior officials, most readers seemed willing to suspend their usual skepticism. But little was written about Xing's flight and afterward.

"Our committee is determined to push the investigation to the end. Anyone involved, no matter how high his position, will be punished. As our premier has pointed out, corruption can be a cancer of our body politic. It is an issue concerning the future of our Party, and our country too."

"Yes, we have to deal a crushing blow to those rotten elements in our Party," Chen said, echoing. "A crushing blow."

"It's more easily said than done, Comrade Chief Inspector Chen. We kept a close watch over Xing, but he got away with his family. How? It still beats me."

"Possibly through his connections—" Chen stopped, not completing the sentence: *at the top*.

"Now he is dragging China through the mire, presenting himself as a victim of a power struggle, and making false accusations against the Chinese government. We have to do something about it."

"How, Comrade Zhao?"

"All the information will be delivered to you. You are in charge of the investigation in Shanghai."

"What am I supposed to do in Shanghai?" Chen said. "Xing is in the States."

"Xing got away, but not those connected with him. Dig three feet into the ground if need be. You are fully authorized by the committee to take any necessary action. You are a *qinchai dacheng*—Emperor's Special Envoy with an

Imperial Sword, so to speak. In an emergency, you are empowered to search and arrest without reporting to anyone—without a warrant."

Chen did not like the term *Emperor's Special Envoy,* with its feudalistic connotation. In a Beijing opera, Chen had seen such a powerful figure with a shining sword in his hand. It was a high title, but it indicated an assignment involving people even higher up.

"But what about my work in the bureau, Comrade Zhao?"

"I'll talk to your Party Secretary Li. It's a case directly under the committee."

Afterward, Chen did not want to go back in. He was not in the mood to return to the hall, where the girl might not have finished her job. There was still some wine left sparkling in the cup.

A short poem by Wang Han, an eighth-century Tang dynasty poet, came to mind:

Oh the mellow wine shimmering
in the luminous stone cup!
I am going to drink
on the horse
when the army Pipa starts
urging me to charge out.

Oh, do not laugh
if I fall dead
drunk in the battlefield.
How many soldiers
have come really back home
since time immemorial?

The poem carried a disturbing premonition. Chen was not a superstitious man, but why his sudden recollection of those lines? Surely Chief Inspector Chen looked like anything but such a general, standing in the corridor with a white towel wrapped about his shoulders.

Across the corridor, the door of the private room opened silently. A massage girl walked out, barefoot, much prettier than those in the hall room, her slender fingers tying up the string of her scarlet silk bralike *dudou* at her back, her hair tousled, her face flushing like a dream.

2

CHIEF INSPECTOR CHEN PLANNED to stay at home the following morning, reading the material about Xing. The initial part had been delivered to him in five bulging folders the previous night. There was also a special one-page document, a statement on the letterhead of the Party Discipline Committee.

"Comrade Chen Cao, of the Shanghai Police Bureau, is hereby authorized by the Party Discipline Committee to take whatever action necessary for the investigation. Full cooperation with his work is expected at all government levels in the Party's interest."

There was not only a red seal of the committee imprinted underneath the statement but also the signature of Comrade Zhao. It was not just a gesture, it could serve like the imperial sword in ancient history: *execute before reporting to the emperor.*

He started studying the file on Xing. Secret surveillance of Xing must have been going on for a long time. Some of the reports were quite detailed, covering the length of several months. Chen had to get a general picture before making a move.

He took only one short break. Around nine-thirty, he went out to a hawking street-corner peddler and bought a small bag of fried buns with minced pork and shrimp stuffing. The hot buns tasted delicious, and he devoured them one by one over the dossier. As he was picking up the last bun, he got a call from Detective Yu.

"You're not coming to the bureau today, boss?"

"No. What's up?"

"You have a special assignment, I guess?"

"Yes. Did Party Secretary Li tell you anything?"

"No. How about meeting you at your place around noon?"

"Great. Come for lunch."

"Don't worry about lunch." Yu added, "Go on with your work. See you soon."

Yu didn't explain the occasion for his visit. The timing concerned the chief inspector. He wasn't supposed to talk about his new work with any of his colleagues. But for Yu, his longtime partner and friend, also the one in practical charge of the special case squad, he had to make an exception.

So the last bun was left there untouched, stuck to the paper, cold, greasy, flaccid, and dispirited. It was almost like his changed mood, as he went on reading the file about Xing.

In the early eighties, Xing had served as the Party Secretary of Huayuan County, Fujian Province. It was then a backward agricultural area consisting of four or five poor People's Communes. For the year-long labor, farmers there made less than a hundred yuan. Xing got caught up in the early waves of the economic reform, setting up several commune factories. Those nonstate business entities enjoyed tax breaks as well as other competitive edges in the new market. Their success soon changed the local economic landscape. Xing became a national model Party cadre in "leading the people on the way to wealth and prosperity." Instead of accepting promotions, he insisted on working as the number-one boss in the county.

As the reform gained further momentum, those companies became private—his companies. His business rocketed up, reaching out into large cities. Like many other upstarts, Xing could not help showing off. If "it is glorious to get rich," as Comrade Deng Xiaoping said, few appeared more magnificent than Xing. He paraded through Fuzhou in a bulletproof Red Flag allegedly manufactured for Chairman Mao. For his family, he built mansions after the fashion of the Grand View Garden. In a visit to his elementary school, he handed a bunch of hundred-yuan bills to a poor old janitor, like a modern-day Robin Hood. Eventually, his excesses caught the attention of some people in Beijing.

Suspicious things were noticed about his business practice. Because of the market competition, a number of his companies suffered serious losses instead of making profits, but he launched into one new grandiose project after another and went on squandering as if there were gold mountains and silver mines in his backyard. The Beijing authorities had been cautious at first. Xing being a much-touted model Party cadre of the reform, no one wanted to "damage a whole pot of soup with one drop of rat dung." A special investigation team was sent to Fujian, and the initial discoveries were shocking. Xing had made his real money through smuggling. It was a gigantic operation that covered an incredible range of goods, including automobiles, oils, petrochemical products, liquors, drugs, and weapons. The operation was run by an elaborate network involving his Party connections at all government levels, from the very top in Beijing to the local cops and customs, with the direct or indirect complicity of hundreds of officials. According to one source, the smuggling operation racked up a billion dollars in revenues—an amount equivalent to the province's annual gross domestic product. No one had taken advantage of the labyrinthine system in a more skillful and more surprisingly simple way—corruption upon corruption.

In order to "get the green light all the way," he bribed all necessary officials. A Party cadre himself, he knew what worked. A "red envelope" of Chinese yuan or American dollars. If an envelope was returned, he increased the amount until it was finally accepted. With connections secured all over the country, he converted a fifteen-story building in Fujian into a pleasure palace for cadres from everywhere. The mansion was called Red Tower, where the Party officials lost themselves in the woods of the sexiest bodies and emerged as the most loyal allies of Xing in China's economic reform.

As more and more irrefutable evidence was gathered, the Beijing authorities became furious. They gave the order to arrest Xing—as a part of the new national anticorruption campaign. But Xing must have been warned at the last minute, for he sneaked out of the country like a rice-paddy eel.

Newspaper reports about Xing began to emerge early in the year, making him the national symbol of the mounting corruption, providing sensational details about fat cats cavorting with young women in the hot tubs of the Red Tower, and speculating about bribery and protection schemes at the highest rungs of the political ladder. But there was something not covered in the media: Xing's application for political asylum in the U.S., claiming to be the victim of a power struggle, and his threat to reveal the criminal activities of high-ranking Party officials if he was deported. The Beijing authorities were worried that these stories might cost the people's faith in the Party.

But what could Chief Inspector Chen do about it?

While Xing's business had reached into a number of cities, he did not have a company or office in Shanghai. All the chief inspector had gotten was a list of Xing's contacts here. Chen could spend months checking through the names on the list—without getting anywhere.

But Chen understood why Xing's case could be so politically significant. China's economic reform had ignited a powerful engine for financial growth, but it had also opened up a Pandora's box of greed and corruption. Given the opportunity, some Party officials pillaged and plundered like pirates, so the reform itself was seriously endangered.

Tapping on the file, he realized Detective Yu would be arriving soon. He stood up and began to straighten some old newspapers and books. Yu had been making an effort to quit smoking, so Chen put away the ashtray. The desk was small, and it served as a tea table in the event of a visitor. The efficiency-like room would have looked overcrowded with both a desk and a table.

As expected, Yu came over around twelve. A tall man with a rugged face, he carried several lunch boxes as well as disposable chopsticks and spoons in a plastic bag, which was a surprise to Chen.

"Peiqin's idea," Yu said. "She insisted on my going to Old Geng's place first. Free lunch."

"Delicious idea."

Yu's wife, Peiqin, worked in a state-run restaurant, but she had a sideline job as an accountant at a private restaurant, enjoying a good extra income, plus free food from the restaurant owner, Old Geng. The private restaurant was expanding, and the sideline job had become practically a full-time one. Old Geng talked about having her as a partner, for he knew what a capable woman she was.

"Still quite hot," Yu went on, opening the boxes. "The crisp skin roast piglet and smoked carp head. Old Geng's specials."

Chen took out a bottle of yellow rice wine. "You have something to ask me, Yu," he said, crunching the crispy pork skin in his mouth.

"It's an anticorruption case under the Party Discipline Committee, right?" Yu said, not really as a question. "Someone high up wants you to do the job."

"Not exactly," Chen said. "Most of the investigation is in Fujian. Xing runs a large corruption empire from there."

"That bastard!" Yu banged the desk with his fist. "You know what? His Red Tower has become a tourist attraction, in spite of its exorbitant admission fee. People pour in, trying to see the place where those rotten officials luxuriated themselves in 'the woods of naked bodies, in the pools of mellow wines.' The local government has to close the building again."

"Indeed, it's such a notorious case that the day the news first hit the press," Chen recalled, "the *People's Daily* sold out."

"With Xing in the United States," Yu said, taking a sip at the wine, "it may be easy for the Beijing government to blame corruption on Western influences—the result of opening the door and 'letting in the flies.' "

"That's way too simplistic," Chen said. "How have you learned all that so fast?"

"This kind of news people learn in no time. Tell me more about what they want you to do."

Chen recapitulated what he had learned from Comrade Zhao and from the file that morning. At the end of his summary, he pushed over the list of Xing's contacts in Shanghai. Yu looked at the list without responding immediately.

"Why can't they have Xing sent back?" Yu said. "Once he's back, he has to spill. All his connections. No need for you to do anything."

"China is embarking on international cooperation in the legal field, signing extradition treaties with several countries. Some convicts have been returned to China. But Xing is seeking political asylum there by claiming to be a victim of a Party power struggle."

"It's a brazen lie. The Americans really buy it?"

"Xing must have planned it for a long time. His family moved to the States several months before his flight, taking much of the evidence with them. That made the investigation really difficult. The evidence we have may not even be admissible in a foreign court, and our demands for extradition can be overruled on technical grounds."

"It's a tough job, boss. Most of the people on the list have high positions, or high connections. Not like ordinary canvassing, a cop knocking on one door after another, without worrying about the consequences. These are the doors of the most powerful, capable of getting you into trouble. They may not be able to wreak their anger against the committee, but it will be a different story for that particular knocker."

"I know. Beijing could have sent someone to Shanghai," Chen said, "someone who does not have to work here afterward."

"And all your knocking will make no difference. It's not a matter of your having the guts. Those officials won't talk to you, not without undeniable evidence, of which you have none."

"It may sound like I'm quoting the *People's Daily,* but corruption is a cancer of today's society. We have to do something about it."

"Well, the recent prosecution and execution of several senior officials may give you the impression that the CCP leadership is committed to this. With all the media operating under government control, however, self-policing may never be practical. It won't work for a ruling party accountable to no one," Yu said thoughtfully. "People say that anticorruption campaigns make a lot of thunder these days, and at first, quite a bit of rain too. Then still some thunder, but less rain. After a while, you won't hear or see anything at all."

Chen was surprised by Yu's eloquence. Yu must have given serious thought to the issue. Earlier, much-propagandized campaigns had given people reason to suspect that most of the officials, especially those at the top, would manage to wriggle off the hook.

"It's like a proverb, Yu. I haven't seen you for a couple of days, and you talk like another man."

"You're a high-profile chief inspector," Yu said, not responding to Chen's comment. "It may only be another sign of the Party's determination."

"No, I don't think so. The Party authorities are quite determined in this. For one thing, they have allowed reports about the case to be published in official newspapers. As Comrade Zhao said, corruption could develop 'to such a serious extent that it will threaten the government.' "

"Come on. At most, the discipline committee functions like a watchdog. The ultimate decision will be made in the interests of the Party. Whatever investigation is done, it's still nothing but a show."

"For me, it's not a show, as you know."

"And that's why it can be so dangerous," Yu said. "Have you heard the premier's statement about one hundred coffins?"

"Yes, everybody has heard it." The premier made it as a gesture of his determination. *Knowing that it is impossible to do, he still tried to do so because it's what he should do.* That was a Confucian statement Chen had learned from his late father. The premier had played an important role, Chen had heard, in pushing for this investigation.

"Even those on the top know it's an impossible job," Yu said.

Yu must have his reason to be so worried, Chen suspected. The pork skin no longer tasted crisp, but the smoked carp head still made a palatable dish for the wine. He put a large piece of the fish cheek meat on top of Yu's rice.

"We have done difficult and dangerous cases together before, Detective Yu, and you have never encouraged me to quit. What do you know?"

"There is one thing I have to tell you," Yu said. "Hua Ting, a veteran cop in Fuzhou, died in a most mysterious way a couple of days ago—within a week after he had taken over the Xing case, a mission similar to yours."

"Any foul play suspected?"

"As foul as you could imagine. His naked body was found in a prostitute's room. An overdose of Chinese Viagra—according to the whore's statement. Stories with such sordid details run like wildfire in tabloid newspapers there. My father, Old Hunter, does not believe it. He knew Hua for years. A family man, and an honest cop, Hua would never have done anything like that."

"That's the worst ending possible for a cop. His name tarnished, and he will never rest in peace."

"Old Hunter discussed it with me and he wanted me to talk to you. You know what? He calls those crooked officials 'red rats,' with the barn of the Chinese society under their control."

"That's a superb metaphor." But Chen did not want to push on. He refused to see the system as a barn run by and for red rats. "It reminds me of a fable written by Liu Zhongyuan, a Tang dynasty poet, about such a rat-ravaged barn. For a short period of time, people gave it up, so the rats believed it was a world of their own. Then one man broke in, and all the rats, so fattened that they could hardly run, were killed in no time."

"It's a fable, Chief."

"Old Hunter and you want me to think more carefully about accepting the job, I understand," Chen said. "But I really have no choice."

"Yes, Chief Inspector Chen?"

"You may well call me impossibly bookish or romantic, but when someone like Comrade Zhao says he considers me one of the few Beijing can trust in a difficult situation—as an emperor's special envoy—what can I say? As Confucius said, 'If people treat me as the man of the state, I have to live up to the expectation.'"

"I have not read the book."

"But I will be careful. You may be right about it possibly being a show, and there's no point in jumping headlong into the muddy river."

"I didn't think I could change your mind," Yu said somberly, "but I had to tell you all that. Having said so, I am still your partner. If you want to work on the case, you have to count me in."

"Thanks. I know I can always count on you," Chen said. "But at this stage, it would be better for you to stay in the background."

"How are you going to proceed?"

"I haven't decided yet. I'll talk to the people on the list, I think."

"It's like touching the tiger's tail," Yu said, draining his cup.

And the tiger could bite.

3

AFTER HIS TALK WITH Detective Yu, Chief Inspector Chen decided to restudy his investigation plan.

Chen took out the folder again. There was one point made by several sources. Xing had made frequent trips to Shanghai, it was said, because of his mother. It was common knowledge in Fujian that Xing was a most dutiful son. His father had passed away when he was only three, and his mother had brought him up all by herself. About two years ago, Xing had bought her a mansion in Shanghai. Several months before fleeing overseas, he had moved her out to the United States. No one seemed to know, however, why, before that, the old woman had chosen to stay in Shanghai, with Xing being kept so busy in Fujian most of the time.

There was no ruling out the possibility of Xing having come here, Chen contemplated, for clandestine business under the pretext of filial piety. Shanghai had been transforming itself into one of the fastest-developing cities in the world. Xing could not have helped putting his capitalist fingers into the socialist pie.

The people Xing had contacted in Shanghai could be classified in two groups. Those with official positions, and those without. A majority were those met at parties and public activities. It was Xing's style to have lavish receptions and banquets, with hundreds of people hand-shaking and business-card–exchanging and connection-building and bargain-making above and under tables. But there were also a small number of people Xing had met behind closed doors, in VIP karaoke suites or private dining rooms. Those were not necessarily suspicious, though. Xing knew the necessity of cultivating connections even when there were no immediate business plans.

Chen did not mind, as an old proverb went, looking for a horse in accordance with a map, but going through the people on the list, one by one, would probably take him months without getting him anywhere. Of course, he might still claim a conscientious job done with a long report to the committee, a report that would be shelved, dust-covered, and eventually shredded.

Instead, he decided to have a focus. A concentration on those with official positions possibly connected with Xing's business, but not those necessarily high in rank. There was no hurry for the latter. Chief Inspector Chen had to make sure what role was assigned to him before throwing himself headlong into it.

So he took an extra step. He went to the bureau, locked himself in the computer room, and spent a whole day researching. There were only two computers in the bureau, and the chief inspector was one of the few with special access to them. There was one inconvenience: he could not smoke in the computer room and had to step out several times. At the end of the day, having plodded through an extensive background check of the possible targets, Chen settled on Dong Depeing, the standing Associate Director of Shanghai's State Industry Reform Committee, for the first potential breakthrough.

Early the next morning, Chen did more-specific research. The Shanghai State Industry Reform Committee was an institution established in the developing economic reform. The committee played a crucial role in addressing the numerous problems facing state-run companies, studying and specifying new policies and practices for them. Like Chen, Dong was considered an intellectual cadre, having obtained an MA degree in business. Xing had five or six meetings with Dong last year. What's more, Chen had accidentally gotten something like a handle he could use on Dong. Chen had been looking for an apartment for his mother, so Mang Ke, one of his acquaintances in the real estate business, had recommended an area to him. Mang went out of his way, providing inside information about the area's potential: a list of the properties bought by senior Party officials. Such purchases were an unmistakable message that the property value would soon rise because of city development project plans known only to these officials. Dong was one of them, listed not with an apartment but with a house—at a price way beyond the income for a Party cadre. That was why Chen remembered it. New homeowners like Dong could easily come up with stories about loans, but holes in those stories could be found as easily.

Chen contacted Zhu Wei, a reporter covering the real estate market for *Wenhui Daily*. When Chen explained his interest in learning about the properties purchased in Shanghai by city officials, Zhu sounded eager to cooperate. Zhu had already considered writing about the topic, but his boss had vetoed the idea.

"Do you know anything about the house purchased by Dong?" Chen said.

"Anything about Dong? He paid for the house all in cash without applying for a mortgage," Zhu said. "Are you investigating something?"

"Oh no, I'm just curious. Someone told me that the property in that area is an incredible bargain, like Dong's house there. I have been looking for an apartment for my mother."

"It's time for someone to touch these rotten Party cadres, Chief Inspector Chen. Have you seen those TV episodes of Judge Bao?"

"I read the Song dynasty stories long ago."

"Have you thought about his popularity in the present-day China?" Zhu went on without waiting for an answer. "People have their hope in an incorruptible official like Judge Bao."

"That's true," Chen said. He refrained from saying that the popularity of Judge Bao came from his being so exceptional, so unrealistic, simply substitutive of people's collective fantasy.

In the afternoon, Chen set out for Dong's office, which was in the Shanghai City Government Building located in the People's Square.

Chen had been a visitor to the building numerous times. That afternoon, as the soldier saluted him at the entrance, he still felt a surge of pride, despite his misgivings at the bathhouse, and despite Yu's warning at his home. The chief inspector, now an emperor's special envoy with an imperial sword, caught a Confucian statement resurfacing in his mind: *A woman is willing to make herself beautiful for the one who likes her, and a man is ready to lay down his life for the one who appreciates him.*

Dong's office was rather an austere one. A short, stolid man in his late forties or early fifties, Dong rose to greet Chen with an air that bespoke awareness of his own position, and of Chen's as well. Dressed in a well-ironed white shirt and black pants and wearing a pair of golden-rimmed glasses, he looked more like a scholar, and he surely spoke like one.

"Welcome, Chief Inspector Chen. You are an unexpected visitor that lightens up this small office."

"Sorry for not having called you first, Director Dong. I had an earlier meeting in the building, so I thought I may as well drop in."

"You don't have to explain. You are welcome here anytime," Dong said. "Have a cup of tea. You like good tea, I know, particularly Dragon Well from Hangzhou, but I have something different here."

Dong put a little green ball into the cup, before pouring out an arch of water from a thermos bottle.

"Thank you," Chen said, surprised by Dong's knowledge. The tea did look quite different. The ball was expanding into something like petals in the water, and a red berry glistened like the pistil in the center. Then he saw a tiny thread: the leaves must have been bound together with the berry inside. "An exquisite tea. How do you know about my tea preference?"

"I still remember that essay in *Wenhui Daily*. I used to know that pretty reporter too, Wang Feng. She left for Japan. What a pity!"

The article in question was a humorous one published a long while ago. No one would have paid much attention to it. What Chen remembered of the article at all was because of the reporter, the image of whose green skirt was still fresh in his mind.

"You surely are well informed—"

"Well, people know a lot about you, our poet chief inspector. Someone just told me about your *hongyan zhiji,* not only in Beijing, but in the United States too."

It came like a seemingly effortless blow delivered by a tai chi master: *we know everything about you, so you'd better look out. Hongyan zhiji* was a classical literary term meaning an attractive female friend who appreciates and understands you: not necessarily a girlfriend, but definitely with such a connotation—an archetypal dream for lonely, unappreciated scholars in ancient China. Tales about Chen and his friend Ling in Beijing might not be too surprising; Ling's being an HCC—a high cadre's child—certainly did not help. Representations of Chen as a political climber holding her hand actually impeded the development of their relationship. But the reference to his American *hongyan zhiji* was alarming. Chen had met Catherine Rohn, a U.S. Marshal in a joint investigation in Shanghai. They liked each other, but nothing really developed. In the Shanghai Police Bureau, no one had ever talked or joked about it, for such an affair would be politically sensitive for an emerging Party cadre like Chen. How could Dong have come up with all that?

Unless Dong, too, had made an exhaustive study of Chen. But the chief inspector had not made an appointment for his visit. He had planned to surprise Dong. Now Dong had more than surprised Chen.

"Come, Director Dong. People exaggerate in their gossip." Chen tried to lead the talk back his way. "We cannot—in our positions."

"You are right," Dong said, nodding. "But in my position, I have to deal with all kinds of exaggerations. The problems for the state companies, for instance. The Party cadres harp on them all the time, in the hope that they can transform and be rid of the state ownership of their companies."

"Yes, your work is quite new," Chen said, "in the historical transition from the state economy to the market economy."

"Are you working on an anticorruption case involving a state-run company, Comrade Chief Inspector Chen?"

"Yes, you are well-informed."

"I merely guessed. A detective doesn't come to my office for nothing." Dong made a pause before going on. "About the corruption in today's society, I have been doing a lot of thinking too. China has made a 'great achievement' in the last ten years. An achievement Western economists cannot explain. But have you ever considered its possible relation to corruption?"

"What do you mean, Director Dong?"

"Corruption may have facilitated our economic development in a large way. It's a paradox, isn't it?"

"I have not studied the issue. You are an authority on the new economic development."

"Well, I have just read about it in an essay," Dong said, pulling out an English magazine from the shelf, which covered one side of the room. There were titles Chen had never seen before. Several bookmarks stuck out of pages, as if showing the owner's knowledge. "According to the author, China's success has been associated with an epidemic of corruption among local officials in charge of the economy. Why? The transformation of Party cadres from unproductive political entrepreneurs to productive economic entrepreneurs. But what pushed those cadres over the edge? A contradiction between the socialist system and the capitalist practice. The time-honored communist propaganda about Party members being selfless public servants of the people excludes explicit incentives and rewards for those cadres. Their incomes are still fixed and unrelated to their performance. Is that really fair? So some Party cadres see corruption as a sort of compensation, like in Western economies. That makes our fight against corruption much harder . . ."

This talk was turning out to be harder than Chen had expected. Dong launched into new theories, as if forestalling Chen from taking a more authoritative position. Indeed, Dong was not merely higher in Party rank, but also more experienced in delivering the "Party talk." Chen decided to come to the point directly.

"Your guess was correct. I am engaged in an anticorruption investigation. More specifically, an investigation of Xing Xing, and it's directly under the Party Discipline Committee. I have some questions for you. Xing made several trips to Shanghai last year, and he met you a few times. Did he talk to you about his business activity here?"

"Xing, I see. He wanted to invest in a state-run company in Shanghai. It's a new phenomenon in the economic reform and he saw a possibility of becoming the largest shareholder of the company. So he discussed it with me a couple of times."

That made sense. Entrepreneurs were now allowed to buy into state companies. If Xing had been contemplating such, he would have come to Dong, an official as well as an expert on the subject.

"What advice did you give him?"

"I encouraged him to explore it further. Privatization will be ongoing. Of course, I did not know about his illegal business practices at the time."

As anticipated, Dong would not really talk. He kept parrying as in tai chi, giving no opportunity for Chen to break in. Chen played his trump card.

"You are a well-known authority. It made sense for Xing to consult you from time to time," Chen said, taking a deliberate sip of the tea. "Great tea. I've just heard something else about you, Director Dong. A coincidence, I would say. My mother is in her seventies, living in an attic. So I have been looking for an apartment for her. I happened to learn about your house in the Hongqiao area. Congratulations, Director Dong!"

"Oh, that," Dong said, staring at Chen. "What a hard time I had borrowing the money from my friends and relatives, you can hardly imagine."

"It's not easy to borrow such a large sum, I know." Chen might be able to discover something not so pleasant for Dong if the chief inspector were to push in that direction. Dong knew that.

"I literally begged around," Dong said, taking a drink of tea. "Let me tell you something, Chief Inspector Chen. When my nephew Junjun was a toddler, I used to buy him Coca-Cola. A luxurious treat then, and I became his favorite uncle. Now only in his mid-twenties, Junjun is a millionaire in the property market. My monthly income is like a bottle of Coca-Cola to him. But for his generous loan, I would have never dreamed of purchasing that house. Indeed, the world has been changing dramatically, as from the azure ocean to the mulberry field."

It might be partially true. Chen understood why a large number of Party cadres were unable to resist the materialistic temptation. As Dong had implied, the system was far from fair. As a hardworking chief inspector, Chen earned about the same state-specified salary that a janitor in the bureau did. Of course, Chen had subsidies in recognition of his position, like the bureau car, a business expense allowance, a special housing assignment, and so on. All these might not be bad, but he could not cash in the car service when he wanted to take a walk. Once he had seen a Ming-style mahogany desk in a furniture store. It took him five or six months to save enough money for it. When he finally went there with the sum, the desk was long gone.

Still, he had to consider himself well off, compared with those working in the state-run companies on the edge of bankruptcy or with those hanging on in the waiting-for-retirement program. Was it really fair for the CEOs, Party cadres or not, to earn hundreds of times more than the ordinary people? A product of his education in the sixties, Chen maintained a nostalgic passion for a sort of egalitarian society. Others did, too—that might also be one of the reasons why people complained so much about corruption.

"So we have to study those new issues in the transitional period," Dong went on, "and find solutions in a realistic way."

Dong had regained his footing, unshakable no matter what the chief inspector might say. It would not be difficult for Dong to have the bank documents prepared, whether through a real nephew or not. Chen was going to try anyway, but it would be pointless for him to stay here any longer, wasting his breath with Dong.

As Chen was about to make his exit, Dong broached a new topic, rising to pour more hot water into Chen's cup.

"In today's world, people have to move around through their connections. No one is an exception, not even you, Chief Inspector Chen. When the water is too clear, there will be no fish left."

"Well, it depends on your definition of connections. I am a cop. I want to do a good job of it."

"Who is going to define it, then? Hardworking Party cadres like you and me—we know how difficult it is to do a job well." Dong went on casually, "Of course, you are more than an ordinary Party cadre. You are also a well-known poet and translator. You have recently published a collection of poetry, I know. And a huge hit too."

"Oh, you like poetry?"

"Not exactly, but a friend of yours, Mr. Gu of the New World Group, gave me a copy. As you may or may not know, he has given copies to a lot of people."

"Really! He never told me anything about it."

Gu was a highly successful businessman Chen had become acquainted with during an investigation. Gu had helped, and been helped, and since then considered himself a friend of Chen's. So Gu had been doing him favors—"out of friendship."

"I happen to know he bought a thousand copies from the publisher even before the book came out," Dong said with a knowing smile. "Publishers lose money with poetry."

So that's all there was to it. The success of his poetry. He should have questioned it from the beginning. The publisher's ravings had for once gone to his head. Still, he was not too surprised that Gu had orchestrated it. But how could Dong have learned all the details?

Dong must have checked Chen's background before his visit. The chief inspector was troubled. He hadn't told anybody about his plan. The only possibility of it leaking out would have been, he realized, through the bureau computer room. Somebody else had accessed his computer research, and Dong had been informed beforehand.

If Dong pushed further in that direction, things between Gu and Chen could be interpreted in a variety of ways. Chen might believe he had not done anything unjustifiable, but others might not see things from his perspective.

"You surely have your expert way of looking at things, Director Dong," Chen said, trying to gain time. Instead of surprising Dong, he found himself being ambushed. The talk was moving in a direction he had not foreseen at all. There might be something in Detective Yu's warning. Knocking on Party doors could be truly dangerous.

But Dong was not going to stop there.

"Things are not fair in China. For example, you do not have a large enough apartment for your mother to live with you. An old woman living by herself in an attic with a dark, difficult staircase could easily have an accident."

"An accident—" Chen was more than alarmed. He wondered whether Dong had brought it up as a hint. "Thank you for your concern, Director Dong."

Without waiting for Chen to respond further, Dong continued, "You have been doing a great job, Chief Inspector Chen. You should have at least a three-bedroom apartment, so your mother could move in with you and you wouldn't have to worry about anything happening to her at her age. You are a son of filial piety, as we all know. And you know what? I might be able to put in a word for your special situation with the city government."

Now that was a hint, Chen had no doubt about it. All of a sudden, sitting before him was a diabolical triad gangster instead of a senior Party cadre. But it was also a turning point. If he backed away like that, Chief Inspector Chen would never forgive himself for being a coward.

"Thank you, Director Dong. I will keep every word of yours in mind, but I really have to go now."

Chen rose to leave, thinking of a poem written before a battle by Wang Changling, a Tang dynasty poet:

The bright moon of the Qing dynasty . . .
The ancient pass of the Han dynasty . . .
Soldiers after soldiers,
not a single one of them ever returns
from the long march—thousands
and thousands of miles long.
Oh with the winged general
of the Dragon City stationed here,
the Tartar horses would never
have crossed the Yin Mountain.

4

IN THE FIRST GRAY of the morning, Chen felt as if he were waking out of the ancient battle of iron-clad horses galloping through the ignorant night, and coming back to reality again. As a cop, he could put himself at risk, but not his mother.

There are things a man should do, and there are things a man should not do.

Nothing should happen to his mother. That was the bottom line for the son who, though far from being a Confucianist, remembered that Confucian maxim.

He brushed his teeth vigorously. There was a bitter, ammonialike taste in his mouth. For years, he had let his mother down, time after time. Through his career choice, his political allegiance, and his personal life. She had dreamed of her son pursuing an academic career like her late husband, staying away from politics, and settling down with a family of his own. She did not care about his Party position. It was only of late—while she was in the hospital—that he and his position had proven capable of providing for her, at least materialistically. Now, because of his position, she would not even be able to enjoy her remaining days peacefully, like an ordinary old woman.

According to another Confucian principle, however, one might occasionally find oneself unable to fulfill political and filial duty at the same time. If so, the former should take the priority. And his mother, though not the scholar his late Confucianist father was, would not forgive him for backing away from his investigation because of her.

He had to find a way to pursue the investigation without exposing his mother to danger. But that seemed impossible. His work was no longer a secret to Xing's circle. His next interview would be like a declaration of war among those officials.

He dug out a copy of *Thirty-Six Battle Strategies,* a book of war stratagems over a thousand years old. Lighting a cigarette, he searched the table of contents before turning to a chapter entitled "Cutting through Chen Trail in Stealth," which was about a battle in the early Han dynasty. General Han built a bridge, leading the enemy forces to believe he intended to maneuver his troops across it, but then he took a trail called Chen Cang instead and surprised them.

The chief inspector had to find his own Chen trail. He was going to focus on the people considered unlikely as interviewees. No one would suspect that he was trying to break the case through them. In the meantime, he would start making formal phone calls, scheduling interviews with the officials on his list, but he would not approach them the same way as Dong. They would conclude that Chen was merely putting on a show.

He took out the list before he started to brew a pot of coffee. It was the last spoonful from the jar of Brazilian coffee an American friend had given him. *Hongyan zhiji.* He whistled wistfully into a bitter smile. He had already kept the coffee for a long period, and eventually, it would have lost all its flavor.

It was a long list. Xing had an incredible reach of social contacts. Some of them, however, were hardly connections. "Nodding acquaintances" would perhaps be a more appropriate phrase. They were the people of little relevance to his business.

As he took a sip of the fresh coffee, going through the list again, a name jumped out as if printed in red.

Qiao Bo.

Qiao had met Xing only once the previous year. Their meeting was mentioned in local newspapers, for Xing donated twenty thousand yuan to Qiao. Not a large sum. Like a single hair from an ox, but it was much reported as an "entrepreneur's generous support to a patriotic project." It was all because of a book entitled *China Can Stand Up in Defiance,* of which Qiao was the author. Not an academic book, it appealed to popular sentiment and became a national best-seller.

Chen happened to know Qiao, however, against a totally different backdrop. In the early eighties, a self-styled postmodernist poet, Qiao had put his works into a manuscript and approached Chen for a preface. His poems attracted a number of young students, but postmodernism was not considered politically acceptable. As a member of the Writers' Association, Chen declined to write the preface. Qiao later attracted far more attention when he went to jail for his "corrupt bourgeois lifestyle." Newspapers came up with lurid stories of his seducing girls in his dorm room. According to his roommates, however, it was those girls who went after him—a young, handsome, romantic poet. Nothing but consensual sex. But Qiao was sentenced to seven or eight years.

Chen was then an entrance-level police officer, and there was little he could do about it. Afterward, he heard nothing about Qiao until the early nineties. Out of jail, Qiao become a bookseller. A poet no longer seemed like a prince on a white horse riding into the dreams of young girls. Poetry, if anything, became synonymous with poverty. Selling books in a store converted out of his one single residential room, Qiao wrote *China Can Stand Up in Defiance,* with a subtitle, *The Strategic Choice in the New Global Age*. It was a project developed out of his business sensibility, for he sensed a need in the market. The book received favorable reviews, and Qiao knew how to "stir-fry"—how to attract public attention. With the forever-turning wheel of fortune, Qiao came once more into the limelight, only it did not last long this time. When the waves of nationalism gained too much momentum, the Beijing government intervened. The book was not banned, but once all the official media was hushed, it soon fell from the best-seller list. Then numerous new books on similar topics came out, quickly overwhelming Qiao's.

Xing had met Qiao before the book had fallen out of the market's favor.

Chen stood up, searched the bookshelf for a long while, and dug out a dust-covered book. It was Qiao's poetry collection, for which he could have written the preface. He turned over several pages to a love poem and skipped to the last two stanzas:

A drunken swan flushes
out of the canvas, carrying
my body to the sea, where
the coral was my eyes shining
in yours. How can I feel
the waves without your breath,
the waves seaweed-tangled, rising
and falling in me?

A blaze in the late autumn woods.
Dawn or dusk vomits blood again.
When you light a candle, will you
blow it out gently, for me?

Not a bad poem, written through a female persona. Rereading it, Chen thought he could understand Qiao's popularity among those girls in the eighties.

Chen decided not to approach Qiao in a conventional way. It was not easy for an ex-poet—or an ex-convict—to survive, and an investigation in the name of the Party Discipline Committee would not make things any easier for his business. So instead of a bureau car, Chen took a taxi to go and visit him.

The bookstore was located on Fuyou Road, one of the few remaining pebble-covered streets in the Old City area. Chen told the driver to stop one block away. Fuyou was a street lined with booths, kiosks, stands, barrows, and shabby stores on both sides. Several stores appeared to be makeshift extensions, or conversions, out of the former residential rooms. A few peddlers did business on wooden tables or white cloths set out on the sidewalk.

It was an age when everything could be put up on sale, and everywhere, too.

He stepped into the bookstore, which consisted of two sections. One selling so-called antiques, and the other selling books.

The antiques section exhibited a hodgepodge of objects. A time-yellowed picture of an old woman shuffling in her bound feet along the Qing trail, a long brass opium pipe immortalized with the moss of ages, a cigarette box card of a Shanghai courtesan flashing her thighs through the high slits of her floral cheongsam. To his surprise, things as recent as the Cultural Revolution were also marked as antiques, cramming a whole glass counter. A stamp of Marshal Lin Biao standing with Chairman Mao on the Tiananmen Gate. Lin was killed shortly afterward in an unsuccessful coup. The stamp was now marked as worth ten thousand Yuan. There was an impressive collection of Chairman Mao badges—plastic or metal—copies of the *Little Red Book of Mao's Quotations,* the four-volume *Collected Works of Chairman* in the first edition . . .

Next to the collection of the Cultural Revolution, Chen saw a poster of Dietrich in *Shanghai Express.* This city seemed to be suddenly lost in a collective nostalgia for the twenties and thirties, an allegedly golden period of exotic and exuberant fantasies. Things from those days were being discovered and rediscovered with a passion. The poster stood as a plastic-covered valuable, fetching a much higher price than a larger portrait of Chairman Mao standing on Tiananmen Square.

Chen took a bamboo shopping basket. He picked a stainless steel lighter in the shape of a Little Red Book, marked for only five yuan. He also chose something like a large plastic Mao badge with a long red silk string attached. Possibly a pendant, but the red string was too short.

Looking up, he saw a middle-aged man in a traditional Tang jacket in a corner partially sheltered by a bookshelf. He recognized him to be none other than Qiao. Qiao, who had changed a great deal, deeply wrinkled like a shrunken gourd, did not come over. Perhaps what Chen had chosen were merely cheap imitation antiques.

Chen then walked toward several special-price bookshelves with some of the books marked as eighty to ninety percent off. Qiao moved over, drawing his attention to a section marked "beauty authors."

"A lot of people buy these books," Qiao said.

Not because of those glamorous authors on the covers, Chen knew, but because of the pornographic contents—allegedly autobiographical. Like Lei Lei, the author of *Darling, Darling,* whose cover bore a blurb praising the book as "a lush, lustful account of her sexual experience with three Americans." Or like Jun Tin, the author of *Peacocks,* notorious through her fight with Lei Lei for the number one Chinese-female-Henry-Miller title. With the first lessening of the government censorship, books featuring sexual descriptions turned into the hottest product. Surprisingly, there was a bronze ancient monster crouching on top of that particular shelf, as if moving out of a Chinese myth.

"*American Lover* by Rain Cloud," Qiao said, picking up a book. "Graphic description of the sexual ecstasy between a Chinese woman and her American lover. The book has caused a sensation because the alleged protagonist's daughter sued the author. Rain settled the case for a large sum, but guess what—the book was then reprinted to roaring success, bringing in far more than what she paid."

"How?" Chen said.

"She claimed that the trial was orchestrated by the government. Once the writer was 'persecuted,' her book sold like hotcakes. It was translated into five foreign languages. People are contrarily curious. Not to mention all the lurid details, much reported during the trial."

"What a shameless profiteer!"

"Is there any ashamed profiteer? Look at that paragraph. 'They write not with their pens, but with their pussies,' " Qiao read aloud from a newspaper clipping taped above the book.

"Well, what else can you say?" Chen picked a couple of different books at random and put them into the bamboo basket.

"Look at this red silk string, so cute," Qiao said, noticing the other chosen objects in the basket. "You can hang it in your car."

"Are Shanghai people so nostalgic for the old days?"

"Are you a professor or a PhD?" Qiao's wrinkles seemed to be expanding in surprise.

"Ah—" That was an allusion to a popular saying: *As poor as a professor, as silly as a PhD.* "I wish I could be either one."

"Traffic is so terrible. Numerous accidents. Taxi drivers are superstitious. To them, the evil spirits must have been let loose on the roads."

"So people believe in Mao's posthumous power as a protector?"

"Oh, you must be cracking another international joke!" Qiao shook his head violently in mock disbelief. "Little evil spirits are afraid only of big evil spirits. Who do you think is the number one evil spirit?"

"Mao?"

"Now, you are not that dumb. I was just joking, of course. The books you have picked are not bad at all."

"I have another stupid question," Chen said. "These books sell well. Then why at such a discount?"

"Because they sell so well, pirated copies come in incredibly large quantities."

"I see," Chen said. Some private-run bookstores had no scruples about ordering through dubious distribution channels, with tons of pirated copies coming in, ending up in the special-price section. "So these books are sold illegally here."

"What do you mean?" Qiao demanded sharply. "All the private bookstores are the same. How else can they make money in today's market?"

"I'm not concerned with other bookstores, Qiao," Chen said, producing his business card. "I think we need to talk."

"Now I recognize you," Qiao said, staring hard at the card. "I've heard a lot about you, Chief Inspector Chen. You didn't come to my store to buy discount books, did you?"

"You are not that dumb."

"There are many booksellers like me. You don't have to be so hard on me, Chen," Qiao said in a pleading voice. "I'm down and out, like a dog already drowning in dirty water. Do you have the heart to beat it to death?"

"You have not lost your poetic metaphors, Qiao. Let's open the door to the mountains. Your books are not my business—pirated or not—but I need to ask you some questions about Xing."

"About Xing? You mean that bastard in the headlines?"

"Yes. You met him last year, right?"

"I did, but I haven't seen him for more than a year. If you've come here because of Xing, go ahead. Any question you want to ask, Chief Inspector Chen."

There was no mistaking Qiao's willingness to collaborate. Qiao had not met with Xing for a period of time, as Chen had learned from the file. There must have been a reason.

"What an exploiter!" Qiao went on indignantly. "Xing just played a cheap PR trick at my expense."

"Please explain it for me, Qiao."

"When *China Can Stand Up in Defiance* was a national hit, he arranged a meeting at the Shanghai Hotel. The meeting was reported in newspapers—the generous support promised by a successful entrepreneur to a struggling writer. But when the initial sensation of the book ebbed, he did not keep any of his words."

"What did he promise you?"

"The larger check he had promised never came. Among other things, a three-bedroom apartment, which disappeared into the air like a yellow crane in that Tang poem."

"He offered to buy you an apartment?"

"No, he said he would give me one when the construction was completed, but then he didn't contact me anymore. I called him several times. He never returned my calls, not a single time."

"Did he put down anything—black and white on paper?"

"No. The sum he gave me there and then was only two thousand yuan. Like a pathetic, meatless bone thrown to a starving dog."

"Now about the construction project—his own property in Shanghai?"

"That I don't know. But it sounded like it." Qiao said with a frown, "Let me think. 'I'll talk to my little brother about it. And he'll give you the apartment key as soon as the complex is done.' I think that's what he said—or something like that."

"Anything else can you remember about your meeting with Xing?"

"We met in a restaurant at the hotel. He talked most of the time. He had a young secretary with blond hair, dyed, and a tall bodyguard. The little secretary made notes of our conversation. She talked to the reporters afterward, I think. That's about all I remember."

"Frankly, I don't think you were involved with Xing. But if you can think of anything else about him, let me know. You have my phone number."

"If I can remember anything."

"I still want to buy this stuff," Chen said, taking out his wallet. "As for your bookstore business, it is not my concern, but it could be somebody else's. You are clever enough to run a decent and profitable bookstore, like the West Wind. You might also try to contact the Writers' Association for help."

"Are you are an executive member there?"

"Yes. I'll put in a word for you," Chen added, "because I did not write the preface. I remember."

"Thank you. I'll think about it."

"I'll come here to buy books. Good books. See you."

When Chen stepped out of the bookstore, instead of getting into a taxi immediately, he decided to walk for a while.

The meeting between Xing and Qiao was perhaps no more than a PR trick—on Xing's part. It was no surprise that Xing didn't keep his word to Qiao, whose value disappeared once his book dropped off the best-seller list. So there was hardly any possibility of Qiao knowing about Xing's business practice here. So far, the strategy of cutting through the Chen trail wasn't working.

After crossing He'nan Road, he turned onto Shandong Road. Like Fuyou Road, it was lined with peddlers' booths. Absentmindedly, he almost bumped into a booth of sugar-covered hawthorn when he saw a girl biking out of a winding lane, carrying books on her bike rack, riding swiftly past as on a breath of wind. She was obviously not bothered by the street commerce.

It reminded him of a scene in Beijing, years earlier, of a young girl gliding out of a *hutong* by the white and black *sihe* style houses, a lone peddler selling orange paper wheels, old people practicing tai chi, a pigeon's whistle trailing in the clear sky, the girl's bike bell spilling into the tranquil air . . . For a moment, it was as if he were back in his college years, standing on a street corner near Xisi subway station, when life seemed to be still so simple. He bought a stick of sugar-covered hawthorn, which was rare for that time of year.

He took a bite of the hawthorn, which tasted different than he remembered. There was no stepping back into the river for a second time. Chief Inspector Chen had to move on.

But why should Xing have chosen to make such a gesture to Qiao? It was a controversial book. Perhaps not a lot to gain from such a gesture for a businessman like Xing. Or could it have been done for somebody else who, much higher in Beijing, favored the nationalist stance? That was possible, but unsupported.

Then Chen thought of something said by Xing—"little brother." It was a term that referred to one's younger brother, or to someone in a triad organization, perhaps a member lower in rank. Xing had no younger brother, but for such a businessman, a triad connection was not unimaginable. Possibly one of his gang buddies from Fujian was doing business in Shanghai.

He dialed Old Hunter, who had once worked on a case in Fujian in the sixties. That was probably how the old man had learned about Detective Hua's death—through his own channels there.

"I'll find out for you," Old Hunter said without asking why, "who this 'little brother' could be. I still have some friends there who acknowledge my old face. It's not a world of rats yet, red or black."

"Be careful, Uncle. Don't let anyone suspect your interest in Xing's case. Not a single word about my investigation."

"You don't have to tell me that, Chief. I have been a hunter for years, and a hunter never retires."

"I really appreciate your help."

"You don't have to say that. Hua was an old friend of mine. If I ask questions there, people will simply think me a retired old busybody." Old Hunter added after a pause, "That's the least I can do for him. You be careful, Chief Inspector Chen. I'm old, but you are still young."

5

THE NEXT ON THE list Chen had circled as a possible interviewee was An Jiayi.

He should have approached her first. For some reason, however, he had chosen not to do so.

But after the talk with Qiao, especially after the new information from Old Hunter, Chief Inspector Chen had no excuse not to. He made up his mind in his bureau cubicle.

Old Hunter's response had come early in the morning. The old man must have moved heaven and earth in Fujian. According to his connections, Xing had a "little brother" named Ming—or a half brother, to be exact. Xing had never openly acknowledged him as such, but it was not a secret among the local people. Xing's father had died when Xing was very young and his mother had had a hard time bringing him up by herself. There were various stories about that period. In one version, she worked as a maid for a high-ranking Party cadre family, where she was said to have had sex with the master, and left to give birth to a son in secret in the countryside. When Xing grew up, he never told anyone. It was said, however, that early in his political career, Xing had been helped by that high-ranking cadre. Also, Xing was a filial son. Since his mother doted on the little son, Xing, in turn, helped Ming in whatever way possible.

Ming had kept a low profile in Fujian, but two or three years earlier, he had started a real estate business of his own in Shanghai. That explained why Xing had bought the mansion for his mother in the city. Then Ming disappeared, allegedly in the company of Xing.

Chen was disturbed. The fact that there was no information whatsoever about Ming in the original file spoke for itself. For a Shanghai cop, the identity of Xing's little brother was a mystery, but it should not have been so with the Fujian police. It should have been followed up on as an important clue.

Chen immediately made inquiries through his private channels into Ming's business in Shanghai. He was even more disturbed by what he came up with. The little brother had connections to a number of big officials in the city. While he kept a relatively low profile here as well, he had hired a PR firm through his company. And that firm was run by none other than An Jiayi.

So An's name had appeared both as a guest at Xing's parties and as a partner in Ming's business.

Drawing in a deep breath, Chen turned to pour himself another cup of tea. The tea tasted stale, the water lukewarm, and the dried jasmine petals yellowish. He hadn't needed to come to the office this morning, but Yu was inundated with the workload of the special case squad, and Chen thought he might be able to help a little. Yu was not in the bureau, though. Chen picked up the list again.

Flowers falling, water flowing, the spring gone, / it is another world.

In the early eighties, when Chen had just left Beijing Foreign Language University for the unexpected position at the Shanghai Police Bureau, he joined a reading group with several other "literature youths." For Chen, it was a halfhearted effort to keep his literary dream alive, as it was, perhaps, for the others, several college graduates state-assigned to jobs regardless of their personal interests. They met once a month to discuss books as well as their own writings. An and her husband, Han, a newlywed couple, both attended. An was an announcer, and Han, a reporter, for the new Eastern TV Station.

The group met regularly for about a year, before Chen was overwhelmed with writing political speeches for Party Secretary Li. An's show had begun to attract an audience, and Gong, a leading member of the group, went to Shenzhen to start his private auto parts business. As in an old saying, there's no banquet that does not come to an end. The reading group eventually dissolved.

Afterward, Chen still saw An on TV, a budding anchorwoman. He heard about some trouble between the couple, allegedly caused by their changing social status. When first assigned to the TV station, there had not been much difference between the two. With Chairman Mao's teachings still fresh in the national memory, everyone was supposed, in whatever position, to "serve people." But things began to change. It did not take long for an attractive young anchorwoman to become a star while Han, an inconspicuous reporter, remained in the background. People started addressing him as "An's husband," like something moving in her shadow.

But Chen was not that familiar with them. Han was said to be a jealous husband, particularly with the people An was nice to. Then he applied to study in Germany, possibly to better himself and so rise to her level. It turned out to be a disastrous decision. Almost immediately driven out of school because of his linguistic problems, he started working in a Chinese restaurant in Berlin instead of coming back. In the meantime, in addition to her anchorwoman career, An started a public relations company.

As a celebrity her attendance at Xing's parties was understandable, but her business relationship with Ming was a different story. It might be nothing unusual for a businessman to engage the service of a PR company. But why An's? Why, with Ming's construction project hardly in blueprints?

An might well know something about Ming, and about Xing as well.

But would she talk to Chief Inspector Chen?

The reading group long dissolved, their paths hardly crossed anymore. At a city congress conference not too long ago, he had seen her at a distance. She was so busy interviewing more important people, he did not even make an attempt to approach her. Now, out of the blue, he was going to try to get information out of her. It wasn't hard to predict her reaction.

He pulled together a dossier on her. There was nothing surprising or suspicious about her career as an anchorwoman. In fact, she'd received a long list of awards for her excellent work. It was also commonplace for celebrities to run businesses on the side, like restaurants with large pictures of them on the wall. It did not take much for people to go to a restaurant, but it took a lot to hire a PR company. What could she do for her clients? An anchorwoman with no experience in that business.

There were stories about her from an unofficial source, but such tabloid stuff might not be unusual for celebrities, let alone an attractive woman with an audience of millions. He lit a cigarette, underlining the paragraph about her "special connection" to high-ranking Party cadres. As in the saying, *It might be like catching at the wind, clutching at the shadow.* But there's another saying, Chen recalled: *No waves will rise without a stir of the wind.*

Those stories alone were far from enough to make her talk. He ground out his cigarette in the swan-shaped crystal ashtray.

He realized it was time for lunch. Three hours already gone this morning and he still had no idea how his Chen trail could work. He walked down to the bureau canteen, which was full of people, as always. He ate a bowl of beef noodles with plenty of red pepper and green onion without talking much to anyone. His colleagues all seemed to be aware of how sensitive his investigation was. The noodle soup tasted heavy, hot, and afterward he felt slightly drowsy. But there was no coffee in the bureau to wake him up. His cell phone rang.

"Long time no see, Chief Inspector Chen," Gu said. "You haven't come to my place for weeks."

"Sorry, I've been so busy—you know how it is."

Unlike other businessmen, Gu knew better than to be a nuisance. It bothered Chen that their relationship had become a handle for Dong. Not really Gu's fault, though: an entrepreneur could not have helped boasting of his official connections and Gu might have been discreet in his way. At least Dong seemed to have learned nothing about Chen's lucrative translation project with the New World. Gu had claimed that it was a favor by Chen, but with such a large fee for the translation, Chen knew better.

"You are always busy, but so are other celebrities. They still come to my KTV club. Liu Wei, he stars in three TV series, and he visits here every week."

"Really," Chen said. Liu was a rising star, notorious for his lusty performance in bedroom scenes. Then something clicked in Chen's mind. "Do you have a lot of visitors from the TV and movie industry?"

"Yes, quite a few," Gu said. "How about this Saturday evening? White Cloud will also be there. A nice girl."

"She's very nice, but I don't think I have time this weekend." Chen said after a short pause, "How about this afternoon? A cup of coffee or tea. Indeed, we haven't seen each other for a while."

"What about the Starbucks near the New World?"

"Great. See you there in half an hour."

Chen left the canteen, and looked around before heading out through the bureau gate. Old Liang, the veteran bureau gatekeeper, saluted him with one hand, the other still grasping a plastic lunch box. The old man had worked dutifully for over forty years, long past his retirement age. The pension fixed in the eighties was not enough to support the retired gatekeeper in the nineties, so the bureau made a special allowance for him to continue to work there.

Chen got onto a bus, which turned out to be a most unpleasant experience. The conductor kept shouting, "Move in! Don't stand close to the door." At each new stop, a fresh wave of people broke in, elbowing and pushing him in still farther. The increasing heat mixed with the sweat smell was almost unbearable. The gap between the doing-well and the not-doing-well was visible everywhere. Nowadays, a successful entrepreneur like Gu would have a private car, and a rising Party cadre like Chen would have a company car, but the ordinary people could only take the ever-crowded bus.

A "provincial sister" standing next to Chen, wearing a black dress with thin shoulder straps, soon found her dress crushed out of shape, and started pushing Chen in frustration. At the next stop, though it was still quite a distance from his destination, he squeezed himself out through the walls of passengers, which caused another angry outburst of curses all around. The young girl followed him out, only to find the buttons on her shoulder straps missing. In embarrassment, she started screaming for the bus to stop, her hair disheveled, her dress rumpled. The bus crawled out of sight, leaving her standing there, holding her straps, weeping and whining, her voice seeming to dog him for two or three blocks.

The cool air from the central air-conditioning of the Starbucks was heavenly. It was one of the earliest American cafés in Shanghai, and its chain shops were rapidly spreading and attracting a large crowd of trendy customers. A new class, conveniently called the white collars, had emerged, most of them with well-paid positions in private or foreign companies. Young, educated, and well-off, they were eager to catch up with the world—through their newly acquired global brand awareness. Sitting in a corner, Gu was waiting for him.

"A cool place," Chen said as he took his seat, wiping the sweat from his forehead with a paper napkin.

"How could the Shanghai people have managed all these years without a good café?" Gu said. "People need a place like this."

"Good question. Old Marx is right again. Coffee belongs to the superstructure—for the mind, not for the basic needs of the body. People must have a solid economic basis before worrying about the superstructure."

"No wonder you're a political star, Chief Inspector Chen. You're capable of applying Marxism to a cup of coffee." Gu chuckled. "A lot of people come here for the feeling of being fashionable in today's society—that's for the mind too."

That was probably true. Sitting in an expensive American café might convince them they were the successful elite. But Chen hadn't come for that.

"A cop cannot afford to be fashionable." Chen decided not to talk about Dong for the moment, with whom Gu might have things to do in the future, as he did with Chen. Instead, the inspector came to the point directly. "I need to ask you a question, Gu."

"Go ahead."

"Do you happen to know An Jiayi?"

"Oh yes, a celebrity."

"Any contact with her?" Chen said. "For instance, has she visited your place?"

"No, she hasn't. As a rule, men don't bring their women to karaoke."

"What does that mean?"

"They come for K girls, my Comrade Chief Inspector. It's no business secret. Now that people have hi-fi stereo systems at home, they don't have to come to my place to sing. Someone like An has to be especially careful. It wouldn't be pleasant for her to be seen in KTV club in the company of another man."

"In the company of another man?"

"Isn't that something you want to find out—whom she associates with?"

"Well, I am curious," Chen said, nodding, before changing the topic. "She has a PR company, hasn't she?"

"I've heard of it."

"Now that's something that beats me. She has no business experience. Nor has she any capital—as far as I know."

"No, that's something you don't know. Today's society is like a huge market and everything is for sale. So is her anchorwoman position. She doesn't need any other capital."

"Enlighten me, Gu. I'm no businessman, you know."

"You think she interviews people for nothing? No, people pay a lot for publicity. What's more effective than a TV show?" Gu took a deliberate sip of his coffee. "She can really help."

"But how could her show run like that?"

"Believe it or not, these celebrities charge even for sitting at your banquet table. At the grand opening of my bar on Hengshan Road, I paid Hei Ling—an actress photographed by Taiwan *Playboy*—a thousand yuan for sitting there beside me. Pictures of her in my bar will appear in the newspaper, and customers will come. So there's a price for it."

"There's a price for everything," Chen said mechanically. And that was the problem. People paid the communist ideology only lip service. In spite of the *People's Daily* and the Party documents, the social reality was that each and every person looked out for him- or herself.

"Of course, she doesn't charge for every show of hers. Still, everybody is looking at the money—nothing else," Gu added with a cynical snicker. "What else is there?"

"But can a TV appearance be worth that much?"

"For some businesses, such an appearance could bring direct or indirect benefits. The image of a successful entrepreneur interviewed by a well-known anchorwoman speaks volumes, more than a whole-page advertisement in *Wenhui Daily.*"

"What you've said about her TV show may be true," Chen said. "So she has made enough money. Then why has she started a PR company? Surely, deals like this must be made under the table."

"How can there ever be enough money? The amount from her TV show is only a small dish. She has other clients. Much larger ones."

"How?"

"Well, because of our bureaucratic system, it may sometimes take government officials months, or even years, to approve a company's request for approval of plans or a deal. It won't do to knock at an unfamiliar door—even at a back door—with a bulging red envelope. You need *guanxi*—the person to knock for you, and to lubricate the bureaucratic machine. That's where her PR company comes in. She knows those officials through her work. It's easy for her to say a word or two in her sweet voice. For a matter of bureaucratic inefficiency, a short phone call might be enough. So companies are quite willing to pay her a sum for the early approval, for it gets them a competitive advantage and opens up other opportunities."

"That makes sense," Chen commented, stirring his coffee. So her company's role was to secure connections. Everything depended on her personal relationship with government officials. "Does she know anyone in charge of the real estate business?"

"That should be no surprise," Gu responded, looking up at Chen. "Land development approval is the biggest black hole today. Before our economic reform, land belonged to the state and it was up to the government to plan any development. Now it's totally different. Private construction companies can apply for land from the local government. Everyone has a good reason, and the officials don't have the time to study all the applications. For the property developer, it's a matter of life and death to get the land, and at a cheap price too. The price varies, depending on the location as well as on the purpose—"

"It sounds complicated," Chen said, recalling similar details about the land application in the New World Project. "I'm learning a lot today. So the government officials have to grant the use of the land in one way or another, but the officials don't have to listen to her, particularly when it's not a simple matter of bureaucratic efficiency. Can a phone call in her sweet voice be so effective? After all, it could be a multimillion yuan deal."

"You really don't know?"

"Know what?"

"About her special relationships with people in the city government." Gu came up with a mysterious smile. "To be exact, with someone in the office of land development. An old proverb has come back into current circulation, Chief Inspector Chen: *People sneer at poverty, but not at prostitution.* When the only criterion for value is a man's—or a woman's—money . . ."

"So you mean—"

"I'll find out more for you. Whatever you want me to do, Chen."

"Thanks," Chen said, though he had not said what he wanted. Gu was a very clever man, capable of hearing the sound vibrating beyond the strings. He wondered how Gu could try to help. As an afterthought, he added, "Oh, you don't have to mention our talk to anyone."

Shortly after Chen left the café, he got a call from Comrade Zhao.

"Xing made a new statement to the local newspapers, saying that he is going to give a press conference soon. He said he will release the names of those officials involved if we do not stop persecuting him."

"Let him do so. The more he blabs, the easier our work will be here."

"Do you think he'll tell the truth? And no matter how blatant his lies, some Americans will use what he says against China."

"What else can we do?"

"Xing may be bluffing there, I think, trying for some sort of deal. We have to push on with our work here."

"Well," Chen said, failing to see the connection here. Nor was he clear about what deal Zhao meant. He didn't want to give any details about his new approach. "I have been doing my best."

"Now, I don't think I have to repeat myself," Comrade Zhao concluded. "You are an emperor's special envoy in Shanghai."

Late that afternoon, Chen decided to pay a visit to his mother. He hadn't seen her since his interview with Dong.

There was not much, however, he could do for her. He had tried to talk her into staying with him, but she had invariably declined. His was a one-bedroom apartment. It would be too inconvenient, she declared, when he had visitors, especially young female visitors. As an alternative, he tried to find her a maid—a "provincial sister" in a live-in arrangement—but she would not listen to this, either.

The traffic snarls were terrible, especially at rush hour. When the car finally came in sight of Jiujiang Road, the lane, enveloped in the graying dusk, appeared shabbier than he had remembered.

In the bureau, he had heard people talking about the possibility of a three-bedroom apartment for him, so that his mother could move in with him. The housing system was still on a dual track. While some people had started buying their own apartments, the majority remained dependent on the government quota. A Party cadre, once promoted to a given rank or position, would be granted corresponding benefits, including better housing in the overcrowded city. The prospect for him was complicated, however, with so many lower-level cops on the waiting list, bickering and complaining. A special housing quota directly from the city government, as Dong had suggested, would have helped.

Around the street corner, he saw several kids playing in the shadow cast by a Coca-Cola umbrella. The red and white umbrellas had mushroomed everywhere. According to *Shanghai Morning,* they were a part of the colorful Shanghai landscape, along with the billboards presenting life-size Chinese stars drinking to their hearts' content. But he was still surprised at the sight of the umbrella there, close to the lane, where most of the inhabitants would find the drink too expensive, if not too exotic.

Aunt Qiang, a short, gray-haired woman who lived next door, stared at him as he got out of the taxi. She had a bamboo basket dripping with shepherd's purse blossom, a rural delicacy he had first read about in a poem by Qiji. She took a step forward and said, "Oh, you. Little—"

It appeared as if nothing had changed from his childhood memories, surely not the fresh, luscious shepherd's purse blossom, but the old neighbors might no longer consider it appropriate to address him by his small name.

He passed by a Chinese chess game in front of a dingy hot-water shop. Usually, the players and the audience would smoke, drink, and sometimes eat inside the water shop. The outside location was perhaps due to one of the players, Wong Ronghua, an ex-member of Shanghai Chess Team, attracting a large audience. Wong, a gaunt, grizzled man, grinned at Chen, revealing his teeth stained through years of bitter tea and poor cigarettes. He straddled one end of a wooden bench, and his opponent perched on the other end, keeping it precariously balanced. The chessboard was placed between them. Stripped to the waist in his black shorts, Wong appeared sallow, malnourished, with his ribs visible, looking like a washboard.

There were three or four hot-water bottles lined along the bench, squatting on the ground like the audience on the other side, who would probably remain in that position to the end. The neighborhood was not exactly a slum, but these were the people left out of the materialistic transition of the society.

His mother was upstairs watching TV in the attic room. The same fifteen-inch TV set he had bought years ago—still at the "state price" then. She had made a scarlet velvet cover for the TV, which must have kept her company a lot. Alone, she did not go out much, much less so after her recent stay in the hospital.

"With the cable, I can watch many stations," she said with a smile, turning off the TV with her remote. She made him a cup of green tea. "The tea's from one of your friends," she said. "I can hardly remember his name. The big buck who came to the hospital, I remember. Specially delivered from Hangzhou. The fresh tea of this year: Before the Rain. Quite an expensive kind, for all I know."

He thought he detected a subtle sarcastic note in her comment, but he said nothing. Instead, he kept breathing into the cup. People described him as a good son, but he was not so sure about that.

In time-honored Confucian doctrine, the worst thing possible for a man was to be without offspring to carry on the family name. That happened to be one of his mother's favorite topics, even though she did not elaborate so directly. To his relief, she did not appear eager to bring up the topic that afternoon.

"You have something on your mind, son."

"Well, no, not exactly."

"I don't know anything about your work, but I know my son."

"I'm doing fine. But there are so many things for me at the bureau. I may not be able to come here as often as I would like. How about moving in with me for a couple of weeks? I can take better care of you."

"Everything is so convenient here. Peddlers deliver fresh vegetables and meat to the room for a yuan. The old neighbors help a lot too," she said. "You are busy with your work. If I stayed with you, then when you come back late, I would be worried."

That was true. Even when he came back early, all the evening phone calls would not be pleasant for her. Not to mention some of his discussions.

"But I'm concerned about you."

"And I am concerned about you," she said, taking an appreciative sip. "All these gifts, and the tea too. Your friends keep sending me presents here."

"Really!"

"Because of your position, I am afraid."

"I understand, Mother. I have known some people through my work, but I draw a line for myself. In fact, the Party Discipline Committee has just assigned me to an important case."

"The Party Discipline Committee? Oh, what kind of case has the committee given you?"

In recent years, the committee had become the institution responsible for fighting corruption. Hence its popularity among the people. She looked both pleased and perplexed.

"An anticorruption case."

"Yes, the committee is like the police of the Party. Corruption is getting out of control with all the officials helping one another. It's time that the Beijing government does something about it."

"Yes, the Party authorities are determined." He went on, taking a sip at the tea. "It may be a tough job, and I am afraid I cannot take good care of you."

"Don't worry for me. You have taken a path different from your father's, but I think he would be pleased with your conscientious work if he could know of it in the underworld," she said slowly. "Of late, I have often dreamed of seeing him. Perhaps the day is not too far away."

"Dreams are dreams, Mother. You have missed him very much."

"I don't know what advice to give you, son, but I remember what your father used to say. *There are things a man will do, and things a man will not do.*"

"Yes, I always remember that."

Another Confucian quote, but he did not know how to apply it in the present case. Such a truism could be applied to anything, depending on the perspective a person took.

"Not all people are in a position to do something," she said.

There had been a subtle change in her attitude, he noticed. She had never really approved of his profession, but of late, she seemed to be more resigned to it, perhaps because she thought her late husband would have approved of her son serving the country as a police officer. She got up, moved to the chest, and produced a silk scroll of calligraphy.

"This is something your father left behind. Better in your apartment. I don't even have the room to hang it properly."

The scroll presented a poem, "River Snow," copied in his father's calligraphy. The verse had been written by Liu Zhongyuan, an eighth-century Tang dynasty poet:

Not a single bird visible
in hundreds of mountains,
nor any footprint discernible
on thousands of trails,
only a solitary boat,
a bamboo-capped-and-clad old man
alone, fishing—
the snow
in the cold river.

Such a lonely world, and such a solitary man, Chen contemplated. The image of the bamboo clothing added to the chilliness of the scene. Chen was struck by the ambiguity of the last few lines—not necessarily angling for fish, nothing but the snow in the cold river. Perhaps more of a gesture.

Liu was the poet who had written the fable about the barn rats. Chen recalled Yu's comment: *It's a fable, Chief.* In real life, Liu had ended up helpless, like the old fisherman in the cold river.

But Chen understood why his mother wanted to give the scroll to him. In spite of her failing health, her mind remained clear because of her studies of the Buddhist scripture: *no illusion of self, so she can see clearly.*

He left his mother's place without having sorted out his thoughts. He could not see clearly ahead.

The chess game was still going on outside the hot-water shop. None of the audience looked up at him as he passed. He was irrelevant to the battle in the world of a chessboard. Only Chang, the owner of the water shop, seemed to be nodding at him, as in the days of his childhood. His mother had hot water delivered to her attic room from time to time. But Chang could have been nodding at a master move in the chess game.

Then Chen was overtaken with an ominous question: why, all of a sudden, had she chosen to part with the scroll she had cherished for years? He struggled to push the unanswerable out of his mind.

Late that evening, a sealed package was express-delivered to Chen at home. No one had told him about such a package. He looked it over in puzzlement. The young, bean-sprout-thin courier refused to tell him the name of the sender.

"No, I can-can-not say," the courier stammered, his face as scarlet as a cooked shrimp. "My customer is strict about it."

"That's fine," Chen said, putting a rumpled ten-yuan bill into his hand. "Thank you."

Closing the door after him, Chen opened the envelope only to have a bunch of pictures fall onto the table.

They were pictures of An in a variety of scandalizing poses with a man. Chen took in a sharp breath. One of her drying herself with a white towel, her bare ass like two shining moons, the man sitting on the edge of a bed, his hand reaching out to her breasts. Another of her throwing her naked body across the bed strewn with pear blossom petals. In still another, the two were sitting up in bed, her bare shoulders flashing out of the blanket, reading, leaning against his . . . The pictures were not of high quality—most of them were out of focus. Possibly taken by a hidden camera in a hotel room.

Whoever the man in the pictures was, it was not Han. Moving the lamp over, Chen took a closer look at the clandestine lover. A tall, gaunt, middle-aged man with gray-streaked hair. There was a mole noticeable above the left corner of his mouth. Chen did not recognize him.

Chen was no moralist. In the mid-nineties, an extramarital affair was no longer seen as something corrupt or scandalous. Not in An's circumstances. In spite of a story of success with fame, family, beauty, and her own company too, he sensed her loneliness behind the glittering façade.

Exquisite as jade,
she cannot compete with the autumn crow flying
overhead, which still carries the warmth
from the Imperial Palace . . .

It was understandable that there was some other man in her life. Or men. Chen did not want to judge, though he could not help feeling slightly depressed.

He could guess who had sent those pictures. He had talked about An with Gu alone. The shrewd businessman hadn't promised anything specific, but the man in the pictures was no ordinary man. So here came the message: a potential lead in the romance. The sender chose to remain anonymous—for good reason.

It was a quiet evening. He pushed open the window and the air seemed instantly filled with the message of the early summer. One cicada started screeching in the foliage, and then a group of them followed in chorus. Still, Chief Inspector Chen did not see the necessity of approaching An in the name of the special investigation. Not immediately.

He returned to her file on the desk. In addition to her TV show and business, she had recently published a book based on her interviews of celebrities. Judging from the reviews, the book provided some interesting anecdotes as well as a number of photos. Popular because of people's interest in the celebrities. Chen had purchased a copy and skimmed it—there was no need for him to read it through. In those pictures, An looked elegant, professional, in sharp contrast to those in the package.

Jotting down some notes on a piece of paper, he picked up the phone.

"Hi, I want to speak to An."

"Who is it?"

"Chen Cao, your old friend."

"Oh, it's you, our famous detective," An said with a surprise of recognition in her voice. "What has made you call this evening?"

"Your book, I've just read it," he said, "and I've looked at your pictures too. So stunningly beautiful, all the geese and fish would dive out of your sight in self-consciousness."

"Come on, Chen. You're not calling to make fun of me like that."

"No, I'm not. People buy the book like crazy because they like you so much. And count me in, one of your greatest fans."

"Well, that I do not know. You must have long forgotten about me."

"How could that be? I've been busy, as you know, but I kept seeing you on TV and I grabbed the book as soon as I heard about it." He added emphatically, "I like your prose style."

"You really do?"

"Definitely. So let me buy you dinner, An, in celebration of your literary success."

"You're overwhelming me tonight, Chief Inspector Chen. When?"

"How about tomorrow evening?"

"Fantastic. I know a restaurant, Golden Island. Still quite new. Not too many people go there, but it's excellent. On the Bund."

"Golden Island. I've heard of it too. On the Bund. You'll sign the book for me, won't you?"

"I would love to. I've been thinking about interviewing you for my show."

"It would be a great honor for me. On your show, in your scarlet cheongsam, you have always reminded me of Li Bai's 'Qingping Tune.' *'The clouds eager to make / your dancing costume, the peony, / to imitate your beauty, the spring breeze / touching the rail, the petal / glistening with dew—'* "

"Cut it out, Chen," she said with a giggle. "You're being hopelessly romantic."

"See you at the restaurant." He added, imitating her tone, "See me on TV."

"Oh, you still remember that."

See me on TV was a phrase she had used years earlier. It was a little flirtatious on her part, then. Still a little flirtatious on the phone, now.

The way he talked shouldn't have alerted anyone. He was notorious for quoting poetry, and perhaps for being romantic too.

She'd better not be prepared for the evening.

6

GOLDEN ISLAND WAS ONE of the new restaurants on the Bund.

For most Shanghainese, the Bund still constituted one of the most glamorous areas in the city, with its picturesque waterfront and the magnificent buildings stretching along Zhongshan Road. In Chen's childhood, most of these buildings, though in government use then, were seen as evidence of the imperialist exploitation, for they had housed prestigious Western companies in the pre-1949 era. In the nineties, the city government had released those buildings to the original or new Western companies. Consequently, high-end restaurants reappeared around the area.

Golden Island was popular not only because of its location but also because of its architectural design. The swelling restaurant had been converted from the original rooftop of an old business building, with ceilings, tall windows, and walls added on a modern note.

As Chen stepped out of the elevator, a young waitress came over to him. "Have you made your reservation, sir?"

"Under the name of An or Chen."

"Oh, Miss An has already reserved a special room. Lovers' Nest, please."

"Oh—"

He had heard of the Lovers' Nest. While the main dining hall did not look so different from other restaurants, across the entrance, on the side overlooking the Bund, stood a row of cubicles named Lovers' Nest, well-known among young people. He had learned about them from White Cloud.

It was a tiny room, with only two bench seats inside, a wood table in between, and hardly enough space for two to dine without accidentally touching each other. Lovers might not mind that, though. The windows boasted a broad view of the Bund with the vessels moving along the river, and those sitting by the window would enjoy a sensation of being up above the crowd.

It was surprising that she had reserved such a room, but nonetheless a good choice, considering what they were going to talk about. He took his seat and noticed that there was a "do not disturb" sign available on the table.

"You can put the sign outside the door," the waitress said with a knowing smile. "We will knock before coming in."

While he waited for An, he took a picture out of a large envelope. He had accomplished only one thing that day—the identification of the middle-aged lover in those pictures. He was Jiang Xiaodong, the Director of the City Land Development Office. It was a relatively new position and not exactly a big fish in terms of the cadre rank, but it was a crucial position in terms of the property market. Especially to the locusts of real estate developers. Now Ming's use of An's PR company made perfect sense. Of course, Jiang might not be the only one behind the scenes. Chen put the picture back into the envelope and picked up the menu.

Chen did not have to wait long. Halfway through looking at the menu, he heard a light knock, and he looked up to see An entering with a familiar smile. It was as if they had never fallen out of touch all these years.

She wore the same scarlet silk cheongsam, high-slitted, sleeveless, and an elegant pearl necklace shimmered around her neck. The dress clung to her body like caresses, hugging her sensual curves as she moved. She looked barely changed from their reading-group days.

"The room is lit by your presence," he said, standing up.

"The room is great because of a great man like you," she said, holding out her hand. "So now we have had our exchange of literary compliments."

Hers, too, sounded like an echo from a classical essay. An was a popular anchorwoman not merely because of her pretty face: she also spoke in a cultured manner.

There was another knock on the door. The young waitress came in and lit the candle in a glass bowl. It added a romantic touch to the occasion. She then placed a bottle of Dynasty on the table and uncorked it for them.

"Compliments of the house."

He shook the glass, sipped at it, and made a gesture of approval.

The candlelight flickered on their faces. The dancing flame carried Chen back to the old days of their passion for reading literature. Now, he joined her in reading the menu instead. The restaurant claimed to have invented a new Shanghai cuisine, which, according to a brief introduction on the front page, consisted of a combination of other cuisines, subtly modified to a taste acceptable to the city. A Sichuan dish was made less spicy, or a Ningbo dish less salty.

"When it is everything," Chen commented, "it is nothing."

"How about lovers' table d'hote? It contains all of our chef's specials. It will be a dinner you two cannot forget," the waitress recommended.

Not a bad idea, he thought, and it saved him from taking the time to choose. The two resumed their talk. It was the first time they had ever been alone together for a dinner. The cubicle felt like a *sampan* room. The river came to life under their gaze, as the neon lights formed and transformed fantastic patterns.

He was not in a hurry to question her. They would at least enjoy some of the meal first. While he might not have much to say about himself, he found it not at all difficult to listen to her story. Perhaps with the unexpected reunion, with the wine, with the scene spreading outside the window, she would grow sentimental.

Hers wasn't a new story, not the personal part of it, which he had already learned from other sources. Narrated from her perspective, though, it sounded nonetheless tragic, albeit ordinary.

"Han says that he will not come back without success. When? God alone knows. But for my mother, who takes care of our son, I couldn't have managed these years all by myself," she said wistfully. "Perhaps I shouldn't have put so much pressure on him."

The color of the fresh willow shoots out there
precipitates her into regret:
She should not have sent him away,
so far away, going after success.

She couldn't be blamed for being such a celebrity, but her husband's dilemma wasn't difficult to understand—it was hard to have such a well-known wife. Still, it was not for Chen to judge who was responsible for her failed marriage. Deep in his heart, he guessed there was something parallel in his life—a peg, a string—he didn't want to touch at the moment.

"Thank you for telling me all this," he said. "Indeed, every household has a difficult account. Look at me. Still a bachelor, about which my mother worries all the time. I wish we could all be back in the days of our reading group."

"No need to be too hard on yourself," she said, reaching across the table to pat his hand. "The past is past, but we still have the future in our hands."

A clever remark, echoing perhaps another book they had read together in the group.

"Gather the flower while you may," he said, taking a drink, "or you have only a barren twig in your hand."

"Exactly." She then tried to make him talk about his work, which he managed to evade.

"You're not that unfamiliar with the official world, An. Nothing but sordid details. I don't think we should spoil the evening with those things. On the other hand, you have a PR company. It's a huge success, I've heard. Tell me more about it."

"How long do you think I can work as an anchorwoman, Chen?"

"What do you mean?"

"It's a star-making age. As a woman, how long can I remain attractive to the public? I have to be realistic. Several people have been coveting my position at the TV station, and you should see them—younger, and much prettier too. In the entertainment industry, new young faces come along every year. Xie Donghong at CCTV, you know, is only in her mid-twenties, and with an MBA degree from an American university."

"But you have so many loyal fans who watch you every night. I'm one of them."

"Come on, Chen. A man may blossom in his forties, but a woman goes downhill in her thirties. I'm thirty-seven. It is a fact I have to acknowledge," she said, gazing into the wine, as if in search of her own reflection. The early summer evening spread peacefully outside the window, while autumn waves rippled in her eyes. "But you are different, a rising star in the political world."

It reminded him of two lines of a poem—*As always, a general is like a beauty, / there's no seeing a white hair.* In China's new cadre policy, age became a crucial criterion. He was lucky, but he had better seize the moment too.

"The car, the apartment, and the new boarding school for my son, all these I have to pay for," she went on. "Do you think my state company salary is enough? I have to earn money for the future of my son, if not for myself."

There was real worry in her voice. Spoiled by her success, she might not be able to envision the life of an ordinary woman. It wasn't something she had planned, but it wasn't something she could help, he understood.

"I know what you mean. I have to do translation to make up for my bureau salary."

"Besides, I have to keep myself busy. Because of my working schedule at the TV station, and my son studying away at school, I am all alone when I come back," she said, taking a sip of the wine. "One or two solitary evenings may not be too bad, but—"

"You are multitalented," he said, in an effort to change the topic. "You have so many fans of your show. Now you have so many clients for your PR company."

"It's nothing but connections," she said. "You can do it too. In fact, you can help me a lot."

Was she going to include him as one of her connections? If so, she would talk more freely.

"Well, you never know," he said.

"Heaven and Earth of Connections. That's the name of another PR company, my biggest rival in the city. The company owner is the son of an ex-politburo member. All he needs to do is to make phone calls to important people, 'Hi, Uncle, my father asks about you,' or 'Oh, Aunt, I've just talked to my father about you,' and he then slips in a few words for his clients. These 'uncles' and 'aunts' are in powerful positions, capable of making decisions. So he charges for the calls—"

Abruptly Chen felt something moving in his pants pocket—throbbing. His cell phone began vibrating instead of ringing. He must have accidentally pressed a button. As he took it out, the caller hung up. He was clumsy with the new gadgets and he fumbled with it a bit, unsure how to restore the ringing function.

She took the phone from his hand, pushed a few buttons, and it rang with a pleasant tune he had never heard before.

"Thank you so much." He refrained from asking how she'd done it. To her, he must have appeared awkward enough.

The lovers' table d'hote started to arrive. First, the cold dishes. One was salted cucumber skin in green rolls, crisp and clear. Another presented red shiny dates steamed with sticky rice stuffed inside. Not only sweet, it was also sensual in its color suggestion, the soft white rice inside the scarlet date skin. It took enormous imagination to invent this small wonder—like something from *The Dream of the Red Chamber.*

"Scarlet and white, as in a classical Chinese love poem," An said. "People call the dish 'your soft heart.' "

She seemed to be at home. Possibly a regular customer in the company of Jiang, or of some high-ranking officials. After the limelight, after the wine, she must have found it hard to turn back to those old days. A company of hers would ensure the luxurious lifestyle she enjoyed. There was perhaps nothing wrong with it in this materialistic time, he admitted.

She drank a little, set the glass on the table, and held a scarlet date between her red lips, her white teeth glistening in an amorous way. There was a subtle, mature voluptuousness about her. She must have sensed his glance, her eyes mirroring the response in his imagination.

According to one of his favorite poets, what might have been points to infinite possibilities. Years earlier, this could have been a most wonderful night, with two of them sitting together there, wrapped in a cocoon of intimacy, ready to burst into unknown realities. But time flies. People change. It was an evening for police investigation. He could not help it. The way he could not help being Chief Inspector Chen.

Another knock on the door. The waitress sent in more dishes. It turned out to be a feast of delicious nostalgia, in tune with the latest trend of the city. He was particularly impressed with the Old Subei Chicken Soup, which smelled rich and pleasant with a subtle flavor of wistfulness. Its very name sounded like a call for a bygone era. Another call was the Granny Pork in the small urn with the shining homely color of brown soy sauce. As in a granny's traditional home cooking style, the pork had been fried and then steamed for such a long time that it melted on their tongues.

An recommended the pigeon of the house, its skin fried to a golden brown, a crisp crust covering the tender meat. She started tearing the bird with her slender fingers. "The wing is the best part, its muscle juicy out of constant movement," she said, placing a pigeon wing onto his plate.

"I have to tell you something, An," he said abruptly and apologetically, putting down the glass as he moved on to explain the real purpose of the evening.

"It is an official investigation under the Central Party Discipline Committee. I need your cooperation," he concluded. "Our friendship is very important to me, but for a cop, work has to come first. That's what I am, whether I like it or not."

"I thought," she said slowly, "that you wanted to see me for old times' sake."

"It's for old times' sake, An, that I wanted to meet you here first."

That was both true and not true. Or, like the much-quoted couplet in *The Dream of the Red Chamber*: *When the true is false, the false is true. / Where there is nothing, there is everything.* An official investigation in the name of the Party Discipline Committee could have a disastrous impact on her business. No one would engage any service from such a PR company. As well as a disastrous effect on her reputation. There would be no way for her—an embodiment of political correctness—to appear on TV again.

"How could you have listened to those people?" she said, her face flushing in indignation.

"I would not have listened, but then I received something." He produced the large envelope that contained the pictures.

Her face blanched at the sight of the photographs. He watched her closely. An was an experienced anchorwoman, her feelings always deftly hidden behind a professional mask, but she failed to conceal her immediate reaction. The hand that held her glass began to quiver. She put her wrist on the table to steady it.

He sat back, crossed his knees, and selected a cigarette from his case with deliberation.

"That's what an old friend is for," she said between her teeth. Putting her spoon into the fish soup, leaving it there, and digging a cigarette from her crumpled pack, she was trying to pull herself together, but not successfully. She was doing anything to keep herself from looking up at him.

"I wish I had an alternative. So I want to talk to you first as an old friend."

"What do you mean?"

"What if I had turned these pictures in to the committee first? You don't need me to tell you. In a worse scenario, if somebody else—not necessarily in the committee—got hold of those pictures, God alone knows what could happen. A unscrupulous rascal could have sold them to a tabloid magazine for a fortune."

She didn't say anything for a minute or two, staring at the pigeon head, which stared back at her with its dead eyes.

"Your company would be closed, your job lost, your property taken, and your apartment would be gone too. What a nice apartment! I don't think it would be easy for you to move back to your *tingzijian* room of eight or nine square meters, An. If that room is still there."

"You don't have to be sarcastic, Comrade Chief Inspector Chen."

He did not have to be sarcastic, but sitting in a "lovers' nest" he had to justify himself. He went on, "Don't believe those high up will try to help you. They have their own necks to save. Beijing means business this time, and they know it. An anticorruption bureau will be set up in Shanghai. Do you want to sacrifice yourself for those who would throw you out as a pawn? In the end, they may get away scot-free, but you'll have to pay the full price."

She studied him up and down, still in disbelief over her humiliating downfall in front of an old friend.

His cell phone started ringing again. "Nothing important," he said, turning it off after looking at the number.

"You think you can pull this off?" she said. "Evidence like this may not be permissible. As a cop, you know better."

"Let me put it this way, An. When I got the assignment, a leading comrade in Beijing joked about me being the emperor's special envoy with an imperial sword. You know what it means, don't you? In ancient China, such an envoy could kill without having obtained official approval first. Believe me, the evidence will be more than permissible."

"So I have no choice? Listen, Chen," she said hoarsely, "I want you to know something—"

He did not say anything, waiting to hear what she wanted him to know. But the waitress knocked at the door again. She came to light a new candle for them, bowing before she left with a smile. In the fresh candlelight, he noticed that An was without makeup. Her face clear and clean, suggestive of an innocent purity, untouched by evil. She looked up at him, in a long gaze, as if the autumn waves were breaking against the shore in her large black eyes.

"Xing has so many connections in Shanghai," she finally said. "But why have you chosen me, a helpless woman, of all the people? Are the others too monstrous for you to touch?"

She was sharp. The accusation hit home. He did not wince. It was not that he did not have the guts, he told himself.

"I have no choice, An. The investigation is under the committee," he said. "If you collaborate, I won't mention your name in the report. I give you my word."

"So what do you want from me?"

"You tell me everything related to Xing—or to Ming—and I'll return these photos to you. Your choices in your personal life are not my business.

The anticorruption campaign, however, is a matter of life and death for our country."

"Can I have some time to think?"

"About what?"

"It may be a matter of life and death for me."

He lit another cigarette for her and pushed the window slightly open. Unexpectedly, a mosquito came buzzing in. An incredible nuisance at such a height, like a tedious song coming from next door during a sleepless night.

An then began to tell about the business deal she had helped to arrange for Ming. A long, complicated story. The beginning part of it had little to do with An, comprehensible only in a larger context. With the development of the economic reform, there were a large number of state-run factories that had fallen into terrible shape. In the old days, they manufactured products in accordance to the state planning, without having to worry about profit or loss. Now they had to struggle for survival in the market economy. Shanghai Number Six Textile Mill was such a factory. Its products were poor quality, and it could not obtain the raw material at the state price as before. Most of the workers, iron-bowl holders, were hardly in a position to help. Still, they clamored for the same socialist pay and benefits, desperate as ants crawling on a hot wok.

According to the *People's Daily,* the problems might be insignificant, "inevitable in the historic transition." But these factories became an increasingly impossible liability. So with a new government policy, a state-run company was allowed—for the first time since 1949—to go bankrupt. Interested entrepreneurs were encouraged to buy them at a discount, and even enjoy a further reduction by retaining its workers. That, too, was considered contributing to the political stability. The buyer for Number Six Mill was none other than Ming, who, without revealing a specific plan, promised to keep five hundred employees and so got the factory at a "symbolic sum." No one knew anything about Ming's coup until after the deal was done. He razed the factory for residential property construction. The location turned out to be close to a not-yet-announced subway route, so it attracted a number of investors the moment word got out. The value of the land proved to be five times more than what he had paid for the factory.

To meet the government requirement for keeping the factory in operation, Ming set up a small workshop of about ten people for equipment maintenance. He reached a housing development agreement with a construction company, through which he was able to retain the ex–state employees as temporary construction workers. Upon completion of the project, he would own one-third of the apartment complex.

In an inside report to the city government, Ming's maneuver was described as one arrow that killed three birds. It helped the state stop losing money through a bottomless hole; it kept ex–state employees holding their rice bowl—though no longer made of iron—for a couple of years; and it met the housing needs of the city. Of course, the report did not touch on the profit Ming had walked away with. He did not pay a single penny out of his own pocket. With an official copy of the factory buying-over document as the mortgage, he had acquired a low interest loan from the government bank. In short, it was like "capturing a white fox empty-handed."

Nor did the report mention a snag hidden in the operation. It was against government policy to turn a factory into a commercial construction lot. Otherwise Ming would not have gotten the land at such an incredibly low price.

Everything had been achieved through his connections, or rather, through Xing's. The large network of corruption worked. The PR service provided by An also contributed: among other things it represented the small workshop for equipment maintenance as the factory's continuous operation, a claim accepted by Dong for the Shanghai State Industry Reform Committee, and it obtained the land development permission from Jiang for the City Land Development Office. All this was not difficult, as An put it, just offering incense to every god in sight. She knew the doors, both the front and the back.

"Perhaps not simply because of your knowledge about the doors," Chen said, casting another glance at the pictures on the table. But the deal was big: even with all her connections, it was probably too big for the sweet words she had whispered on the phone or in the bedroom. Still, there was no denying her part.

She did not respond to his remark.

He said simply, "Now tell me more about Ming."

"Ming keeps a low profile. He stays in the shadow of Xing. As far as I know, he's focused in Shanghai, and Xing takes good care of his little brother. They are much closer than ordinary half brothers. Xing does whatever his mother says, and Ming is her favorite son."

"Really!"

"Xing is not a monster throughout. A filial son in his way, like you," she added in hurry. "Of course, I'm not talking about you as a monster."

"No one is good or evil a hundred percent. You are right about it."

"But they didn't tell me everything. Like the inside information about the subway—neither Ming nor Xing mentioned a single word about it to me. That's the most important part of the operation and a number of people higher up were involved."

The Bund was enveloped in the night. Across the river, numerous neon lights on the eastern bank started projecting fanciful attractions for a new part of the city. She might have been telling the truth, except the part about her own activities.

"How did you get those photos?" she said.

"Somebody sent them to me. Don't worry about it. No one knows anything about our meeting tonight. No one could have suspected—in a lovers' nest."

"A penny for your thoughtfulness."

"Now, you mentioned that Ming contacted you as late as the Chinese New Year. According to my information, Xing got away in early January. If that's true, Ming got out later than Xing."

"I can't be sure of the exact date. Ming may still be here, I've heard something about it, but I'm not sure. I'm going to make phone calls, and I'll let you know as soon as I find out."

"That will really help. You know how to contact me." He put down his cell phone number on the back of his business card and rose from the table.

At the restaurant exit, the elevator door opened like a grin, and she leaned over, whispering in his ear, "You promise that you will return the pictures?"

"I give you my word."

"Get rid of them in your memory too."

He was surprised at the coquettish way she made her second request. It was not like her—not in the days of their reading group. But he did not know her anymore, not after so many years.

"I will, An."

"I will come or call, Chen," she said. "If not tomorrow, then the day after tomorrow."

7

AN DID NOT COME or call the following day, nor the day after it, as she had promised.

Chen did not want to think too much about it. He tried to put his father's calligraphy scroll on the wall. Liu Zhongyuan was a great Tang poet, and like some of his contemporary intellectuals, Liu had been politically disappointed—with those red rats controlling the court—but it was in his exile that he wrote his best poems. Chen wondered whether this could be the reason why he wrote so little of late. Then his mind wandered away, thinking of several lines by another Tang dynasty poet who also wrote in his down-and-out days:

> *You say you will come, but you do not keep your word,*
> *you're gone, not a single trace left.*
> *The moonlight slant on the tower,*
> *at the fifth strike of the night watch.*

Chen recalled those lines in a self-deprecative mood. But he was not exactly worried. There was no telling whether Ming was still hiding in the city, and it would take time for An to find out. Still, she would cooperate. After all, he had the pictures in his hands.

In the meantime, he kept himself busy interviewing other officials on the list. He made a point of being perfunctory and polite, never pushing anyone too far. The message would be clear: he had learned the risks involved from Director Dong and now Chief Inspector Chen was merely putting on a show—that's all it was.

He also made inquiries into Ming's business—through his personal connections, under the excuse of apartment hunting. He had been talking about buying his mother an apartment for some time, so his questions about real estate companies seemed natural. Ming having disappeared, his company had gone temporarily into disarray, but the housing project was said to be moving forward with no real disruption. Before his mysterious evaporation, Ming sold the company to someone named Pan Hao. Pan was a mystery man, allegedly from Beijing, with several large companies under his name. So the financial future of the new company seemed to be secure.

He got a call from Detective Yu in the afternoon.

"In a press conference held yesterday," Yu said, "Party Secretary Li bragged and boasted about your work under the Party Discipline Committee."

"What? He promised not to tell anyone about it!"

"He mentioned you as our ace detective, and your assignment as another proof of the government's determination to fight corruption."

"It's really becoming a part of a show, as you've said."

"The publicity won't do you any good."

"No, it won't. But my assignment was probably no longer a secret after my talk with Director Dong. Not in that circle anyway."

"Director Dong—any new development?"

"Not yet," Chen said. "I'll keep you posted."

For quite a long while afterward, Chen remained upset with the news. Why should Party Secretary Li have trumpeted his investigation like that? It was putting him on the grill of public attention. Not to mention the political.

He made a few more calls for interview appointments.

An still didn't call. Chen gazed at the scroll and lit a cigarette. The ashtray was already full. It was shaped like a shell, as if trying to catch a message from the distant oceans. He was seized with a portentous feeling. She should have touched base with him, progress or not. So he called her. No one answered. Neither in her office, nor at her home.

Around six o'clock, he opened a can of Qingdao beer with a pop, and again dialed her home number. It was answered by an unfriendly, unfamiliar male voice.

"Who are you?"

"Oh, I'm a friend of hers," Chen answered. It was not her husband Han, that much Chen could tell immediately.

"A friend of hers—" the man said. "What's your name?"

Chen wondered whether it could be someone she was seeing—possibly none other than Jiang. But the way the man asked the question was ridiculous. Whoever Chen was, the man had no reason to be jealous. An was probably not at home, otherwise she would not have permitted another to talk like this.

"What's that to you?" Chen said, ready to hang up. "I'll call back later."

"Don't hang up, man. It's useless. I've got your number."

That was strange. Caller ID was still something rare in the city. She might have it at home, but what could the man do? Chen took a gulp of the cold beer and said, "What do you mean?"

"Tell me who you are, and your identification card number too, or we'll find out, and then it will be big trouble for you."

"Are you a cop?"

"What the hell do you think I am?"

"What do you think I am?" Chen snapped.

"Listen"—the man at the other end of the line raised his voice—"I am Sergeant Kuang of the Shanghai Police Bureau."

"Listen—I am Chief Inspector Chen Cao of the Shanghai Police Bureau."

"What—oh, I am so sorry, Comrade Chief Inspector Chen. It's like the flood washing away the Temple of the Dragon King."

"What has happened, Kuang?"

"An Jiayi was killed early this morning."

"What?" Chen was stunned. "So you are there in charge of the homicide case?"

"Yes. I've just arrived."

"Where was her body found?"

"At home. She was supposed to appear at the TV station in the afternoon, but she did not turn up. People called everywhere, without success. She had never missed a show before. According to the secretary at her PR company, An complained about not feeling so well the last few days. So the station sent someone over to her home, and they discovered her body."

"Don't move the body or do anything," Chen said. "I'm on my way."

"I won't. Celebrity cases can be too tough for our ordinary homicide squad."

Chen detected the sarcasm in the response. Kuang wasn't eager for his cooperation. Every now and then, Chen's special case squad had to take over the politically sensational cases—which was not pleasant for him. Still, such a division of labor was far from pleasant for people in the homicide squad too, depriving them of the limelight as it did.

The traffic was bad, as usual. Along Yen'an Road, the taxi simply crawled, like a disoriented ant. It had grown dark when the taxi finally arrived at the high-end apartment complex on Wuzhong Road. There were a couple of guards standing at the entrance. Apparently it was a secure, high-class neighborhood.

The apartment building in question had already been roped off. A man in plainclothes standing near the entrance recognized the chief inspector, nodding vigorously, but Chen failed to place him.

Kuang was waiting for Chen outside the apartment on the third floor, waving a newspaper like a fan. A short skinny man in his early thirties, Kuang had protruding eyes like a special kind of goldfish Chen had seen in his childhood.

Chen went up and said, "Well?"

"Doctor Xia has come and left," Kuang said. "According to him, she was strangled to death early in the morning. Possibly around two o'clock. Having had sex shortly before. Rape of some sort. The criminal used a condom."

"That's uncommon in the best area of Shanghai. The murderer might not have been a stranger to her."

"That's possible. He could have committed the crime after having consensual sex with her. There is no sign of forced entry, no bruises on her body, no noise heard by the neighbors. The location of the apartment complex makes the scenario of a stranger breaking in hardly possible."

It was not unimaginable for a woman like her, with a husband away in Germany for years, to have a lover, in the city of Shanghai, in the nineties. She had had one at least, Chen knew.

He walked with Kuang into the bedroom, where her body had not been moved yet. On her back on the carpet, An lay spread-eagled, wrapped in a white terry robe that slipped high up, revealing her bare thighs and belly. Her silk lace panties were removed, not torn, but crumpled into a ball beside her. Her face turned to one side, already bluish under the light. He noticed that her skin was slightly waxy. Her fingernails and toenails, painted scarlet, looked unbroken, unsoiled.

He had seen her numerous times on TV, always elegantly dressed, reading the news with a halo of political correctness. He had never imagined his last image of her would be like this. It would perhaps haunt him for a long time.

He knelt down and gazed into her eyes, which stared back, unblinking. The corneas appeared cloudy, which reinforced Dr. Xia's estimate of the time of death. He studied her face for a minute before touching her eyelids. He muttered almost inaudibly, "I'll catch the murderer, An."

To his astonishment, her eyes closed slowly, as if in response to his words.

"Wow! It's like in those old stories," Kuang exclaimed in a low, shocked voice. "Your touch worked the miracle."

In a story Chen had heard long ago, a murdered woman refused to close her eyes until someone swore her revenge. Kuang, too, must have heard it. Chen was also aware of the consternation implied in Kuang's comment. For in that particular tale, the man who swore her revenge was romantically involved with her. It wasn't the moment, however, for Chen to be concerned about his colleague's interpretation.

He remained standing beside her, staring, trying and failing to imagine what could have crossed her mind in her last moment. The effort was momentous to him, sort of establishing a bond of pledge between the living and the dead.

Beside him, Kuang started elaborating his theory of a rape murder case in detail.

Chen listened, nodding, his eyes now fixed on An's family picture in a crystal frame on the nightstand. An, Han, and their son, all of them smiling and basking in the happy sunlight on the Bund. Possibly taken in the days before Han's departure to Germany, their marriage probably already on the rocks. The picture still told a story expected by the camera. Smile—click—done. But the fact that the picture remained on the nightstand in her last days saddened Chen.

The scene behind An's family might not be far away from Golden Island, for he noticed the neon sign of Kentucky Chicken, which had enjoyed a tremendous success in Shanghai, in a colonial building at the corner between Yen'an and Zhongshan Roads. The building had been named East Wind Restaurant in the seventies, and even earlier, at the beginning of the twentieth century, it was the Shanghai Club, a prestigious establishment that catered to English expatriates and featured the longest bar in the world at the time. Whatever its names, the building had a much longer life.

Chen did not say anything to Kuang. An's death must be related to the Xing investigation, but he saw no point in discussing it with the young cop.

Kuang might have been baffled by the inscrutable chief inspector, who made little response to his analysis. For Kuang, there were also earlier questions left unanswered. Chen's call to her, for one.

When the morgue people came to carry away the body, Chen said to

Kuang that he would like to stay there for a while, alone. Kuang nodded and left in respectful confusion.

Chen stepped out onto a tiny balcony overlooking the area. It was a high-end subdivision. Down there were parking spaces outlined for the residents. He didn't know which car was hers. He then noticed a broken guitar, apparently long untouched, dust-covered, in a corner of the balcony. Once again, a poem came to him out of the unlikely moment, this one by Li Bai, a Tang dynasty poet from hundreds of years earlier.

The moon touching the autumn's first-born frost,
she still wears her silk dress
too flimsy for the night,
playing the silver lute,
long and hard,
in the courtyard,
unable to bring herself back
to the empty room.

Chief Inspector Chen was not intent on searching the room one more time. Had there been something important, it must have been taken away. Still, he wanted to hang on there.

He pulled out the small drawer of the nightstand. Among some scrap papers was an address book. Its cover bore the faded emblem of the TV station with the year 1982 printed. He opened it and found it belonged to Han. Most of the addresses and phone numbers must be outdated. On a page he saw a quote from the beginning of *A Tale of Two Cities.* It was perhaps from their reading-group days. The address book might have been there only for sentimental reasons. Still, he put it in his pocket.

Now, in the room where she had spent her last days, he chose to see her life in a new light. He did not want to see An simply as someone in a corruption case. Her involvement was admittedly a mistake on her part, but could she have done all that because of her loneliness? People had to keep themselves busy with one thing or another, like himself. A public relations company might not have been a bad idea in itself, and it was natural for someone in PR to work with businesspeople like Ming. As for her personal life, Chen thought he was no judge—he knew he wouldn't like to be judged by others.

What would her life have been like if things had remained as they were in their reading-group days? Both An and Han might have been here, like so many others. A contented wife, opening a colorful career album over the weekend . . .

He pulled himself back from these useless thoughts. Some people had complained in the bureau that Chen wasn't meant to be a cop—and perhaps he was indeed still too romantic for such a career.

But it was a battle of life and death now. An was not innocent, but she could have lived with her problems. It was his investigation that had led to her death. And the least he could, and should, do was to bring the criminal to justice for her.

Someone had forestalled him. In spite of his precautions, the path had been anticipated and blocked as soon as he had turned mistakenly pleased with his Chen trail—in targeting someone not conspicuous, and in a roundabout way. All his efforts had fallen through and he did not know which link had gone wrong. That was the terrifying part. It appeared he remained in the light, while the enemy remained in the dark, ready to pounce on him.

There were a lot of things he did not know, but he was almost sure—no use pretending to himself—that she had alarmed some people in her effort to find the whereabouts of Ming. She must have made phone calls.

So that would be the direction for him: her telephone records for the last few days. But the case was not assigned to the special case squad. His pushing Sergeant Kuang would be like attempting to cook in somebody else's kitchen.

What was worse, if he himself was under watch, as he suspected, any steps taken by him could have consequences, not only for him. He thought of what Dong had ominously suggested.

That night, he failed to fall asleep for a long while. A cricket chirped intermittently, not too far away, rubbing its wings in a corner of the room. He stared up at the ceiling like one possessed. In his police experience, he had occasionally speculated on the possibility of investigating a victim close to him. An was not exactly close—never had been. Still, she had been nice to him in the reading-group days. More than anything else, he cherished the memories of their literary passion then.

One evening, he recollected, after their reading activity, four of them walked into a shabby ramshackle eatery near the Bund. Han, An, Ding, and he, sitting around a rough wood table. They were poor, ordering plain noodles, sharing a tiny dish of roast Beijing duck, and spending two hours over a poem, to the great annoyance of a white-haired waiter.

Tonight, the same night cloud, the same siren over the river, the same petrel flying, perhaps, as if out of a calendar, in spite of all the changes . . .

Lying on his bed, he also thought of Han, who by now must have learned about his wife's death, and of Ding, who seemed to have disappeared in the south. Chen, alone, was the one still hanging on there. He should be grateful, he contemplated, for being able to do something for those not as lucky.

And he fell asleep with a new plan for his action.

8

CHIEF INSPECTOR CHEN ADOPTED a different approach with Jiang Xiaodong, the Director of the City Land Development Office.

It was an attempt with dual purpose. He had to investigate Jiang's involvement in both the An case and the Xing case.

According to the information initially given to Chen, Jiang had never met Xing in privacy. Nor was there any record of his meeting with Ming. But for those pictures with An, no one could have suspected there was anything untoward about the approval of the land development.

But Chen was not going to use the pictures too early. The scandal would spell the downfall of the corrupt director, but it would not necessarily prove Jiang a murderer nor lead to a breakthrough in the Xing investigation.

So Chen started by focusing on something small, the company car service for Jiang. In China, a Party cadre, once promoted to a certain rank, would be provided with a company car. Theoretically, the car was meant for business use only, but a dinner or karaoke party could be claimed as necessary for business. No one would raise any question about those requests. At the rank of a chief inspector, Chen had the use of the bureau car, though not exclusively, and not with a designated driver. At Jiang's rank, a car and driver were at his service, but they were not available twenty-four hours a day or parked at his residence. Jiang still had to call beforehand. So the chief inspector would check through the Chen trail first.

Early in the morning, Chen went to Jiang's office, which, like Dong's, was located in the City Government Building. Instead of entering the building, he headed straight for the parking lot, where he saw a small office with a couple of people dispatching various cars. It took him no time to find out that Jiang's driver was Lai Shan. Lai had already left to get the car maintenanced that morning, so Chen had to wait there patiently.

Around ten-thirty, someone in the office said to Chen, "Lai has come back. He's probably going to have lunch in his car. A couple of steamed buns—you know."

Chen stepped out to find Lai, but quickly changed his mind. He walked out to the square and hailed a taxi to Xinya Restaurant on Nanjing Road. It took him only five minutes to get to the restaurant, where he had the taxi wait for him. He chose a roast Guangdong duck, had the chef slice it, meat and skin together, and put it into a plastic box. He had the duck bones put into a larger plastic box and, in addition, he got steamed buns and a six-pack of Budweiser. He then rushed back.

Lai was a man in his early fifties, short, swarthy. He was reading a newspaper in the car, yawning, staring out at the approaching cop. Chen handed in his business card with a plastic lunch box in his hand.

"I'm Chen Cao, of the Shanghai Police Bureau. I have a couple of questions for you. Nothing wrong with you, Comrade Lai. Don't be alarmed. I happen to know you have not had lunch yet, neither have I. So how about us talking over our lunch together?"

"Fine. I only have cold buns," Lai said, eyeing him up and down. "If my boss needs me, I have to move immediately."

Chen moved in and put the plastic box between them. A popular way to eat a roast duck was to have the duck slices wrapped in pancakes, but it was not too bad wrapped in the soft, warm buns from Xinya. When Chen popped open the beer, it was like opening the chatterbox between them.

"Guangdong roast duck is different from Beijing roast duck, not so fatty. So I had the chef slice the meat and skin together."

"Yes, I had Beijing roast duck last night. Nothing but crisp duck skin in pancakes, with green onion and Beijing sauce. Really tasty, but I like duck meat too. Guangdong roast duck is better for me."

"It's a pity that we can't have the duck bone soup here," Chen said, finishing the second bun. "It has to be hot, with a lot of pepper."

"Exactly, that's one of the three celebrated ways to eat a duck," Lai said, smacking his lips. "Thank you so much for the lunch. I have heard your name before, Chief Inspector Chen. No free lunch in the way of the world, I know. You are a busy man with a lot of questions. So go ahead."

"Did Director Jiang use your car last night?"

"No, Jiang didn't request the car service last night. I was at a wedding. My friend's daughter got married at Yanyun Pavilion." Lai took a picture out of his wallet. "Look at the picture. What a grand wedding. Twenty-five tables altogether. And an impressive array of luxury cars. The bride had an uncle coming in a Mercedes, and they insisted on my driving the Lexus there too."

Chen took a glance at the picture. The date was imprinted on the right corner of it. No mistake about the date. The part about luxury cars also sounded true. It was an age when being rich meant being glorious. For a wedding, people would show off their wealth in whatever way possible.

"Let me ask you a different question. Does Director Jiang use your car all the time?"

"Theoretically, my job is from eight to five, but as you know, there're a lot of dinner parties in the evening. To be fair to Jiang, he makes a point of discussing his schedule with me. So like today, I took my wife to hospital in the morning. And he gives me twenty extra hours every month. That helps."

"So he uses your car all the time—late into the night?"

"For really personal business," Lai said slowly, "Director Jiang does not always request my service. Taxis are available outside that famous subdivision of his—Riverside Villas. It takes too much time for me to get there."

"I see. Does he ever drive himself?"

"No, he doesn't. So he doesn't have the car parked in his subdivision. It saves me one and half hours of taking the bus home, the tunnel is usually terrible with traffic congestion."

But that didn't necessarily mean Jiang stayed at home last night. In fact, Chen himself didn't request car service all the time either. For his visit to the bathhouse, for instance, or his date at Golden Island. As a fast-rising Party cadre, he had to be careful about his image. He thought he detected a slightly sarcastic note in Lai's emphasis on "really personal business."

"One more question—what is his schedule for the day?"

"He's going to Qingpu in the afternoon. Then there will be a dinner party there. I don't think I will make it back until after ten. Is there something you want to talk to him about today?"

"No, I've finished all my questions. The last one was really for the duck bones. You'd better keep them in a refrigerator if you're going back home so late."

"I see. Yes, there's a refrigerator in the office."

"That'll be great. To make the duck bone soup, you have to cook them over a small fire for two hours at least, I think, until the soup turns milky white. You can add some cucumber slices into the soup with a handful of black peppers," Chen said, pushing open the door. "It's been a wonderful lunch, Lai. I don't think you need to mention it to anybody. Bye."

"Bye. Chief—" Lai reached out of the car, a piece of duck in his hand and puzzlement in his eyes. It could have appeared like a free lunch to him, an inexplicable one. Chen did not think Lai would talk to Jiang about it.

Chen then hailed a taxi, telling the driver to go to Riverside Villas in Pudong.

"Go through the tunnel?" the driver said.

"Yes," Chen said. "It's quicker."

"Perhaps, if there's no traffic."

Pudong had once been a largely rural area east of the Huangpu River, with a few old factories interspersed here and there. In his days of English studies at Bund Park, the view across the river was mostly an expanse of somber-colored farmland. There was a popular saying at the time, he remembered: *A bed west of the river is better than a room east of the river.* At the end of the eighties, however, the city government began a tremendous effort to turn Pudong into the Wall Street of Asia, declaring it a special zone and offering attractive government policies for foreign investment. The landscape soon underwent a fundamental change; new buildings shot up, and housing prices soared to the skies.

Chen had heard of the Riverside Villas. It was one of the most expensive new residential areas in Shanghai, bordering on the eastern bank of the Huangpu and boasting a superb view of the river and of the Bund across it. People described the area as another Bund, even more modern and magnificent. Such a change no one would have dreamed of half a decade earlier. Jiang must have purchased the apartment here through his insider knowledge.

Riverside Villas was a high-end subdivision, where a security guard stood in front of its gate with an archlike top. There was a booth with a phone, a desk, and a chair. Once more Chen had to produce his badge. The middle-aged security guard named Aiguo cooperated zealously. According to him, the gate closed at midnight, and residents returning later had to speak to the night security through the intercom before getting in. Aiguo happened to be the one working here last night.

"Oh, you've been working continuously for more than forty hours," Chen said, glancing at his watch.

"It's not a fancy job, but I can doze, off and on, in the booth at night," Aiguo said, scratching his head. "There were only two who came back after twelve last night. Jiang was one of them, around one, in a taxi. I had to put it in my time sheet."

It did not exactly fit with the time of death the police estimated for An, Chen thought.

"In addition, I had the taxi license number copied," Aiguo went on. "If you want to know more, I can call for you here, Chief Inspector Chen. The taxi belongs to the People's Taxi Company, I know."

"I appreciate your offer, Aiguo." Chen was surprised by his eagerness to cooperate. He wondered whether Aiguo bore any personal grudge against

Jiang. "But tell me first a little bit about Jiang in general. He's lived here for a couple of years—one of the earliest residents in the subdivision, I've heard."

"Who can afford to live here?" Aiguo responded. "Corrupt officials and big-buck capitalists. At the price of twelve thousand yuan per square meter, I could save all I earn for ten years, without eating and any other expense, and I still would not be able to buy a bathroom in the area. The gap between rich and poor is really like that between cloud and clod. When Jiang bought it, he paid only one thousand yuan per square meter, not to mention a special discount no one knows about. Is that fair in our socialist society?"

"No, it's not fair."

"But what can you do? Jiang, like other residents here, simply takes a security guard like me as trash. Especially Jiang, one of those damned night animals. It seems as if they never have to sleep, like rats. Two or three times a week, he comes back after the closing of the gate. Sometimes two or three o'clock. I have to get up to open the gate for him. But I'm a man, and I need to sleep. Right now it's not too bad to get up a couple of times at night, but in the winter, it's hell. I shiver like a straw man. They have heating at home, but there is nothing in the booth here. Nothing but an old army overcoat. And what can he be up to until two or three at night? Not official business, surely."

"It's hard for you," Chen said, nodding. Aiguo's animosity was understandable. And it was an opportunity for Chen. He might as well gather as much information as possible here, even if Jiang's nocturnal activities were not related to An's case.

"Now, one night's expense for people like Jiang can be far more than one month's pay for me, Chief—" Aiguo made an abrupt halt as a black Lexus came rolling into view.

Out of the car emerged a middle-aged man Chen recognized from the pictures as Jiang.

"Hello, Chief Inspector Chen," Jiang said in a loud, warm voice, walking over in strides. "You are looking for me, I've heard."

It was an encounter Chen had not anticipated. Jiang must have cut short his visit to Qingpu. But it was an inevitable encounter, Chen reflected, considering the photographs in his briefcase.

"I've heard a lot about the area. I happen to have a meeting in Pudong this afternoon, so I wanted to take a look here."

"Now that you're here, why not come in?"

"Yes, in front of a temple, I'd better go in to kowtow to the clay image."

"Well, you won't go to a temple without having something to pray for."

Aiguo listened to the exchange of proverbs between the two with a knowing smile, waving his hand at Chen as he walked in with Jiang.

Jiang's apartment was on the top of a twenty-two-story high rise. The suite was renovated, featuring a spacious living room and a bedroom on one level and another bedroom and a study on an added second level. It looked like a townhouse in a new style called *fushi,* popular for its economical use of space in the overcrowded city.

But this apartment, Jiang explained, had been designed for a different purpose: Jiang's paralyzed wife. The barely furnished living room was simply a larger area where she could move around in her wheelchair. His wife managed to hiss out a greeting in a raucous voice.

"She was paralyzed fifteen years ago in a car accident," Jiang whispered. "It affected her speaking ability too."

The normal sexual life for the two might also have been affected, Chen observed. Still, Jiang had been nice to her in his way, at least in designing the interior of the house. But did that justify his affair with An?

They went upstairs to the study in silence. Jiang closed the door after him, and they sat on either side of the desk. Chen could hear the wheelchair rolling about downstairs.

There was no point in beating about the bush. Chen started talking about the Xing investigation, focusing on the approval Jiang had given Ming's land development request.

As Chen had anticipated, Jiang made a total denial, as if he could push out the moon by shutting the window.

"I didn't know anything about Ming's relationship with Xing, Chief Inspector Chen. The land development was approved because I didn't see anything wrong with the plan in itself," Jiang said with a serious expression. "You question the part about the continuous factory operation, but it had been studied and approved by Comrade Dong of the State Company Reform Office before it had been submitted to me."

"So you have never looked into the matter yourself."

"Do you know how many applications I have to read every day? No way can I do careful research on a particular one. The market is money-oriented. Property development involves a lot of risk. No businessman wants to do things for others, or for the country. So it was with Ming's application, but other than that, I didn't find anything out of the ordinary."

"Well," Chen said, knowing he had no choice but to play his trump card. "Can you tell me where you were last night, Director Jiang?"

"What do you mean?" Jiang snapped, staring at Chen with daggers flying out of his glare. "How can you talk to me like that?"

"I am talking to you as an emperor's special envoy—that is Comrade Zhao's term—directly under the Party Discipline Committee," Chen said, producing the authorization on the committee's letterhead. "I would hope you would cooperate with me."

"An emperor's special envoy? It's almost the end of the twentieth century, Comrade Chief Inspector Chen. I feel ashamed for you." Jiang made a visible effort to control himself. "I have explained to you everything about that matter with Ming. He disappeared several weeks ago. Why, all of a sudden, do you want to know my whereabouts last night?"

"Why can't you give me a direct answer, Director Jiang?"

Chen's cell phone rang. It was Aiguo. Chen excused himself and walked to the window.

"I've already learned something from the taxi driver. He picked up Jiang around twelve last night at a bathhouse called Niaofei Yuyao."

"Niaofei Yuyao, I see," Chen said. An ironic coincidence that they had visited the same bathhouse. *The one who retreats for fifty steps should not laugh at the one who retreats for a hundred steps.* "Thank you so much, Aiguo. That's very important."

But that practically ruled out the possibility of Jiang's being the murderer, Chen contemplated, turning off the phone. He sat back down at the desk and said to Jiang, "I apologize for the interruption, Director Jiang."

"Now you'd better give me an explanation, Chen," Jiang demanded. "I'm a Party cadre of eleventh rank. What do you really want with me? You approached my driver stealthily this morning, and then the security in the subdivision."

"Lai told you that?"

"He tried to put the duck bones into the refrigerator in the office, and I found everything out."

"Now let me tell you something, Director Jiang. Because I took into consideration your cadre rank, I tried to conduct the investigation in an inconspicuous way, and to approach Lai and the security informally first. Why? One of the people involved in the land approval was murdered last night."

"What? Are you considering me a suspect in a homicide case?" Jiang rose in indignation.

"Calm down, Comrade Jiang. As a police officer, I have to check into everything. I have evidence about your involvement with her."

"Her? Evidence! Don't bluff me like a three-year-old kid."

"Have you heard of the death of An Jiayi?"

"You mean the anchorwoman. Yes, I read about it in the newspaper today. A shameless slut on the sly."

Chen was infuriated in turn by Jiang's callousness.

"You knew the slut only too well on the sly, Jiang," he said, also rising from the desk. He tossed the pictures on it. "Take a damned good look at them. And then you can say that to me again."

Jiang stared at the pictures in disbelief, as if he had too hard a time changing back from the lover in the pictures to a high-ranking Party cadre in his study. His face turned to white, then to red, and he was unable to say a word.

The sound of the wheelchair rolling around on the floor below came up to them through the silence.

"Undeniable evidence," Chen said in a low voice.

"How could you have stooped so low?"

"Will you believe it if I tell you, Director Jiang, that people have been watching you for a long time? There's one thing I can assure you. I didn't do it. Nor do I know who did."

It was true, and full of implications too.

"So what do you want me to do, Chief Inspector Chen?" Jiang said. "I was with some friends last night. They can prove it."

"In a private massage room, with another naked girl serving you hand and foot."

"You—" Jiang stammered in astonishment.

It was only a guess, but Jiang's reaction proved it. Panic-stricken, he believed that he had been followed everywhere.

"Let's not talk about last night yet. Tell me what you know about Ming. And about An," Chen said. "I don't want to brag about my special position, Director Jiang, but I can do something with the 'imperial sword' in my hand, I want you to bear that in mind. For instance, I can withhold these photos from the higher authorities, and I can also give them to *Shanghai Morning.*"

"Now that I have learned of Ming's relation to Xing, Chief Inspector Chen," Jiang started on a different tune, "how can I not try to help? Ming could have used An as his PR person, I see, in a devious scheme. As for An, her marriage was long on the rocks. In the Western world, she would have automatically divorced her husband—such a long separation. And my married life was totally wrecked in the car accident."

"That's neither here nor there, Director Jiang."

"But if you think the approval for the land development went through because of her relationship with me, you are wrong, Chief Inspector Chen. Such an application has to travel from one office to another, either through the front door or the back door. Not only in Shanghai, but also in Beijing—with other connections at a much higher level."

"Connections at a much higher level." Chen had thought about that. After all, Jiang had functioned only as one link in a long chain, all of which Chen had to trace. In order to minimize his responsibility, Jiang might be willing to drag some others into the mire. "Tell me about them."

"Yes, I think—I think I know some names possibly connected," Jiang said hesitantly. "But it's such an important case, and with a murder involved, that I have to verify some information first. It won't do to throw out irresponsible accusations."

"You know I can't wait. So you may give me the names. I'll do the background check first."

"Like the background check you've been doing on me?" Jiang said with a bitter smile. "It'll take only a couple of days for me to find out. I can't tell you anything at this moment."

"You don't have to go into details," Chen said, wondering whether Jiang had recovered from the blow and begun procrastinating. "Anything you can think of. I have to make my report to Comrade Zhao."

"If you really can't wait for a day or two, Chief Inspector Chen, you may go ahead and do whatever you have to do. I have been a Party member for many years, and I know better than to destroy other hardworking Party cadres—like me—for things they might not have done."

Those pictures would be more than enough to crush Jiang's career. Once Chen turned them over, however, he would have no cards left in his hands. Jiang would be a dead pig, and the water, no matter how steaming hot, made no difference. His confession about his adulterous relationship with An might be hot in tabloid magazines, but that wasn't what Chen wanted to read. As Jiang had said, Ming's deal was not one Jiang alone could have approved. It might be true that he had to verify something first, and that he had reasons to be very cautious about things at a "much higher level."

Downstairs, his wife burst into a violent fit of coughing.

"I'll give you a couple of days," Chen said, rising again. "But no more than that. I have no choice, you know."

In the meantime, Chief Inspector Chen would keep a close surveillance on Jiang, who, like An, might have to contact others in desperation.

9

BUT CHIEF INSPECTOR CHEN did not have much time to follow the latest development in his investigation.

A cricket was still screeching in the fragmented dream of the early morning when the phone in his room shrilled. He rubbed his sleepy eyes in disorientation. It was a long-distance call from Chairman Wang Yitian, of the Chinese Writers' Association in Beijing.

"Chief Inspector Chen, we have a very important assignment for you. You are going to serve as the head of the Chinese Writers' Delegation for the America-China Literature Conference in Los Angeles next week—to be exact, the day after tomorrow."

"You cannot be serious, Chairman Wang. For such a conference, I would need a lot of preparation. No way can I leave at such short notice," Chen said, blinking in a crack of the sunlight that glared through the early summer trees. A peddler started hawking fried dough sticks in the first wave of heat. It was said the much-used oil might contain alum from the dough sticks, but he felt strangely hungry at the moment. "I have no idea what this conference is about."

"We understand," Wang said. "In fact, we've been talking about it with the Americans for months. Comrade Yang Jun had been chosen as the delegation head, but all of a sudden, he fell sick. We have to have someone to replace him."

"But how can I replace him? Yang is a writer of international renown. There are so many better-known writers, senior and more qualified, in the Writers' Association. Who's the one after Yang in the delegation?"

"Bao Guodong. A senior working-class writer, but it would have been an international joke to appoint Bao as the head. He doesn't speak English, nor has he any knowledge of American literature. Once, he made a point of calling Americans by the Chinese equivalent. So Dr. Hegel became Dr. Hei, which in Chinese could mean Dr. Black."

"But it doesn't have to be Bao. Anybody else can do it."

"It's a conference that a lot of people are watching. The first one between the two countries since 1989. Not simply any writer may fulfill the position."

"What do you mean, Chairman Wang?"

"It's an urgent matter of improving our international image. So it takes an experienced, talented, politically reliable writer like you to head the delegation. As a young Party cadre writer, you are the best candidate we can think of. A modernist poet and translator, you have an intimate knowledge of Western literature, and you have experience in receiving foreign writers. Besides, you can speak English to your American counterparts, while they cannot speak Chinese—a plus for our collective image. Of course, the appointment is not made just in consideration of one's status as a writer." Wang paused before moving on. "Politically, you have to know what to say, what not to say. As a representative of Shanghai Congress, you are surely qualified to head a government delegation."

"I'm honored that you have thought of me," Chen said, trying to come up with more official-sounding excuses, for he was disturbed by the timing of the assignment. "I'm too young and inexperienced. I don't see that my Party position has anything to do with the assignment."

"It has everything to do with it, Comrade Chen. You are a Party cadre, and I don't think it necessary to discuss that part."

"To be honest, I don't think I am so popular, as you know, among old writers. So far, I have only published one poetry collection. That's far from enough for a delegation head."

"Many writers are not always easy to get along with, but you are not exactly one of their circle. That should help. I don't think the old writers will make things hard for you."

"Because of my law enforcement background?" Chen said alertly.

"You don't have to think that way. But now that you have mentioned it, I don't think it will be hard for you to enforce discipline—if need be."

"To enforce discipline, indeed—"

"This is an assignment you cannot say no to, Comrade Chen Cao. It's in the interests of the Party."

"In the interests of the Party!" Chen ground out his cigarette in disgust, a gesture invisible to the chairman in Beijing.

There was no immediate response from the other end of the line. Wang might be waiting for him to go on. A small commotion seemed to be breaking out in the street. He looked out to see a dog barking in a red convertible stuck in the traffic congestion. For the first time, the word *pet* had become a reality in Chinese life. He had never before seen such a scene except in American movies.

"As you may or may not know," Chen went on, "I'm engaged with a special investigation under the Party Discipline Committee."

"We know. We've talked to several leading comrades here."

"Oh, you have?" Chen said, not really surprised. For such an assignment, his background check might have been made by the very committee.

"They all have a high opinion of your work. Your temporary assignment is only for a couple of weeks, so they think it will not be a problem. By the way, Comrade Zhao Yan has left for Shanghai."

"Really. Do you know why?"

"No, I don't. Old comrades like Zhao usually go somewhere else in the summer. He will probably contact you too, I think."

"I see," he said, coming to the realization that it would be futile to argue any more. "I'll call you back, Chairman Wang."

Long after the phone conversation was over, he could not brush aside a feeling of uneasiness.

Could it really be a coincidence?

As a cop, he didn't think so. But he didn't think that Jiang could have orchestrated such a surprising move only one night after their talk. Besides, what was the point? Chief Inspector Chen would be back.

10

WHEN HE ARRIVED AT the bureau office, the documents for the writers' delegation had already been delivered there. Things could be efficient in China when the Beijing government gave the order directly. On top of the stack was a camera-ready copy of his business card for his approval:

> **Chen Cao** *Poet, Translator, Critic*
>
> Head of Chinese Writers' Delegation
>
> Member of Shanghai People's Congress
>
> Member of Chinese Writers' Association
>
> OFFICE PHONE: 280-9435

Whoever had designed the card knew better than to list his police position. Chen crossed out the third line. For the coming trip, he was supposed to be a writer, not a politician. The phone number was that of the Writers' Association, Shanghai Office, which was not unacceptable. He went there from time to time.

Then he dialed Jiang's office. Jiang was not there. According to his secretary, Jiang was having an important meeting in Nanhui for the day. He did not have a cell phone, which was hard to believe, but the secretary said he might call in during lunchtime.

Chen then dialed Sergeant Kuang, who hadn't made a report to him, but it wasn't really something officially requested. After all, An's death wasn't assigned to the special case squad.

Presently a large envelope came through the bureau mail. It was from Kuang, containing a transcript of An's phone calls for the last three days. Sending it instead of bringing it to Chen's office in person was perhaps Kuang's way of showing Chen the reluctance of his respect. Chen began reading the transcript at once. Over the last three days, An had made six phone calls. Three to her son's school. One to her company assistant. Two to someone in the city government about a possible cultural festival. Not a single call was remotely related to Ming, or to Xing.

Was it possible that something had been deleted from the records? Chen didn't think so. There was also a short note in the envelope, saying that Kuang had been making a list of the people she had met in the last few days. The list could be a long one. It had obviously not been traced as far back as Chen yet, but it would be, eventually.

He tried Kuang's number, but the line was busy. So Chen came back to the delegation file on the desk.

Nominally, the Writers' Association was an unofficial organization, but it was largely controlled by the government through its funding. One of the main functions of the association was to provide for a number of "professional writers," who would be able to concentrate on writing without having to worry about nine-to-five jobs. Each of them would get from the association a *gongzi,* an amount equivalent to their otherwise regular salary. In the pre-reform years, it had meant a lot to be initiated into the association. It was a high honor, and there were a lot of benefits too. In fact, all the writers chosen for the delegation were members of the association, and all of them were professional writers except Chen. He had chosen not to be one because of the imposed limitations. He would have had to write more "officially"—in tune with the government. The financial aid came with a political tab.

The mid-nineties brought dramatic changes everywhere, and in the literary scene too, in spite of the government control. For one thing, the book market became increasingly money-oriented. The new royalties system made a small number of writers financially independent, while those whose works could hardly sell in the market, like poets or critics, got nothing but the basic professional-writer pay from the association.

The delegation contained writers in a variety of genres. On the top of the list was Bao Guodong, a poet whose work was not unfamiliar to Chen, especially what he had produced during the Cultural Revolution. Even after all these years, a few lines came back to his mind easily—

The fish cannot swim without water.
The flower cannot blossom without sunlight.
And to make revolution,
We cannot go without Mao Zhedong Thought.

The poem had been made into a popular song broadcast all over the country. After the Cultural Revolution, Bao wrote little, but he remained on the literary scene, as an administrator in the Beijing office of the association. Now Bao also served as the Party Secretary of the delegation.

The next one was Zhong Taifei, a playwright better known for his life story. As a Rightist, Zhong spent his best years in a faraway labor camp, where his "black" class status excluded any possibility of romance. Then, during the Cultural Revolution, he fell on his hardest time yet, being physically starved as well as sexually starved, literally more dead than alive. But as Lao Zi writes, *Luck turns at the lowest point.* A widow cook, illiterate, older by more than ten years, took inexplicable pity on him. He survived on the steamed buns she stole for him. As a result of mysteriously misplaced yin and yang, they came to live together. In the eighties, Zhong wrote a play based on his experience in the labor camp. It was a huge hit. His life story got much exposure, along with the picture of "her white hair shining against his red cheeks," which added to the popularity of his works.

Then was Shasha, a "beauty author" before the invention of the term. Born of a high-ranking cadre family, she chose for herself an unconventional path, first as a dancer, and then as a novelist. There were notorious stories, however, attributing her literary success to her unconventional life in the circle of high connections. One of the stories claimed that half of the politburo could have met in her "scented bedroom of red sweat." Those tales might not have been reliable, but it was undeniable that her literary achievement was not "pure and simple."

And then was Peng Quan. Peng had written celebrated essays before 1949, but in the years afterward, as a "historical counterrevolutionary," he had produced nothing. Unlike Zhong, Peng kept silent even after his rehabilitation. Having survived thirty years of self-reforming and self-criticizing, he might have been totally brainwashed. Nothing left of the talented essayist of forty years earlier. Why Peng was chosen for the delegation, Chen had no clue.

Finally, there was Huang Jialiang, a young interpreter for the delegation and a recent graduate from the Beijing Foreign Language University, where Chen had studied in the early eighties.

But Chen didn't want to spend too much time looking through all the information. There was no rush on it. He was going to be with those people for two weeks. Instead, he moved on to the activities of the delegation. Except for some formal speeches, he realized that he would not have much to do. So he might as well follow the time-honored doctrine of Taoism: *Doing nothing does everything.* The established writers should know better than to cause trouble, and contrary to Chairman Wang's suggestion, he didn't see any point in supervising them every step of the way. There was only one official responsibility specified in the document: he was going to organize daily political studies for the delegation, but that too would merely be a matter of formality.

He made a phone call to the Shanghai Library, requesting some books. He didn't have much time to prepare for the conference, but he would try to read those books during the flight. Then, as he was going to call Detective Yu, unexpected phone calls came into his office.

Zhu Wei, the *Wenhui Daily* reporter, wanted Chen to purchase for him the latest edition of a GMAT reference book in the United States. Zhu must be a well-connected reporter to have learned about his new appointment so fast. The second phone call was from Xi Ran, the Secretary of the Writers' Association, Shanghai Office, asking Chen to carry copies of *Shanghai Literature* to the conference. To his surprise, the third was from his mother. Party Secretary Li had already informed her of the delegation assignment, assuring her that the bureau would provide any help she needed during his absence. She wanted Chen to buy some genuine American ginseng for her friends. Then she switched the topic.

"Perhaps you'll see your American friend there."

"I don't think I'll have the time," he said, aware of what was running across her mind. "She may not know about my visit. There are rules about the government delegation activities and I am the delegation head."

One of the regulations stated that members were not supposed to meet their relatives or friends without official approval. Especially politically sensitive contacts, let alone the "American friend" mentioned by his mother. Though he had thought about the possibility even before her call came in.

By the time he was ready to leave his office, having gotten several more congratulations calls, he was beginning to have second thoughts—anticipatory ones—about the visit. It was an enviable opportunity, all the more so in the name of a government delegation, and the calls proved that. For Chen, it was also an opportunity to polish up his English. Not to mention the fact that it would add to his status as a writer. Last but not least, the appointment as the head of a government delegation was a political boost.

All was well except the timing. As he walked out of the bureau, Chen called Jiang again with his cell phone. Jiang was not back at his office, or at home. His secretary apologized profusely. It was possible that Jiang had been trying to avoid him. Perhaps Jiang already knew about his trip. Since Chen had only one day left in the city, Jiang might gain a break for two weeks by not taking his phone call. Of course, Chen could turn over the pictures. But what happened then would be totally out of his control, especially since he would be visiting abroad. The pictures were the only trump card he had, and there was no point throwing it away like that. He knew that, and Jiang did too.

But Chen didn't think that he had to worry too much. As long as he had those pictures, he didn't believe Jiang could get away. It was only a matter of two weeks.

So he went to the Shanghai Library and got his books. He then decided to pay a visit to Gu at his KTV office. He should inform Gu of the trip, and more importantly, of An's death. He didn't want anything to happen to his businessman friend.

But Gu appeared to have already heard about it and was not eager to talk on the subject. "I am a law-abiding businessman, Chief Inspector Chen. I've not done anything out of way, have I?"

"Of course you haven't."

"People should have known better than to stir up a sleeping snake." Gu changed the topic, producing a bulging envelope and a small package. "For your trip. Now, I'm not offering you anything, Chen. I'm asking a favor of you."

"How can that possibly be?"

"Shoot pictures for me in the United States of those ultra-modern or unique shopping malls. It would be really useful for my New World project, you know. Film may be expensive and I can't let you put down your money for me. For a delegation member, the foreign currency allowance is only a hundred dollars."

So once more it was Gu "asking a favor of him," rather than the other way around. The shrewd businessman seemed to have all kinds of pretexts up his sleeve. It was true, however, that in accordance with the government regulation, Chen had only one hundred dollars as his personal allowance. China Bank did not allow people to exchange foreign currency without official permission, and Chen didn't want to go to the black market for that.

"Whatever you say, Gu. I'll shoot pictures and keep the receipts for you. Thank you."

"Don't mention it," Gu said. "Oh, please ask about your American friend. What's her name? She's beautiful."

"Catherine Rohn, but I'm not sure I'll see her."

"Here's a small present from me in case you do." Gu took out a brocade-covered case containing a Chinese brush pen, ink stone, ink stick, and a lion-headed seal chop with a tiny bowl of red seal ink. "She has a passion for Chinese culture, I remember."

"It's very considerate of you, Gu," Chen said. Indeed, Gu could be a man full of surprises, and full of resources too. "Now, there's another favor I have to ask of you."

"Anything you say, Chen."

"For the next two weeks, my mother will be all alone. She is in poor health, as you know."

"Yes, you're right. What about sending White Cloud over? Last time she helped in the hospital. A clever, capable girl."

Not too long ago, with his mother in the hospital and himself busy with a translation project for Gu, White Cloud had been assigned to him as a free "little secretary." The old woman had thought highly of her, though he had refrained from telling his mother what "little secretary" meant in today's society.

"She's very nice, but I don't think my mother likes the idea of having anyone stay in her room. I've suggested a temporary maid for her, and she won't listen." He added emphatically, "Several robbery cases have occurred in her neighborhood recently."

"Got it," Gu responded promptly. "Nothing will happen to her. I give you my word. I know some people in both the black and white ways."

The black way referred to triad organizations, in contrast to the white way of the government. If it was a matter of a rough neighborhood, Gu's connection with the black way should be more than enough, and that was probably why Gu gave his word so promptly.

"I don't know how to thank you enough, Gu."

"Don't say that, Chen, if you take me as a friend. With the long, long road, you know a horse."

What else could Chen say, as a cop, to an entrepreneur with his triad connection?

Afterward, Chen thought it would indeed be helpful to have some extra dollars. Not that he would have a lot to purchase abroad, but there was no telling what he might have to do there.

As for the reunion with his "beautiful American friend," he was not sure about it. Since their joint investigation in Shanghai, they had hardly kept up a correspondence, except some holiday cards. The contents on the cards could have been examined by others. Of late, even those cards had become fewer and fewer. But he should have prepared some present for her, like Gu. He recalled her interest in Chinese literature. Then he had an idea. Something really special, he thought.

It was the first time that he felt any sort of eagerness at the thought of the trip.

Water flows in the rippling
of her eyes. Mountains rise
in the knitting of her brows.
So where is a traveler going to visit?
The enchanting landscape of her eyes and brows.

Whose poem it was, he forgot, whistling in the breeze. Possibly a Tang dynasty poet. Chen thought that he, too, might be able to produce a couple of lines during the trip.

11

IN THE MIDST OF his delegation preparations, Chen also managed to find out which hotel Comrade Zhao was staying in. The Western Suburb Hotel.

The day after he had learned about Zhao's arrival in Shanghai, he had not yet received Zhao's call. The chief inspector waited until the early afternoon before he dialed the hotel. The operator refused to confirm that Zhao was staying there, much less put him through. It was little wonder with that particular hotel. So Chen decided to go there. The old man would not be too displeased with his unscheduled visit. While he did not think Zhao would make any change regarding his delegation appointment, he might be able to find out something behind the sudden decision.

The Western Suburb Hotel, located not far from Hongqiao Airport, was a high-class hotel not yet open to the public. The hotel consisted of a group of villas with woods and lakes enclosed in high surrounding walls. In its facilities, the hotel was perhaps on a par with those new, five-star American hotels in Shanghai, but it remained for the exclusive use of senior Party leaders during their visits here. In the last few years, when there were no important guests staying there, it would occasionally open its restaurant to outside business. The hotel itself remained enveloped in mystery.

At the hotel entrance, Chen showed his identification to an armed sentry. A chief inspector's rank meant nothing here. He had to wait for the "leading comrade" to signal approval. Comrade Zhao must have said something to the sentry, who saluted Chen on a suddenly respectful note, saying, "Yes, please come in, Comrade Chief Inspector Chen. Comrade Zhao is waiting for you. He stays in Building B, close to the end of the complex."

It was an independent, two-storied, white colonial building shaded in green foliage. A young maid in her pink uniform opened the door for Chen. "Comrade Zhao is in the living room."

Chen saw a long mahogany desk in the center of a spacious living room, which was furnished in a traditional Chinese way, with long silk scrolls of painting and calligraphy hung on the walls. The desk was covered with white *xuan* papers, ink stone, ink stick, and books. There was a curl of smoke rising from a small tiger-shaped bronze incense burner on a mahogany corner table.

"Welcome, Chief Inspector Chen," Zhao said, coming out from behind a mahogany bookshelf, carrying a large book in his hand.

Zhao was a man in his early or mid-seventies, white-haired and browed, with a ruddy complexion. Dressed in a silk Tang costume, he looked well preserved and spirited for his age. He showed Chen to a sofa and seated himself opposite in a hardback mahogany chair.

"I apologize for not having called for an appointment, Comrade Zhao. Chairman Huang of the Writers' Association told me that you had come to Shanghai," Chen said. "I tried to call you, but without success. I have to leave for the United States tomorrow."

"I have heard about your upcoming trip," Zhao said. "I was thinking of calling you too. Phone calls have kept coming in."

"You are on vacation here, I understand, but I have to report my work to you."

"You have made your reports," Zhao said, handing a cup of tea over to him. "A leading comrade in Beijing has discussed your work with me. I have said to him, I think, what you are probably going to say to me. So we may spare some repetitions."

"Oh, a leading comrade in Beijing." Chen was disturbed by the appearance of an unidentified "leading comrade in Beijing." Whoever it might be, the discussion and decision must have been made at a higher level than the Writers' Association.

"While we're well aware of the urgency of your investigation, he did not think it would matter for you to be away for a couple of weeks."

"It's only a couple of weeks, but in the middle of an anticorruption case under the Party Discipline Committee—under you?" Chen said. "There are so many writers qualified for the position."

"That is for the Writers' Association to decide," Zhao said with a smile, producing a folder out of the desk drawer. "As for the battle against corruption, it will be a long one. Let me show you something I have been working on."

It was a draft on ethical regulations for Party officials. Zhao started by giving a comprehensive definition of corruption. The regulations forbade Party cadres from using their position to obtain improper benefit, to conduct business on their own account, to convert public property into private, to use their powers or influence to help others, to receive above-standard official treatment, to convert public facilities for private use . . .

"Corruption, especially within the Party cadres, is one of the most serious problems facing China today," Comrade Zhao said, his silver hair shining like a dream in the sunlight. "People complain about corruption being institutional or a result of the one-Party system, and about absolute power leading to absolute corruption. I think that's too simplistic. But we have to deal with the problem in an institutional way. We cannot content ourselves with one or two isolated investigations. As a relatively new system, China's socialism may experience all sorts of bumps along its way. We should never lose our faith in it."

"Yes, we have to come to the root of the problem," Chen echoed, choosing to say little. Some had been talking about his being too liberal. But would such a Party document prove to be the solution? A few conscientious

Party cadres, like Judge Bao of the Song dynasty, might follow the regulations. Only there was no guarantee. Neither institutional nor legal guarantee. After all, the Party Discipline Committee had to serve the ultimate interests of the Party.

Chen started to feel irritated with the direction of the talk. He hadn't come here for a lecture, one day before his trip, two days after An's murder, and in the middle of an investigation that was reaching a crisis point. For all he knew, he had gotten on somebody's nerves, which had led to An's death and to a "leading comrade" saying something in the Forbidden City that resulted in his delegation assignment. He decided to push a little.

"You have given a most profound analysis, Comrade Zhao. As you have pointed out, we must carry the anticorruption work to the end," Chen said. "It's the first time for me to be engaged in such a case, and the leading comrade has discussed my work with you in Beijing. Has he made any specific suggestions or criticisms?"

"You are a young Party cadre full of drive," Zhao said slowly. "That's very good, but it is also very important for someone in your position to bear in mind the ultimate interests of the Party."

"The ultimate interests of the Party? I am a Party member and a police officer. I remember what my Confucianist father has taught me. *A man lays down his life for the one who appreciates you, and a woman makes herself beautiful for the one who likes her.* Because of the Party, I am what I am today. Now you have entrusted me with an emperor-special-envoy task. How can I not fight for the Party's ultimate interest?"

"We know, but there's always room for improvement in our work. For instance, the investigation could be conducted more discreetly. Someone has complained about your passing confidential information to the media."

"No, I have never talked to the media about the case . . ." Chen sensed something wrong. He had mentioned Dong's name to Zhu Wei, the *Wenhui* reporter, but not in the context of the Xing case. It might not have been too difficult for a reporter to associate it with the investigation. Still, the chief inspector was not held responsible for speculations. How could the accusation have made its way into the Forbidden City so fast?

"I have been fighting for the sacred cause of our great Party all my life,"

Zhao said. "Now China is finally making great strides in the right direction. Our anticorruption work is to ensure the success of this historic reform. But there are people anxious to make something out of it. To present a totally rotten picture of China, as if all the corruption occurred because of our Party system. And they attempt to stir up trouble through the media both at home and abroad."

It was a difficult talk, almost like a high-level tai chi performance. *Diandaojizhi.* Zhao would never push or punch all the way. Just one light touch, sometimes a gesture in a direction, and Chen had to figure out how to respond.

"But it's not true. I have never talked to the media about the investigation. How could that leading comrade in Beijing have believed it?" Chen said. "Does my delegation appointment mean a stop to the investigation?"

"No, you mustn't think so. Don't ever consider the trip to the United States as a stop to your investigation. As an experienced investigator, you know that there are different perspectives from which to look at one thing. Don't worry about what people may say about your work. I trust you."

"Thank you, Comrade Zhao," Chen said.

Was it possible there was something else in Zhao's statement? If not a stop, then a continuation of the investigation? Chen thought he caught a subtle emphasis on "the United States," and "different perspectives." It suddenly occurred to him that Xing was there too. Was that a hint? There seemed to be something else Zhao could have said, but he didn't.

Instead, Zhao produced a silk scroll and spread it out on the desk. The scroll presented a poem entitled "The Guanque Pavilion," written by Wang Zhihuan, a seventh-century Tang dynasty poet.

The white sun declining
against the mountains, the Yellow River
running into the oceans, you have
to climb even higher
to see further—thousands
of miles to the distant horizon.

"I copied out the poem last night. Since retirement, I have learned only one small skill—how to make silk calligraphy scrolls. So this is one for you. Keep it, or give it to one of the American writers there. It may make a good gift."

"No, I will never give it away, Comrade Zhao. It is special for me. I'll hang it on the wall."

Chen was no judge of Chinese calligraphy, but he liked the poem. A silk scroll in Zhao's handwriting with his red chop seal on it would be spectacular on Chen's wall. He appreciated the gesture made by the old man.

"Let me add one line," Zhao said, standing up and writing with his brush, "To Comrade Chen Cao, a loyal anticorruption soldier."

Was the poem also a subtle hint?

A hint about the necessity of climbing higher to see further. It could be just another reference to the political catchphrase *daju weizhong*—to take into consideration the interest of the situation in general. Or to the necessity of approaching the investigation from a different perspective.

There would be no point in pressing Zhao for an explicit explanation. The old man had said all that could be said, as well as the unsaid, as in a classical Chinese poem. Politics could be like poetry. A figure of speech whose meaning Chen had never considered before.

"I have one more question, Comrade Zhao," Chen said, pushing a little again. "So far I have made no real breakthrough, but there are some leads that should be followed, I think, during my visit abroad."

"Well, you're in charge of the investigation. Do whatever you think necessary."

"Thank you." That was better than he had expected. "Comrade Detective Yu Guangming has worked with me for years. A capable and loyal comrade. During this period, can he act on my behalf if need be?"

"Of course. If need be, he can also come to me. I think I've heard of his name." Zhao added, "Any special idea or target?"

"No, it's just that the case can be complicated. Anything could happen in two weeks, I'm afraid. And I'll keep in close contact with you, Comrade Zhao," Chen said, rising, "while in the United States."

"It may not be so easy to make phone calls there. An old Chinese saying puts it well: *When a general is fighting along the borders, he does not have to listen to every order given to him by the emperor far away in the capital.*"

That had to be a hint, Chen concluded.

And he was going to think a great deal about it. He left the hotel, carrying the scroll. After a while, he put it on his shoulder, like an imperial sword.

There was a flash of light in the tree—a hummingbird flapping up toward the sun.

On his way home, Chen called Peiqin, the wife of Detective Yu.

"Tomorrow morning, I would like to have breakfast with Yu."

"Come to our restaurant," Peiqin said. "Our new chef is good."

"Old Half Place is closer," Chen said. "Yu has become a loyal noodle eater there, you have told me."

"Then he will be there." She added, "Second floor, there are nice private rooms there. I'll make a reservation for you."

Peiqin was a smart woman. Chen didn't have to say more. She must have guessed why he had chosen to call her. In one of their previous investigations, he had also contacted her when he had to take extra precautions.

12

THE FIRST FLOOR OF Old Half Place was as crowded as Detective Yu had anticipated, and even more noisy than he had remembered.

The restaurant was known for its noodles with the legendary *xiao* pork, and perhaps more for its exquisite taste at a relatively inexpensive price. So it attracted a large number of not-so-well-to-do gourmets.

Looking around, Yu couldn't help shaking his head as he moved upstairs. There was a huge price difference between the first and the second floor. Peiqin had reserved a private room upstairs—for him and Chen. There were hardly any customers visible there. Such a luxurious room was unnecessary. She could make much ado about his work, especially with Chief Inspector Chen in the background.

A waitress led him into an elegant room with antiquelike table and chairs. He was impressed by silk scrolls hanging on the walls and fresh flower blossoms in the vases. There was also a spell of southern bamboo instrument music wafting through the air. The mahogany chair, however, was not that comfortable. Sitting there, he felt out of place, picking up the menu.

It was not the expense that Yu worried about. Chen wouldn't have asked him out simply for breakfast. Not on the morning of his visit to the United States. He knew his boss too well.

In the bureau, Chen's new appointment was a topic much discussed. Something could have gone terribly wrong.

The waitress put four tiny dishes on the table. Pickled garlic, fried peanuts, sliced ginger, and sugar-covered dry plums. After pouring a cup of tea for him, she stepped back and remained standing behind him, like part of the room—silent, still, and almost contemplative.

When Chen finally walked into the room, Yu was reading through the menu for a second time and feeling that he'd been waiting there for a long while.

"Nice to see you here, boss," Yu said. "Peiqin has chosen the private room for us."

"It's a nice place," Chen said, taking the tea from the waitress. "Elegant atmosphere and service."

"Most of the customers for the restaurant are gray-haired retirees. They have few coins jingling in their pockets. Three or four yuan is about all they can afford—on the first floor. It's far more expensive on the second floor, let alone a private room."

Yu then handed the menu to Chen.

"Today you choose," Chen said with a smile. "Peiqin says you're a regular customer here."

"Don't listen to her. Mr. Ren insisted on treating us a couple of times after the *shikumen* case. That's about it."

Yu chose his noodles with dried shrimp and green onion; Chen had his with deep-fried rice-paddy eel. In addition, they ordered a small bamboo steamer of pork-and-crab soup buns with the lotus leaf–covered bottom. And two side dishes of the famous *xiao* pork.

Handing the menu back to the waitress, Yu said, "You may leave now. We want to discuss business. If we need anything else, I'll let you know."

"Business expense, of course, on the Central Discipline Committee," Chen said as the waitress turned to leave.

"Don't worry about it. That much I can pay," Yu said, draining his tea in one gulp. "Something serious, boss?"

"Not that serious. I'm going to the United States for a couple of weeks. It's a great opportunity, as most people will say, only it comes in the middle of the investigation."

"Yes, the timing. Why do they want you out at such a juncture?"

"I don't know. They of course have their reasons. Official reasons."

"Xing is in the States, isn't he? So now you're going there too, I think."

"I wish that could be the reason, but no, they didn't say anything to me about it," Chen said, picking up a dried plum with his chopsticks. Yu's instinctive response was sharp. Chen hadn't been aware of such a possibility until at Zhao's hotel. "For the last few days, I haven't really discussed the case with you. Not because of any confidential regulations or considerations, but because of little progress—"

"You don't have to talk like this, Chief. It's a case under the Party Discipline Committee, I understand."

"Now I want to discuss with you some new developments. Have you heard about the death of An Jiayi, the TV anchorwoman?"

"Yes, I've heard. Found naked and strangled at home. Sort of a celebrity, but not that well known—not politically. So the case went to the homicide squad. Kuang is working on it. Was she involved in your investigation?"

"She was. I'm not sure if her death was also involved, but the timing was suspicious—it was shortly after I interviewed her, and before she gave me some crucial information."

"Those monstrous rats are capable of doing that," Yu said. "Don't you see a similarity between her and Hua in Fujian? In each case, a naked body after sex."

"I don't know much about the Hua case in Fujian, but those behind Xing could be connected. So, do a couple of things for me during my visit in the States: in an address book left behind in her room, there are some phone numbers. It's quite an old address book, but it may still be worth checking into. Also, look into her phone records for the last several weeks, especially after the special investigation group was formed in Beijing."

"Hasn't Kuang checked the phone records?"

"He did, but according to him, she made no more than six or seven phone calls in the last three days, all of little relevance," Chen said. "Kuang doesn't seem too eager to share his information with me."

"I see. Anything else you want me to do?"

"It may not be easy. You aren't officially on An's case. Kuang is not cooperative—for a number of reasons. In fact, you'd better not tell Kuang about your interest in the case."

"I won't say a single word about it. Not to Kuang. Not to anybody."

"Follow the An case as closely as possible. I've put together a list of people, either interconnected with An or with Xing. Among them, Jiang, of the City Land Development Office. I want you to pay special attention to him. Any unusual move made by him, like going to another city or applying for a passport. Also, keep this small package for me."

"I'll put the name down," Yu said, taking the padded envelope and producing a notebook. Chen did not explain about the contents of the package. It wasn't characteristic of his boss, but Yu didn't ask.

"And Dong, of the State Company Reform Committee, also in connection with Ming's company." Chen put down his chopsticks and wrote several names on a piece of paper.

"Tell me more about these people."

So Chen began with a detailed account of his work, focusing on the involvement of Jiang and Dong, and on the possibility of Ming still hiding in Shanghai. At the end of his narrative, he added, "I need to ask a personal favor of you."

"What's that?"

"Call my mother from time to time. She's in rather frail health. You don't have to go there. Or perhaps Peiqin can call. Does Peiqin know her?"

"Yes—remember the dinner in Xinya? We both met her there."

"Old Hunter is still making his rounds patrolling as a traffic control advisor, I know. He may occasionally make his rounds there too."

"Tell me what's on your mind, Chief."

But there came a knock on the door. The waitress returned with their noodles and other dishes.

"The soup in the bun can be very hot. You may use the straw," she demonstrated amiably, "to suck out the soup carefully first."

It was not exactly soup in the bun, but hot, savory liquid with a rich flavor made of crab ovary and digestive glands. But Detective Yu did not have his heart in the food.

"Yes, we will do that," Yu said to the waitress curtly. "Please leave now."

"The *xiao* pork is wonderful too," Chen said politely. "Thank you."

As soon as the waitress left the room, Yu resumed, "What's on your mind?"

"I'm concerned not just about her health, but her safety too."

"Has somebody made a threat against her?"

"Not explicitly, but I have to be careful. In a real emergency, you may also contact Ling—my friend in Beijing. I've put down her phone number too. She may be able to help."

"In a real emergency," Yu repeated. "That's too much. You must have moved in the right direction, or those bastards wouldn't have tried to play this kind of dirty trick. They know you are a filial son. It's not your case anymore, it's mine too, Chief. I have to do something."

"I'm sorry to drag you in like that."

"I don't read much, you know, but I remember the saying in the *Romance of Three Kingdoms*: '*Not born on the same day, we want to die on the same day.*' The three sworn brothers—Liu, Guan, Zhang. So how can I stay outside alone? Let's have some wine."

"Why?"

"I am a lucky guy—a great wife, a wonderful son, and a real friend. Now I have something worth fighting for. So we'll drink."

"Let's drink tea instead. I'm going to a government office in the morning."

"Tea is fine," Yu said. "Now, what do you think of Comrade Zhao? He's in Shanghai, isn't he—because of the investigation?"

"Comrade Zhao may be one of the last Bolsheviks, like Old Hunter, but you can't expect him to go out investigating by himself. A high-ranking revolutionary of the older generation, his hands are bound with all the doctrines," Chen said, taking a sip at the bun. "Oh, I have met with him at the

Western Suburb Hotel and mentioned your name to him. He has heard of you too."

"Me? That's not possible."

"But that's true. I suggested to him that you be permitted to act on my behalf during my visit abroad, and he agreed."

"Any specific instruction?"

"With this case, anything is possible." After a pause, Chen said, "If need be, you may go to him in person. But you don't have to. You're an emperor's special envoy too, and can do whatever you believe necessary. Here is the statement signed by Comrade Zhao on behalf of the Party Discipline Committee. I have added one line to it."

Yu took the statement printed on the letter of the powerful committee. The line in Chen's handwriting read, "Comrade Detective Yu Guangming of the Shanghai Police Bureau is hereby authorized to act on Chief Inspector Chen Cao's behalf during his trip out of China." Chen had put the line under the original statement, but above Comrade Zhao's signature, together with his own signature. Yu wondered whether Chen had done that in the presence of Zhao.

"How can I contact you in the United States?"

"You don't call me. I will try to call you—in our weather jargon."

In one of their earlier cases, worrying about the possibility of their phone lines being tapped, they had successfully practiced their special weather jargon. Phrases like "cloudy with the possibility of rain," or "the possibility of the sun breaking out in the afternoon" had served their purpose well.

"And you can't be too careful," Chen concluded, draining the cup.

"Don't worry, Chief."

But, at home at the end of the day, Yu was worried.

Peiqin was busy warming dishes in their room. She was dressed in white and blue floral pajamas and a pair of transparent plastic slippers he had never seen before. He made himself a cup of tea, going over what he had done during the day.

Not much, he admitted, spitting out a tea leaf. Instead of talking to Kuang, Yu had approached a young cop working with Kuang, and the information he had obtained about An's phone records did not reveal anything new or different. For an anchorwoman, her phone calls seemed to be surprisingly few. As for Jiang and Dong, it was out of the question for him to go to their offices. And he did not know any people working there.

"Time for dinner, Guangming," Peiqin said. "There is a dish in the microwave."

He put the tea on the windowsill and took out a dish of salted pork fried with fresh leek. Peiqin was ladling out a bowl of rice for him.

The dish was steaming hot and good, in spite of its coming out of the microwave. The appliance was a housewarming gift from Chen in celebration of their moving into the *shikumen* room. A well-chosen gift, especially for Peiqin, who insisted on having hot meals at home. She could not, however, bear the idea of the shiny white microwave being smudged by the wok fumes in the common kitchen area, so she put the microwave in their bedroom, which also served as the dining room.

Theirs was not exactly a multiroom apartment, but it was still a huge improvement on what they had had—staying under the same roof with Old Hunter and sharing everything. It was at least a room under Yu's own name.

It was a simple meal for only the two of them. Their son Qinqin studied hard at school and would normally stay there until after nine. Earlier this evening, he had called, saying that he would be studying even later for a coming test. It was a crucial period. They did not have to wait up for him. With the partitioned outer room, Qinqin could come back late without waking them up.

Peiqin made a point of preparing special dishes only when Qinqin was home. It was a priority of necessity, to which Yu had no objection. Qinqin should have a different life, and for that, a good college education was a must. They had to save every penny for the boy. So the only fresh dish that evening was the hot and sour soup made of the ingredient package Peiqin had bought at a food store. She also sliced a thousand-year egg with a thin thread, which took no time, and divided the small dish of leftover soy-sauced pork with leek he had taken out of the microwave.

She, too, had been extremely busy. In addition to her accountant job at the state-run restaurant, she helped more and more with the private-run restaurant. She did not have as much time to cook at home. But the soup tasted good, enhanced with an egg and a handful of chopped green onion.

Over the meal, Yu told her about Chen's new assignment. That was the question she was going to ask, sooner or later.

"What about his anticorruption investigation under the Party Discipline Committee?" she asked, without looking up from her rice bowl.

"It has to wait until he comes back. The delegation assignment was a decision made at a higher level."

"So he has to go."

"He can't help it."

"But it's—" she said in an elated voice with the spoon between her lips, "it's also a good opportunity for him."

"Why?"

"He may meet that American woman officer again—what's her name?"

"Catherine Rohn."

"Yes, that's her name. She really likes things in China. She studied Chinese in college, I remember, but for one reason or another, she ended up being a cop. In that, she's like him. They are both in a career they hadn't planned for themselves. She had dumplings with us at our old home, don't you remember that? We still have the food mixer in our kitchen cabinet."

"I remember, that's a gift from her. But I doubt whether they will meet there. As the delegation head, he will be in the political limelight—and then with her?"

"Your boss is still single." Peiqin did not respond to the question directly. "I'm not talking about the one in Beijing. Such a distance between them. And such a gap too. I don't think that's good for him."

She ladled some more soup onto her rice, and then added a little water. It might be too spicy for her. The instant food was not that good after all.

"Well, he mentioned his Beijing girlfriend Ling today."

"In connection with his investigation?" She looked up sharply.

"In a way, yes. He mentioned her when he talked about his concern for his mother. No one takes care of her during his trip abroad."

"The old woman is in poor health, I know, and his HCC girlfriend Ling is in Beijing."

"Yes, he wants me or you to call her regularly. I mean his mother." He added, "And I also have permission to contact Ling in an emergency."

"Really!" She raised her chopsticks involuntarily. "That's not good. Now, is it just because of his mother's health?"

"He's concerned with her safety too. He gave me Ling's number."

"That sounds worse."

"I know. It's the first time he has talked to me about her. He usually avoids the topic, you know. According to someone in the bureau, their relationship has been strained. I doubt whether she would help him."

"Things might be more serious than he has told you, or he wouldn't choose to play the last card—I mean Ling. What else does your boss want you to do?"

"He also wants me to follow up some possible clues. Nothing officially," he said vaguely, and checked himself at the sight of her chopsticks coming to an abrupt stop in midair, like a wand in a magician's hand.

"Your chief inspector may be a capable cop—but he may not be so capable of staying out of trouble."

"What do you mean, Peiqin?"

"He is part of the system, so to speak," she said, dipping a slice of a thousand-year egg into the soy sauce. "He may fix a small problem here and there, like a loose screw, or a broken nail. But when the whole system is in a mess, what can he do? What, but put on a show—nothing but a show—whenever there is anything remotely like a stage?"

"He's above that," he said, surprised at her harshness. "At least, he doesn't believe he puts on a show."

"The system has not treated him too shabbily. His position, his room, his car, and whatnot. He may believe he's in serious business. It's useless."

"I've tried to talk him out of it, Peiqin, but as a cop, he has his responsibilities. And he insists on carrying on with the investigation, so—"

"So you have to throw in your lot with him. The government may try to expose a couple of red rats, but there are hundreds or thousands of them carrying on under their eyes, and they choose to do nothing. Why? It's their foundation. How can they do anything to shake their foundation?" Peiqin went on, putting a slice of the egg into Yu's bowl, "Do you know who's really behind Xing's case? Somebody too high, too powerful. That's why Chen is worried. So what's the point of dragging you into it?"

"Do you think I have a choice?" Yu said. "He is a good boss. And a good friend too. I can't stand aside with my arms crossed."

"He may be an honest cop, but this case involves too high a price tag. As a celebrity cop, he may be able to get away with it. But what about you? It's not even your case."

"He's not required to do anything while he is abroad. But he says he has to, as an investigator, and he needs my help," Yu said. "There aren't many cops like him left today. If I don't help, who will?"

"Sometimes, you talk like your Chief Inspector Chen," she said, shaking her head. "There must be somebody like Judge Bao, or the grand stage will not attract any audience."

"I haven't read many books, Peiqin. There are things I don't have to do. But if I don't, I can't sleep with an easy conscience." He said after a short pause, "Remember, Chen didn't have to go out of his way to help us with the apartment, but he did."

"*Yiqi,* the oughtness of the situation. I knew you would come to that. The obligation for you to pay him back," she said. "Don't take me wrong, Guangming. As long as you try to stay out of harm's way, I'm not opposed to your helping him."

"I will. In fact, I'll hardly do anything except keep an eye on some people. I am being more than careful. That's why I want to suggest that you call his mother."

"I'll do that. Things may not be so easy for him." She changed the subject abruptly: "By the way, have you heard about a plan for a high-end commercial complex in our neighborhood? If so, this old *shikumen* building of ours will be torn down, and as compensation, we may have a brand-new apartment."

"I think that's why he insisted on us taking it. He might have used some inside information for us."

"Yes, he did, and I should say, not for his own benefit. However, what will eventually happen to him? I don't mean the case, but the way he stays mixed up with those 'inside people' and connections?"

"Let's not worry about things too far in the future," he said.

"Qinqin is going to an English camp in Hangzhou," she said, switching to yet another topic. "Three weeks. Possibly a large sum. If we are going to move again, there will be another expense. I'd better put in more time at Old Geng's, and you have to take good care of yourself."

Yu did not make an immediate reply as she stood up to clean the table. He helped with a wet mop in his hand.

It was about ten when they went to bed.

"Oh, he wants me to keep this envelope for him," he said, reclining against a propped pillow. He took out the padded envelope, opened it, and the pictures fell out on the bed.

For the next few minutes, Yu and Peiqin gaped at the lurid photos without uttering a sound.

"It's An Jiayi," Peiqin finally said, her hand grasping his on the towel. "They killed her, didn't they?"

"Chen interviewed her two days before her death."

"That's too much." She suddenly rested her head against his chest. "Why did he give those pictures to you?"

"I don't know," he said. "I don't think he wants to carry them with him."

It was probably not true, he knew. And she knew too. Neither of them wanted to discuss it. He caressed her hair in silence.

One of the pictures appeared to be staring back at them. An nestled against a man on the bed, her bare breasts hardly covered by the quilt, her long black hair streaming like a fall.

Yu lost his mood, holding on to Peiqin, feeling her toes pressed against his leg.

That night, he lay awake for a long while. Beside him, she began snoring, lightly, worn out with work and worries.

He tried to think about things he could do for Chen, but without much success. Finally, sleepiness seemed to come over him in a confusion of fragmented images.

Among them, a very blurred image of several crabs bound together with a straw rope. For a moment, he seemed to be one of the crabs, caught out of water, producing bubbles of crab froth for each other's survival in the dry night, and the next moment, it was Chen who was the crab, waving its claws in a futile attempt to scissor through the silence. In bewilderment, Yu turned to touch Peiqin's bare shoulder. She turned over, nestling herself against him in sleep.

He realized that she had been worried about him. Her reaction at dinner could have been an effort to stop him from joining Chen in the investigation, but she did not really push. The same way he had earlier tried to talk Chen out of the case. He took another look at his watch in the dark. It was almost eleven-thirty. Qinqin was not back yet.

And the chief inspector must be flying over the Pacific Ocean, wondering what Detective Yu was doing at this moment in Shanghai.

13

I left the city of the White King
in the morning, in the midst
of the colorful clouds,
sailing thousands of miles
to Jiangling, all in a day's trip,
the monkeys crying on
along both the banks,
and the light boat
speeding through mountains.

CHEN QUOTED THE TANG dynasty lines as the airplane was beginning to land at the Los Angeles airport. He added in a hurry, "Of course, ours is a Boeing, not a boat."

Perhaps he should have chosen another poem, more appropriate for the occasion, in the company of these established writers. The flight had been delayed for ten hours in Tokyo. Nor had any monkey been heard or seen throughout the journey. It was not like in his bureau, where, whatever the chief inspector chose to cite, his colleagues would raise no question. Still, reciting the lines seemed to have relieved his tension. So far, everything had been smooth sailing, in spite of the delay, in spite of unexpectedly finding himself the delegation head.

Chen knew he wasn't a popular choice as head of the delegation. It wasn't difficult to understand their reservation, if not resentment. His police background projected him as sort of a politically reliable watchdog, hardly anyone had read his poems, and except for Little Huang, the interpreter, Chen was the youngest in the group. It was a pleasure to meet and talk with these well-known writers, but not necessarily so to serve as their boss.

But he had little time to worry about those things.

It was early morning in Los Angeles. The American host waited for them at the airport—greeting, handshaking, self-introducing and introducing each other, business card–exchanging, all the polite, meaningless, yet necessary, talking. Boris Reed, a history professor of the University of California and one of the original sponsors for the conference, was overwhelming in his welcome speech.

What happened next was like a surrealistically hectic montage. What with the jet lag and the culture shock, Chen and his writers remained disoriented during the long drive through the awakening highway, through the unfamiliar skyscrapers and unbelievable slums . . . Because of the delay at the Tokyo airport, the delegation arrived in the morning instead of the previous evening. As the first session of the conference had been scheduled several weeks in advance and a couple of American writers were there for only one day, the Chinese barely had time to check into the hotel before they had to hurry over to the conference hall.

It was a huge, impressive hall with Chinese and American writers sitting around tables set up in an oblong ring. In spite of the simultaneous interpretation equipment, Chen made his speech first in Chinese, and then in English. A speech of formalities, decked with quotes from classical Chinese and modernist Western writers. Then he was repeating the Tang dynasty lines in conclusion.

"Li Bai's poem reminded me of another poet," Chen said in his opening speech. "An American poet. I read his poems years ago in Shanghai. Now it's morning here, and it's evening in Shanghai. *'Let us go, you and I, / when the morning and the evening / are joining against the sky.'* "

"A different delegation from a different China," an American critic commented. "Now we can really talk. Whether from East or West, we are writers."

As if in contradiction to the American's comment, Bao took the floor. It was a speech full of clichés from the *People's Daily,* but thanks to Pearl, the talented American simultaneous interpreter, it sounded quite smooth in English. The audience politely applauded.

American writers spoke too, one after another. It was the first conference after the interruption of 1989. They had a lot to tell, and a lot to ask too. When Professor Reed began to talk about the significance of their meeting, Chen was hardly able to keep himself focused, though he kept nodding and applauding as before. The jet lag had started kicking in. And there was something else waking up in the back of his mind.

But the conference went on. Every attendee, Chinese or American, was supposed to talk for five to ten minutes, interesting or boring. Chen felt like lighting a cigarette, but there was no ashtray on the table.

An unexpected topic came up in the discussion. As most of the Chinese writers introduced themselves as "professional writers," James Spencer, an American poet, took a great interest in it. "I wish there were an institution here like your Writers' Association. A sort of government salary for your writing. It's fantastic. In the States, most of us can't make a living on writing. That's why I teach at a university. We all envy you. I would love to go to Beijing and become a professional writer too."

The American poet would have to live in China for years, Chen thought, before learning what a "professional writer" was like. Chen chose not to make any comment. Zhong said, however, with a sarcastic note discernable perhaps only in Chinese, "You are most welcome, James."

After lunch, the Chinese visited the campus bookstore. Bao frowned, muttering, "I have not seen any of our works here."

"It's not a large bookstore," Chen said.

"It's not just the size of it," Zhong said, siding with Bao.

All the other writers took the issue seriously. In China, they were considered the leading authors in their respective genres. So they had taken for granted their popularity in the States, but they found it far from so. The Americans had hardly heard of their works, except a few university professors specializing in modern Chinese literature. And only one touched on Chen's translation in his speech during the morning session.

So in the afternoon session, Shasha launched into an unrehearsed topic. Wearing a scarlet sleeveless silk cheongsam, she spoke in an authentic yet graceful way.

"I am going to address an important issue—the imbalance in the Chinese-American literature exchange. If you ask a college student in Beijing—not necessarily even one majoring in Western literature—he or she will reel off a list of American writers. Not only Mark Twain and Jack London, but a horde of contemporary writers, including some of you sitting here today. We have a dozen magazines devoted to the translation of Western literature. One Chinese critic saw the influence of Oates in my novels, and she's right. Mr. Chen, our delegation head, has translated Eliot and other American poets. Very popular translations. But what have our American colleagues done about modern Chinese literature? Little, I have to say. Very little."

Bao nodded. Little Huang was busy making notes. Peng, too, assumed a serious expression. Zhong took the floor. "There seems to be a political tendency. Those Chinese writers translated here—such as Sun Congwen or Zhang Ailing—are hardly relevant today."

Zhong had a point. For more than thirty years after 1949, the history of modern Chinese literature had been written to one overt political criterion. Those not affiliated with the Party or the socialist revolution were either criticized or ostracized. On the other hand, studies of modern Chinese literature in the West turned out to be exactly the opposite. Those writers were chosen in terms of their intrinsic value, and for their antigovernment stance as well.

Bonnie Grant, a sinologist who had translated Misty poets, commented with a hardcover in her hand, "There are Chinese writers writing in English here, and their books sell well. Perhaps there's something wrong with the translation of your work."

"We are in a commercial market," James Spencer said, once more trying to make the point. "It's a matter of selling one's product. The bookstore can think about nothing but profit."

"Not just in the bookstore," Bao cut in. "I cannot find my book even in the university library. I have asked Pearl to do a search for me during the lunch break. You have a Chinese department here, haven't you? That's a matter of cultural hegemony."

The conference atmosphere became tense. Bao might have been used to those political phrases, but the Americans were not. The discussion appeared to be going out of control. Chen had been aware of an anti-American undercurrent among his group but he wasn't prepared for this sudden shift.

Fortunately, the time for the cocktail party came. Their argument stopped as abruptly as it had started. Amidst the toasts, once again the writers were shaking hands and expressing their best wishes. Shasha plucked from her hair a fresh white jasmine petal and put it into a cup of tea, to the delighted surprise of Americans who surrounded her.

14

THE TROUBLES WERE NOT confined to the conference hall.

Afterward, in the evening "political study" in his room, Chen listened patiently as his delegation vented their frustrations.

"No thermos bottle in the hotel room," Bao started the angry chorus on a small note. "I cannot even have a cup of hot tea."

"Nonsmoking area," Zhong joined in. "Is this a free country? Nothing but hypocrisy. The Americans dump their cigarettes in China. They rip us off in a big way. Now we are not allowed to smoke the cigarettes bought with American dollars."

"It's not just us. Everyone in the hotel has to obey the rule," Chen said, though he felt constrained too.

"It's like the Opium War," Zhong went on. "They knew opium was a drug, but they dumped it on China on the grounds of free trade."

"I talked to an American student today," Little Huang said. "They believe that Hong Kong belongs to Britain, and that we do not even have the right to take it back. They know nothing about the Opium War. There is nothing in their textbooks."

"You know what?" Shasha said. She had changed her clothes again, and now in her pajamas, barefoot, she appeared at home. "Pearl told me that Pizza Hut is a cheap fast-food restaurant here. In Beijing, it is a high-end place. A pizza costs more than an ordinary Chinese worker's daily income. That is capitalism."

In the end, the Chinese writers were aggravated by the Americans' ignorance of their works. They had checked again in the late afternoon. Not a single translation of their works was available either in the bookstore or in the library.

"We are guests here," Chen said. "They have done a good job arranging this conference."

"We did a far better job in China," Bao cut in again. He had attended an earlier conference held in Beijing, before 1989. He talked with an unquestionable air of authority. "The best hotel in Beijing. Their delegation head got the presidential suite."

Peng was the only one in the group that spoke little, sitting in a corner. Chen failed to recall what Peng had said in the meeting.

Still, it was a lively political study, not so political as Chen had dreaded. Afterward, they talked about other things, without leaving his room immediately and not all at once. Shasha was the last one to stand up, just as Bao stepped out, but instead of leaving, she turned around again.

"Oh, I need to discuss with you the issue I raised in the afternoon."

"Yes, you made a good point today."

He had no idea why she didn't discuss it earlier, with others in the room. In fact, they had already touched on it, though not with serious concentration. It might not be a good idea for him to stay alone with her, so late in a hotel room. She was said to believe in her irresistible charm to men. But it wasn't a good idea for him to show his misgivings, either. He'd better not make any of them feel uncomfortable in his presence.

"Indeed, your writing is as graceful as your dancing, Shasha," he started on a casual note. "In my college years in Beijing, I saw your performance, in the Red Pagoda Theater."

"Really! You should have told me earlier."

"I was a poor student then, sitting at the end of the theater, worshipping the moonlike beauty rising on the stage."

"Come on, Chen. You don't have to say that to me. No one can dance forever. Beauty fades quickly, like a flower. So I moved from stage to page."

It was clever of her. Now she had her words dancing in fairy tales. She was a best-seller whose books were being made into TV series.

"But you have not come to Beijing so often—to your girlfriend Ling," she said, abruptly changing the subject.

It was probably no secret to the circle Shasha moved in, the story of him and his HCC girlfriend. Still, no one had brought up the subject to his face before. He wondered why she wanted to discuss that with him.

"I'm very busy in my work," he said.

"You don't have to explain to me, Chen. What's going on between a man and woman, others will never understand. Whatever people may say, you cannot live in their expectation or explanation."

"Yes, you put it well, Shasha."

So they kept chitchatting. Shasha did not turn out to be a siren as in the stories about her. She struck Chen as an understanding and titillating talker, though occasionally intimate in an unexpected way. When she rose to leave, it was ten-thirty. They had not really touched upon the issue she had mentioned. Why had she chosen to stay on behind? he wondered. Perhaps she knew jet lag would keep her from being able to fall asleep. Perhaps as an acknowledgment of their common friend in Beijing. Perhaps she was just like that, flirtatiousness being second nature to her. Perhaps, with her extraordinary connections, she had a mission unknown to him—the mission of watching over him. It was not much of a possibility, but he could not rule it out.

As a result, Chen had no time to make a phone call back to Detective Yu in Shanghai. It didn't seem a good idea to call from the hotel room. The bill probably wouldn't be covered by the Americans, and the delegation had only a small budget. Nor was he sure if the room was bugged. His cop background must be no secret here. Perhaps he should try to use a pay phone. He copied some numbers on a scrap of paper.

As he was about to walk out of his room, there came a light tap on the door. Not again, he thought as he steadied himself in resignation and opened the door. To his surprise, it was Dai Huang, an old poet from Shanghai, standing in the doorway.

"Sorry to approach you like this," Dai said shamefacedly.

"Oh, come on in, Mr. Dai. I didn't know you were here."

Chen had met Dai in the Shanghai Writers' Association. Dai had studied abroad in the thirties, served as a bank manager on his return, and written modernist poems in the pre-1949 era. In spite of his strenuous efforts to reform himself in the socialist revolution, Dai lapsed into silence in the late fifties, and it was not until the mid-eighties that his work was reprinted. He was not a writer chosen for the conference.

"The Greyhound had an accident on the way, so I have just arrived here," Dai said, wiping his feet on the doormat.

As it turned out, Dai happened to be visiting a relative in San Francisco. He heard of the conference and hurried over by bus. He had intended to stay with a friend in L.A., but his friend had just left for a business meeting. It was late, and Dai could not afford to stay in a hotel nearby. He contacted Bao, who suggested he touch Chen, on the grounds that his room was the largest.

Chen thought that he had to help. He liked Dai's poems. But for the political considerations, Dai would have been chosen as a delegation member—and stayed in the hotel. With a king-sized bed in his room, Chen didn't think it would be a problem.

In spite of the late hour, neither wanted to go to bed immediately. Chen used the coffeepot to make hot water. Dai carried Dragon Well tea with him. The water was not too hot, but the tea tasted good.

"Isn't life full of ironies?" Dai started. "In the fifties, I gave up my properties to the government, including an inherited house in the States. In an effort to make myself a member of the proletariat, but what then?"

Chen had heard the story before. The brainwashing campaign was effective in those years, and Dai had wholeheartedly believed the communist propaganda. During the Cultural Revolution, however, his self-reforming effort was condemned as abortive camouflage to buy himself a Party membership.

"Think about it. The interest from selling the house could have covered my hotel expense here for a month," Dai said, not trying to conceal the bitterness in his voice. "I am staying with my niece in San Francisco, room and board. A nice girl, she gives me a hundred dollars as monthly pocket money here. I don't have the old face to ask any more of her."

What could Chen say? His own father, a neo-Confucian scholar, had donated to his college a collection of rare books, which were later exhibited as criminal evidence against him and burned at the beginning of the Cultural Revolution.

"Don't worry, Mr. Dai. The university will take care of your problem tomorrow morning," Chen said. "It's an honor for me to share this room with you. I read your poems as early as in middle school. Now you go to bed first, Mr. Dai. I'll look through the schedule."

After Chen glanced through the schedule, he took out his notebook, scribbling down several lines. It was out of the question to call Yu with Dai in the room.

Finally, he went to bed. Lying uncomfortably on one side, staring at the ceiling, he knew he would not be able to fall asleep anytime soon. The old man, exhausted by the long hours on the bus, started to snore. Chen soon got up and moved over to the sofa. Sitting with his legs resting on a chair, he tried to think over the day's events.

But his mind was tired, unable to focus. English seemed to be jarring against his Chinese subconscious. Then he thought of Xing again—who was also in Los Angeles. But Chen was not a cop here and he had no idea how to proceed. In a way, he didn't even know what he really was, with the old poet snoring in the bed. He thought of a poem written by Su Dongpo, a well-known Song dynasty poet, in his exile. Chen particularly liked the ending of it.

Long, long I lament
there is not a self for me to claim
oh, when can I forget
all the cares of the world?
The night deep, the wind still, no ripples on the river.

The poem was about Su being shut out at midnight because his houseboy slept too soundly, snoring like thunder. He could only stand outside, listening to the sound of the river, while he thought about the loss of his self in the midst of all his worries. Chief Inspector Chen was in quite a different situation. He was in his own hotel room, with his career in a steady rise, though the snoring that came to him in the depth of the night was perhaps as loud.

After a while, he rose again and took two sleeping pills. He started jotting down notes for a speech on the second day. When he finished with the notes, however, the pills still hadn't started working.

His mind wandered further away—to An. The memories of her black braid flapping in their reading-group days, of her politically correct image radiating on TV, and of her naked body lying spread-eagled in her apartment. A nocturnal confusion of juxtaposed images. And then their meal in the restaurant on the Bund. He had a feeling he had missed something in his earlier reconstruction of that evening. Once more he tried to recall what they had said, minute by minute, in the Lovers' Nest. As he had experienced before, the effort only wore him out without yielding any clue.

It was almost three-thirty, the window revealing the first gray light, when sleepiness finally began to overtake him. Perhaps Dai would get up soon. Still, Chen tried to set the alarm clock. The instructions were in English and took him several minutes to figure out. He was mechanically clumsy. Then something rang in his memory.

It was not what she said, but what she did in Golden Island.

That evening, he had had a problem with his cell phone. He must have accidentally touched a button, and he had had no clue how to put it back to the normal ringing. She had taken it from his hand and restored the ringing in no time. He was amazed, her slender fingers touching his, but he did not ask her how she did it.

"It's easy," she said.

Not easy for the chief inspector, who now realized the importance of the incident. *She must have had a cell phone too.* Or she could not have fixed the problem so easily. He had to find her cell phone records.

15

THE SECOND DAY IN Los Angeles was like the first day, busy with meeting, visiting, dining, and discussing. And now it was the third day, which would probably turn out to be just like the day before, Chen thought, waking up early in the hotel room.

In the midst of all the delegation activities, Chen managed to do a few things on his own.

With an international phone card, he had called Detective Yu, his hard-working assistant in Shanghai, who had hardly anything new to tell him. *The weather remains cloudy, with little change in the air.* If An had been murdered in connection with the anticorruption investigation, it might have been planned at a high level. So getting information would be difficult for a low-level cop like Detective Yu, let alone one without access to the investigation. The people Yu watched showed no unusual signs. Jiang was back in office, and in the newspaper too, the day after Chen had left, delivering a speech on the urgency of making the land development process transparent to the public. Sergeant Kuang kept plodding away at the An case without giving away any details. Yu had to find his own way of exploring the case. Separately, a short poem by Chen appeared in the *Shanghai Morning* with a note about his new status as the delegation leader. After Yu's report, made mainly in the weather terminology, Chen told Yu what he had thought of during the night Dai was snoring in his room. The chief inspector found it hard to explain in their agreed-upon jargon, but he believed that he had managed to convey his meaning.

He also called his mother. The old woman was pleased with the phone call from Peiqin and with the visit from White Cloud. In addition, Party Secretary Li had sent a small basket of fruit. Everything appeared to be fine there.

And here, he put Dai in the hotel as an honorable delegation member, a proposal Professor Reed had readily agreed with. Dai had a poetry collection translated into English, so there was no question about his writer status. Bao alone seemed not too pleased. Both Zhong and Shasha were on Chen's side. Peng nodded, as usual.

Also, he delivered a speech on the translation of classical Chinese poetry. Afterward he had a fruitful discussion with a group of people interested in the topic.

So he had been doing an acceptable job for the delegation, he thought, in a number of ways. Little Huang was not always up to the task of literature translation; Chen helped whenever he had time. With his educational background, he also provided a sort of cushion for the culture shock of the delegation.

But the third day in L.A. turned out to be different from the first two. The American host suggested that the Chinese take a day off, considering they had had meeting after meeting without a break. So the day was rearranged to be one of free exchange among the writers. There were informal discussions and seminars on campus, and they could choose the topics they liked.

There were several American writers staying in the same hotel, and they talked over breakfast. Not exactly a productive literature discussion, Chen contemplated. The morning newspapers arrived, with both English and

Chinese articles about the conference, carrying Chen's picture in one of them—under a larger picture of a Chinese supermarket.

Some of the members of the delegation were having a hard time adjusting to the American breakfast. There was a microwave in the hotel canteen and they could easily warm up Chinese food for themselves. The Americans had no objection to the request.

Sightseeing was on the day's agenda. Zhong suggested that they go out in the morning, and while sightseeing, they could do some shopping too. The delegation got into a van, driving all the way to Chinatown. Once the van came in sight of those familiar signs and characters under an arch with tilted glazed eaves and dragon-embossed pillars, the visitors felt as if they were arriving home. There, they did not have to move in a group and no one would get lost. Chen stepped into a grocery, where he saw a dazzling array of Chinese products, perhaps even more various than in a Shanghai supermarket. He discovered a small bottle of Liuheju Fermented Bean Curd, a special Beijing product with a pungent flavor. A pity that he could not take it back to the hotel, where Americans might protest against its smell. He did buy a stick of green bean candy, *dougen,* a Tianjin product. He had so enjoyed it years earlier, sharing a small piece of it with his friend Ling. A small wonder, its rediscovery in another country. He paid for it, tore away its plastic wrapper like an impatient child, and popped it into his mouth. It was not the same taste as in his memory, but like a lot of things in the world, that could not be helped.

He heard no one speaking English in the store. There was only an old American couple examining herbal Chinese medicine in silent curiosity, and all others were Chinese, shopping, bargaining, and speaking in their respective dialects. A middle-aged woman was tearing the yellow leaves off the green cabbage before placing it into her plastic bag, a familiar scene which reminded Chen of Aunt Qiang, who lived down the street from his mother. He came to a counter that displayed cell phones and calling cards. A prepaid cell phone caught his attention. It was expensive, but affordable with the advance from Gu. Chen also purchased a new phone card, one that was cheaper than the one he had bought in the university store. According to the instructions on the back, it cost only ten cents per minute to call China, a benefit of competition. In China, telecommunications was still a state-controlled industry.

He stepped out of the store carrying the phone card. Before he discovered a public phone booth, he saw Pearl coming over with a cell phone in her hand.

"Somebody has been looking for you everywhere," she said with a smile.

"Thank you," he said, taking the phone. "Hello, this is Chen Cao."

"I am Tian Baoguo. Still remember me, old friend? The same Little Tian who shared the dorm desk with you for four years in Beijing Foreign Language University."

"Of course. Old classmate. How can I forget those long nights, of talking about the night rain south of the Yangtze River, and of scrambling eggs over your little alcohol stove?"

"I read the news. I saw your pictures. It had a biographical note about you: the distinguished poet and translator. Only one Chen Cao under the sun. I made so many calls. Now I have finally got hold of you. Where are you?"

"Chinatown. In front of a Chinese grocery store called Central Trading."

"Don't move. I'm running over. Five to ten minutes. We'll have lunch together."

"I would love to, Tian, but I'm here with my delegation."

"The delegation's lunch is on me. A small way of showing my respect to you writers—on behalf of my company. The best Chinese restaurant here. See you soon!"

When Chen discussed Tian's invitation with others, no one had any objection. They were intrigued at meeting a prosperous overseas Chinese still interested in the literature of his country. With no special activity arranged for that afternoon, Pearl, the American interpreter-escort, did not insist on their dining in the hotel.

And in less than five minutes, Chen saw a tall man striding over and recognized him immediately as Tian, though they hadn't seen each other for more than ten years.

"As our ancient sage says, there are three wonderful moments in one's life," Tian said, grasping his hand. "When one's name appears at the top of the civil service examination. No more civil service examination today, but your high-ranking position counts. When one gets married with the candle of happiness illuminating the wedding room. I have just married a second time. When one meets an old friend in a faraway place. All apply to us. Isn't today a perfect day?"

"You still talk like in the old days, Tian."

"Now I've come here in the name of my company too. You have to give me face by condescending to dine with me. Every one of you, my respected masters."

It was a banquet set in a magnificent Chinese restaurant. Tian had reserved a private room. At his insistence, the restaurant owner, too, came out to toast the "great Chinese writers." To the pleasant surprise of everyone, Tian had also prepared his special present. Ten bottles of deep sea fish oil—each with a gold "Made in the U.S.A." label pasted on top—for each member of the delegation. An offer that made not only him, but Chen as well, immediately popular.

"It's a popular product of our company. The best on the market. Please accept it as a token of our appreciation of your wonderful writings," Tian said with undisguised pride. "I used to major in Chinese literature. I cannot express how I admire you. Deep sea fish oil will be good for hardworking intellectuals like you."

"Thank you for your present," Zhong said. "The fish oil will be good for my older wife."

"You have to write a report about his pioneering business in the *People's Daily*," Shasha said with a giggle. "Good for his business."

It was an impressive feast by any standard. The host and guests kept raising their cups. The restaurant owner brought out a bottle of Maotai as house compliment. "Drink to your hearts' content. I've had it for over ten years. No fake products those days."

It sounded like a not-too-subtle reference to the rampancy of fakes in present-day China. Still, everyone at the table cheered.

Tian made a passionate welcome speech, concluding with a couple of lines from Wang Wei: "*'Drink one more cup, my dear friend! / Out of the Yang Pass / to the west, you'll find / no companion of old.'* "

"Now we are way out of the Yang Pass," Bao commented, echoing from the well-known poem, "but we still have a good friend like Tian."

Because of the banquet, of the wine, of the fish oil, when Tian invited Chen to his home, no one had any objection, despite the delegation regulation against a member going out with a friend without an official approval. Several urged Chen to go.

Bao also said, "Enjoy yourself in the company of your friend. I'll take care of things."

"Anywhere you want to go," Tian said as soon as Chen got into his car. "Anything you want to do. It's your first trip here. Casino, club, bar, topless, bottomless. You name it."

"I would like to go to your home," Chen said. "To meet your young wife. And you may tell me your success story along the way."

"It's anything but a success story, Chen. But it's a long drive, so I may as well tell it from the beginning."

In the mid-eighties, Tian came to the United States to further his studies in comparative culture. He made a career change, however, while working on his dissertation. Devastated by the divorce from his first wife, who saw no hope of his finding a job here, Tian started practicing acupuncture and herbal Chinese medicine. His studies in comparative culture were unexpectedly useful. His eloquent and frequent talk about the balance between yin and yang, about the mysterious interactivity of the Five Element System, about the omnipresent Way of Qi—all in English—prompted local newspapers to report on his "groundbreaking" medical work on the new continent. He was soon enjoying success among American as well as Chinese clients, who stood waiting in long lines outside. He began making herbal pills, which, too, proved to be popular with people who had no time or earthenware to prepare medicine in the traditional Chinese way. He then bought a run-down warehouse and turned it into a workshop for herbal medicine production. Because of the FDA regulations, he called the pills health products.

"But I don't see how the deep sea fish oil came into your product line," Chen commented with a smile.

"When the wheel of fortune turns, no one can stop it. You don't even have to oil the wheel."

"Fantastic, Tian. Tell me more about it."

"I made my first trip back to China several years ago. I met up with Yan Xiong. He majored in French and lived in the same dorm building with us, remember?"

"Yes, he wrote his thesis on French symbolism."

"He must have forgotten all about the symbols—except what stands for money in this materialistic age," Tian said. "Yan is now a cadre in charge of export and import in Ningbo. He offered to collaborate with me on the health products—on the condition that he and his wife act as the exclusive agent."

Tian then went into a detailed market analysis. As the economy in China improved, people became aware of the need for those health products. It was in line with the time-honored tradition of *bu,* the necessity of providing something beneficial to one's yin and yang system. They did not believe, however, in the locally made pills. There were too many reports about knockoffs. The emerging middle class was willing to pay a couple of dollars more for a product with a "Made in the U.S.A." label.

"The Yans know the market, and they have the connections. One of my products, deep sea fish oil, was a huge hit. Natural omega in the depth of oceans, which sounds both mysterious and miraculous."

"It's true," Chen said.

"My company has obtained several patents. The American customers are drawn to the part about the ancient Chinese tradition, and the Chinese customers to the part about modern American technology. What an ironic joke!"

"It's good that you take it as a joke, and laugh at it too. After all, a successful joke."

"But how far have I moved away from the dreams I had in Beijing Foreign Language University? We talked about the value of life, about the aroma of newly printed pages, about the reflection of White Pagoda in the

Northern Sea, about the bamboo music in the quaint teahouse. Now I am a businessman, reeking of copper coins all over."

"How far have I moved, Tian? I didn't read mystery novels then. Now I have translated several of them—for money. And I am a cop, like one prowling in those pages. In fact, I don't know why I have come here." Chen changed the subject: "You should have contacted me in Shanghai."

"Well, the first time I went back, I heard a lot about your work. I thought it might not be so convenient for me to approach someone in your position. Then for the following trips, I was overwhelmed with business—including that of marrying Mimi."

Tian couldn't help being effusive at the unexpected reunion. There was no doubt about his sincerity. Still the same bookish, honest Tian as in their college years. It must not have been easy for him to take a day off for an old friend, with so much business for him to take care of in L.A.

"You know a lot of business people here, Tian?" Chen said, with an idea flashing through his mind.

"Some, I would say."

"Do you know Xing Xing too?"

"I have heard of him—and seen him at an antique auction, at a distance. The local Chinese newspapers were full of his stories."

"Well, I'm a cop, you know." He knew he was taking a risk. *While a general is fighting along the borders, he does not have to listen to every order given to him by the emperor far away in the capital.* And a general could not fight alone. He had to depend on his allies. For the moment, he had only Tian—or had his only hope in Tian. Tian was trustworthy, he judged. Besides, Tian had business in China. Such a businessman would probably not give away a Chinese official in an important position. "So let me tell you something—between you and me. I was investigating a case concerning Xing before I came out."

Chen began to talk about his work—part of it—to Tian. Tian slowed down before turning into a rest area off the highway. Then the car pulled up in the cool shade of a blossoming tree. There were several cars and trucks there. A few Americans stood drinking or smoking. Chen and Tian did not get out of the car.

At the end of Chen's account, Tian said quietly, "It's about time that the Beijing government did something about corruption. I'm so glad you still trust me like in our college years. You are doing a great job, Chen. I'm proud of having you as a friend."

"The authorities have been trying hard—" Chen did not go on, for he himself was not so pleased with the editorial-like defense of the government. "Xing stays in Rowland Heights, right?"

"Yes. I know something about the area. The people there buy a lot from my company."

"Really! I need to find out something. Maybe you can help me. For instance, who does Xing associate with here? And if possible, I need to know in what ways."

"That shouldn't be too difficult," Tian said.

"But you can't canvass—knock on one door after another. Everything should be done without Xing's knowledge."

"I have an idea. I might be able to break through using the kids of the ex-official families there. Totally spoiled, they brag and boast as if the world were a watermelon in their hands, which they can cut and eat to their hearts' content. A little Chinese girl once offered to pay the private school tuition for her American friend, claiming that there was too much money in the banks for her father to count. Sure enough, her father, a former mayor of Liaoyang City, promptly signed a check for her. So I'll approach their kids. Birds of a feather gather together, and they may tell me something."

Chen had heard stories about corrupt officials fleeing overseas with tons of money and squandering the stolen money like children throwing pebbles into water. He made no comment.

"And I have another idea," Tian went on. "Let me drive you to Rowland Heights this afternoon. It may help your work."

"I don't think a visit there would lead to anything. I'm not supposed to do any official investigation. It's out of the question for me to knock on his door."

"We may still find something there. You never know, Chen."

Chen didn't think so, but like a Tang dynasty general, he could hardly resist the opportunity of observing the enemy at close range. Besides,

Tian appeared to be in such high spirits, he would probably keep talking all the way.

"Well, if that's not too much trouble for you."

"No trouble. It's not just for you, but for China too. I've got my citizenship here, but China is still my home country," Tian said excitedly. "Let me tell you something. Last year, I watched the soccer game between the U.S. and China on TV. To the annoyance of my American neighbors, I cheered the Chinese team all the time."

"Yes, I understand."

"So that's it. We'll go to Rowland Heights, but a little later on: it'll be better in the evening. Come to my home first."

So they arrived at Tian's house, which was located in a new subdivision. A new red brick house with a back garden. Not large, but nice. According to Tian, it was worth more than a million in the area.

Mimi, Tian's new wife, wearing a pink T-shirt and white shorts, barefoot, soared out like a butterfly. She was about twenty years younger than Tian, handsome, tall, moving softly with a suggestion of voluptuousness. Tian had met her during one of his trips to China, and brought her here by having married her there, about ten days after their first meeting. The marriage was also seen as part of his success story.

"Old Tian has told me so much about you, Chen," she said sweetly. "You look so young."

In spite of Chen's protest, the Tians started to prepare a barbeque reception in the backyard, which boasted a swimming pool, and a white pavilion in enjoyable relief against the green foliage. Soon, the ribs sizzled deliciously over the antique grill made of an old-fashioned tank. They sat close to a corner overgrown with weeds. Cicadas started chirping, distantly, different from those heard in Beijing. Against the rugged mountain lines, the afternoon sun on the back of a wild goose seemed to be still coloring a corner of the sky.

They did not resume their talk about Xing immediately. Mimi kept coming to them with drinks and snacks in her hands, an amiable, competent hostess, walking light-footed over the green grass. She finished a Qingdao beer with them before she went back into the living room for her favorite TV program.

"By the wine urn, the girl is like the moon, / her white wrists like frost, like snow," Chen quoted a couplet in a moment of impulse. He immediately regretted it. It was out of place.

"I first met her in a bar in a Qingdao hotel. She worked there—a Budweiser girl," he said, brushing the sauce on the slightly burnt ribs. "So your guess is close. Except there's no wine urn there, but a beer barrel."

"She's so pretty. I could not help quoting."

"Except that we are no longer so young," Tian said, in a reference to the ending of that celebrated poem too: *Still young, I am not going back home, / or I'll have a broken heart.* Heaving a long sigh, Tian took off his toupee. His bald skull shone in the afternoon sunlight, like a boiled egg.

"Tell me more about Rowland Heights," Chen said, changing the subject again.

"Well, it is an open secret. The area has embraced a recent influx of extraordinarily wealthy Chinese. A new breed of immigrants, small in number, but conspicuous as hell. They buy million-dollar houses and pay all in cash. So many Chinese officials in charge of government or state-owned business money have disappeared, only to resurface here with their families in tow, with the missing money channeled into their personal bank accounts."

"Yes, the capital flight amounted to several billion over the last two years, a large part of it embezzled by officials on the run."

"We'd better leave now," Tian said, looking up. "It's getting dark."

Chen called the hotel and spoke to Bao. "There's no special activity for the rest of the day, so I think I'll stay on with Tian. You'll have to take care of the political study in the evening."

"I'll take care of everything," Bao said.

Chen and Tian set out around five-thirty. Mimi accompanied them out to the car. "Come back, Mr. Chen. I'll make you a seafood dinner, Qingdao style."

The traffic in L.A. was crazy, cars speeding recklessly like headless flies. Tian, too, drove fast, but he kept talking, as if still sitting at leisure in his own backyard. A sign for Rowland Heights soon came into sight.

Tian must have been a regular visitor to the high-class subdivision. There was a guard with a phone sitting in a booth at the entrance. Visitors had to be announced before being admitted. But the guard apparently recognized Tian and waved him through without asking him to do anything. They drove through the entrance, turning into a driveway lined with tall palm trees. After making two or three turns, Tian pointed to a secluded section and whispered, "Here is Xing's house."

It was a majestic mansion looming through the dusk, with a marble arch towering over its door, and a couple of stone lions squatting in front of the entrance, which reminded Chen of the celebrated bronze ones on the Bund.

"Four or five million dollars at least," Tian said, estimating in his businessman's way, "Xing's house."

They saw a stolid man in black sitting on a rattan chair on the porch, resting his feet on a white plastic chair, drinking from a bottle of beer. It was not Xing. That Chen could tell.

"Possibly a bodyguard," Tian said, slowing down as he made a show of looking for the house number.

The guard looked up in alert, putting the beer down, but the car did not stop, rolling out of sight.

"We'll come back," Tian said. "Xing has connection with local triads. Those tangs and bangs are capable of doing anything."

"Do you mean Xing belongs to the secret society in Los Angeles?"

"I'm not sure, but with his money, he could have easily rented those thugs for protection."

"Money can make devils pull round the mill like blindfolded mules," Chen said. "Is Xing still doing business here?"

"No, not that I've heard of. He'd better stay low. The money he has plundered will let his next three generations wallow in obscene luxury."

"Has his case made a big buzz here?"

"It did, but Chinese people here don't care much about the politics back home—thousands of miles away in the Forbidden City. Look at this white five-storied mansion next to Xing's. It belongs to the son of a politburo member. Little Tiger, that's his nickname, I think."

"What is he doing here?"

"He's barely in his twenties. Instead of studying, he's been partying everywhere, drinking, dancing, and mah-jonging night and day. He has a large import and export company—at least under his name."

"You know a lot of people."

"The Chinese community here is like a small world. Folks keep bumping against one another."

In the midst of gathering dusk, they were driving round to Xing's house again.

"I'll ask for directions," Tian said, pulling up before Chen could stop him. "You stay in the car."

Tian apparently knew some residents here. The black-clothed guard stood up and pointed in one direction. Tian went on with his questioning, as if still lost. The door behind them opened. A white-haired woman appeared with a string of large beads in her hand. The guard said something to her, and the door closed again. But in a swift glance, Chen saw the hallway inside enveloped in incense. Then the door of the white mansion opened again, and a young man came out. The guard bowed to the young man respectfully as Tian moved back to the car.

"Sorry, I've got nothing for you," Tian said, sitting beside Chen. "The guy would not even say whether Xing is at home. I didn't want to sound too inquisitive. No point stirring a sleeping snake."

"No," Chen said. "I really appreciate all your effort. So the old woman must be Xing's mother."

"Yes, Xing is a filial son. When he first came here, he often appeared in his mother's company. I have seen her picture in the local Chinese newspapers too."

"Is the old woman a Buddhist?"

"I think so. I have read something about it, but I'm not sure."

"That's interesting."

"Why?"

"Oh, my mother also believes in Buddhism," Chen said. "Is that young man Little Tiger—the next-door neighbor to Xing?"

"Yes. Perhaps more than a next-door neighbor. Tell you what. I may be able to find out more. My company has ads in most of the Chinese newspapers here. The editors owe me some favors."

"No, I don't think it's a good idea to contact those people. Xing may be well connected here."

Warmed with his first detective experience, however, Tian continued to make suggestions on the way back. Some of his ideas might be worth trying; others were totally impracticable. Chen listened and then glanced at his watch.

"How far is it from the hotel?"

"About fifteen minutes."

"Let me down here. You'd best not be seen too much in my company. Now about Xing, don't do anything without consulting me first."

"I'll be careful. No one will ever suspect me."

"Don't call the hotel. I bought a new cell phone here. Call this number only," Chen said, writing the number down on a scrap of paper. "Better call me only from a public phone."

"That sounds more and more exciting, like in a thriller movie, Chen. Any special directions for me to follow?"

"I don't know. Little Tiger, his next-door neighbor, might be someone worth checking into. As a cop, I don't believe in coincidence."

"What do you mean by coincidence?"

"Xing's connected at the very top," Chen said. "Drop me here. I'll take a taxi the rest of the way."

16

IN THE HOTEL ROOM, Bao found himself unable to fall asleep. It was only eight-thirty. He should not have gone to bed so early, but there was nothing else for him to do. Shasha and Zhong were out of the hotel, following Chen's example. The political study was canceled without anyone consulting Bao. No one paid much attention to him.

He tossed about on the mattress. How could a human body feel comfortable on the steel springs? In Beijing, he slept on *zhongbeng,* a sort of mattress woven of twisted palm fiber—hard, airy, reliable—and he fell asleep the moment his head touched the pillow.

What kind of a bed was provided in Chen's suite? he wondered. Nominally, Bao was the Party secretary. Only it did not work here. His Party position was not mentioned. Thanks to the first letter of his name in the Chinese phonetics, he was put directly under Chen. Other than that, he was treated exactly like other members. It was an unacceptable yet undeniable fact that Bao had to move in this young man's shadow.

He took out from under the pillow a book of his poems from the seventies. He had intended to give it to an American writer. So far, no one seemed to have read him. Unbelievable. He got up, turned on the TV, and cursed in spite of himself. All the channels were in English. He tried to use the coffeepot for hot water, without success. Chen had shown him how, but it was a different pot, with the instructions in English. He did not want to ask again. Even the interpreter seemed to take him as an old fool.

Everything was weird here: the windows could not be opened. What's the point? The carpet exotic, sweaty under his bare feet, almost slimy in a sultry evening. In several rooms, smoking was not allowed—in a country of so-called freedom. Absurd to suffer the restrictions in a hotel room that cost more than a hundred dollars a day. More than his monthly income, come to think about it. He ignored the rules. Lighting a cigarette, he dashed the ash into a plastic cup as he slumped into a chair close to the window, resting his foot on the windowsill. In the spiraling smoke, he watched the fragments of his life moving around to form a new, meaningful whole.

Bao's literary career had started in the early fifties during the nationwide Red Flag Folk Song Campaign, which pushed workers and peasants to the fore as "proletarian writers." Following Chairman Mao's doctrines about literature and art serving politics, it was a matter of necessity that proletarian writers should play a principal role. So an old editor of *Shanghai Literature* came to the Beijing Number One Steel factory, where Bao, a young apprentice then, was cracking a handful of soy-sauce-fried watermelon seeds. As the editor explained the purpose of his visit, Bao burst out laughing.

"What can I say? Nothing an uneducated worker says will ever interest you," he responded, spitting the husk into his palm. "Look, such a small seed can only grow into a tiny watermelon. There's nothing you can do about it."

"Hold on. That's fantastic, Comrade Bao. That's brilliant. Thank you so much," the editor said, scribbling lines in his notebook. "I'll contact you again."

Three days later, the editor contacted him again, showing him a copy of *Liberation Daily* with a short poem published there:

What kind of seeds grow what kind of melons.
What kind of vines produce what kind of flowers.

What kind of people do what kind of things.
What kind of classes speak what kind of languages.

The poet was none other than Bao, with an editorial note underneath: "In a simple yet vivid language, the emerging worker-poet Bao speaks the truth: the class struggle is everywhere. While the class enemies will not change their true color or their true nature, we, the working-class people, will always be loyal to our revolutionary nature. The first two lines are hidden metaphors, juxtaposing the image with the following statement."

A huge hit, the poem was reprinted in the *People's Daily* and other newspapers. Radio stations interviewed him. Magazines covered him. He was admitted into the Chinese Writers' Association. Instead of working in the steel factory, he became a professional writer with more published poems. One couplet even appeared in textbooks. *A shout from our Chinese steel workers, / And the earth has to tremble three times.* Then Bao married a young college student who worshipped his poems. During the Cultural Revolution, because of his working-class origins, Bao became a member of the association revolution committee. One of his new poems was even made into a popular song. With the end of the Cultural Revolution in 1976, however, troubles came his way. Those who had suffered under the revolution committee criticized him. What's more, he was no longer capable of publishing his work. People called his poems political doggerel, and his working-class status hardly helped anymore.

Still, he had to consider himself lucky with his position intact as an administrator in the Writers' Association, and the occasional appearance of his name in the newspapers. The Party authorities tried to keep a working-class poet on the literary scene in a symbolic way. Now in semi-retirement, Bao was given the chance to visit the United States. Bao could have said no to this trip, but he was going to retire soon, and then he would lose all his privileges, including the opportunity of a government-paid trip. It would be a terrible loss of face for a writer of his status to step down without having visited the States. The opportunity was like a chicken rib: not meaty, but too chewable to throw away.

It was then that the phone rang. He wasn't really in the mood to talk to anybody, but to his surprise, it was Hong Guangxuan, someone he had known in the mid-sixties, in the Beijing Workers' Culture Palace, in his poetry workshop. Sitting in the audience, Hong listened to his talks and turned in the homework to the "master." So they became acquainted. After Hong emigrated to the United States in the early eighties, they had lost contact.

Bao moved down to the lobby in strides, carrying that poetry collection. Hong had a Chinese restaurant here, Bao had heard.

"I'm so glad to see you, Master," Hong said, rising respectfully as in the old days.

"You have not forgotten me, Hong." *Master* was a word Bao had long missed. Now thousands of miles away, someone still remembered him as such. He was touched.

"How can I! Those days in the Worker's Culture Palace," Hong said. "I heard about the delegation two days ago and I thought about you. In the local newspapers, I read the name of the delegation head—never heard of him before—Chen Cao, but only this morning did I learn from someone else that you were here."

"Oh, I'm the Party secretary of the delegation," Bao said. "The Party position won't be mentioned in the newspapers here."

"Yes, that's right," Hong said. "It's about ten years since we last met. Things have really changed, as from azure oceans to mulberry fields. How about a long talk over a night meal? There are excellent Chinese restaurants in L.A. As genuine as you can find in Beijing."

Bao was not hungry. But the prospect of a genuine Beijing night meal was tempting—the more so with someone who shared the memories of the Beijing Workers' Culture Palace. As he was going out, he thought about giving Chen a call, but he decided not to. It would be a loss of face to seek Chen's approval in the company of Hong.

Hong moved to a black BMW convertible parked in the driveway, from which he took out a cell phone, pressed a few buttons, and spoke in English.

"You don't have to drive me around, Hong. No point in going to fancy places. Let's just go to a quiet place where we can sit and talk."

"Well, come to my place then. Not a fancy restaurant, but we'll have our privacy, and my chef will do his best."

"That sounds like a plan."

Hong's restaurant turned out to be a small one located close to the old Chinatown area. In spite of the red paper lanterns and golden plastic lions at the entrance, the restaurant did not have something like a private room. Instead, Hong treated his "distinguished guest" in a low-ceilinged office above the landing of the narrow staircase. The chef was none other than Hong's brother-in-law, who served on the desk four cold dishes, cucumber in sesame sauce, sliced pig ears, smoked carp head, and pickled napo cabbage with plenty of red pepper. Hong also took out a bottle of Beijing Erguotou.

"My wife brought it over years ago. The old wine of our Beijing. I have saved it for an occasion like tonight. To your health, Master!"

"Thank you, Hong. It's just like the old days," Bao said, raising the cup.

"Just homely dishes, far from enough to show my respect to you. The restaurant is not prepared for your honorable presence tonight," Hong went on with a touch of bookishness, "which brightens the whole humble place."

"You don't have to say that. These dishes are great. In Beijing, I have not had pickled cabbage for a long time. Why? It's too cheap for restaurants to make profit."

"They should serve the working-class people."

"Chinese newspapers don't talk about the working-class people anymore. The best customers are big bucks. Banquets of fifty or sixty courses. We don't have to imitate those bourgeois apes."

"You are right. I have read about the so-called middle or bourgeois class in China. The world is turned upside down! Let's talk about something else. To the success of your visit."

"Thank you. To your success too."

"By the way, who is Chen Cao? Never heard of him. What does he write?"

"A modernist poet."

"Oh, one of the Misty poets no one can understand?"

"Well, his poems are said to be not that misty," Bao said, taking a sip at the wine, "but to be honest, I can hardly understand one single short poem out of his whole book."

"He looks quite young in his picture."

"In his mid-thirties."

"How can he serve as the head of the delegation?"

"Yang fell sick, so Chen replaced him at the last minute. A decision made by some people high up there. Chen has published only one poetry collection."

"He must have connections at the top."

"That I don't know," Bao said gingerly. "He's from Shanghai. I don't think too many are familiar with his work."

"As Chairman Mao said, literature and art should serve the broad masses of workers, peasants, and soldiers. Only a handful of intellectuals would enjoy those obscure poems," Hong went on, draining his wine in one gulp. "I came to know your work, 'The Working-Class Are Strong-Backboned,' I still remember, through a song in the radio. '*We the working-class are strong-backboned. / Following Chairman, we march forward, / With the country and the world in our heart, / We do not stop on the road of the revolution. / Holding the red flags high, we move on courageously. / We're the locomotive of the new era.*' So clear, and so powerful. I memorized it, indeed—"

"Let's talk no more about it," Bao said. "You know an old Chinese saying: An aged hero does not want to talk about his glorious past."

"Think about it. Chen must have studied your famous poems as a middle-school student."

"Well, because of the new cadre policy, people of his age with a higher education have been rocketing up."

"Does he work in the Writers' Association?"

"No, he's a cop in Shanghai, but he's a member of the association."

"Now that's something. A cop. He could have some secret mission for this trip."

"Not that I know of," Bao said vaguely, "but anything is possible with him."

The chef served on the table an earthen pot of fish soup. The soup was steaming hot, red with dried peppers and indescribable herbs. Bao helped himself to a spoonful, which was so spicy that he felt as if there were thousands of ants crawling on his tongue. He had to take a gulp of cold water.

"This is a world changed beyond our comprehension." Hong smacked his lips, launching into another topic. "Don't think life is easy for me here. In the restaurant business, so many Chinese are struggling for one small bowl of rice in cutthroat competition. People work like dogs, seven days a week. Visitors from China marvel at my house, at my restaurant, and at my cars, but they don't know everything here is on the loan. I am breaking under the burden."

"I know," Bao said, wondering at Hong's sudden change of subject. "Visitors from China" might have touched Hong for money, but Bao had never thought about doing that. "You earn every penny the hard way."

"Those good old days of the Workers' Culture Palace. We were the backbone of the socialist China. Our songs were loud and clear. If I can manage to go back next year, I'll revisit the palace."

"Don't mention it again. It has been turned into an entertainment center. Karaoke, belly dance, massage, whatnot! I fought hard against it, but to no avail."

Their talk was once again interrupted by the chef, who brought in a platter of steaming pork-and-cabbage dumplings with white garlic and red pepper sauce.

"The socialist China is going to the dogs," Hong said with a sigh. "I still remember an old Beijing couplet: *The most delicious is having dumplings—with garlic, and the most comfortable is lying on a bed—with a book.* At least we are enjoying dumplings with garlic tonight, and then I'll read your book on my bed."

The Erguotou was smooth, yet strong. Bao felt the liquid shooting all the way down like an arrow. It was not common for him to have such a devoted audience, and it seemed only to add to his frustration. Then the discussion came back around to the delegation again.

"Has Chen done anything in secret—a cop in a writer's clothing?" Hong resumed, twirling the cup in his fingers.

"No, I don't think he spies on the others. To be fair, he knows how to show off. He speaks a little English and tossed in a handful of new terms. I guess that's why he was chosen. A new image."

"A new image? I don't buy it. As you have said, we, the working-class people alone, are the revolutionary models for the socialist society."

"You are right. Chen does not even make a good model for the delegation. According to the regulation, no one should go out without having obtained the delegation approval. But Chen went out with his buddy this afternoon. What was he really up to? No one can tell."

"I can," Hong said. "Topless or bottomless shows. A lot of Chinese visitors are drawn to them like flies drawn to blood. A friend of mine has a tourist business here. An expert for delegation activities, he always arranges such a show at the top of the activity list. These visitors do not have to worry about the expense—the receipts will declare it as decent business expense without giving them away."

"Really?" Bao said. "That's a possibility."

"Let me do something for you. Tell me what you know about Chen, about his activities here. I may be able to find a queue or two of his. It's so unfair. We need to do something about it."

In the Qing dynasty, a queue—a braid of hair worn at the back of the head—could be grasped by an opponent in a fight. In the Cultural Revolution, Deng Xiaoping had once described himself as "an Urgue girl with so many queues." Later on, he got into trouble because of his queues being pulled by Mao.

"Don't go out of your way for me, Hong."

"Not just for you, Master Bao. People like Chen will be no good for our socialist literature. Believe me, my heart always remains a red, loyal Chinese heart."

"Well . . ." So far Bao did not really have anything to complain about regarding Chen. But Hong had his point. With people like Chen in power, the future of Chinese literature would be predictable. If evidence of Chen's inappropriate behavior could be obtained . . . "Oh, I remember one thing. He made phone calls—not in the hotel room, but at a public phone booth. A couple of times."

"That's very suspicious."

"Yes, the Americans are covering the hotel phone bill, I think. He doesn't have to save a few pennies for them. He may be making contact for those shows."

"That's important. I'll check into this," Hong said, not trying to hide his excitement as he raised the cup again. "To your greater success—with people like Chen out of the way."

To his dismay, Hong found the cup empty. So was the bottle. He looked out with an apologetic smile. Customers still came in at this late hour. There was only one waitress bustling around with platters overlapped on her bare arms. The chef must have been too busy to come back to them. The dishes on the desk turned cold. Bao contemplated, digging into a fish head.

Hong seemed to be growing sentimental as he got further in his cups, his face flushing like a coxswain's. "Did I have a choice when I left China? The state-run factory was losing money, unable to pay its employees. I could not make a living writing poetry. So I came out. Not easy for me to start all over. All these years, I've written only a couple of lines: *'Washing possible recollection / from a greasy mop, I'm ladling / my fantasies out of the wok.'*"

"That's really not bad, Hong."

"I remember the lines because I have come up with nothing else, because it's a true picture of my life, day in and day out," Hong said, draining the last drop before he produced an envelope. "Don't look down on me, Master. Here is five hundred dollars. I am not rich, but that's a token of my respect to you."

"No, I cannot accept it."

"It's nothing. As our old saying goes, *you can be poor at home, but not poor on the road.* So give me an opportunity to pay respect to my respected working-class master."

"I don't know what to say, Hong."

"And here is a prepaid cell phone. Call me when you want me to do anything—or when you want to tell me something about Chen."

"That's expensive. Chen alone has such a cell phone in the delegation."

"You are the Party secretary. Of course you should have one too. If we workers don't help each other, who will?" Hong said. "Oh, by the way, do you know the name of Chen's friend?"

"No, I don't, but he has a hi-tech company, I think, like those upstarts in China."

"It is so unfair."

"Yes, even in the hotel, Chen alone is given a suite."

"I have read that he shared the suite with somebody else—two men on the same bed. Some Americans must have made a joke about it."

"Oh, Dai, that capitalist poet. He's not a member of our delegation. So he touched Chen for the night. But it was my idea."

Hong really knew a lot about Chen. Was Chen reported so much here? Bao felt uncomfortable. It was time for him to stop drinking, he knew. He did not want to go back to being a drunkard. It was against a working-class poet's image, which he had cherished for years.

17

THE CONFERENCE WENT ON as before, though not without a few skirmishes between the writers from the two countries. In spite of his earlier, pacifist intentions, Chen could not help getting into heated discussions.

One particular topic that came up upset the Chinese. In the contemporary Chinese literature sessions, the Americans kept talking about a handful of dissident writers, making it seem as if they were the only worthy ones. Bonnie Grant, a senior sinologist with an exclusive translation contract with Gong Ku, a leading Misty poet who had killed his wife and then committed suicide, praised him at the expense of other Chinese poets.

"Those Misty may not be bad," Chen responded, "but that does not mean they are the only good poets. Their introduction to the Western world could have been done in a more objective way."

Bonnie hastened to defend her choice, concluding with a sarcastic note, "Gong wrote under a lot of political pressure. For instance, the last two lines in his poem 'After Rain,' '*A world of colorful poisonous mushrooms / after a sudden rain.*' Why poisonous? It's not about mushrooms, but about new ideas. New ideas that are poisonous to the official ideology. As a member of the Chinese Writers' Association, you were probably not aware of any political pressure."

That rattled Chen. It was so ironically untrue. Some Chinese orthodox critics had condemned his own work as being "modernist decadent" too. Chen had intended to argue that the Misty poets had courted Western attention through their political gestures. Instead, he checked the notes and counterargued by pointing out her erroneous rendition, particularly with regard to the image of poisonous mushrooms.

"Your interpretation about 'poisonous mushrooms,' I have to say, is far-fetched, though you are certainly entitled to your reading. After all, every reading is said to be a misreading in deconstruction. But I happened to be with Gong that day—at a conference in the Yellow Mountains. As always, Gong wore a self-made tall red hat, imagining himself to be a child lost in the woods. That was his adopted persona, and he played that role so completely that he could hardly distinguish between it and his real self. That day he talked about picking mushrooms. It was after a rainfall, the hillside was a riot of them. He declared that he would make mushroom soup that evening, and I told him that some mushrooms could be poisonous—"

"But we can judge only by the text, not by the real or imagined experience behind it," Bonnie interrupted. "Writing is impersonal, Mr. Chen, haven't you learned that?"

"You don't have to use Eliot's theory to show off to me," Chen retorted. "In the fifties and sixties, we judged Chinese writers only by political criteria. That was wrong. But today, there seems to be another trend, the opposite political criteria. I liked Gong's poetry because it was fresh from his deliberately childish perspective—fresh after the Cultural Revolution. How can such a child be so political?"

Chen's speech nettled Bonnie, but she was at a disadvantage. Chen was far more familiar with the background of the lines she had quoted. The Americans did not make an immediate response. Zhong applauded, and the other Chinese followed. Afterward, Martin Beck, an American publisher, asked Chen to write an article for his magazine.

As they left the conference hall at the end of the morning session, Chen got an unexpected call from Tian. It would be unrealistic, Chen had believed, to expect any breakthrough from a bookish businessman who had had no experience in investigation, but Tian surprised him with new information.

"Xing's mother will go to the Buddha Glory Temple this afternoon. She is a devoted believer. She goes every Thursday afternoon, her weekly routine, like other people going to church here. And Xing will be with her."

"That's something, Tian. What does she do there?"

"Burn tall incenses, I think, and draw bamboo sticks of divination."

"I see," Chen said. Buddhism remained popular among old Chinese. His mother, a passionate believer, kept burning tall incenses to a Buddhist shrine in her attic home, praying that Chen might settle down with a family of his own in the near future. Years earlier, she had taken him to an ivy-mantled temple in Hangzhou, he remembered, where she drew bamboo sticks of fortune shortly before the outbreak of the Cultural Revolution, but that marvelous oracle did not prove true. Her husband passed away with the Red Guards' slogans rattling the window over his deathbed. And her son later became a cop. "And what does Xing do there?"

"He keeps her company. He has made several donations on her behalf."

"How have you learned all this, Tian?"

"I called local Chinese newspaper editors. Now don't worry, Chen. I haven't approached any of them directly. Xing's going to make another statement exposing and condemning his persecution by the Beijing government. So they brought up the subject."

"Thanks, Tian. That may be really important to my work."

That afternoon there was a scheduled visit to Disneyland, Chen knew. During the lunch, he found himself finally embraced as "one of us," as approval poured in from the delegation members.

"You have reasons, and you have principles, Chen," Zhong said.

"You have said what we all would have said," Peng nodded vigorously.

"I am glad that Beijing has chosen you." Shasha patted his hand. "You are experienced in dealing with those Americans."

"Those Misty poets are groveling dogs," Bao said, "chewing a pathetic bone thrown out by the foreigners."

Chen complained of a headache, making little response.

Shasha said that Chen looked pale, touching his forehead. Zhong claimed that the delegation head had worked too hard. That was probably true. Bao, not unpleased to assume his Party secretary responsibility for one afternoon, urged Chen to take a break in the hotel. Chen agreed reluctantly, like a responsible delegation head.

The moment the delegation left the hotel, Chen changed into a T-shirt and jeans, picked up a mini recorder, and sneaked out. There seemed to be no suspicious-looking people outside. He hailed a taxi.

"To the Buddha Glory Temple," he told the driver.

It was a long drive. Sitting in the back of the car, he tried to think of a plan for the afternoon. It was out of the question for him to approach Xing. No point revealing his identity as a Chinese investigator. He wondered whether he would be able to talk to Xing at all. Perhaps, as in a proverb, he told himself, *there will be a road with the car reaching the mountains.*

The temple turned out to be a rather splendid one, made of red walls and yellow roofs and upturned black eaves decked with mythological figurines, like those seen in Suzhou and Hangzhou. There were not only Chinese monks and believers kowtowing and scripture-chanting in the courtyard, but also Americans, some in Asian costumes or with a large Chinese character *Fo*—Buddha—printed on their T-shirts. No one paid him any special attention.

He walked to the large main hall, in which towering clay images sat majestic in the front. There was a huge bronze incense burner before the gilded Buddha. He bought a bunch of incense, put it into the burner, and imitated others by clasping his palms piously. He then turned around, noticing an oblong mahogany table at one side of the hall. There were books and bamboo containers holding bamboo sticks on the table, behind which stood a middle-aged, deep-wrinkled, clean-shaven monk in a scarlet and yellow patchwork gown, apparently in charge of interpretation.

The monk reminded him of one he had seen in his mother's company, years earlier. He suddenly remembered a Beijing Opera seen also in her company, perhaps even earlier, and it gave him an idea.

He moved over to the monk.

"What's your honorable name, Master?"

"My monk name is Illusionless. What can I do for you, my most reverend benefactor?"

"My mundane surname is Chen. I am an ignorant scriber in the world of red dust," Chen said. "I need to ask you a favor, Master. For a book project, I need to have the experience of serving as a fortune-teller in a monastery. So can I stand in your place for a couple of hours?"

"No, that's impossible. A bamboo stick divination reader is no fortune-teller. It takes a lot of training to give accurate interpretation. We cannot misguide our benefactors."

"I have read several books in the field. So I think I'm qualified to try. You don't have to leave me alone here, my profound master. If I say anything wrong, you correct me. Please, let me be your student for one afternoon." He took out an envelope containing three hundred dollars. "Here is my tuition for the afternoon."

"Well, I cannot take it, but I'll put it into the donation box, my benefactor."

Chen wondered whether the money would eventually go into that particular box. As a student, it did not take him too long to acquire the basic technique from the master. There was a large *xuan* paper book spread out on a wooden stand next to the table. When a pilgrim picked out a bamboo strip bearing a certain number, Master Illusionless would open the book, turn to a page with the matching number, and interpret the poem on the page in a sort of fortune-telling way. The master could hardly justify the practice, however, in the light of Greater Vehicle, or of Lesser Vehicle, which Chen managed to quote for the occasion.

"Everything comes up in illusion," Master Illusionless said solemnly, "and interpretation evokes illusions too, all of which make up our world."

"So we are looking for the ox while we are riding on its very back," Chen said, paraphrasing a Zen paradox he still remembered.

"You have something of a Buddha root, Chen. Try your hand here." Master Illusionless nodded his approval and turned to a small monk. "Bring over a *kasaya* for him."

The little monk returned and handed the *kasaya* to Chen with a bow. Master Illusionless said, "You may don the gown. I hope you won't let me lose face."

"No face is face, and face is no face." Chen was getting warmed up with the practice of paradox. The *kasaya* was a patchwork gown worn by a Buddhist monk of enlightenment, which carried a halo of authenticity. And it really helped. *Buddha needs his costume,* and so did a monk or a would-be monk. Wrapped in the *kasaya,* Chen, too, felt like someone of sacred erudition. With so much unknowable in the world, a divine interpretation might be as good as any other help to a person. The chief inspector could use one himself.

But Chen did not have much time for metaphysical speculation. Pilgrims came over to the table, and he started practicing. It turned out to be not too difficult. In his college years, he had made a special study of Empson's book on ambiguities, learning how to give different interpretations to one poem. In the temple, he saw no difference except for making his own interpretation as convincing as possible. Master Illusionless kept nodding beside him.

Presently he saw an old woman in a satin dress shuffling into the hall. Following her was a short man wearing a gray wool suit, sporting a crew cut, beady eyes, and a nose like crushed garlic. He was followed in turn by a tall man in a dark martial costume. Chen recognized the short man as Xing, and the tall one, possibly the triad bodyguard he had seen in Rowland Heights.

After kowtowing to the Buddha image with the incense in her hand, the old woman moved toward the table, leaning on a dragon-headed bamboo stick. She appeared to know Master Illusionless well.

"Is there another master reading with you today, Master Illusionless?"

"Yes, madam. This is Master Chen, a man of profound learning. I told him what a great benefactor you have been to the temple, so he came all the way to help. He may relieve the unnecessary worries of your mind."

"That would be great. I am worried about so many things."

Chen noticed Xing standing at a respectful distance, showing no impatience or curiosity, and the tall man standing with arms crossed and a fierce expression on his face, barring others to move close to the table.

"Can we try something different today, Master?"

"What do you mean, madam?"

"Instead of the bamboo strip divination you've performed, can you practice the reading of a Chinese character for me?"

"Well . . ." The master sounded hesitant. It was another form of divination through analyzing the component parts of a Chinese character. A sort of glyphomancy, even less Buddhist in its possible origin. Master Illusionless might have not practiced it.

"Sure, I'll read it for you," Chen responded with an air of utter confidence. "When Chuangjie first created the system of Chinese written characters, every archetypal stroke of a character came out of the cosmos in miraculous correspondence to the omnipresent *qi,* and that in turn, in correspondence to the microcosmos of an individual human being. So that's called *tianren heyi*—heaven and human in one. For a virtuous woman like you, whatever character you may write in a moment of faith, there will be elements recognizable from the mysterious correspondence."

It was too fabulous an opportunity to miss, Chen thought excitedly.

He had never learned the technique properly, but he had seen its practice in *Fifteen Strings of Coppers,* the Beijing opera seen at his mother's side. In the opera, a disguised judge tricked a confession out of a criminal by performing the character divination. A Chinese character has multifarious meanings in itself, as well as in its combination with other characters. And a character can also be broken down into radicals or component parts. So the possible interpretations were unlimited. What's more, a written character reading would involve a lot of interactivity. He could try to interpret in a way that she was going to believe and respond to, and if at all possible, he would get her to reveal some information in the process.

"Really, Master Chen!" she said. "I have never heard of such a profound theory before."

No one had ever heard of it before. It was a hodgepodge of the moment, invented to impress. He had scrambled together all he had heard and read into this improvised mumbo jumbo, since few knew anything about the theory of the practice. Still, he told himself, he based most of it upon classics rather than superstitions.

"Everything comes out of your heart, madam." He lit a stick of incense, closed his eyes, and breathed deeply, as if in meditation. "Write a character on the paper, and I'll tell from it."

As the monk ground the ink stick on the ink stone, the old woman picked up a brush pen, took a deep breath, and wrote the character *xing* on the paper.

"Xing . . ." Chen studied the character in deep concentration, as if lost in communication with it. "Is it about yourself?"

"No, not about myself."

"I see. For this character, *xing* by itself means travel or movement. Some trip must be involved, pleasant or not pleasant."

"You are absolutely right, Master Chen," she said eagerly. "Can you tell me if it will be a smooth trip?"

The question was made in the future tense, and his performance proved to be smoother than expected. She swallowed it hook, line, and sinker. His comment about travel was but a guess, though it would not have been too off the mark, with Xing's flight out of China not too long ago. But apparently it hit home. The old woman's response showed that she was concerned about a future trip. Since Xing was standing right there, she must be worried about somebody else, about Ming, her son left behind. That meant An's assumption was correct—Ming was still in Shanghai.

"Let's move further. Judging from the left radical of the character, double person radical, it involves two. The right part of the character is unusual. For the top section, the horizontal stroke is *yi,* meaning one, and for the bottom section, it makes a partial character *ding,* meaning a boy. So you may be worried about your sons, or at least one of them."

"Master Chen, you are divine. Now you have to tell what will happen to my sons."

"Let me be frank with you, madam. *Ding* with a horizontal stroke weighing above does not look so good, for *ding* may be associated with death or other tragedies, as in *dingyou* . . ."

Now he was stretching it way out of proportion, especially the connotations of *ding*. But the practice was not without its ironic precedent, he realized. Ezra Pound, an imagist poet, had played the same trick by deconstructing a Chinese character into component ideograms—except that Pound had done so for poetry.

"You have to help me, Master Chen. I will be grateful to you all my life."

"What I can tell you, madam, is from the character alone. Fortune or misfortune is self-sought. Human proposes, heaven disposes." He paused significantly before going on. "But I may be able to read a little more out of it if you can tell me what you really want to know. For instance, the time and the direction of the movement you are concerned with."

"Yes, my little son has not come out yet," she said hesitantly. Xing might have warned her about talking to strangers. "I don't know when he can make it. Or whether he can make it."

"Now excuse me for saying so, but the horizontal stroke looks like a sword weighing over his head," Chen said, pushing it as much as he could. "I am afraid he may be in some sort of danger."

"Oh you almighty Buddha, protect him. I know he's in danger, Master Chen," she said in a tearful voice. "Xing, come over here. I have met with a great master today. You have to write a character too."

"You have done an interesting job!" Xing said to Chen, moving up, producing a hundred-dollar bill, and tossing it on the table. "For candles and incenses."

"Illusion rises from your heart, sir. What is interesting to one may not be so to another. There is no door for fortune or misfortune. The world depends on your thought to be good or bad," Chen said, switching on the mini recorder in his pants pocket as he dipped the brush pen lightly in the ink. Thanks to his voracious reading in his college years, those old phrases came to him naturally. "But if we can see something from a character you choose in correspondence to Way of the Heaven, it may help."

"Can you read such a lot from one single character, Master Chen?"

"I do not claim that a character can tell you everything, but it can reveal a possible direction in which things might be going. Go ahead and write the character with the question in your mind. If you think my interpretation is neither here nor there, you can take back the candle and incense money."

"You may have something," Xing said, looking him in the eyes. "You do not sound like a local Chinese?"

"Who is a local Chinese in Los Angeles? But for the request by Master Illusionless, I would not have come over today." Chen then added, improvising on a Tang poem, "*The Buddha Glory Temple / stands amidst the deep green, / the temple bell carrying / the evening far in a breeze. // A straw hat fastening / the setting sun, / I retreat alone into the blue, / distant mountains.*"

Xing might not necessarily be a man of high intelligence, but he was definitely not a gullible one. Chen had to risk being seen as a quack—or worse, as a disguised cop. It would then no longer be a matter of facing the possibly armed bodyguard standing in the background. The exposure of Chen's secret police activity here—under the cover of the government delegation—could lead to diplomatic troubles. But so far he had succeeded in tricking the old woman, and he might be able to do so with Xing. He could always try to give Xing's reading in metaphysically ambiguous sentences. A fortune-teller didn't have to be responsible for his superstitious claptrap. What really mattered was fishing something crucial out of Xing. For this to work, he had to include the old woman in the talk too.

"As madam has demonstrated, a character arising from the heart of her hearts will tell. The choice of the character is simply made by you, but more by the divine power of the universe, so it contains the *qi* from you, as well as from everything else, including this great temple, including your great mother."

"That's right. The temple makes a difference too," the old woman said, nodding vigorously. "Write your character. It's too good an opportunity for you to miss."

"Well, the same character then." Xing wrote it on the paper. *"Xing."*

"Now, is it about yourself?" Chen said, studying the character anew.

"Yes, it's about myself."

"The same character, but with all the different *qi* from your heart," Chen said. "Let me say one thing first. Your handwriting is bold and powerful. The shape of the character bears a certain resemblance to dragon. Very impressive, like in a proverb often used to describe Chinese calligraphy, *'like a dragon moving and like a tiger walking.'* It's in line with the meaning of the character *xing* too. So I would say there is something of a dragon in you."

Chen knew Xing had been born in the dragon year. A dragon was generally considered a lucky, masculine symbol in traditional Chinese culture, with the connotation of great power. It was a compliment Xing would snatch up, Chen supposed, and Xing nodded approvingly.

"You are no ordinary man," Chen pushed on. "In your case, the double person radical may not be just about two. Your movement concerns a lot more. It's difficult to see the direction for the moment. Also, the character *xing* for you means, among other things, a sort of business center, possibly with a great deal of money at your disposal, as in *yinghang.*"

Chen watched Xing's reaction. He had to convince Xing of his authenticity by throwing out information unavailable to an ordinary quack, but at the same time he should not go so far as to arouse Xing's suspicions. His interpretation had to remain open, ambiguous, yet specific enough for Xing to think in the way Chen had planned. Only through that could Xing let out some information, unwittingly, in his anxiousness to obtain "divine" advice.

"More and more interesting!" Xing said composedly. "What else can you read in the same character?"

"What time period do you want to know about?"

"The near future, I think."

"If it's about traveling, the people with water element in them may not be good for you."

"What do you mean by water element?"

"*Wuxing*—five elements, as you know. For instance, those with their names containing water radical in them, like Jiang."

"Names containing water radical, like Jiang," Xing repeated without making an immediate response.

"Yes. Don't you remember the man in charge of land development in Shanghai, Xing?" the old woman said, growing pale. "His name is Jiang—river, water radical, no mistake. Both you and Ming have met him a number of times. He's in trouble now, you have told me."

"Mom, you don't have to believe too much in those things," Xing said, frowning. "What else, Master Chen?"

Chen restudied the character for another two or three minutes, resting his forehead on his hand, with his eyes half closed, before he resumed, "There's something strange. It is a very complicated situation."

"A man asks about misfortune, not about fortune," Xing said. "Don't worry. Go on with your interpretation."

"I'll be frank. There's another character: *xing* plus the plant radical. Also pronounced *xing,* but it means floating without a root. Now it's unusual for somebody of your weight. In a flight of association, with the plant radical plus the character *zhong,* or weight, it brings in somebody surnamed Dong into the picture. He may not be helpful to your movement."

"Dong, anybody surnamed Dong, Xing?" the old woman asked anxiously. "Dong?"

"That's weird," Xing said, visibly shaken. "Dong Deping. He's in charge of the State Industry Reform Committee in Shanghai. He also helped with that land deal for our little brother."

"Is he also in trouble?" The old woman was growing hysterical, grasping at Xing's sleeve.

"I don't know, but he took a big red envelope from us," Xing said to her. "So did Jiang. The amount was large enough to lock them up for life. Their days may not be easy with the investigation going on."

"Then my little son is really in trouble. Master Chen knows everything," she said, sobbing. "If anything happened to him, how could I live?"

"Don't worry too much, Mother. I don't think they know anything about our little brother's whereabouts."

"Oh Buddha, protect my little son, and I'll gild all the images in the hall." She turned to Chen with the string of beads trembling in her hands. "Master Chen, you know everything. Please tell us what to do."

"Again, we are talking about movement," Chen said, facing Xing. "For a mighty man like you, your movement means something. As in the proverb, it's like the movement of a dragon and a tiger. However, I wonder if you are associated with someone named 'tiger.' Someone close or staying close to you. A neighbor or something like that. Now be careful. A dragon and a tiger may eventually not go together. Needless to say, the tiger in question could come from the top."

"Now what are you talking about?" Xing took a step back, glaring at Chen in spite of himself.

"I am talking about what I read from the character, sir. Still, things might have a turn in the near future. Both good and bad involved."

"Can you be more specific?" the old woman cut in again.

"You may believe you have someone powerful behind you." He paused significantly before looking at Xing. "Believe it or not, what will help you comes from your heart."

"How? I'm totally confused."

"The fact that both you and your mother have chosen the same character speaks for itself. The Way of Heaven is mysterious, but filial piety always comes first. *Who says that the splendor / of a grass blade can prove / enough to return / the generous warmth / of the ever-returning spring sunlight?*"

It was not really advice, but he'd better not push things too far. All this might sound compelling to the old woman, but after the initial shock, Xing would come back to himself. As in those stories he had read, a mediocre fortunc-teller usually ended up by giving some sort of "do good things" advice.

But Xing decided it was time to leave. Perhaps he was too shaken to stay on. It was just as well. Xing would probably not reveal any more.

"You have spent a long while with us. Here is your fee," Xing said, putting another hundred-dollar bill on the table. "Don't say to anybody what you have said to us today."

"Of course not."

As the Xings walked quickly out of the sight, Chen turned to Master Illusionless with a smile.

"I don't know who you are," Master Illusionless said, scratching his clean-shaven scalp, "but you are no ordinary man."

"I don't know who I am. As the scriptures say, identity is an illusion too," Chen said. "At this moment, I am your apprentice. Now I have to go, like a tumbleweed turning and turning around the distraction of humdrum vanities."

18

EARLY THE NEXT DAY, Chen had a Chinese newspaper delivered to his room.

Chen's speech the previous day got them an article in the local newspaper entitled, "A Chinese Writers' Delegation in Reform." It described the conference as a "successful one, which not only deepened the understanding of two great cultures, but also strengthened the friendship of two great countries."

And Chairman Wang of the Chinese Writers' Association said practically the same thing, in an international phone call, speaking highly of his work as the delegation head. Wang did not know anything, of course, about his work as an investigator.

In that morning's session about Chinese drama, Chen said little. It was not his field. Sitting in the conference room, he took the opportunity to mentally reexamine the developments in the Xing case.

Detective Yu had gotten hold of An's cell phone record and transcripts of her calls—with the help of Old Hunter. An had talked to several men, asking about the whereabouts of Ming, but none seemed to know. So those phone calls, while valuable in tracing those possibly connected to Ming, failed to produce a breakthrough at the moment. Yu said that he would go on exploring in that direction and that there were several names he hadn't known before. Yu didn't exactly go into detail, and there was no point in mentioning all the names on the phone. No matter how hard they tried to keep to their weather terminology, those names had to be real names.

For the same reason, Chen did not tell Yu about his fortune-telling experience in the temple. It took too much explanation on the phone, but he did ask Yu to check into a company under Little Tiger's name, which had its offices in Beijing.

The morning session went on. Chen rose to get himself a cup of coffee. Leaning back against the chair, he reviewed the temple scene. Xing's talk about Jiang and Dong was crucial. So Chen had some more cards to play, though he was not in a hurry to do so. As for Little Tiger's involvement, it was like a random harvest, and it could be a possible new direction for him.

During the intermission, he excused himself and went to the university library. He knew no one would miss him during the remaining session. Both Shasha and Bao were absent. Chen threw himself into research on the library computer. It was really convenient here.

At the Shanghai Police Bureau, there were only two computers, and many people waiting for access. What was worse, most of the search engines were blocked by the government. What information came up was that available in official newspapers, which helped little. Besides, Chen did not want to do the job in the bureau with all his colleagues moving around. Here on the campus, he worked on the computer without worrying about the possible consequences. The information gathered about Xing was far more detailed, and analytical too. He was beginning to obtain a comprehensive picture of the whole matter.

He worked on for hours, skipping his lunch.

Later in the afternoon, he had a discussion with the American host about the delegation's activities after they left L.A. Their visits to various cities had been scheduled long in advance. According to Professor Reed, however, Perry Turner, the American playwright in charge of their activities in Chicago, had been injured in a car accident. Reed suggested that instead of going to Chicago as scheduled, they might choose a different city.

"Let's go to that city. I have forgotten the name of it," Bao, who made a point of presenting himself at such meetings, suggested in high spirits. "Master Ma used to draw his inspiration from it."

"Master Ma—" Little Huang was totally lost.

"Which Master Ma?" Chen cut in.

"How many Master Mas are there in American literature?" Bao asked back. "Of course, the master who wrote about—em, the corruption of the American election system."

"The election system—" The interpreter remained puzzled as before.

"Oh, 'Running for Governor'," Chen said, turning to Huang. "I have read the story. Let me interpret for Mr. Bao."

In the sixties, translation of Western literature into Chinese had been subject to the political criterion. Mark Twain was one of the few chosen because of his "anticapitalist stance," and the hilarious "Running for Governor" was included in Chinese textbooks as a lampoon against hypocritical American democracy. Bao must have read the story, but the interpreter, born in the seventies, had used different textbooks.

Chen took over the interpretation. Bao's idea was not bad, and his constant unhappiness would be appeased by Chen's choosing to second the proposal and even to interpret it for him.

"According to Mr. Bao, the hometown of Mark Twain will be a point of interest to us," Chen continued. "He has been very popular in China."

"Yes, Hannibal. That's not far away from St. Louis. You might spend a day or two there too."

"St. Louis," Chen responded. "T. S. Eliot was born in the city."

"Great. So it's decided," Reed said. "You've translated 'The Waste Land.'"

Not merely for this reason did the city interest Chen, but he saw no point elaborating on it there. He was glad that Reed made the suggestion, which was readily accepted.

It was not lines of Eliot but those of Feng Yanshi, a tenth-century Chinese poet, that came to his mind as he left Professor Reed's room with Bao.

So many days, where have you been—
like a traveling cloud
that forgets to come back,
unaware of the spring drawing to an end?
Flowers and weeds spread untrammeled along the road
on the Fold Food Day.
Your scented coach is tethered to a tree—
by whose gate?

Recalling Chinese poetry was perhaps more becoming to the head of a Chinese writers' delegation, more culturally correct, he reflected with a wry smile, when his cell phone rang again. The number on the screen showed that it was Tian, who spoke with urgency in his voice.

"Can you come out? You are leaving, I know, but I've got something important for you. I'm in the café across the street."

"I'll be there," Chen said simply.

In the café, Tian was waiting at a table against the window, and he rose as Chen stepped in.

"Remember the white mansion I pointed out to you the other day?" Tian said before Chen was seated.

"It belongs to the politburo member's son, Little Tiger, right?"

"Exactly. As a matter of fact, it was Little Tiger that arranged for Xing's arrival in L.A. He made the down payment for Xing's house months earlier."

"How did you learn all that?"

"Mimi has been talking about buying a new house in a better area, like Rowland Heights. It prompted me to talk to Shan, a real estate agent. He happens to be the one who arranged the deal for Xing's house. Little Tiger put down two hundred thousand dollars. Shan gave me all the detailed information."

"That's incredible!" Chen said. "But why tell you his business secret?"

"Well, most of the houses there are in the range of one and half million dollars. So at six percent, the agent gets around ninety thousand dollars. He would do anything for that fee. Indeed, he'd sell his soul to get me to buy in Rowland Heights—except he's no Dr. Faust."

"You know a lot about real estate business, Tian."

"Well, my ex-wife's present husband is a real estate agent. A man with only a middle-school education, who doesn't even need that for his business. He simply drives his clients around, with a smile heaped on his face, but he earns more than a professor. Little wonder my ex-wife dumped me for him."

"You have proven to be far more successful," Chen said, understanding why Tian would have a grudge against real estate agents.

"So Xing and Little Tiger must have been in the same boat for a long time. Partners in their common smuggling business. Xing must have connected at the top in Beijing."

"Xing may have lots to do with Little Tiger, but not necessarily with his father."

"Come on, Chen. It's such a notorious case—a teenaged son would not have the guts to keep his involvement from his father."

Chen nodded, as the politburo link also accounted for Xing's flight at the last minute. The information came from the very top because people at the top had their own interests at stake. Chief Inspector Chen was not simply dealing with a corrupt official with connections, but with the very *connections* that made the country what it was.

"And there was something else," Tian went on, "something I can't understand."

"What?"

"Xing has talked to Shan about selling his house. Shan asked him why. Xing said that he can hardly pay his legal fees."

"That's impossible! With so much stolen money in his hands, that doesn't make sense."

Xing's plan to sell the house was a surprise, though of course, he would not have told the true reasons to a real estate agent. So could there be other possibilities?

The information Chen had gathered here led him to believe it was a huge gamble that Xing would be granted political asylum in the United States. He might be able to afford the exorbitant attorney fees, but the evidence he had produced so far was hardly convincing. Several experts considered the odds of his being granted asylum extremely slim. The American government was also under pressure from the Chinese. Once deported, Xing knew his fate would be sealed. So what did that mean?

"I've been busy with Shan, looking for houses," Tian went on. "I almost forgot to choose a present for you. So Mimi has wrapped a case of fish oil for you. And I have just dug out a scroll I bought last year. Allegedly the work of Zhu Sishan, a calligrapher at the beginning of the twentieth century," Tian said, taking the scroll out of the box. "Possibly a fake, but at least not one of those mass-produced imitations you buy in China."

The calligraphy was angular and spirited, as if subtly animated with the *qi* of the calligrapher. What impressed Chen was the poem copied on the scroll. The poem was entitled "Fisherman," written by the eighth-century Tang dynasty poet Liu Zongyuan.

His sampan moored overnight
by the western hills,
the old fisherman fetches
the clear water at dawn, and cooks
with the southern bamboo.

Disappearance of the smoke
against the rising sun
reveals no one in sight—
the mountains and water green
at the sound of the oar, the sampan
is seen streaming down
to the horizon,
only the white clouds left
to chase each other, inadvertently,
over the rocks.

A reminder of the "River Snow" his father had copied. By the same Liu Zongyuan. Whether the scroll was genuine or not, what mattered for Chen was the spirit of the poem, lonely yet uncompromising. It would make an excellent present for his mother. Possibly a message to her as well. Her son might not have followed her husband's academic path, but there was still something in common between the two.

"I don't know how to thank you," Chen said. "Remember the lines we read together in Beijing? '*When you have a good friend in the world, / no matter far away, he's like your next door neighbor.*'"

"Of course I remember. We read it together while cooking a small pot of white cabbage over an alcohol stove," Tian said, taking a look out of the window. "Oh, isn't that the antique worker-poet in your delegation?"

Sure enough, it was Bao standing outside the hotel, looking in the direction of the café. Then came another surprise. Bao produced a cell phone out of his pants pocket and started dialing. As far as Chen knew, Bao had a hard time making ends meet in Beijing. Now, all of a sudden, Bao had a cell phone here. An unnecessary luxury, which alone would have cost more than his delegation allowance. The hotel phone was covered by the Americans, at least in Los Angeles.

If the phone call was about Chen, as Chen suspected, what could it possibly mean?

After Tian left, Chen continued to think about Bao and his cell phone. Things had been strained between Chen and Bao. Not simply a matter of men of letters belittling each other. In modern Chinese literature, Bao had left his mark as a representative of a particular period, and the foreign visit before his retirement should have been a crowning experience for him. But Bao must have found it hard to swallow a younger man's having been appointed as the delegation head. Bao bore him a grudge, he understood, but there was something more than that.

Instead of going back to the hotel, Chen used his phone card at a pay phone in the café.

"I've been expecting your call, Chief," Yu said.

"How is the weather in Shanghai?"

"Cloudy, but there seem to be some dark clouds approaching."

"What does that mean?"

"It's difficult to describe the weather on the phone, you know, so unpredictable."

Indeed, it was too difficult to talk the way they had agreed on. The weather terms had worked before, but not this time. There were so many new, unforeseeable factors involved. He wanted to know what Detective Yu had learned.

"Forget about the weather," Chen said. "Let's talk."

It was a risk they had to take. Yu's home line might not be tapped. Chen had not mentioned Yu's assistance to anyone except Zhao.

"Kuang has found out about your phone call to An. And he talked to Party Secretary Li about a romantic night you had with her in a fancy restaurant. Little Zhou, who was driving Li that afternoon, overheard the talk. And he told me."

"I interviewed An for Xing's case. In order not to arouse any suspicion, I talked in a flirtatious way."

"You don't have to explain to me. I know that, but others don't."

"I'm not worried about that. Another romantic anecdote probably won't be the end of the world."

"But there may be someone behind Kuang. Otherwise he wouldn't have the guts to mention it to Li."

"Any new discoveries in An's cell phone record?"

"Nothing yet."

"Anything else?"

"Oh, Comrade Zhao is still in Shanghai. I don't know what he's doing here."

Chen then told Yu what he had just learned about Little Tiger in relation to Xing, in the vaguest terms he could think of.

"Now we are really touching a tiger's backside," Yu concluded.

19

IN SPITE OF HER efforts against it, Peiqin found herself getting more and more involved in the investigation.

She reflected with a self-deprecating smile as she stepped into the hot-water shop. It was located at the entrance of the lane Chen's mother lived on. Putting on a black, soot-spotted apron, she stood beside the huge coal stovc as a "temporary helper." There was a small cracked mirror on the somber wall. Studying a slightly soot-smudged reflection, she thought she did not look too bad in her late thirties.

It was hot. One third of the shop consisted of the stove with a gigantic pot and long, serpentine pipes. It was an antique coal-devouring monster, possibly one of the last few remaining in the city. The only thing that might have kept the stove from being put into a city museum was a thermometer, supposedly showing the temperature of the boiling water. She had to shovel coal into the stove regularly.

She wiped her forehead with a smeared towel, taking another look around the room. She noticed a wood screen close to the back door. Behind the screen, there were several soft-cushioned chairs and a table covered with a plastic foam top. The space was like a private room. She wondered who would need the luxury here.

Ironically, it took Peiqin some effort to obtain a temporary position—without pay—at this shabby water shop.

It was all because of Old Hunter's worries. Since Chen's departure with the delegation, Old Hunter had patrolled the lane several times, and he thought he had sniffed something. Being an old-fashioned cop, however, he did not think it right for him to patrol an area too much without an official assignment. Besides, it would not be that safe for him to circle the lane time and again. He could be recognized. So Yu wanted to patrol instead. It seemed to Peiqin that both the father and son were overreacting. As diabolical as Xing and all the red rats might be, what could they gain by hurting an old woman? If anything happened to her, Chen would surely fight back with a vengeance.

Still, Peiqin had volunteered for a day's reconnaissance in the neighborhood. She happened to be in a position to help. She had talked so much about the legendary chief inspector to Old Geng, the owner of the private restaurant, that the latter mentioned that he was related to Chang Jiadong, the owner of a hot-water shop at that lane. So Peiqin offered to work there for one day. Both Geng and Chang proved to be very understanding. They made the arrangement for her without asking her any questions.

For the first half hour, there was no business in the water shop. No one seemed surprised at the sight of her working there, either. With so many people laid off in the city, a middle-aged woman like Peiqin perhaps would consider herself lucky to get any kind of job.

She decided to read for a while. Nowadays she did not have much time for herself. Even in her state-run restaurant office, things had begun to change. For the sake of profit, there were three shifts instead of one, and she still had to do all the accounting by herself. She took out the dog-eared book, *The Dream of the Red Chamber*. It was a classic novel she had read numerous times.

She occasionally wondered why the saga of a Qing aristocratic family so appealed to her. In the novel, what happened to those beautiful, talented yet ill-fated girls was preordained, prerecorded in a mysterious register in a heavenly palace. It was fiction, she knew. She did not believe in the supernatural yin/yang arrangement that prevailed in spite of tragic human effort. But she had come to see her life as a sort of a parallel. For one thing, she had never read any mysteries in her school years during the Cultural Revolution, when she was panic-stricken at the sight of policemen like those who had taken her father away. Afterward, however, she married a police officer, and now she was becoming something like the officer's private assistant and acting like a character in those mysteries.

But she did not think she was tragic like those characters in *The Dream of the Red Chamber*—"her hope as high as the sky, and her fate as thin as the paper." She considered herself as fairly lucky; Yu working with a secure job at the bureau, and Qinqin studying hard for college. Only all of that could be jeopardized because of those "red rats"—she liked the term coined by Old Hunter. In traditional Chinese culture, *red* had a lot of connotations. Red was about sensual vanities of the human world, like the red chamber in the novel or the Red Tower in the Xing case. And these red rats were surely sexually depraved. She thought of those pictures of An and her man.

Failing to concentrate on the book anymore, she thought she had an excuse for putting it down. A hot-water woman holding a classic novel would attract attention. Placing the book back into her bag, she decided to look again around the lane. It might once have been a decent neighborhood, but with so many new tall buildings rising around like bamboo shoots after a spring rain, the area had turned into a shabby "forgotten corner."

Nonetheless, it was a convenient corner. Beside the water shop was a small husband-and-wife grocery store. On the other side of the lane entrance was a public phone booth. Then she noticed something. Opposite the lane entrance across the street, there was a middle-aged peddler perching on a stool, and his goods on the white-cloth-covered ground caught her attention. Snuff bottles. She had read about snuff bottles as far back as in *The Dream of the Red Chamber*. People today still liked them as inexpensive imitation antiques with the painting on the inside of the glass bottle. It took a lot of training to paint with a miniature brush inserted through the tiny opening. But there were no customers there, like at the water shop.

And unlike a water shop, a snuff-bottle peddler usually had to station himself near a tourist attraction, like the Bund. How could the poor residents here afford to be interested in those useless bottles? Still, the peddler could be someone living in the neighborhood.

Poking at the fire, she tried to refocus her thoughts on the investigation. So far the only progress made was transcripts of An's cell phone calls. Old Hunter had moved heaven and earth in his efforts to get them. But no matter how the father and the son cudgeled their collective brains out, the record failed to lead to anything suggestive of a possible breakthrough.

Things seemed to be getting really tough for Chen too. According to Yu, people in the bureau had been looking into the relationship between Chen and An, thereby turning him into a possible suspect. They probably would not be able to bring Chen down so easily, but a subtle suggestion of a scandal could be obnoxious enough.

Indeed, Peiqin found it hard to figure out this chief inspector. A successful survivor in the jungle of politics, he could nonetheless be stubborn, unbelievably bookish, sticking to a cop's responsibility like his Confucianist father. And as long as Chen persisted in scouting in the woods, Yu had to stay there too.

A little girl came over with two bamboo-slice-covered thermos bottles, making one careful step after another.

"Five pennies in a bottle," she said to Peiqin. The coins fell from her hand and sparkled in a tin can.

In her childhood, Peiqin had run the same errand for her family, with the bottles in her hands that were covered with frostbite like a map . . .

She then looked up to see an old couple shuffling over from a side lane. They had no kettle or thermos bottle in their hands. The man with a maze of white hair wore a rumpled black jacket, as thin as a bamboo stick, his face wrinkled, weatherbeaten as seen in a postcard of a Shanbei farmer, and the woman was much shorter, rounded like a wine barrel, in something like much-patched-up pajamas. They stepped into the shop, nodding at Peiqin, as if she had been working there all those years. Perhaps because of their cramped living conditions in the lane, the shop had become sort of a daily resort to them. They moved straight to one of the tables and seated themselves side by side on a bench. It would be understandable for customers to come here in the winter, but in the summer, Peiqin failed to understand.

They must have reached some agreement with the owner of the water shop for them to hang out there. They carried their own tea leaves, took cups from a small cabinet in the shop, filled their cups with hot water without paying a single penny. Then the old woman produced a plastic-wrapped homemade cake and put it on the table.

"Taro, you eat first."

"You eat first, Chrysanthemum."

Taro and Chrysanthemum sounded like their intimate nicknames, Peiqin observed. Chrysanthemum broke the cake into two, gave one half to Taro, and dipped hers into the hot tea. She started chewing it with great gusto. Eating, they chatted to each other without paying any attention to Peiqin. She had no objection to their noisy presence.

She wondered whether they had spent all their lives in this shabby lane. Whatever their life story, their little indulgence toward the end of it was no more than cups of tea and hard, cold, homemade cake in this ramshackle place. But Peiqin looked on with admiration rather than anything else. Dramatically as the world might have changed, they seemed to have a world of their own, in which they had each other.

"Holding your hand, I'll grow old with you." That was one of her favorite lines in the *Book of Song,* years earlier, when her father still had had the energy to teach her those classic poems. In the nineties, in one of the popular songs, she had heard a variation, *"It's the most romantic thing to grow old by your side,"* with the image of an old couple shuffling into the distance on a karaoke screen, and wealth and fame drifting away like the clouds in the skies.

It might have little to do with being romantic, but it was infinitely touching. Peiqin was sure the old couple were hardly aware of her presence in the store, so she took out the transcript of An's cell phone calls. She wanted to reread it. Some of the phone conversations were perhaps valuable only in the names they provided as possible leads, yet because of their high status Yu was in no position to question either the people An had spoken with or the people mentioned. Nor were the conversations really incriminating. Everyone involved could say that they knew Ming but had no clue about Ming's relation to Xing.

But one short phone conversation intrigued Peiqin. It was between An and Bi Keqin, a senior city government official in charge of the textile industry export and import. As with other phone calls, An approached Bi directly about the whereabouts of Ming, but Bi's answer was a strange one.

> "Come on, An. How can I know? It's like in that Tang dynasty poem. 'You ask where the tavern is, / and the cowboy points toward apricot blossom village.' "
>
> "Oh, thank you so much, Bi."
>
> [An turns off the phone.]

It was strange. In Peiqin's circle, Chen was the only one who quoted poetry in his daily conversation. But she doubted if Chen would have quoted in a short phone conversation. And then An thanked Bi—for what?

Peiqin knew the poem. A Tang dynasty quatrain. The first two lines read: *"With the continuous rain on the day of Qingming, / people feel brokenhearted, on the road."* What Bi quoted were the next two lines. In the original, whether "apricot blossom village" was the name of a tavern or the village in which the tavern was located, she failed to recollect.

Then she remembered something. In one of his investigations, Chen had quoted a poem to say what was impossible for him to say under the circumstances. If Chen had done that, so could Bi. So "apricot blossom village" might be a hint.

There was a restaurant called Apricot Blossom Pavilion on Fuzhou Road, but no Apricot Blossom Village. Nor a hotel by that name. With so many new restaurants or hotels in the city, however, she didn't think she knew every one of them. Especially the expensive ones, since neither she nor Yu paid much attention to them. Someone else might, she knew. She took a look out of the shop. No one was coming in its direction. She ran across to the phone booth and dialed Overseas Chinese Lu, a card-carrying gourmet owner of Moscow Suburb, and a buddy of Chief Inspector Chen.

"Apricot Blossom Village? Oh yes, it's an exclusive club. Not a karaoke club, but a real one," Overseas Chinese Lu said. "Super class with the most wealthy members. The chef there used to work in the Forbidden City for Chairman Mao. Mao's Pork is his famous special. The nutrition goes directly to the brains. Mao had to eat a large bowl of it before finding his inspiration for a national movement. You have to taste it to believe it. The pork simply melts on your tongue, and then in your brains. Also the South Central Sea Carp. The fried fish is served on the table hot with its eyes still rolling, its tail still twitching—"

"Have you been there?" She had to cut him short, knowing Overseas Chinese Lu would hardly stop once on the topic of food.

"Only one time. Obscenely expensive. Most of the people going there are club members, those new upstarts showing off or those high officials squandering money out of the government's pockets."

"Thanks, I think that's all I need to know," she said.

At least it was a possibility. For people like Ming or Xing, nothing could have been too expensive.

When she ran back to the shop, the old couple inside started talking to her.

"How much does Chang pay you?" Chrysanthemum said.

"Not much," Peiqin said. "Better than nothing. A beggar cannot complain."

"Don't be too disappointed. No more than fifty yuan business a day here, I would say," Taro said. "With more and more families having propane gas tanks at home, people do not come to the water shop like before."

"You are right," Peiqin said. So far she had made only ten cents. "Old Chang could turn it into a teahouse."

"Not in our location. Poor people can't afford it, and rich people won't come," Taro said. "Chang hangs on to it because people say a subway station may be built here. In that event, a store will be worth more in terms of government compensation."

"Chang makes most of his money with the mahjong table," Chrysanthemum said. "He charges a different price for a cup of tea."

"I see," Peiqin said, nodding. Mahjong had been a popular game for years. It was not exactly gambling, but it was no fun without small money put on the table. Since 1949, mahjong had been banned. Of late, however, the city government had legalized the game—on the condition that no money was visible on the table. So that's why the screen was in the shabby water shop.

In the midst of her off-and-on talk with the old couple, Peiqin kept a lookout at the lane.

Around eleven, she saw Chen's mother walking out of her building. The old woman was not alone, but with a tall, slender girl supporting her. Could she be Chen's new girlfriend? There was perhaps nothing to wonder at, Peiqin thought, as far as Chen was concerned. Still, this girl looked a bit too young for him. Only in her early twenties, and too fashionable. She wore a short, sleeveless top with her belly button revealed, swaying her hips seductively in her transparent high-heeled shoes.

"What a dutiful daughter or daughter-in-law!" Peiqin said, turning toward the old couple.

"She is neither," Taro said. "I don't know who she is. Possibly a temporary maid hired by the old woman's son. Chen is somebody."

"No, not a provincial maid," Chrysanthemum said. "Not the way she is dressed. Way too flashy."

"The old woman seems to be very fond of her," Peiqin said. "Her son's girlfriend?"

"No, I don't think so." Chrysanthemum shook her head again. "I've never seen her in his company. Now that he's visiting abroad, she comes with small and large bags in her hands. Perhaps she's really after him. The old woman calls her White Cloud, or something like that."

"White Cloud." Peiqin had heard the name before. A temporary "little secretary" for Chen during a translation project not too long ago. Yu had joked about Chen's peach blossom luck, but as far as she knew, nothing had developed out of it. And Peiqin found it hard to imagine the chief inspector growing old with the fashionable swell girl, sitting in her company in a place like the water shop. "Wow, he has hired a young girl to take care of his mother."

"He's a big bug, capable of doing that." Taro took a long drink from his tea. "When he was still a nose-running kid, I already predicted a great future for him. He comes back here regularly to visit his mother."

"Then why hasn't he let his mother move in with him?"

"His mother won't do so," Chrysanthemum said. "Still a bachelor, he has numerous girlfriends knocking at his door. The old woman doesn't want to cause him any inconvenience."

"Well," Peiqin said. People understandably exaggerated the lifestyle of a rising Party cadre in their imagination. Chen did not have "numerous girlfriends," she knew. She chose not to say anything about it. After all, it was not inconceivable for a man in Chen's position.

"His friends know what a filial son he is. So they come here too. A large number of them."

"Really!" she said. "How do you know?"

"All those luxury cars. When they park near the lane entrance, and visitors walk into this building with bags and boxes in their hands, you can be pretty sure," Taro said, starting to cough with a hand pressed to his mouth. "In our lane, there's only one man with all those enviable connections."

"For a Party official, everything is possible in this age of connections and corruptions," Chrysanthemum said, turning back to him and patting him lightly on the back. "Everything okay?"

Peiqin did not have to comment. The old couple seemed to be withdrawing back into their own world, murmuring, in the midst of his coughing and her comforting, only to each other.

Then Peiqin looked up to see the snuff-bottle peddler rising and moving after the two women. Her earlier suspicions came rushing back. No wonder he had been sitting there so contentedly—with no business at all. He was no peddler, but someone stationed there to watch for Chen's mother. For surveillance? Peiqin did not think so. What could the old woman do? So it must be something against Chen. In retaliation for Chen's move, or in an effort to stop Chen's possible further moves. Peiqin was inclined to the second scenario. Kidnapping the old woman to hold her as a hostage was a plausible course of action. And the peddler might strike out at any time.

Peiqin had to make a decision fast. She immediately thought of Ling—

someone to contact in an emergency, as Chen had told Yu. But could that work? *The water too far, and the firs too close.* Things being so complicated in Beijing, hiding the old woman out of sight would perhaps be all Ling could do.

Peiqin could do that too, and more quickly.

She thought of Old Geng's apartment, which he had just purchased without having moved in yet. With all the help she had given in the restaurant, she was sure that he would let the old woman stay there for a short while. White Cloud and she could help take care of the old woman.

In one of those stories she had heard from Yu, he had once exited through an unknown back door to shake off a follower during a dangerous investigation. She failed to recall the exact details. Or she might have read the story in *The Song of Youth.* She was momentarily confused, but that was not important. She scribbled a few lines on a piece of paper.

"I need to make another phone call," she said to the old couple in the shop. "Can you look after the shop for me—just two or three minutes?"

"Those provincial workers may come here during lunch time," Taro said. "They cannot afford to buy lunch at those eateries. So they buy one penny's worth of hot water for their cold rice."

"Come back soon," Chrysanthemum said, looking up at the clock on the wall. "We are going back home for lunch too."

Peiqin dialed Yu at the public phone booth. "Come in a taxi, and wait in the taxi at the back exit of the lane. His mother's lane—you know." Earlier, Peiqin had walked around the lane several times. She was able to reach the back lane exit through a side lane, a route invisible to anyone stationed opposite the front lane entrance.

"Why, Peiqin?"

"I'll explain to you later."

"Fine, I'll be there in about fifteen minutes."

"Wait in the taxi for me."

By the time Peiqin made it back to the shop, the old couple were standing impatiently by the door.

"We'll take a nap after lunch," Chrysanthemum said. "We'll be back around two."

"Thank you. And see you."

Their departure was timely. After adding more coal into the stove, Peiqin stepped out of the shop again. Sure enough, she caught a glimpse of the two women coming back toward the lane and, not too far behind them, the snuff-bottle peddler. Peiqin plucked a hairpin from her hair and stepped back.

The two women were passing by the hot-water store again. Chen's mother nodded slightly at Peiqin without showing any sign of recognizing her.

"Oh, young girl, you have just dropped something," Peiqin exclaimed, holding out her hand.

"What?"

"A hairpin!" She made a gesture to White Cloud.

The girl was all surprise, taking the hairpin from her hand.

"That's—"

"You're White Cloud, aren't you?" Peiqin whispered in a hurry. "I'm Peiqin, Chief Inspector Chen's friend. My husband Detective Yu Guangming is his assistant. His mother knows me too. Come back with her to the hot-water shop."

"Oh, yes, that's the hairpin my sister gave me," White Cloud raised her voice. "Thank you so much."

White Cloud was a clever girl. Instead of turning into the lane, she kept on walking with the old woman on her arm, moving past the lane entrance, strolling for another round, whispering in the old woman's ear.

The snuff-bottle peddler also passed by the shop, his head hung low, without casting a glance at Peiqin.

Peiqin then ran through the back door to the back exit of the lane. She caught a glimpse of a red taxi parked there. She hurried back, feeling guilty. She had done a lousy job for the shop. After fifteen minutes or so, she saw the two women come back. This time, they stepped into the water shop.

"A pot of good green tea," White Cloud said.

"The best tea, and the best seat," Peiqin said, showing them to the table behind the screen, before she leaned down to the old woman. "You still remember me, Auntie? I'm Peiqin, Detective Yu's wife."

"Oh, yes, in Xinya Restaurant, I remember. My son keeps saying what a wonderful wife Detective Yu has."

"It's an emergency. We have to move you to somewhere else. Temporarily. For the sake of your safety."

"What—" The old woman quickly regained her composure. "Can I take something with me?"

"Don't worry about that. We may not have the time."

"Do whatever you think necessary, Peiqin. I sensed something, I think, before Chen left with the delegation."

"Give this note to Yu," Peiqin said to White Cloud. "He's waiting for you at the back exit of the lane. He knows where to take you. You have to be with Auntie all day today. Don't tell anybody. I'll come over in the evening."

"It's for Chief Inspector Chen, I understand. I'll do my best."

Peiqin ran to the back door. There was no one out there. She came back to the table and showed them to the door.

It was not the end, she knew, but the beginning of her adventure.

The snuff-bottle peddler was perched on the stool in the same old position, across the street, whistling a tune.

20

THE DAYS AFTER THEIR conference in L.A. were like repetitions with little variation, at least as far as the delegation was concerned.

The cities they visited were different, but what they did there was similar. Meeting after meeting, handshaking with a poet, business-card exchanging with a novelist, greeting a critic, discussing with readers. Chen had to make his much-rehearsed speeches again and again. The other members were also becoming more experienced in "literature exchange." The initial culture shock turned into culture critique, and each of them spoke from his or her own perspective. Bao alone seemed to remain true to what he called the real color of a Chinese working-class poet, condemning whatever he saw in the United States as bourgeoisie decadent or as capitalistic rotten.

Their travel between cities was partially by air, partially by bus. The American host had arranged a special bus for the trips between nearby cities. It was a practical arrangement for the delegation. They enjoyed the view of large cities as well as small towns. Occasionally, the bus also stopped by rustic inns and roadside pubs.

While moving from one city to another, Chen also managed to move on with his investigation. There had been some progress in Shanghai, but not all of it positive. His mother had been moved to a safer place. Again, Yu didn't go into details on the phone but Chen knew his assistant would not have done so without a reason. Perhaps it was even the very reason that had worried Chen. Jiang could have been behind it. The chief inspector was coming back with those pictures in hand, so it was not unimaginable that Jiang had tried to get something in his own hand, something that could hold Chen in check. Or, in a worse scenario, it was orchestrated by somebody higher than both Jiang or Dong.

Yu's work on An's cell phone record seemed to have bogged down. According to Yu, those that An had contacted were all in powerful positions. It was out of the question for Yu to confront them; furthermore, the phone conversations were hardly incriminating.

Nor was there anything new from Tian, though what he had provided was already more than Chen had expected.

All along the way, Chen had been continuing his Internet searches and research, working on one computer after another in different cities. There were things he still did not grasp, but he had confirmed his impression that it wouldn't be easy for Xing to get political asylum and that few really believed his stories of political persecution. Still, it could drag on for a quite long time before any ultimate decision was made in court. In the meantime, Xing made one statement after another, mixing false information with facts, to the great annoyance of the Beijing government.

Between his responsibility as a delegation head in public, and as a cop incognito, the days passed quickly. Somehow he could not shake the ominous feeling that things were moving, like water in the dark.

On the fifth or sixth day, Chen was sitting uncomfortably at the back of the bus. The imitation leather covering of the seat felt rather sticky against his back and the air was stuffy. The effect of the long, continuous journey was beginning to tell.

Dozing with his head against the window, he thought of two famous lines by Yue Fei, a patriotic general in the Song dynasty. *"Riding through eight thousand miles under the moon and the clouds, / fight for thirty years with achievement in sand and dust."* Shortly after the composition of that poem,

General Yue was ordered to die, in spite of his legendary loyalty to the emperor. Chen felt disturbed at the thought of it. Looking out, the bus was moving near the bridge spanning Illinois and Missouri.

Little Huang, the interpreter, was the first to point out, "Look. The Arch of St. Louis!"

For the first minute or two, Chen did not respond like a tourist upon arrival in a new city. The novelty of their trip had worn off. Then he realized that it was not just another city, like all other cities, scheduled on the delegation itinerary.

"Yes, Master Ma's old home," Bao said with a broad grin.

"Not in St. Louis, but in Hannibal," Zhong said.

"It's close."

Once the bus crossed the bridge, the high buildings of the city made for an impressive skyline, but there were also occasionally poor, dilapidated buildings along the way, forming a sharp contrast in the downtown area of St. Louis.

It did not take them long to arrive and disembark at the Regency, a high-end hotel attached to an ex–railway station, which was remodeled into a large shopping mall. It was a clever design, Chen thought, for the hotel residents could look out at what had been a railway platform, musing about the bygone days.

A familiar smell dragged Chen back to the present. Possibly that of green onion sizzling in a wok. Sure enough, he discovered a food court at the other side of the mall. A variety of restaurants and snack bars, including a Chinese eatery under a glittering neon sign of a gigantic wok. It was an added convenience for the writers. They did not have to ask the local escort to take them out to Chinese restaurants.

The local escort showed up. He was a tall young American who spoke no Chinese and kept raving about the location of the hotel. "Look, the Arch is within walking distance, the landmark of this city, where the frontiersmen started their journey westward long ago."

"Yes, we can walk there in the evening," Little Huang added.

The escort helped at the front desk. Everyone had his or her room key in no time and all their luggage was piled up in a cart to be taken to their respective rooms. As usual, they exchanged room numbers. Chen had a suite with a Jacuzzi bath on the third floor. A privilege for the delegation head, which everybody took for granted now.

Chen was tired, perhaps more so at the sight of the comfortable bed and of the glistening white bathtub. But he had no time for a break. He had to make phone calls—in the mall underneath the hotel. First to Detective Yu. It was still early in the morning in Shanghai, so Chen had a good chance of catching him at home.

Stepping out of the room, Chen saw Huang walking over in his direction.

"The hotel sucks," Huang muttered.

"Why?"

"The hot water does not come."

"Really? Try mine."

The hot water worked all right in Chen's room. Possibly a problem only with Huang's.

"You may use my tub," Chen said.

"What about yourself?"

"There's a bookstore down in the mall. I may find some interesting mysteries." That was true. A publishing house in Guiling had been pushing him for new translations. In spite of his workload, he had no objection to translation. It kept him reading and writing, even though mechanically, with his imagination crumpled like a dirty mop.

The phone in Chen's room rang. It was Shasha. She, too, was interested in the ultramodern bathtub. "You have a Jacuzzi in your room, I've heard."

"Try it if you like. Little Huang is in my room right now. Come in forty-five minutes," Chen said before turning to Huang. "Take your time."

"Thank you, boss. It'll take me no more than fifteen minutes."

"Don't worry. Leave the door closed after you finish." He spoke into the phone again. "I'll leave my key at the front desk, Shasha. I'm going to take a walk—in the home city of T. S. Eliot."

"Oh yes, Eliot made you."

It was a well-meant joke, which also sounded like an echo from a poem. Perhaps by Eliot. He was not sure, however, whether it took an American poet to make or unmake a Chinese cop.

Chen went down to the mall. It was late afternoon, and shoppers were pouring in. He saw a Chinese family walking in front, a young couple with a little boy. The woman wore silk embroidered satin slippers, shorts, and a silk vest like a *dudou,* and the man was in a white T-shirt with a gigantic beer mug imprinted on it. Both were carrying large plastic shopping bags. Holding a red balloon over his head, the boy jumped along, as if on invisible tracks, imitating the toot of the bygone trains. Presently Chen discovered the woman was American dressed in an overtly Asian way. Perhaps it was fashionable here, he did not know.

There were several pay phones scattered throughout the building. He chose one partially sheltered in a corner, and he dialed Yu's number. But no one picked up. Strange. It was still morning in Shanghai. At least Peiqin should be at home.

He took out his address book and found another number—a local St. Louis number. But he hesitated. It might put him in a difficult situation—in China—if she contacted him. As a Chinese police officer, he had to report any call from an American police officer. He dialed the number. No one at home there either. A click, and the answering machine brought out her voice.

"This Catherine Rohn's residence. Sorry I can't take your call. Please leave your phone number and a detailed message, and I'll call you back as soon as possible."

He hung up without speaking. Not a good idea to leave his cell phone number, and he hadn't remembered to bring the hotel number with him.

Leaving the public phone, he was in no mood for window-shopping. But there was no reason for him to hurry back. Huang might still be enjoying himself in the tub. And then it would be Shasha's turn, like a lotus flower blossoming out of the water. He turned into the bookstore, where he saw several shelves marked "mystery." All the authors were listed in the alphabetic order of their names. It was a far more popular genre here. In China, only in the last two or three years had a new type of literature called "legal system literature" emerged, as the legal system itself was new. Most of the writing in that genre, however, had little to do with the real police work, for the Party authorities always acted like a god at the last minute.

Chen picked up a hardcover—a naked girl with Chinese characters tattooed on her back. Glancing through a few pages, he knew that he wouldn't be able to choose in so little time. Instead, he picked up a newspaper and a map before heading to an affiliated Starbucks café. The familiar fragrance seemed to bring back what he had discussed with Gu at the franchises in Shanghai. Looking up, he saw a variety of names on the coffee list, in English and in other languages as well, which he hardly knew how to pronounce.

"A cup of regular coffee," he said.

The coffee tasted hot and strong. After a refreshing gulp, he started studying the map, but he failed to locate the Central West End. Frustrated, alone, he felt out of place.

Finally, he made up his mind to walk out. With his English, he should have no problem finding his way around. No time to visit Eliot's home this evening, he knew, though it was the first American city to bring out a feeling of déjà vu in him. In his college years, he had cherished an ambition of writing a book about Eliot, believing he had a singular Asian perspective. He had read books about the poet, and about the city too. Now with the project irrecoverably shelved, he found himself in that city, lighting a cigarette in the cool evening air.

In spite of the map in his hand, it did not take him too long to get lost. All of a sudden, the streets appeared deserted, except for an occasional car speeding along recklessly. There were no pedestrians like him around. In less than fifteen minutes, he must have made several wrong turns. Thanks to the pinnacle of the hotel shimmering in the sunlight, he managed to trace his way back.

Several people had already gathered in his room. They must have come in after Shasha. She was wrapped in a white robe, stretching on the sofa, her shapely bare legs stretching out like lotus roots. Zhong smoked like a chimney, as if trying to create a smoke screen to shield her out of sight. Peng slouched in a corner, silent as usual. Bao strode in, burping noisily with unusual satisfaction on his face.

"There's a Chinese buffet restaurant down in the mall," Bao said, wiping his mouth with a paper napkin. "The owner's from Shandong, my old home. We talked a lot. He gave me a box of fried dumplings for free. Genuine Shandong taste. A good-hearted overseas Chinese."

"He may have kept his Shandong taste, but not necessarily his Chinese heart," Zhong responded. "I saw the restaurant too. Far more expensive than the express bar."

"Why so hard on him, Zhong?" Bao retorted with blue veins standing out in his temples, throbbing like the earthworms in one of his poems. "The price is different—buffet—as much as you can eat. I've never had buffet in China. It's not easy for a Shandonese to get along in this foreign country."

"An American student told me that buffet is characteristic of the Chinese. That's so untrue," Shasha commented languidly. "The same with fortune cookies. What an irony. We have never had fortune cookies in China."

Chen looked at his watch: seven-twenty. It was about time for their routine political study, and everybody had come in except Little Huang. Usually, the young man was punctual. According to Zhong, Huang had headed out alone. Little Huang might have strolled out after the bath and lost his way.

"We don't have to wait for him. He'll come back," Bao said, "with the hotel card and phone number in his pocket. Don't worry."

Chen was not worried. Huang spoke English, was capable of making it back to the hotel on his own. The meeting did not last long. People had many different things to do, with the mall located underneath the hotel. Chen, too, sneaked out again and made another call, but he got the same message.

When he got back to the room, he took a Budweiser from the refrigerator and turned on the TV. There was a show about people talking in a bar, hilariously, with an invisible audience bursting into constant laughter. While he understood most of the dialogue, he failed to make out the occasion for the audience's guffaws. And he felt inexplicably frustrated.

Around nine-thirty, he called Little Huang's room. No one answered. Because of his interpreter position, Little Huang had never missed a group meeting or stayed out late by himself. Nor had he mentioned any friend or relative in the city. Chen contacted the front desk. The night manager promised she would check and call back with any information. Chen took his shower.

Around eleven, the night manager, too, became concerned, and she called Chen. After a short discussion with Chen, she contacted the local police about a possible missing person. It was not an ordinary tourist, but a Chinese delegation member.

The response came shortly after midnight. A body had been found on the corner of Seventh and Locust Street. There was no identification on the body, but it was a young Asian male.

Chen rushed out in a hotel car. There was hardly any traffic at this late hour. The car drove straight to the mortuary. There, a night-shift clerk led him to a room and pulled out a stretcher. The dead man under the white sheet was none other than Little Huang—his glasses missing, his hair disheveled, and his face already waxlike.

The body had been discovered by a patrolling cop. According to an initial report, the victim's skull had been crushed by some heavy, blunt-edged object. Possibly with one blow. The estimated time of death was between five-thirty to six. The report pointed to a possible robbery case gone wrong. Huang's wallet and other identification had all vanished. There was no sign of struggle before his death. No bruises or any other wounds on his body.

Shortly afterward, Jonathan Lenich, a local homicide cop, arrived at the mortuary. A dapper man with gray eyes and silver-streaked temples, Detective Lenich appeared sleepy and grumpy. He looked at the dead body, and then at Chen.

"A visiting Chinese writer?" Detective Lenich said.

"An interpreter for the delegation," Chen said.

"He looks like a visiting Chinese."

There seemed to be an emphasis on the word "visiting." Chen wondered what his American counterpart was driving at.

"A Chinese local would be dressed more casually, a jacket and jeans, but a Chinese visitor dresses far more formally—black suit and scarlet silk tie. And look at his shoes, another telltale sign."

Chen nodded. The American had a point, though how the shoes could have made such a difference, Chen wondered. Also, would a mugger have observed that carefully? "So you think he was an easy target here?"

"Well, that's not exactly what I mean."

"A robbery and homicide case?"

"We'll need to wait for the autopsy report—but we won't learn much from that, I'm afraid. We'll need statements from you and other members of your delegation."

"I understand," Chen said somberly. "But what about the location? The hotel is at the center of downtown, and Huang could not have walked far. It's hard to imagine how somebody could have been mugged and murdered there. And it was still light—"

"That's something you don't understand, Mr. Chen. Downtown isn't safe, even in broad daylight. St. Louis has a very high crime rate."

But Chief Inspector Chen couldn't help but think of other scenarios. Perhaps he needed to explore Little Huang's background first. With his own experience in the Foreign Liaison Office, he knew people working there usually had special backgrounds. At the least Party membership and approved political status, and often much more than that; sometimes they were even directly trained and controlled by Internal Security. What about Little Huang? Not just an interpreter, but one for a delegation visiting the United States. It was an extraordinary opportunity for a young person like Little Huang. Could he have been assigned a secret mission? If so, anything could have happened.

"A high crime rate indeed—it happened only about two hours after our arrival here," Chen said, trying to respond, and to clear his own thoughts. "As for a robbery-murder scenario, he was killed with one blow . . ."

"At a close distance."

"Do you think an ordinary mugger could have hit like that? One single blow delivered from behind, the victim unaware of the approaching danger."

"That's a good point, Mr. Chen. For a poet, you seem to know a lot about homicide."

"I have translated American mysteries."

"No wonder you speak English well. Killers can be desperate or demented, different from the people in your poems," Detective Lenich said. "My colleague is making a list of people with a history in the neighborhood. I'll start checking their alibis early tomorrow morning—or rather, this morning. Then I'll come to speak to your delegation members."

"What can I do?"

"Go back to your hotel. I'll come over later in the morning."

By the time Chen got back to the hotel, it was almost four o'clock. The first gray light came filtering in through the blinds. He slumped across the bed, worn out yet intensely wakeful, like a bulb before exploding.

The murder had happened while he was serving as the delegation head, and he had to hold himself more or less responsible. If no one had been allowed to go out alone, the tragedy might have been avoided. Bao had grumbled about Chen's laxity in enforcing delegation regulations, though as the Party secretary, Bao would share equal responsibility.

But what if there was something else behind the homicide? What if one of the Chinese writers was involved?

Chen got up, took a cold shower, and started making notes in an effort to brainstorm. He started by ruling out possibilities.

Little Huang seemed to have gotten along well with the writers. He knew his position, so to speak, and he showed proper respect to everyone. It was true that his English occasionally caused miscommunications. Shasha had once declared that she didn't trust him, but her remark could have been made for Chen's benefit. Bao was perhaps the only one who had seriously complained about Little Huang, claiming that the interpreter curried favor with Chen. Even so, it would be hard to imagine that Bao or any of the others would have committed murder because of such grudges—unless there was something else between Little Huang and them that Chen didn't know about.

In another scenario, Little Huang might have had an antidefection mission for the delegation. In that event, someone with such an intention might have panicked and killed Little Huang. But defection was less common in the nineties, and Chen didn't see why any of his fellow writers would have any reason to do so.

Chen composed a fax requesting Little Huang's detailed file from the Writers' Association in Beijing. He also made a long-distance call to Fang Youliang, one of his former schoolmates now teaching at the Beijing Foreign Language University. Some interpreters were enlisted by the Foreign Liaison, Chen knew, as early as their freshman year. Fang promised to provide any information about Little Huang from the college.

Of course, there was one more direction, Chen reflected, but he didn't want to think too much about it for the moment. It was already nearly six A.M. He reminded himself that there were more phone calls to make—as delegation head.

21

AT HOME, DETECTIVE YU looked at an ashtray that was already full in the morning and made himself a cup of extra-strong Uloon tea.

He had taken the day off for a number of reasons. Peiqin had been busier than ever, working at a state-run job as well as a private-run job, leaving home before six, so it was up to him to take care of some things at home. He had to pay Qinqin's English camp fee at the district school office. He had to buy fresh noodles for the evening. Most importantly, he had to check into a room-exchange proposal. Someone had offered to exchange a new two-bedroom apartment with bathroom and kitchen for their one-and-half room unit without bathroom or kitchen. The deal sounded too good to be true. Peiqin attributed it to the possibility of their area being turned into a high-end commercial complex in the near future. Still, a bird in hand is worth two in the woods. She was greatly tempted by the offer. After all, there was no telling what would happen next in China. She wanted Yu to take a close look at the apartment, lest there was something wrong with the feng shui of that new building. In Shanghai, most people were still dependent on government housing like Yu, so a room-exchange decision could be a very important one, in spite of the fast-developing new housing policy.

But for Yu, it would also be a day for him to think about what he could do for Chief Inspector Chen.

He had a hunch that the murder was somehow related to the Xing investigation, though it occurred thousands of miles away. He did not have anything to prove it but, as a cop, he didn't believe in coincidence. As with An's death. He couldn't shake off a feeling that, for some reason, Chen hadn't told him everything. People like Jiang could have hardly ordered a murder, even in the United States. So someone at a much higher level might be involved. It was a matter of life and death for Chen—to be exact, for both Chen and Yu.

But the only real help Yu had provided—together with Peiqin—was in moving Chen's mother out of danger temporarily. Still, time was not on their side. Yu might not be able to keep the old woman in hiding for long. Party Secretary Li had already approached him about the whereabouts of the old woman.

"You don't know where she is?" Li said sarcastically. "It's like the sun rising in the west."

In the bureau, Kuang had gone so far as to taunt Yu with Chen's connection to An in front of other cops.

"Your boss has really enjoyed the peach blossom luck," Kuang declared in the main office of the bureau. "A tit-tat meeting with that beautiful anchorwoman in a 'Lovers' Nest'—a couple days before her death."

Yu ignored it as a joke, which it wasn't. Kuang must have heard something, or he wouldn't have had the guts to speak of Chen like that.

But the only thing Yu had so far was An's cell phone record, which he had studied for days without discovering anything substantial. It was out of the question for him to approach those officials. He had thought about doing research on them, but he would have to get special access permission for the bureau computers. And that might not be a good idea, as others might trace his work. Everybody knew about his relationship to Chen.

He didn't have a computer at home. Among his friends, no one had one at home. Not even Chief Inspector Chen.

Spitting out a loose tea leaf, he remembered he had seen a laptop in Chen's home. Not Chen's, but one lent to him for a translation project by an upstart named Gu—a computer as well as the college girl, White Cloud, as a "little secretary," who was "lent" to Chen's mother this time.

It wasn't difficult to guess why Gu had befriended Chen. It was an investment for future return. But since the shrewd businessman saw potential in the chief inspector, Gu might help his assistant as well.

Yu took a taxi to the Dynasty Karaoke Club. He still had many things to do afterward, so on the way there, he got the money for Qinqin's English camp out of the bank.

As soon as Yu sent in his business card, Gu came out and welcomed him into a spacious office. A tall man in a Western-style suit with Chinese-style cloth-heeled shoes and green jade neck decoration, the entrepreneur was gracious to the detective. Yu lost no time explaining the purpose of his visit, though he refrained from mentioning any specific details.

"It's something important for Chen, Mr. Gu, or I would not have come to you like this."

"You don't have to explain," Gu said, picking up the phone on his desk and giving instructions to his secretary outside the office. "We haven't met before, but Chen has talked such a lot about you. It's like I have known you for years too."

A young waitress in a pink cheongsam came in with a new laptop still in the box, and another, in a green cheongsam, with a platter of fruit enveloped in a mirage of spiraling mist. "Tropical rainforest," she said. She also had a bottle of foreign wine in an ice bucket and opened the wine with a pop.

"If you are not in a hurry," Gu said, raising the cup, "I'll have one of our best K girls for you in a private room. My treat. You have really given me face today."

"Thank you, but I'm really in a hurry. Next time, Mr. Gu."

There would be no next time, Yu was sure. He had heard stories about K girls in private rooms and he had to think of Peiqin. That was bottom line.

"It's an honor that you thought of me, Detective Yu. I am a businessman, but a man of *yiqi* too. I am willing to have my chest pierced with knives for a friend."

It sounded sort of like triad jargon. Detective Yu was confounded that someone with triad connections would make such a statement to a cop.

"We have already cooperated," Gu went on warmly. "Between your wife Peiqin and White Cloud. What a master stroke Peiqin made in the water shop."

As Yu was about to leave the club with the laptop, Gu said casually, as if in afterthought, "You have a room in the Luwan District, close to the intersection of Huaihai and Madang Road, right?"

"Yes . . ."

"Don't exchange it with others. There are huge potentials there. If you really want to move to a larger apartment, let me know. I'll give you a new three-bedroom apartment in a decent area—plus a hundred thousand yuan in cash."

"No kidding!"

"Think about it. You don't have to give me an answer right now. Not a single word about it to anyone else, of course. You are my friend and I'm not an unscrupulous businessman who would rip off a friend like you."

Probably not, Yu observed. Stepping out of the Dynasty, he thought about calling Peiqin, but he saw no sign of a public phone booth there.

Connections and corruptions, Detective Yu pondered, walking. It could be hard to draw a clear-cut line between the two. In fact, he had got the room through Chen's help—with the inside information from Chen's connection. Still, Chen got nothing for himself, and Yu deserved a room—even according to the official housing committee of the bureau. So Yu could say that he had done all that, like Chen, not for himself . . .

He decided not to think about those things anymore.

Back home, Yu started searching on the computer. The computer provided more detailed information about the people An had contacted in her last few days, yet invariably in official language. According to the government-controlled media, these officials, instead of being crooked, were actually communist models. When he gathered everything together from various sources, he was still unable to make any use of it.

Then the phone rang. It was from Peiqin.

"You are still at home, Yu?"

"I've just got the money from the bank. Everything will be taken care of. I'm leaving soon."

"Don't forget your lunch. Make a purple seaweed soup for yourself. There's a pack of it in the kitchen cabinet."

"I won't forget."

Peiqin had left several steamed buns at home. He warmed two up in the microwave, but they turned out to be drier, and harder too. A mistake. He should have resteamed them, remembering what Peiqin had done. He tore a sheet of the purple seaweed to pieces, poured in hot water and soy sauce, making a palatable soup with chopped green onion and sesame oil floating on the surface. He washed down the buns without much difficulty, when he realized, picking his teeth, he had forgotten to tell her the news about their unit's value. She would not come back until the evening. He was tempted to light another cigarette, but he thought the better of it. Cigarette smoke could be bad for the computer, he recalled.

Occasionally, Peiqin could be like Chen, with leaps and bounds in her thinking. Yu admitted she had helped in her way—her decision to move Chen's mother was timely and effective. Still, he had not thought much of what she said about Apricot Blossom Village. Perhaps Yu was too used to the company of Chen, who threw poetry into his speech like pepper in a hot Sichuan soup.

Now on the computer search, Yu thought of Peiqin and typed in Apricot Blossom Village. It turned out to be a new, exclusive club, not like the Dynasty, but one with elite members and expensive fees. From one of the links, he found an article about the lavish parties held there—including Xing's parties. Xing had entertained in fancy restaurants or hotels in Shanghai. But at Apricot Blossom Village Xing had held three consecutive parties where his guests included high-ranking cadres from Beijing. The article had been published before Xing had gotten into trouble.

Yu continued his research about the club. The general manager was surnamed Weici, a man of mysterious background. No information about the founding of this club with exorbitant membership fees. In fact, it was the first time Yu had read about such a club. According to the introduction, people had to pay an unbelievable membership fee—fifty thousand yuan as a down payment and then a monthly fee of three thousand yuan. The monthly fee was equivalent to the combined monthly income of Peiqin and Yu. Rich people burned money.

So it was a place Detective Yu should check into. Apricot Blossom Village could have a special connection to Xing, and to Ming too. If so, Bi's quote had been a hint to An. It was a long shot, but one worth trying. With pictures of Ming in his hand, Yu might be able to ask some questions there, though not as a cop, which would only alarm people. He'd better go there like a would-be club member—with the English camp money, plus his secret nest of three hundred yuan he had saved from his pocket money by quitting smoking periodically.

But another problem arose. Even with all the money, he did not look like a likely visitor there. In the club pictures, the members appeared elegantly dressed. Yu was dressed in a three-year-old shirt with a dispirited collar and faded black pants. He could even be barred from entering the place.

It was out of the question for him to call Peiqin for suggestions. Those swell places were just as foreign to her. His only suit was bought in the eighties—for his wedding—and was now too small. Earlier this year, for the dinner at Xinya, he had tried to put it on; Peiqin had joked about him looking like a bursting bag.

Then his glance fell on a magazine Qinqin had brought home. In that magazine, he remembered a picture of a movie star playing golf. The club boasted one of the largest golf courses in China. Yu might dress himself up like a golfer. He dug out the magazine. To his relief, the movie star was dressed in a simple way. A white T-shirt, shorts, and tennis shoes.

Simple, but of expensive brands. There was a logo of a man riding a horse on his T-shirt. Yu happened to have one with a similar logo, a knock-off. It could pass, he thought. The shorts he dug out did not look much different. Only he did not have tennis shoes. Then he thought of Qinqin's favorite shoes, Nike. They were the only brand-name shoes Peiqin had bought for her son, insisting on them in spite of the ridiculously high price. Yu failed to see anything special about the shoes worth nine hundred yuan—except something like a red check. But she didn't want Qinqin to feel inferior at school and the boy wore the shoes only on special occasions. The father and son wore the same size.

Finally, he finished grooming himself with the magazine spread out before him. He found the image in the mirror not so different from the star, but drastically different from Detective Yu. It was a weird sensation.

He also chose his route carefully—the bus, the subway, finally a taxi. He had to arrive there in a car, but he did not have to take it all the way. Nor could he afford to.

Apricot Blossom Village was located in Fengyan Country, a large complex surrounded by high walls and tall trees. Yu got out of the car. A uniformed security guard at the entrance bowed to him. People were driving in and out in their own luxurious cars, apparently club members. The only section of the club open to nonmembers was a large reception hall adjacent to the entrance. There was also a bar there, where people could drink, talk, and enjoy a tantalizing look at the magnificent golf course that stretched into the distance. Yu saw a row of white villas beyond the lush meadow.

He took his seat at a table and picked up the menu. The minimum was five hundred yuan. Perhaps nothing to a genuine would-be member, which he had to play for a short while. He had no choice. He would never become a man, he knew, "catching up with the trend"—an old phrase with a new connotation, suddenly popular in the newspapers—so he did not bother about things other than his job in the changed world. Still, a cup of black tea for two hundred fifty, with a tea bag instead of real tea, proved too much for him. It tasted odd, and he had a hard time not scowling.

A model-like hostess walked lightfooted over to his table, her hair highlighted like a golden dream, her willowy figure fetching, as if copied out of a fashion magazine. She carried a large club brochure in her hand.

"Yes, tell me something about your club," he said simply.

So she put a map of the club on the table—tennis courts, swimming pool, golf course. Her blue-painted fingernails flipped like butterflies over the drawing. She talked about the benefits of being a member here.

"It's a super heavenly place. For a busy and successful man like you, only in this club can you totally relax and enjoy the precious moments of your life."

"Really!" It took him about two hours, not to mention the bus, subway, taxi fare, to reach the place. He could have taken a nap at home and dreamed of heaven—if there were indeed one.

"The best golf course in Asia. Shanghai is the most happening city in the world, as an American magazine just voted. Look at the splendid meadow, the bosom of the nature. Such a golf course membership card is a must for people like you," she went on glibly. "The golf course alone is worth the money. Not to mention all the rich and successful people you'll meet there. Nothing's like that for building your relationship network."

In truth, Yu had never touched a golf ball before. It was said to be symbolic of one's social status in new China. The rich might need something for them to believe they were really rich. The white ball worked like nothing else for that purpose. But, more than that, for people like Xing or Ming, the lush meadow was also super for cultivating their connections of corruption.

"And you can bring your friends to dinner here," she went on. "The best chef in China, he used to cook exclusively for Mao. Five Ways of Eating an Australian Lobster is today's special."

"Is that included in the monthly fee?"

"You must be joking, sir."

He was not joking. There was no point in pretending anymore about potentially belonging to this different world. The Nike shoes had started pinching his feet terribly.

Detective Yu took out a picture of Ming and asked, "Have you seen this man here?"

She took a look at the picture, and the brochure nearly dropped from her hand.

"You aren't really interested in becoming a club member here, are you?" She regained her composure, looked over her shoulder toward the gate, where the security stood like a statue.

It was not the time for a confrontation. Not only was he not authorized to investigate here, but he wasn't supposed to let anyone know of his interest. Any misstep would jeopardize the whole thing.

He whipped out a wad of money without counting it and pushed it into her hand—like a really rich man, the way he had seen in an American movie, putting a finger to his lips.

"Well, you have never asked me any questions, and I have never seen you here," she said nervously, inserting the money into the brochure. She cast a glance—or he so thought—toward those white villas across the golf course.

That wasn't an answer Yu had expected, but it wasn't a simple "No" either. It meant something, he reflected. If she had never seen Ming, she would have simply said no. Rather, she initially appeared nervous, nearly panicked, and that, together with her insistence on having not met the detective or heard the question, was more than suggestive: she not only knew Ming, she also knew how critical the knowledge was.

But for the moment, there was no point in his staying here and pushing anymore. He rose and left.

Out of the club, he found he had less than twenty yuan in his pocket. Not enough for a taxi home, or even to the subway station. It was an area with very few people walking. It took him five minutes to find someone, from whom he learned the way to the nearest bus stop. He had to walk quite a distance.

As he dragged his steps along his long way home, the initial excitement over the hostess's reaction began ebbing. Whatever the possible interpretations, there was hardly anything he could do. It was impossible for him to obtain a search warrant for the high-class club without evidence or a witness, even if he was officially assigned to the investigation. Perhaps he had better not call Chen about it unless he made further progress. Only he had no idea how.

And his steps grew heavier, almost lead-laden, as he visualized a stormy evening waiting for him at home. He had not done anything Peiqin had wanted him to. On the contrary, he had spent Qinqin's English camp money, plus his own savings, on a cup of tasteless teabag tea.

He then found a little comfort in a new idea. Peiqin would be overjoyed to learn the value of their present room unit. Consequently, his failure with the day's responsibilities was less significant. After all, they could have exchanged their room at an enormous disadvantage without his visit to Gu. And Yu might be able to pay the camp fee the next day. That meant he had to get the money from other sources. Difficult, but not impossible. As a last resort, he could turn to Old Hunter. The old man would probably approve of anything done for the sake of the chief inspector. So Yu did not have to tell Peiqin the exact truth.

He quickened his steps again. If he were lucky enough, he would still be able to buy the fresh noodles, which cost less than two yuan at a small store near home.

The bus stop came into sight.

22

BY EIGHT THIRTY, EVERYBODY in the delegation had heard about the tragic death of Little Huang.

The telephone kept ringing in Chen's room like a funeral bell.

Bao was the first to come rushing into his room, declaring in a thundering voice, "It's absolutely unacceptable. How could something like that have happened to a Chinese delegation? We have to hold the Americans fully responsible."

"They have been working on the case," Chen said. "I met with a local cop assigned to the case last night."

"We have to inform the Chinese embassy of the case."

"I've already done that. The embassy people are contacting Huang's family. They may fly over as early as tomorrow."

"We have to report this to the Foreign Ministry in Beijing. It's a serious diplomatic incident."

"Yes, we'll do that, but the embassy must have notified Beijing."

"Now what are we supposed to do here?" Shasha cut in, in her terry robe and slippers, her toenails painted like blood.

"We may have to stay here for the time being. To cooperate with the police. The American investigators will come for our statements."

"That's absurd," Zhong said, striding into the room. "The American government has invited us over. One of us was murdered here, and we are going to make statements to their cops?"

"Don't worry about the statement. Nothing but routine questions. It doesn't mean that you are a suspect." Chen added, "That's also the opinion of the Chinese embassy—that we should cooperate in whatever way possible."

"In addition to giving statements," Zhong said, "what else can we possibly do?"

"It will be hard to continue the delegation activities as scheduled. The news must have attracted negative media attention and the university is concerned about it. So we'll wait until further notice. In the meantime, we have to be careful."

"Who will serve as our interpreter then?" Shasha said.

"I'll help as much as I can," Chen said. "I'll talk to the Americans about it."

Chen spent the next half hour making phone calls, making explanations, and making notes whenever he had a minute. The two local institutions originally responsible for the day's activities were universities. One of them, Washington University, with a Chinese department, promised to send over help for interpretation.

Shortly before nine, the front desk called up, saying Detective Jonathan Lenich had arrived at the hotel in the company of a new interpreter. They were both waiting in the lobby. Chen and Bao immediately went downstairs.

"Oh, you must be Mr. Chen Cao," a young blond woman in a white blouse and blue jeans stood up, speaking in Chinese. "I am Catherine Rohn. The university sent me over as your new interpreter. You speak English too, I know."

"Oh, Catherine—" Chen was practically speechless at the meeting, before he realized her self-introduction in Chinese was not meant for him. "Thank you for your help, Miss Rohn."

It was clever of her to have announced her temporary identity as an interpreter-escort. There must have been a reason for her to be sent over in that capacity. It was a sensitive case; at least, so it must have seemed to some people here. Otherwise a marshal wouldn't have been dispatched incognito.

For Chen, there was no point revealing their former relationship, either, though it could be the very reason that she was assigned here. It would have led to unnecessary speculation among the Chinese. For the moment, it was nothing but business. He'd better not to mention anything to her, not even in English.

Whatever the reason was, she was someone he thought he could trust. But then again was he really so sure—after all the silence?

So many days, where have you been—
like a traveling cloud
that forgets to come back,
unaware of the spring drawing to an end . . .

"You must have heard of the situation," Bao started sternly. Because of the linguistic barrier, he had been unable to say anything as the Party secretary of the delegation. A barrage of questions came from Bao, but they were neither here nor there. It was hard for her to answer them—or not to answer them.

"I've heard there was an accident," she said, handing over her business card to Bao. "Washington University called me early this morning to provide interpretation service, but they did not tell me anything else. You will have to speak to Detective Lenich about it."

"She is a temporary interpreter," Chen said to Bao, glancing at the bilingual business card, which declared her as a senior interpreter from a local translation agency. "We don't have to discuss the case with her."

Catherine translated his remark to the detective.

"I'm in charge of the case," Lenich said. "You can discuss it with me."

But Bao's questions sounded too official, as if echoing from his office in Beijing. Talking about responsibility did not help at this stage, Chen thought. With Bao occupied with his official talk, however, he stole another glance at Catherine. She looked hardly changed from his memory—tall, slender, her face animated with an inner glow, and her hair cascading halfway to her shoulders. But in that instant, he thought he also saw one tiny difference. The color of her eyes appeared to be brown instead of blue, though as serene, vivid as he had remembered. Because of the sunlight in the hotel lobby?

It is difficult to meet. A line from Li Shangyin came to assume a different meaning. Difficult not so much in terms of distance, but what to say to each other at the moment of their meeting? Perhaps just like in that Tang dynasty poem: *what is not said speaks much more than what is said.*

She was busy translating for Bao and Lenich, occasionally looking back at him with a familiar yet not so familiar smile.

Other writers came down. They, too, started questioning the Americans. She had a hard time interpreting for all of them.

"I like China. Not too long ago, I made a trip to your wonderful country. I had a memorable experience with an excellent escort. So I will do my best. Trust me."

She made the statement for him, he knew. It was also a reassuring one for the other writers, who now had to depend on an American instead of Little Huang.

"An unlucky trip from the very beginning. Doomed," Zhong commented. "Remember the unexpected health problem of Yang? Problems even before the beginning of the trip."

Chen tried to talk more with Detective Lenich, but it was difficult for them with others continuously cutting in. The hotel manager approached them. A group of agitated Chinese talking in the lobby did not present a pleasant scene, especially with the prospect of journalists coming over soon. So the manager offered to provide them a conference room with a small enclave attached to it.

"You have a lot to do, Miss Rohn, with so many Chinese writers on your hands," Chen said before moving into the cubicle with his American counterpart. "I'm glad you are here. We appreciate all you are doing for us."

"Call me Catherine. I'd love to help, Mr. Chen."

The discussion with Detective Lenich did not produce anything new. The American cop held onto his earlier assumption: it was a street homicide case, in which the victim happened to be a Chinese delegation member. He had his assistant checking the alibis of the possible suspects in the area, and he wanted to start interviewing the writers in the hotel.

So the writers had to come in, one by one, to give a statement. Zhong was the first interviewee and Catherine followed him in. Chen and the rest of the delegation remained in the larger room. They did not talk much. Chen made several more phone calls. Eventually, Zhong emerged with a livid face. Then it was Bao's turn. Presently Chen heard loud voices from the smaller room. Catherine must have had a hard time interpreting so, after a while, Chen went in too. For Detective Lenich, it might have been a matter of formality, but Bao fought back by talking about the Americans' responsibility all the time. Chen's effort to intervene was far from successful.

Unable to break the impasse between the two, Chen recommended a pause.

"Well, it's time to have a lunch break," he suggested.

"Let's eat here," Bao said. "It's not safe outside the hotel, is it? There is a Chinese carry-out down at the mall. They'll deliver."

With a sideways look at Chen, Catherine translated Bao's suggestion selectively. Chen and Lenich agreed to the idea of having Chinese food delivered to the conference room. When Chen spoke to the writers, however, Shasha asked if they could have lunch in their respective rooms instead and take a short break afterward.

After briefly conferring with Lenich, Chen agreed. "You can all head back to your rooms," Chen said. "I'll stay here with the Americans."

When the food was delivered, Detective Lenich decided to take his back to his office, promising to return in an hour. Catherine and Chen were left alone in the room, the long conference table between them. He sat with a portion of sweet and sour shrimp with walnuts, and she, a portion of Chinese barbequed pork. Their moment alone overwhelmed them in awkward silence.

"How did you come to be an interpreter today?" Chen asked, disposable chopsticks in his hand.

"I've been studying Chinese for years," Catherine said. She sounded not so pleased with his question—the first of their reunion. "You didn't tell me about your visit."

"I tried—several times—but either your line was busy, or others interrupted. There are delegation regulations, you know. Yesterday afternoon I called you again, but I got your machine. I didn't leave a message because I forgot my room number."

"You weren't calling from your hotel room?" she asked sharply. Without waiting for an answer, she went on, "I thought you must have forgotten about me."

"No. Of course not, but I did wonder if it was a good idea for me to contact you, being what I am."

"That's so considerate of you," she said, taking a drink from her cup. "Anyway, they approached me for information about you—being what you are."

"Oh, they . . . I should have realized that."

"As the delegation head, you must have a lot of responsibilities—special responsibilities, since you were appointed on such short notice."

"Oh? You heard about that? You know a lot—" Chen stopped midsentence.

They were certainly being mistrustful of each other again, he thought, just as they had been the first time they met in Shanghai. It wasn't difficult for him to pick up that much.

Still, how would he react in her position?

But there was something she hadn't told him either. Surely, she wasn't assigned to the Chinese delegation just because of the homicide case.

"I've missed you," he resumed on a different note. "You remember Mr. Gu of the Dynasty Karaoke Club, where you were introduced as my girlfriend?"

"Yes, I remember. That sly businessman."

"I talked to him about you, and he wanted me to bring you something—to my 'beautiful American girlfriend.' It's in my room upstairs."

"What did you say to him about me?"

But before he could respond, they were interrupted by Bao, who returned carrying a large portion of fried dumplings, declaring he had more questions for her.

"Comrade Bao is a well-known Chinese writer, as well as the Party secretary of our delegation," Chen said by way of explanation, barely able to conceal the frustration in his voice. It was no surprise that Bao showed off his official responsibility from time to time, but he seemed to make a point of not letting Chen out of his sight for very long. It was all the more exasperating now with Catherine here. "He has to show his concern for the case—even during the lunch break."

"When a case like this happens," she said, "everybody must be concerned."

"Really. What is the American government's response?" Bao said. "How could you have allowed this to happen to a Chinese delegation?"

"There's no point repeating these questions to her, Bao. How can she answer for the American government? She's been busy working all morning," Chen said curtly. "Catherine, if you want, I'll show you to my room and you can take a short break there."

But his room was still being examined by two American cops. Little Huang had taken a bath there before stepping out. Chen had to think of some other excuse for them to be alone.

"We'd better speak to the hotel security," he said. "I am not familiar with the hotel management here. You have to help me, Catherine."

"Let's do that," she said.

But that didn't work out either. His cell phone rang. It was a call from the Foreign Ministry in Beijing. A call of diplomatic formalities, but he had to listen and answer attentively. She stood at a distance, leaning against the wall with her ankles crossed, the same way she did back at the Peace Hotel in Shanghai. Then Detective Lenich returned to the hotel, wanting to speak with Chen again. Then Shasha showed up in the lobby and started to talk to Catherine.

As it turned out, the American cop had a new scenario: the murderer was a delegation insider, or at least was connected to an insider. Detective Lenich's theory was based on a detailed analysis of the crime location. He took out a city map and stared drawing red and blue lines across it. It was not uncommon for a tourist to stroll around upon arrival in a new city, but usually not very far. A couple of blocks, a breath of fresh air, and a first glimpse of the city landmarks. The hotel location made such a supposition quite plausible. The hotel opened onto Market Street, a prosperous street in the downtown area, with the Arch not far away to the east. It was reasonable to assume that Little Huang got out to Market Street and turned right in the direction of the Arch. But his body was found on a shady street quite a distance from the hotel, farther to the south. As a tourist, how could Huang have ended up in such a desolate area? He might have gotten lost, but with so many high buildings nearby, it was hard to imagine he would have strayed so far in that direction.

Based on that analysis, Inspector Lenich developed a new theory. Huang might not have been murdered on that shady side street, but rather somewhere closer to the hotel. As further evidence for this, foreign fibers were found on his clothes, possibly from a car in which his body had been moved.

Lenich had a point. This could be a far more complicated case. Chen also realized that there was something unusual about the trip—not just concerning Little Huang, but other members of the delegation as well.

Bao, for instance, seemed to be following Chen in a mysterious way. Bao had been grumbling about Chen being in charge, but that could hardly account for him spying on Chen. Shasha, too, puzzled Chen with her inscrutable inquisitiveness. And Peng, with his baffling reticence. Indeed, why was he included in the group? He hardly wrote anymore, or even talked like a writer. Was his presence simply symbolic? As for Zhong, he made a point of calling back to China. Supposedly to his old wife in Nanjing, but once, when consulting Chen about the instructions on the back of the phone card, he let slip the area code, revealing that his call went to Beijing instead. Any one of them could have been entrusted with a secret mission unknown to Chen, the delegation head appointed at the last minute.

He didn't discuss any of this with Detective Lenich, yet it made sense, Chen agreed, for the American to check the Chinese writers' alibis—except Chen himself. Someone in the bookstore had already confirmed that Chen was reading and drinking coffee during that time period. He remembered

Chen as being the only Chinese there, that he spoke "slightly quaint English with an accent."

The other delegation members were not so lucky. Shasha was the one who had followed Huang in the sequence of using Chen's bathroom. She had only her own word that she hadn't seen him since. Bao claimed that he went to the Chinese buffet restaurant, spending about two hours there because of "eating as much as you can." Afterward he chatted with the buffet owner, yet the latter couldn't remember when Bao had arrived at the restaurant. Peng said that he took a nap as soon as he checked in, sleeping until the time of the political study. While it sounded plausible for a man of his age, no one could prove it. Zhong maintained that he strolled around the shopping mall before eating at the Chinese Express. No one there remembered seeing him, with customers coming and going all the time, and Zhong did not see Chen or Bao.

So Detective Lenich had a lot to do, following up on his new direction.

It was not until after five that the American cop finished talking with the writers. Chen, too, felt obliged to talk to the delegation. A speech of formalities, though not a long one.

"We have to be more careful," Chen said. "To ensure the safety of the delegation, we have to reemphasize our disciplines. And I want to repeat a few of them: Do not go out by yourself. Do not go out without reporting to the delegation head. Do not meet with unknown people. In addition, turn in your passports, so they will be under my special care."

These were not new rules. During the early stage of China's first opening its door, Chinese delegations abroad had had to follow the rules literally. A considerable number of people had defected then, either by disappearing or seeking political asylum. So they were supposed to go out only in groups, with one watching another, and with their passports under the care of the delegation head. But things had since improved. Most of the delegations were made up of those doing well in China. They would be unlikely to gamble on an uncertain future overseas.

"If you have any questions, you can ask our interpreter, Catherine Rohn," Chen concluded. "She has been doing a great job for us."

"But what do we do in the evening?" Shasha said. "She won't be here with us all the time."

It was a good point, so Chen requested that Catherine stay with them at the hotel, at least for one or two days. It appeared to be a very reasonable request. Chen himself was busy with many things, and there needed to be an interpreter around for the Chinese writers.

She agreed quietly. "It'll save me downtown traffic in the morning."

The hotel manager cooperated promptly. Instead of giving her the room Huang had occupied, he promised her another one on the same floor as the delegation. Chen was pleased with the arrangement. Perhaps later, after the delegation political study, he would run into her in the corridor.

And he did, only earlier. As the delegation was having their evening political study, Catherine called into Chen's room.

"Miss Rohn wants me to come and discuss tomorrow's activity," Chen said to the delegation at the end of the phone conversation. "Americans like to stick to their schedules."

"That's true," Shasha said. "They have to cook with the recipe in their hands. No improvisation or imagination. But she is so attractive, and speaks good Chinese too."

To his surprise, Chen found Detective Lenich in Catherine's room. Her true identity, as a U.S. marshal, was no longer being kept from the American investigator. She was dressed in shorts, sandals, and a light yellow T-shirt. She must have taken a shower, her hair still wet. She started making a fresh pot of coffee for Chen.

Detective Lenich elaborated on his theory. "The murder was a collaboration between an outsider and an insider. An insider to point out the target, and an outsider with a car to move the body. My colleagues have made a more thorough search of Huang's room. Nothing there matched the fiber found on his clothes, and the bus in which the delegation traveled to St. Louis is equipped with imitation leather seats."

But this theory opened up a number of new questions, Chen observed.

For such collaboration, the plan must have been made far in advance. That afternoon, the delegation was originally scheduled to arrive for lunch at the hotel, but, because of a traffic accident along the highway, they had arrived several hours late. Then there was the unforeseeable factor of Little Huang's bath in his room. So the outsider in Detective Lenich's conspiracy theory would have had to wait hours outside of the hotel, and the insider—a delegation member—would have had to be there too, see Little Huang walking out, and point him out to the murderer. And during that time period, there must have been some contact between the insider and outsider.

Lenich had checked with the hotel phone service. Nothing. It was no surprise, Chen thought. He himself had made a point of not using the hotel phone except for official business. For such a murderous conspiracy, the hotel phone would have been unacceptable. The only phone calls Detective Lenich had discovered were from Shasha's to Chen's room. And another one from the lobby house phone—possibly a wrong number, since no one spoke when it bounced back from Chen's room to the hotel operator.

"A room-to-room call," Detective Lenich commented. "It was around five-forty. No one picked up. It proves only one thing. Little Huang must have stepped out of the room by that time. Incidentally, that also rules out Shasha as a suspect."

They then discussed the delegation activity for the next day. Lenich thought the Chinese writers had better remain in the hotel, but Chen said that they had been complaining. It would be hard to keep them in for another long frustrating day.

"Let's go to the Arch," Catherine suggested. "It's close to the hotel. If there is any new development, Detective Lenich can come over."

Lenich and Chen left her room around ten-thirty. She walked them to the door with a wan smile. It had been a long, exhausting day, and she looked pale in the corridor light. Chen then accompanied the American cop to the hotel's front gate.

Back in his room, he found several fax pages about Little Huang from the Chinese Writers' Association. The information from the official channels showed nothing suspicious in his background. He didn't start working for the association immediately after graduation; he was assigned to teach a middle school. He got the job at the Writers' Association when another interpreter suddenly quit. He was reliable and easy to get along with; though not a Party member, he was given the opportunity to serve as interpreter for delegations visiting abroad. This was Huang's third trip out of China. The last page of the fax also detailed a change in the arrangements for Little Huang's family's trip to the U.S. His father had suffered a severe heart attack upon learning the news.

There was also a fax from Fang, his former schoolmate at the Beijing Foreign Language University. It provided more background information about Huang in his college years. A hardworking student from a poor family in Anhui Province, he had worked as a TA for a professor and as a part-time English tutor over weekends. In his student years, Huang hardly had any time for political activities. "He also liked poetry," Fang added in conclusion, "like you. I think that's why he went to work for the Writers' Association."

Around eleven-thirty, a call came from Catherine.

"Sorry to phone you so late, Mr. Chen," she said. "I hope you're not in bed yet."

"No. I'm not. I thought about calling you too, but a fax came in."

"I just wanted to double-check our schedule. Eight-thirty tomorrow morning, right?"

"Yes, eight-thirty. Down in the lobby."

"It's the first interpreter-escort experience for me. I don't want to let our Chinese writers down."

"You are so conscientious."

"Detective Lenich is an experienced investigator. Don't worry. Whatever I can do, let me know." She added, "It's been a hectic day. Don't stay up too late."

"No, I won't. You take good care of yourself too."

Nothing but business talk between a Chinese delegation head and an American interpreter. Both knew their telephone lines might be tapped.

Still, she didn't have to make the call.

Afterward, he looked out of the window, thinking of a Tang dynasty poem Ezra Pound had also translated. He might include it in his talk on the translation of classical Chinese poetry, if he was going to give another one during the remaining days of the visit.

Waiting, she finds her silk stockings
soaked with the dew drops
glistening on the marble palace steps.
Finally, she is moving
to let the crystal-woven curtain fall
when she casts one more glance
at the glamorous autumn moon.

23

IT'LL BE A HECTIC day, Catherine awoke thinking, as if still echoing last night's conversation, *in the company of Chen.*

But it was too early. Alone, in her hotel room, she did not want to get up immediately. It was sort of an indulgence to let her mind wander, like a horse unbridled for a short moment, before she braced herself for the day's work.

She wondered what Chen was doing at the moment, on the same floor, in the same hotel.

She had heard about Chen's visit before his arrival in the U.S. The CIA had approached her. The unexpected appointment of Chen must have appeared suspicious to them, more so because the change came at the last minute. The CIA was well aware of Chen's background and his work on an important anticorruption case, which was further complicated by Xing's application for political asylum. They wondered whether Chen was really here on an untold mission under cover of the literature conference. The Beijing authorities could just have easily chosen somebody else for the delegation.

She hadn't told anything to the CIA. She didn't have anything to tell.

Since their difficult yet memorable joint investigation in Shanghai, they had barely been in contact with each other, both being aware of their positions.

In China, they had talked about a reunion in the U.S. She had been looking forward to it. So had he, she believed. But when he did come over, he never called her. Busy, understandably so, with a government delegation under him, but not too busy to phone—unless he really was engaged in a special mission. Still, she had expected to hear from him. Even when he arrived in St. Louis, except for a silent message on her answering machine, she'd heard nothing. She didn't really blame him, but his priorities were obvious.

What had happened to him since their parting in Shanghai, she didn't know. Smooth sailing in his political career, she supposed. His delegation position spoke for itself. She believed, however, that he had got the position on merit. If Beijing had wanted him to work on the Xing case here, a much better cover should have been arranged. In fact, the CIA learned about his investigation by reading about it in the Chinese newspapers.

Nor did she know anything new about his personal life. He had a girlfriend from a high-ranking cadre family in Beijing, but the relationship was described as "not exactly working out." On the immigration form, he had still circled himself as single. Then she checked herself, sitting up on the bed and hugging her knees against her chin. She was a marshal and assigned to a homicide case here.

She moved to the window. Looking out, she couldn't see the U.S. Marshals office building, which wasn't far from the hotel. This was her city, the streets not yet jammed with the traffic, hardly a pedestrian in sight. Those mornings in Shanghai, strolling on the Bund, seemed so long ago, irrecoverably blurred. A cloud was riding across the sky, steady in its direction.

They had worked together on an anti–illegal immigration case in China, and come to know each other with mutual admiration. But their work came to a conclusion, and they parted, as in the poem he had read to her, rubbing her sprained ankle, in the ancient Suzhou garden, *"grateful, and glad / to have been with you, / the sunlight lost on the garden."* It was a moment they'd shared and lost. *So that's about it,* she told herself again.

When her boss had wanted her to join the delegation as an interpreter-escort, it wasn't exactly a surprise. She wasn't so sure, however, about the triple task the CIA specified: finding out Chen's real mission, helping to solve the homicide, and preventing anything else from happening to the delegation.

The first part was practically impossible. Whatever the circumstances of their meeting, she hardly expected him to give her a straightforward answer. He was a conscientious Chinese cop, and a Party cadre—no mistake about it. As he had quoted from Confucius, *there are things a man can do, and there are things a man cannot do.*

For the second part, she didn't think she could help much, not having been trained as a homicide investigator. That was up to Lenich and his colleagues. Still, she wondered about the possibility of a political conspiracy behind the homicide case. She was going to try her best. She shuddered at the possibility of anything happening to Chen. Her personal concerns aside, a disastrous international case wouldn't serve the interests of either country.

The phone started ringing. The call was from her boss, Director Spencer, of U.S. Marshals, St. Louis Office.

"You made the right decision in staying at the hotel with them," Director Spencer commented in approval. "Both the CIA and the marshals will do whatever necessary to help. Just tell us what you need."

"What I really need is more background information on the Xing case," she said, "not just because of how it relates to Chen, but because it might be relevant to the homicide case as well. As detailed as possible."

"That can be arranged."

"I'll need a laptop. So I can work from my hotel room."

"I'll have it delivered. By the way, does Chen have a computer with him?"

"I don't think so, but I'll double-check."

Shortly after she hung up with him, a call came in from Bao. "Can we go out in a group today?"

"I think it's okay, and we are going to the Arch—in a group."

"Really! You should have told me earlier."

"Mr. Chen, Detective Lenich, and I discussed it late last night. He may not have had the time to tell you."

The next call was unexpected, from Zhong, just as she was about to head to the shower.

"I thought about it all night. I don't think Little Huang went out with any special plan. Before he left, he took a long bath in Chen's room. No less than twenty-five minutes. I should have discussed it with Detective Lenich, but no one would have taken such a long, luxurious bath if he had some plan in mind."

Again it was difficult for her to respond. Zhong might have a point, but how could he be so sure that the bath took "no less than twenty-five minutes"? Perhaps Lenich was right. There was something strange about the delegation. She had a feeling that she might have to be here for quite a few days.

"You should raise this with Detective Lenich today."

"He's going to be with us all day again today?" Zhong snapped. "That's absurd!"

"Oh, we are going to the Arch, but he won't be with us. He'll be working in the hotel, and you can always contact him."

It couldn't be easy to be an interpreter-escort under normal circumstances, let alone this far-from-normal situation. The Chinese seemed to be in a collective lousy mood; the investigation meant a prolonged stay in St. Louis, with all sorts of restrictions imposed. Detective Lenich's questions, while quite routine, must have sounded unpleasant to the Chinese, she thought as she took her shower. As she stepped out, still wrapped in a towel, the phone shrilled again.

"Sorry to call so early in the morning, Catherine," Chen said.

"You aren't that early. This is the third or fourth call this morning." She took a look at the clock, drying her hair with the towel. Not even eight yet. "I'll come down. We're meeting at eight-thirty, right?"

"Yes. Yesterday I tried to talk to hotel security, but we didn't have time. So this morning I thought you might be able to help me before we leave. Just a few questions. It won't take too long."

"Fine, I'll be down in one minute."

She dressed quickly and headed down to the lobby. She saw him standing in a corner, toying with a cell phone in his hand, a plastic bag on the chair beside him. He was dressed in a three-piece black suit with a scarlet silk tie. He looked like a Chinese official.

"Good morning, Miss Rohn."

"Morning, Mr. Chen."

"Look, I called you with this cell phone," he said smiling. "Last night, Detective Lenich talked about the hotel phone records. There's one thing I forgot to tell him. Two of us also have cell phones. Bao and I. I have to call China while traveling from one city to the next; my mother is in poor health. The prepaid cell phone is expensive. I don't know how and why Bao has one. I don't even know his number."

"I'm sorry to hear about your mother's health," she said. But the part about the cell phone was strange, she thought. He could have told Lenich about it. It was an odd thing to say to her first thing in the morning. She looked up at him and he flipped the phone closed emphatically.

"Oh, this is for you," he said, already changing the subject as he handed the plastic bag to her. "Last night, there were people in my room, and I came over in a hurry. The writing set is from Mr. Gu. The book is from me. You like Chinese poetry, I know."

"Thank you so much, Chen. Can I take a look? The Chinese way is to open the present later, I know."

"Now we are in St. Louis, so do as St. Louisians do."

Shasha's appearance in the lobby, however, interrupted their conversation. "Oh, you two are down early," Shasha said in mock surprise.

"Miss Rohn has been doing a great job for us," he said. "To express our gratitude, I am giving her some small gifts."

"The writing set is expensive," Shasha said, picking up the miniature water ladle and turning it over to read the tiny engraving on its back. "Eighteen-karat gold. I have a similar set at home. Four or five thousand yuan."

"Really!" Chen exclaimed. "A friend gave it to me, and I think it will make a good present for Miss Rohn, a would-be sinologist."

He didn't reveal that it was a gift to her from Mr. Gu and Catherine knew why.

"A new book by you?" Shasha went on, picking up the book.

"An advance copy," he said. "A collection of classic Chinese poetry in translation."

"You never told me about it, Chen. You must have prepared the present just for her," Shasha said smiling, turning toward Catherine. "Our poet must have brought the book all the way here for you."

Catherine smiled without making a response to Shasha. "Thank you, Mr. Chen. I like Chinese poetry. It's a wonderful present."

Shasha turned to the inscription page, on which were two lines he had copied in English: *Anguish of separation is like spring grass: / the farther you go, the more it grows.* The couplet might be from a poem in the collection, but Shasha didn't read English.

The other Chinese began to show up. It was the time for them to set out for the Arch. Catherine clapped her hands for attention.

"I've talked to the city government. Your prolonged stay here may cause you inconveniences, they understand. So they'll try to do everything possible to make your visit to the city a comfortable one. For one thing, if you would like to call back to China, they have offered to provide you with prepaid international phone cards. As for those of you with cell phones, you may also have prepaid cards. You have a cell phone, Mr. Chen, don't you?"

"Yes. As the delegation head, I have to take care of a lot of things, but I have just put enough money onto my cell."

"I have a cell phone too," Bao said.

She was aware of a surprised murmur among the Chinese, and of a subtle glance from Chen. "Let me put down the number and the mode, so the phone card will work with yours, Mr. Bao," she said, taking the phone and jotting the number on a notebook. "Now let's go to the Arch."

The hotel had arranged a minivan for them. Most of the Chinese carried cameras in their hands. In spite of the interpreter's death, they wanted to have a memorable day with the celebrated Arch towering overhead.

Once they arrived at the Arch, the tallest man-made monument in the United States, the Chinese writers started wondering at close range, touching the individual slabs of stainless steel and imagining how all of them had been put together. They began to take pictures, posing with the Arch shimmering in the background.

Visitors usually wanted to go to the top of the Arch and the Chinese proved to be no exception. Catherine went to buy them the tram tickets. There were a lot of people in line for the tram, and their turn wouldn't come for about forty-five minutes. Looking back, she saw the Chinese were still busy taking pictures. It appeared that Chen was a popular photographer among the group.

So she was left alone. She sat on a bench near the tram entrance. It was ironic. In Shanghai, Chen had played a similar escort role. If there was any difference, it was that he tried to do more than the Chinese authorities had instructed him to. Now things seemed to be coming full circle.

She started thinking about the CIA theory regarding Chen's secret mission. She failed to see how, what with his delegation responsibilities, and in the midst of his fellow writers, it would be possible. According to the CIA, Chen hadn't yet made any suspicious moves except for calling on pay phones instead of using the hotel phones. Chen wouldn't have come all this way to make phone calls.

And Chen apparently had his own suspicions about the homicide case. He agreed with Lenich about probing among the writers, and then there was his hint about Bao's cell phone earlier this morning.

She opened the book he had given her. A bound galley of Chinese love poetry translated by Chen and Yang, a celebrated scholar persecuted to death during the Cultural Revolution. According to Chen's introduction, most of the work was done by Yang, Chen only added a few poems not included in the original manuscript. She turned to a poem entitled "The Lines Written in Dinghui Temple, Huangzhou," written by Su Dongpo, a Song dynasty poet she'd liked in her college years. Chen liked Su too, she remembered.

The waning moon hangs on the sparse tung twigs,
the night deep, silent.
An apparition of a solitary wild goose
moves like a hermit.

Startled, it turns back,
its sorrow unknown to others.
Trying each of the chilly boughs,
it chooses not to perch.
Freezing, the maple leaves fall
over the Wu River.

A footnote by Chen said that it wasn't necessarily a love poem. Still, she wanted to read it as one—in a way that she wanted to be moved. For the lonely wild goose could be about him, and about her as well.

Then she put down the book, frowning, as she took out her ringing cell phone. She recognized the number.

"He's a conscientious head," she briefed David Marvin, the CIA officer assigned to work with her, "busy with his delegation responsibilities. I don't see how he could have the time or energy for another mission, whatever it might be."

"We've just learned that he wasn't with the delegation for two afternoons in L.A. One afternoon he spent with an old friend of his, and on the other he claimed he wasn't well, staying at the hotel instead of going to Disneyland with the delegation. Besides, he seems to have spent some time on the computers at a number of college libraries."

"What did he do there?"

"Mostly Internet searches on Xing and some companies possibly related to him."

"When I was in China, I tried to get onto American Web sites, but most of them were blocked. So he may be trying to get information about Xing while here." She added after a pause, "Still, he didn't come all the way here for computer research, did he?"

"Well, I wanted to keep you posted. If you have anything, let me know."

"I will. Bye."

It was time for the Chinese to move over to the tram station so she led them to the line there. Underneath the towering Arch was a museum called Westward Expansion. They only had three or four minutes before their turn, but Zhong and Shasha moved over and started taking pictures again. Chen smiled at her apologetically, holding the camera.

When their turn came they had to go on two tram cars. Shasha, Bao, Peng, and Zhong sat in the first one, Catherine and Chen, the second. They were not alone, though. There was also an old American couple sitting in the same car, who probably couldn't speak or understand Chinese. However, both Chen and Catherine felt they had better talk in a guarded way as the tram started to climb, in jumps and jerks.

"Thank you for your idea about the cell phone card. It was brilliant."

"You think there's something wrong about his cell phone?"

"I'm not sure, but it's too expensive for him. And he doesn't know many people here," he said, before changing the subject. "I've got faxes about Little Huang from China. There was nothing in his background. Nothing that justifies it. Such a young interpreter."

She knew what he was driving at. In a case of premeditated murder, there had to be a motive, but Chen didn't see one. Huang wasn't a plausible target for Detective Lenich's theory.

They were in the dark, as the tram bumped up through an almost vertically rising tunnel, with nothing but the somber concrete walls surrounding them.

"Your delegation appointment was made at the last minute. So you may not know everything." Anything was possible with Chen: that was one thing her boss had said to her.

"I have thought about it, and the others might be possible but not Little Huang."

Before they could discuss it any further, the tram jerked to a stop. They stepped out with the old couple. The top level of the Arch was like a long, narrow corridor crammed with people looking out of small square windows along the both sides. They had a great view of downtown and of the murky, ship-studded Mississippi River. She'd lost sight of the other Chinese, who must have moved on ahead. She stood beside Chen, whispering in his ear.

"We know what case you were investigating in Shanghai."

"How?"

"Xing applied for political asylum here. It's been widely reported in the American newspapers. It's a quandary for our government so we've paid close attention to the development of the case in China."

"I'm not here because of Xing," he said.

"But it doesn't take a chief inspector to lead a writers' delegation." She had a sense of déjà vu. In another city, she had voiced similar questions. *It didn't take a chief inspector to act as a tour guide.* But it was more than that—there was their reversal of roles for the part of tour guide.

"Things in China are complicated. Honestly, I don't know why I was chosen to head the delegation. What I was investigating in Shanghai might not have been pleasant to some people, I think. That's a possible reason why they sent me out."

"Sent you out? What do you mean?"

"As a delegation head, I had to stay away from the investigation."

"But that's only a matter of two or three weeks. What's the point—"

Then the Chinese writers discovered them and came over excitedly.

"We've been looking everywhere for you," Zhong said.

"The tram ride is not for the claustrophobic," Shasha said with a giggle.

Afterward, in the midst of the Chinese, Catherine had hardly any time alone with Chen.

That evening, they went to a dinner held at a magnificent Chinese restaurant on Olive Street. A banquet of *yajin*—to relieve the shock. A representative of the city government also attended. There were speeches of formalities from both sides. In spite of all the condolences, people did not lose their appetite. It was a long and good meal and they didn't get back to the hotel until after ten.

Back in her hotel room, Catherine wondered whether Chen would phone her again. He didn't. Others kept calling in, however, including her mother. She decided not to mention Chen to her mother, who would perhaps ask questions for hours.

She then tried to do some research on Xing on the laptop, which had been delivered to the room. It was a long and fruitless search. She was tired and sleepy. Absentmindedly, she keyed in the name of Chen Cao in Chinese. There were a number of articles about his police work. Quite a few about his writing too. She found a recent poem of his entitled "35 Birthday Night."

2:30 A.M. A dog barks
against the moon-bleached night.

Is the dog barking into my dream
or am I dreaming of the dog?

There was a siren against the night sky. She rubbed her eyes. She was awake, alone, reading a poem in the hotel room.

24

FURTHER CHANGES TO THE delegation activity schedule appeared inevitable. The long-planned visit to Mark Twain's home was canceled. Zhong raised the safety issue regarding the caves, where people could easily get lost, and Bao, who had passionately proposed the visit in Los Angeles, became the one against it in St. Louis. Chen wasn't so keen on going to Hannibal, either.

Catherine was busy making new arrangements for the delegation, and Detective Lenich wasn't coming by until later that morning. But Chen had a visitor in his room after breakfast. It was Shasha. She'd come to thank him. While in Los Angeles, he had interpreted for her when she spoke to an American agent. The agent had phoned, saying that a large publisher was interested in her books.

"Thank you," she said. "You are a good boss. And a good friend too."

"I have done nothing. It's your book, Shasha."

"I wish I could do something for you too, Chen. You seem to have so much on your mind."

"The investigation of Little Huang's death is going nowhere, and we are stuck here in St. Louis. As the delegation head, I can't help but be concerned."

"It's not your fault. You were dragged into the delegation. I don't think anybody could have done better in your position."

"Now that we are on the subject, Shasha, I have a question for you. Chairman Wang called me just two days before the trip. I knew little about the conference, or about the delegation. Now the Americans believe that except for you and I, everyone else in the delegation could be a suspect."

"Why?"

"From five to six-fifteen that afternoon, I was reading in a café down in the mall, and a bookseller there confirmed my alibi. You called from your room to my room around five-forty, and the front desk also remembered you picking up my room key shortly afterward. In other words, you and I alone have solid alibis."

"You are a cop, Chen," she said sharply, "I don't think I am in a position to discuss this with you."

"No, I don't suspect anyone in our delegation. But to discuss the case with Detective Lenich, I need to know more about them."

"Well," she said slowly, looking at him in the face, "I would like to ask you a question first."

"Go ahead, Shasha."

"You already knew Catherine, didn't you?"

"Yes, we met in Shanghai," he said, surprised by her observation, but determined to say no more than necessary.

"The way she looks at you, I knew," she said. "You may take me as a busybody, but to tell the truth, your friend Ling wanted me to keep an eye on you. Now don't get her wrong. Whatever problems there may have been between you two, she's concerned about you."

"Yes, you move in the same circle, I should have known, but let's not talk about her for the moment—"

"Let me finish. She told me she had her reasons to be concerned about you—*about* you, not because of your relationship, you know what I mean, though she didn't go into any details with me."

"I see," he said somberly. Ling could have called him directly, although the details of her concerns wouldn't have been pleasant or positive to him as a cop, especially in the midst of an investigation on the number-one corruption case in China, he supposed. "Thank you, Shasha."

"That's why I have been concerned too. Ling is a good friend of mine. Not every high cadre's child really wants to be an HCC—not me, not Ling. Now, what do you want to know?"

"How were the people selected for the delegation? For instance, Peng doesn't write anymore, and he hardly speaks at the conference. Considering what he suffered during all the political movements, some compensation is understandable—"

"Who didn't suffer those years?" Shasha said with a cynical smile. "But his daughter has married an HCCC."

"HCCC?"

"High Cadre's Children Cadre. In other words, those HCC themselves have become high cadres. Peng's son-in-law has been rising fast—already a member of the Central Party Committee. So he put in a word for Peng with the Writers' Association. 'The old man has suffered enough. We have to think of a symbolic compensation for him. It's also good for China's image. Perhaps you may arrange a visit abroad for him.' "

"So he was chosen because of his son-in-law," he said, "not because of his work."

"And Bao was chosen for symbolic considerations too, though different ones. He complained to everybody—as a representative of the working-class writers left out in the cold in the nineties. As for me, nobody put in a word for me. The people at the Writers' Association know more about my connections than about my writings. Now Zhong might have come into the delegation on his own merits, but his mistress in Beijing, a well-connected writer, must have made phone calls for him too."

"Oh, I didn't know that," he said, but now he knew why Zhong kept calling back to Beijing. "Still, I'm not qualified to be the delegation head. Why would they choose me?"

"You keep saying that you aren't qualified. But who really is? Don't be so hard on yourself. In China today, with everything turned upside down, make the best of the situation for yourself—as long as it isn't at the cost of others. What else can you do?"

"Thank you for telling me all this, Shasha."

"One more thing," she said rising. "Because of Ling's request, I have been observing things happening around you. All of a sudden, Bao has a cell phone. One evening, I overheard him talking on the cell phone, mentioning your name."

Shortly before lunchtime, Catherine proposed her new plan for the day: an evening of opera at the Fox Theater, and before that, shopping at Asian grocery stores on nearby Grand Avenue. Chen made a different suggestion. A visit to Eliot's old home in the Central West End. No one else seemed to be interested, though.

"T. S. Eliot is the *guiren* for you," Zhong said with a smile.

Chen smiled by way of response. In Chinese, *guiren* meant an unexpected helper, as if preordained. It was true that a large number of readers came to know Chen through Eliot.

"Really!" Catherine feigned surprise.

"Well, the success of the translation came more from Eliot's status as a modernist. Some critics claimed—tongue-in-cheek—that it was necessary to understand modernism for the realization of 'four modernizations' for China."

"Yes," Shasha cut in with a giggle, "a young girl put a Chinese copy of 'The Waste Land' as something symbolic of her modernist knowledge on top of her dowry in a tricycle, parading the book all the way through Nanjing Road."

"No wonder," Catherine said. "Mr. Chen wouldn't miss this opportunity for the world."

So they reached a compromise. As Peng wanted to take a nap after lunch, the delegation was going to the groceries in the late afternoon, and then to the theater as suggested by Catherine. Chen was going to the Central West End, alone, "like a pilgrim," as Shasha commented.

Not exactly alone, though.

"I don't think there's a need for me to interpret at the Chinese groceries. Nor at the theater, people are not allowed to speak there. The minivan driver will take you there, and then bring you back after the opera. There are several Asian restaurants in the Grand area. Choose one you like." Catherine went on, turning to Chen, "Let me drive you to the Central West End, Mr. Chen. We'll discuss more about the schedule changes on the way."

"Yes, that's so considerate of you, Catherine," Shasha commented. "Our poet has been working hard. He deserves a break in his favorite area."

"Sounds like a plan," Chen said. "Comrade Bao, you'll take care of the group."

It was a practical arrangement. No one raised any objections, except Bao, who declared in a miserable tone, "It's really *yangzhui* to watch opera. I would rather stay in the hotel."

"Yangzhui?" Catherine repeated it in puzzlement. She hadn't heard the Chinese expression before.

Literally, *yangzhui* meant "foreign or exotic punishment or torture." In its extended usage, it could refer to any unpleasant experience. For Bao, an opera in a foreign language for three hours would indeed be long and boring. Chen chose not to explain. He simply said, "Comrade Bao may be a bit tired."

But Bao changed his mind. In spite of his disinclination, he agreed to take the delegation to the theater. "One of us has to be responsible for the delegation, Chen. So you can go to the Central West End."

Outside the hotel, Catherine had a greenish car of German make. Not Volkswagen, but a brand not available in Shanghai. Chen took his seat beside her. A seat belt slid across his shoulder automatically. The moment she put the key into the ignition, however, her cell phone rang. She started the car and began to drive with the phone in her hand. It didn't sound like a business call, he thought. He leaned back and looked out of the window. In spite of the time he had spent studying the St. Louis guidebook, he couldn't make out the direction. Fumbling in his pocket for the city map, he noticed the car already slowing down.

"Euclid," she said, flipping the phone closed. "Central West End is over there."

Central West End was an area with a marked difference. Small streets, quaint buildings, sidewalk cafés, colorful boutiques. The streets also boasted the city's oldest and most impressive private homes. To Chen, all this seemed to have changed little from Eliot's day.

It took her quite a while, however, to find a parking place. As they walked out, turning into a side street, the evening breeze came like a greeting from a half-forgotten poem. They were in no hurry to talk about the delegation schedule. It was an excuse, they both knew.

For this evening, for the moment at least, at Central West End, he wanted to feel like a Chinese poet, walking along the streets an English poet had walked.

And to feel like a man walking in the company of a woman he cared for. It was the first time that they were really alone.

Whatever might come next, he didn't want to think about it. She didn't seem to be in a hurry to talk about their work, either.

"It's pleasant to walk here on a summer evening," she said.

"Yes, it's so different here."

Fragmented lines came with the evening spreading out against the sky; he contemplated, against all the possibilities . . .

Do I dare, do I dare?

Perhaps it was here a poet had once had the impulse to say the words, but failed to bring himself to the task. Perhaps too meticulous to roll the moment into a decisive ball . . .

He checked himself. It was absurd of him to think of Eliot. A cop, at this moment more than ever, he should be aware of his responsibility, with a homicide case on his hands, another related murder case in China, and in the company of another cop.

"What are you thinking, Chen?"

"I'm glad to be here with you."

"Did you ever think about an evening like this?"

"Yes, a couple of times."

She walked by his side, their shoulders occasionally touching. She wore a black dress with thin straps. Possibly the same dress she had had on the night of the Beijing opera at the Shanghai City Government Auditorium.

A squirrel jumped over a tiny rainwater pool. He saw a gray-haired woman walking toward them, and he approached her. "Excuse me, do you know where Eliot used to live?"

"Eliot? Who is he?" the woman said in surprise, pushing the gold-rimmed spectacles up her nose ridge. She looked like a schoolteacher, carrying a plastic grocery bag in her hand.

"T. S. Eliot, you know, the poet who wrote 'The Waste Land.' "

"Never heard of him. Eliot. I've lived here for twenty years. What is the waste land?"

"Thank you," Catherine cut in. "Central West End is quite a large area, Chen. We can ask at the bookstore."

"Yes, the people there are nice," the woman said, eyeing them for the first time with interest. "Sorry, I can't help you."

"Don't expect everybody to be so knowledgeable about Eliot," Catherine said. "Let me tell you something, Chen. Last year, I saw a movie called *Tom and Viv.* A choice made under your influence. As it turned out, I was the only one in the audience."

"Really! I've read about the movie. Too much of a feminist emphasis. Vivian might have been a poet in her own right, but praise of her shouldn't come at his expense."

"I'm not going to argue with you about feminism this evening," she said with a wistful smile. "That evening, I wished that you were sitting there with me. I didn't understand some references in the movie, but I could figure out Vivian's crush on him. So let us go—to the bookstore. Eliot always comes first for you."

"No, you know it's not true," he said, meeting her eyes, but she looked away. In the dusk, he was not so sure about the color of her eyes.

The bookstore in question proved to be nice, one of the few independent bookstores that survived in the city, she explained. The manager was young but knowledgeable. "Oh, it's not too far away. Eliot's old home is a brownstone," he said amiably, accompanying them to the door. "Go straight from here. Westminster Place. You won't miss it."

Walking out of the store, Chen saw a café to its left, with white plastic tables and chairs set outside under colorful umbrellas. There were several people sitting there, talking at leisure, stirring memories or desires in their cups. It was like a scene he had read. Then it was juxtaposed with another he had seen. A picture she had given him at the end of their joint investigation in Shanghai. He turned to her.

"Oh, remember the picture you gave me? The one of you sitting at a sidewalk café."

"That café is on Delmar," she said. "My apartment is close."

"I would love to go there," he said sincerely.

The visit to Eliot's home turned out to be a disappointment. It was one of the ordinary-looking old houses in a quiet, private neighborhood. The umber-colored front with the symmetrical black shutters gave the impression of an apartment building rather than a family house. Still, he climbed up the stone steps to the door, and she took a picture of him standing there, with a small historical-site sign behind him bearing the name of Henry Ware Eliot. He wondered whether it would be appropriate for him to knock at the door.

She solved the problem by taking his hand in hers and leading him into a lane to the back garden. There was an ancient board saying "I'm in the garden" on the garden door. She stood on tiptoes on a ridge, peeking over the tall fence. He followed her example, looking over her bare shoulder. He saw nothing there except a tree draped with green vines.

A neighbor came out, saying the house was now owned by a well-to-do high-tech entrepreneur who was on vacation somewhere else.

"The swallows, visitors / to the mansions of those noble families / in the bygone days, are flying / into the houses of ordinary people."

"You're in a poetry-quoting mood again?" Catherine said.

"I wonder whether this is Eliot's house."

"I'm sure it is, but even if people welcomed you in, you wouldn't see much inside after so many years."

"You are right."

They started heading back. They weren't in a hurry to return to the hotel. The visit to Eliot's home was an excuse, like all other excuses. They had things to discuss.

"Let's go to a café. We can sit and talk," he said.

So they walked to a café, which was larger than the one next to the bookstore. A performance might have been going on inside. The café window presented dancing music notes in neon lights. There were also chairs and tables outside, where an old man sat drowsing over an empty paper cup.

She said, "Let's sit outside."

He had an espresso, she had a glass of white wine.

He knew they had to talk about their work. This was an opportunity he couldn't afford to miss. Still, he didn't start immediately.

But she said, "Tell me more about your investigation in China." It was a simple, direct question. She had been thinking along the same line.

She had to know what he'd been doing, he knew, and it was a risk he was going to take. After all, he had thrown in his lot with her—in another city, in another investigation. And here, she had already shown she trusted him by playing that trick with Bao's cell phone. They had been collaborating as partners.

They were sitting close. Chief Inspector Chen was not going to be doing anything against the interest of the Chinese government, he thought, as long as he didn't give out specific details about those high-ranking officials. A general picture of China's corruption was nothing new, particularly as Xing's case was being widely reported here. So he told her about the Xing investigation under the committee and brought in his theory about An's death. She was an attentive audience, responding with occasional questions and suggestions.

"She might have contacted her people after the talk with you," she said.

"Yes, that's possible."

Nor did he try to conceal his own suspicion about the delegation appointment, though he gave her all the official reasons Chairman Wang had given him.

"They wanted to get you out of the way," she added, thinking, "but only for a couple of weeks?"

It was a question she'd raised on the top of the Arch, where he didn't have the time to discuss it. She had a point. If people had intended to put him out of the picture, they could have easily done so without bothering to arrange a trip like this.

"I've been thinking about that too," he said. "It doesn't make sense unless dramatic change was anticipated during this period, but I can't think of any."

"Let me ask you another question, Chen. Were you told to do anything about Xing here?"

"No, no one told me, trust me, Catherine," he said, reaching to take her hand across the table on impulse. "There's no point sending someone like me for the purpose."

She nodded, her hand remaining in his.

"Nobody told me anything," he repeated. "I've only groped in the dark."

"What do you mean?"

"I'm not a cop here. What can I do?" He decided to be vaguely honest. "Groping for information about Xing is about all I can possibly do here."

"What's the point?"

"Difficult to say. Perhaps it's like playing *go* chess. Occasionally you have to move anyway, though the move itself may seem pointless for the moment."

So he summarized what he had tried to accomplish without giving specific details or revealing the names of the people involved. After Little Huang's death, he couldn't be too careful.

"It could be dangerous," she said, tightening her grasp. "If your investigation became known—to Xing, and to people in Beijing."

"I know. But I also remember what my father once told me, '*A man has to do what he should do, even if it is impossible for him to do.*' "

The waiter came over to them with the menu. Neither was hungry. But he thought he should order something. He looked at the wine list, which presented all the unfamiliar names.

"You choose," he said.

She did, pronouncing a wine name he hadn't heard before, in French or in Italian. She then leaned back and crossed her legs in a leisurely manner. The wine came and she took a small sip, nodding her approval. He was becoming slightly uncomfortable. He wondered whether he would come to be like someone in that TV series, at home in an American bar.

The evening clouds started unfolding in sensual peace, as if being smoothed by long, slender fingers. Among the glasses, among the talk, among the indistinct shadows on the sprinkled street, he felt disoriented.

In a couple of hours, the delegation would be going back to the hotel, but it didn't matter much if he returned late. Everybody was aware of his passion for Eliot. "Lost in the 'Waste Land,' " he could joke about his absence.

He didn't want to spend the evening just talking about a corrupt Chinese official hiding away like a fattened rat. He was sitting with her, their fingers entwined, in a café in the Central West End. In an evening Eliot, or Prufrock, dared not to dream about, with the streets muttering into retreat, against a hundred visions and revisions.

"China man, Chinglish!" Several kids appeared to come out of nowhere, shouting, scuttling along on their scooters, and pointing their fingers at him. The scooters resembled a miraculous vehicle in a children's book of mythology he had read at their age.

What they had discussed here had already started him thinking in a new direction. Discussion helped, he knew. There could be something terribly wrong in his work, he suspected.

"I have something for you," she said, producing a folder. "A transcript of Bao's cell phone calls. Perhaps you may make something out of it."

"Oh, you are so effective."

"Our people in L.A. have been following Xing and his associates closely. Especially his mysterious next-door neighbor. The man who called Bao had been seen in their company, so they tapped his line as well."

The first page was from a phone call to Bao on the day of their arrival in St. Louis. From L.A. The caller must have known Bao well.

> "I have phoned your hotel several times, Master Bao, and they told me you have not arrived yet. I was worried. So I'm making this call on your cell phone."
>
> "Don't worry. The highway traffic was terrible. We have just checked in."

"Is that the hotel you have shown me in the list?"

"Yes, it's a good hotel. A five-star one, close to the Arch. I don't know how to pronounce its name in English."

"That cop still has the best room?"

"Don't mention him again. He alone has a massage bath in his room. And he simply takes it for granted. He must be luxuriating in the American bubbles right now, I bet."

"A typical bourgeoisie—you are absolutely right, Master Bao. It's depressing even to talk about him. I'm calling you because I know someone in the shopping mall under your hotel. Old Fan, the owner of a Chinese buffet. Mention my name, and he will probably give you a treat. He may not have read your poetry, though."

"Yes, I'll go there."

"Well, I'll call you again if I have some other information."

There were several earlier phone records. Chen knew he did not have the time to peruse all of them. That call alone was enough to arouse serious suspicion. The mysterious caller might have been a fan of Bao's poetry, but a fan, however passionate or devoted, would not have made a long-distance call, from a public phone, to his "master," talking about the luxurious room of another writer, or about another restaurant owner he knew slightly. Furthermore, they must have had earlier discussions about Chen. At the least Bao had shown him the itinerary of their visit—including the name of the hotel in St. Louis.

"According to Detective Lenich," she said, "a Chinese man asked about your room number at the front desk, and then made a call in the lobby."

Chen recalled now. That afternoon, upon his arrival, a call came into his room. When he picked it up, the caller hung up.

He didn't give it a thought at the time.

He knew he was in more serious trouble than he cared to admit. A possibility he had so far refused to acknowledge scuttled across the floors of his subconscious. He took a drink, trying not to show any change in his expression.

"There's one thing about being a poet," he said. "Occasionally, you may be followed by your fans all the way."

"Here is the tape. The transcript was done in a hurry. So you can listen more carefully."

"I don't know how I can thank you enough, Catherine."

"I'm concerned about you. It's also in the common interest of our two countries that nothing else happens to your delegation," she said, glancing at her watch. "It's time for us to go back, I think."

"Yes, I'm afraid so."

It was a fact, he knew, but it disappointed him. He didn't want to talk about it. The music from the café seemed to be slowing down with a dying fall.

There was a black bat flitting around over their heads.

25

THE FOLLOWING MORNING PROMISED to be an easy one for Catherine, with the delegation scheduled for a visit to Washington University.

"You must have stayed up quite late," Shasha said to her over breakfast. "Chen could be a romantic poet."

Catherine smiled without giving a response. It was true that she had stayed up late last night. Back from the Central West End, she had had a long discussion with Detective Lenich on the phone. He stuck to his theory of insider involvement. For such a hypothesis, Little Huang had to be somebody of secret significance. According to Chen, however, there was nothing to support that. She believed her Chinese partner and Lenich had not been that pleased with her inclination. Then she did more research on her laptop, late into the night.

When she finally went to bed, she read a couple of short poems in the collection Chen had given her.

The moon rising above the sea
we share, far, far away
as you may find yourself.
Sad, sleepless, in the long night,
in separation, I think of you.
The moon so touchingly bright,
I extinguish the candle and step out,
my clothes wet by dew.
Alas, I cannot hold the moonlight
in my slender hand. I go back
into the room, perhaps
to dream again
of reunion.

It was a touching poem, but how could a Tang dynasty poet be so sure of someone far, far away missing him like that? That was the last fleeting, self-contradicting thought in her mind before she sank into a dreamless night.

When they arrived at Washington University, there was a group of Chinese-speaking staff and students assembled to welcome the delegation. They were quite eager to talk to the visitors in Chinese, so she didn't have to interpret that much.

She didn't have any opportunity to talk to Chen. At least he didn't appear concerned now that he had studied Bao's phone record. He talked with Bao in high spirits. He moved around like a fish in the water—at the university founded by Eliot's grandfather. Chen took pictures of the bronze plaque indicating that at the front entrance. He was eager to find out more about Eliot, he declared. In contrast to the other delegation members, all of whom dressed formally, Chen wore a white jacket with the emblem of Washington University. It was a present given to him by the dean of the Arts and Sciences school in return for a copy of his Chinese translation of Eliot. Chen had put the jacket on immediately.

Bao succeeded in finding a copy of his poems in the East Asian Library, and discussed them with an old professor who had studied Chinese poetry in the sixties. Shasha was radiant. Several students who had read her books gathered around asking for her signature. Peng started reading Chinese newspapers in the library. Some of the Taiwan and Hong Kong publications were not accessible on the mainland. Zhong was nowhere to be seen at first, but it was then reported he couldn't tear himself away from the sound system of the university theater.

There would be a lunch reception in honor of the Chinese delegation around twelve. A lot of people were coming. Some from other schools, some from the local Chinese community. Chen was going to give a talk in the early afternoon. As Catherine started walking toward him, an old gray-haired American woman approached him first.

"Oh, you have come back, Professor Pu Zhongwei!"

"You—" Chen turned around in astonishment.

It was a mistake—an understandable one with his jacket bearing that emblem. As the old woman shuffled away with a profusion of apologies, Catherine felt a sudden chill pouring down her spine.

To some Americans, Chinese people must have looked more or less alike. If Chen had been taken by mistake here, the same could have happened to Huang outside of the hotel. So somebody else—Chen—could have been the real target. The murderer might have followed Huang out of Chen's room and killed him without taking a close look.

It was not a likely mistake, but not unthinkable for a hired killer who knew nothing about Chen except his room number. Huang's emerging out of Chen's room, having taken a bath there, and then closing the door after him would have been enough. Huang, about the same height as Chen, actually bore a slight resemblance.

Thoughts came in somersaults across her mind, as Catherine stood transfixed there, watching Chen talk to American students about T. S. Eliot.

"A Chinese reader once told me that he quoted Eliot to impress his girlfriend because the poet was considered a modernist. Now a successful entrepreneur, he is trying to introduce the musical *Cats* to a Shanghai audience. He says he can make a huge profit of it, and he makes no mistake about making money . . ."

The murderer must have realized his mistake since then, she contemplated. So the effort would not be dropped. What had prompted him to strike in St. Louis, she didn't know, but Chen's investigation must have come close to hitting home. So Xing and his associates had to get him out of the way. With the cops on the scene, the murderer might be more careful, prowling in the dark, but still capable of striking out at any moment.

The police might do a good job of protection here, but there was no guaranteeing Chen's safety elsewhere in the U.S., or back in China, as long as he persisted with the investigation. Nothing could help Chen except a fundamental change of the situation—in which the people posing the threat no longer had the capability or necessity to do so.

Chen moved on to talk with Professor Thurston of the Chinese studies department, she observed, about Ming and Qing short stories. She edged close to him. Chen tried to respond with the newest terms favored by the serious sinologist.

"I don't know how to deconstruct a Chinese story, or how to read it in the light of New Historicism, but for a text formed in the process of passing it from one storyteller to another, generation after generation, some dissimilation would be imaginable in terms of re-creation through readers' response."

"You have put it well," Professor Thurston said. "That's why I've included a detailed bibliography in the anthology."

"Oh, what's up, Catherine?" Chen appeared relieved at the sight of her.

"People don't need my interpretation. I think I'll excuse myself for a couple of hours. Things are piling up on my desk, you know. I'll come back for your reading."

"Take your time." Chen added, "It's just a random talk about Eliot in China."

"I'll be back in time," she said. "It's your favorite topic. I wouldn't miss it for anything."

Instead of going back to her office, however, she headed to her apartment, which was close to the university. Taking a shortcut through the overpass across Mallinckrodt Road, she walked fast. She nearly stumbled at the end of the staircase. She didn't think she'd sprained her ankle, but she slowed down, recalling what she'd experienced in a dusk-enveloped garden in Suzhou.

The moment she got to her place, she kicked off her shoes. Her ankle wasn't swollen, but it hurt. She slumped onto the sofa. It wasn't the time for a break, she told herself. So she got up and made a pot of coffee. Another habit picked up in his company.

She shuddered again at the possibility of Chen being the real target. There was a lot Chen might not have told her, and there were things Chen himself might not have known. But he must have considered this possibility too. She paced about the room, barefoot, on a wool rug brought back from Shanghai. Out the window, cars and buses rolled by like waves along the street, and people moved on, hurrying to their own destinations. All of a sudden, she wished that Chen could be one of them, walking toward her apartment at this moment. Perhaps she was still under the spell of a poem she had read last night.

She stands leaning against the balcony,
alone, looking out to the river
to thousands of sails passing along
none is the one she waits for,
the sun setting slant,
the water running silent into the distance.

But it was only the fluctuation of a fleeting moment, she knew. There was no possibility of his stepping back into her life like that.

Across the street, she saw an old couple standing by a red-painted newsstand, unfolding the newspaper, pointing, talking, and patting each other's shoulder, so meaningful to themselves, but inaudible, incomprehensible to others. Distantly, it reminded her of a shadow play in the Forbidden City.

She took out the transcript of Bao's phone conversation the first day in St. Louis. It made more sense now. The phone call was really about Chen.

What about the information she had about Xing? If she couldn't make use of it, it could be the result of her insufficient background knowledge. These corruption cases in China were extremely complicated, involving high-ranking officials in a maze of connections.

Her mission was one of damage control, and among other things, it was her responsibility to prevent anything else from happening to the delegation, and to Chen. It would be in everyone's interest for the conference to come to a conclusion without further incident. What she was going to do was justified, she decided, even from the perspective of her government.

She was ready to pass to Chen the information about Xing's activity in the U.S. It wasn't just for the sake of Chief Inspector Chen, she told herself, as she turned on the computer.

According to the CIA file, Xing had been making frequent phone calls to China. Aware of possible surveillance here, he spoke cautiously, both on his home phones and cell phones. What made those conversations difficult to decipher was his use of the local triad jargon. Also, he referred to his contacts by their nicknames, such as "Small Boss," "Crocodile," "Big Brother." Who these people could possibly be, the CIA had no clue. Still, there were a couple of points the CIA interpreters underlined.

Xing had mentioned several times that his mother was worried about somebody, the "little boy," still in China. Who this "little boy" was, the CIA had failed to figure out. In one of the calls, Xing seemed to have lost contact with the "little boy," and he asked about his whereabouts anxiously. After a number of phone calls, he must have got in touch with the "little boy" again.

Another point was Xing's connection with the local triad. There were discussions about triad protection of Xing in L.A. Several nicknames were brought up in that regard, like "Black Shark" and "Little Tiger," most of which sounded characteristic of those organizations. Still, in spite of the considerable amount paid for his personal protection, Xing hadn't made any requests for an attempt against anyone else. In one of the highly jargonized conversations, the head of the local triad seemed to have mysteriously made contact, as Xing said to somebody else, with a high-ranking official in Beijing.

In addition, he seemed to have made more phone calls in the last few days. While the contents of the conversations remained largely inexplicable, Xing sounded anxious or even desperate, seemingly under extreme pressure.

Catherine then tried to listen to the phone records herself, but after a short while, she gave up. Xing spoke with a strong Fujian accent. She barely made out a fifth of the contents, which were further muddled by all the jargon thrown in.

But it might not be so obscure to Chief Inspector Chen, who had been working on the case, with access to lots of information unknown to her. He might be able to get some clues out of it, and to make a difference. She printed out the transcript. After a moment's thought, she also copied the transcript onto a floppy and picked up a cassette tape of the phone calls.

She put everything in her bag. Rubbing her ankle, she was ready to go back to Washington University, where Chen would deliver his talk on "Eliot in China."

26

IT WAS STILL EARLY in the morning when the phone rang in Detective Yu's small room. He took a look at the radio clock on the nightstand. Not six yet. Peiqin was still asleep, her bare legs and feet reaching out, so white against the light green towel blanket in the pale light. He picked up the phone and moved down, so as not to wake her up. But there was not much space for him to do so. Qinqin was asleep in the back part, which was partitioned out as his room.

"A very important development, son," Old Hunter said. "Now I know why the Beijing government sent Chen out with the delegation. A devious conspiracy indeed."

"What is it?" He had to push the old man. Old Hunter, otherwise nicknamed Suzhou Opera Singer, could go on delaying and digressing for an hour before coming to the point. "Please tell me, Father. I'm leaving in five minutes."

"Now it's from a most reliable source, this information I'm going to tell you. But I have to begin from the beginning. Now, Hua had a sworn brother at the passport office of the Shanghai City Government, Miao

Zhiying. I have just learned that from Hua's widow. Hua sheltered Miao for weeks during the Cultural Revolution. Miao was then on the wanted list issued nationwide by a Red Guard organization. Hua's a golden-hearted guy, as I have told you. So I went to Miao, who, a man in his late fifties, burst into tears. You know what he said to me? 'If you can do something for Hua by cutting my head off, Old Hunter, strike, and I will not groan.' So I asked him to check any suspicious movement made of late by those rats, and he promised to help. Early this morning, through one of his colleagues, he found out that a Canadian visa—for 'personal business'—had been recently granted to Jiang, the director of the City Land Development Office. The application and approval were conducted in a secret way, completed just two days ago. Miao called me immediately."

"So Jiang's trying to run out, before Chen comes back."

"That's possible. Those rats have had their passports ready long beforehand, Miao told me. It is said that people nowadays can sort of get Canadian citizenship through investment. Two million yuan, and the visa would be granted. Now, how has Jiang gotten all the money? We have to act quick. Or there will be another damned red-topped rat carrying its huge storage of stolen money abroad."

"No, he won't be able to get away," Yu said. "I'm going to the bureau. I'll call you back."

"Chief Inspector Chen should be coming back soon," Peiqin said quietly the moment Yu hung up. She must have woken up during their conversation, yet was still curled up under the blanket. "You may as well wait for a couple of days."

"Oh, you're awake. Old Hunter always talks like that."

"That's a way of prolonging his old professional pride, I understand. It wasn't easy for him to have obtained the information," she said, getting down and putting on a fluffy robe. "But I don't think Jiang could have sent Chen out with the delegation."

"Nor do I. But those rats may get away in the twinkling of an eye," he said, reaching out to the nightstand, out of habit, for a cigarette. He picked up his watch instead. "I'd better do something."

"What can you do?" She walked barefoot to the microwave and started warming two bowls of water-reboiled rice. "But you're right, I think. Things can't wait. We have to do something."

He was pleased with her use of "we." Like Old Hunter, she, too, had thrown herself into it. She had stayed late with Chen's mother last night. White Cloud was too busy with her studies or something else in college. Peiqin considered her too busy and modern a girl for Chen, and for the old woman too.

"I'll make some phone calls first," Yu said, finishing the watery rice with a piece of pickled green cabbage. "I know someone working at China Airline. He may find out whether Jiang has booked the ticket."

"That's a good idea. You need to check other airlines too," she said. "Call me if I can do anything. I'll be at Old Geng's place in the morning, and at the other restaurant in the afternoon. Don't skip your lunch."

Around eleven o'clock, Detective Yu hadn't received a response from his contact at China Airline. Just as he was going to go down to the bureau canteen, his phone rang.

To his surprise, it was Chen, who had made a rule of not calling into his office.

"The weather is really bad. So I think you'd better check on what the K man gave you immediately. Or the fish may go bad."

"Yes, it's not good here." He was so confounded by Chen's sudden switch back to the weather terminology, he had a hard time figuring out how to inform Chen of the latest development here in their agreed-on jargon.

"We have to be careful," Chen moved on before Yu could respond. "Let's hope it will change for the better—as quickly as possible."

And with that, Chen hung up, leaving Yu in confusion.

To an eavesdropper, this international call could hardly make any sense except that the chief inspector proved to be an impossible gourmet. Thousands of miles away, he was still concerned about a fish, possibly given by a peddler in a K market. Perhaps no one would believe it. But Yu, too, failed to make heads or tails out of it, whatever fish it could be.

That was the drawback of their jargon communication. Chen must have a reason for it. Yu went over the short conversation in his mind. It was not about any fish, but who was the K man? He tried to recall all the people he had contacted, one by one, during the past week. The effort was not successful. He refocused on the people who had given him something. Then Gu and the laptop came to mind. With karaoke girls commonly called K girls, it would make sense to call Gu a K man, even though there was no such term in current circulation.

Skipping his lunch, he hurried out of the bureau, heading home.

Sure enough, he had mail from Chen on the computer that Gu had loaned him. It took him a while to download the attachment with Xing's phone transcript. Yu didn't know how Chen had gotten it, but he knew Chen wanted him to study it carefully.

Reading through the phone transcript, he didn't succeed in producing a comprehensible picture. Something had been going on between Xing and his associates in China, particularly in the last few days, that Yu could tell. Many calls had been made, only most of the details were couched in triad jargon. There were names he had seen or heard before, some of them Chen had given him earlier, including Jiang and Dong. The context surrounding their names remained far from clear, except that they still had contact with Xing one way or another.

Then Yu got the call from China Airline. Jiang's name didn't appear on the list. It wasn't exactly high season yet; people could get a ticket one or two days beforehand.

Lighting a cigarette, he read the transcript more closely. All of a sudden, he alighted on a name: Weici.

Weici was an extremely rare family name. Yu had heard of it only once, in a Tang dynasty story. He had not met anyone with such a family name. But at Apricot Blossom Village, the club to which An's phone calls had led him, the general manager was surnamed Weici. So he reread the part containing the name, which happened to be in connection with Ming. He found the name of Weici was mentioned on three occasions.

"I have just learned, Xing. Weici is a man. Your little brother should be fine there," someone said to Xing, possibly in response to his inquiry about the whereabouts of the "little boy."

"Thank God. Weici is a reliable guy. I don't have to worry," Xing said to another man, nicknamed Ginger.

But most importantly, the name appeared in a phone call Xing made to a place that seemed to be Weici's office. *"Your boss has changed his cell number again. Let Weici know I appreciate all he does for me and for my little boy. The green mountains stand, the blue waters flow, and we will meet again."*

That was an unmistakable indication that Ming was hiding there—or at least, that Weici knew the whereabouts of Ming.

Detective Yu had to take action at once, but he didn't want to discuss his plan with Chen. It was a long shot, and full of possible consequences. Chen might try to delay him, being reluctant to expose his assistant through the investigation. A well-connected man like Weici wouldn't be easily bluffed by Yu, even with the emperor's special envoy authorization in his hand. A search of the club, even if permitted, didn't guarantee results. Bringing in a large enough group of cops to do a thorough job was out of the question. Besides, Ming could have moved, and then Weici could make things troublesome for the detective.

Still, Yu wanted to strike without his boss telling him to. Then any responsibility would be his alone. He owed that to Chen.

He took out the emperor's special envoy authorization with both the signatures of Chen and Zhao on it. He also picked up his gun. Still, it would be discreet to discuss his move with someone else first. So he called Old Hunter. The old man was doing his traffic patrol in the Old City area, and he, too, seemed to have something to discuss with him.

They met in a small, shabby teahouse not far away from the Old City's God Temple Market. It was fairly noisy with some performance going on in a corner of the teahouse. For once, however, Old Hunter listened to his plan without interrupting.

When Yu finished talking, the old man didn't immediately comment, only nodding once or twice, holding the purple sand teacup in his hand. During the unusual silence that ensued, Yu heard something like a Suzhou opera singer performing on a *pipa.*

"You are making a difficult decision," Old Hunter finally started. "But what if your plan does not work? Someone like Weici—he'll hit back."

"I have to try it," Yu said, "regardless of the result."

"Now you sound like Zhuge in the *Romance of Three Kingdoms.* 'I'll try my utmost, unforeseeable as the prospect of success or failure may be,' " Old Hunter said slowly, putting down his teacup. "If so, go ahead. Do whatever you believe you should, and you won't rue it. What a coincidence! The Suzhou opera singer here is narrating an episode from the *Romance of Three Kingdoms.*"

"What a coincidence," Yu repeated without really getting the old man's point.

"You have to bring me along. Without a search warrant, you will have a difficult time cracking the hard nut alone. I am an old hand, and I may be able to trap some rats for you."

It wasn't a good idea to bring Old Hunter along with him, Yu contemplated. If things went wrong, the old man's position as a traffic control advisor would be jeopardized, and Weici could complain about a retired cop intruding without any legal authorization.

"You're like Huang Zhong, the old gallant general in that historical novel, Father. Your advice means a lot to me, but I think I'll go there alone."

"No, you are not familiar with the book at all. We are more like General Guan and his son, fighting a battle for the just cause. We have never worked on a case together, father and son." Old Hunter took a final long sip at his tea. "It's an opportunity I have been waiting for, with my Blue Dragon Moon Knife still so sharp."

Yu didn't respond, as if having found an excuse for silence in drinking the tea with his head low.

"We cannot afford to fail, son," Old Hunter went on. "Because of Chief Inspector Chen, because of you, because of our first collaboration—father and son. But more than anything else, because of Hua, my buddy for so many years. In the early sixties, when millions of Chinese died of starvation during the Three Red Flag Movement, Hua came to Shanghai, bringing me a bag of cookies confiscated from a Taiwan smuggling ship. It did not become a cop to keep something seized, he knew, but you and your sisters were too starved to weep at the time. So I have to do something for him. If not, I won't be able to sleep with an easy conscience for my remaining days."

"If you insist on going with me," Yu said reluctantly, "you have to let me do the talking there."

"That will be fine. In a Suzhou opera, one plays the red face, and the other plays the white face. I am quite content with a white face role. It's settled. Let us go."

"I'll call Little Zhou first. He's reliable," Yu said. "In the meantime, let's finish the tea and discuss our tactics."

Little Zhou, a driver at the Shanghai police bureau, soon came over to the teahouse, leaving his car parked outside.

"Both you and I are Chief Inspector Chen's men," Little Zhou declared at once. "You have never used my car. You say it's for Chen this afternoon. And you don't have to say more. It is a Mercedes, the best car of our bureau. No one knows I am here."

They arrived at the club around three o'clock.

A hostess walked over to them. Yu recognized her as the one he had met. Handing his business card to her, he said, "Take us to your general manager Weici."

They were led into a spacious office. Weici was a stout man in his mid-fifties, with success and confidence written on his face in spite of the heavy bags sagging under his eyes. He was taken aback by Detective Yu's visit.

"So tell us where Ming is," Yu said, having made clear the purpose of the visit, and produced the authorization on the Party Discipline Committee letterhead. "As you can clearly see, it is an investigation under the committee."

"I don't know what you are talking about, Officer Yu," Weici said, taking a glance at the document. "I don't know anything about Xing's smuggling business, nor anything about Ming. It's the first time that I've heard that he is Xing's half brother. Before their sudden disappearance, they had a couple of parties at my club. At the time, however, they were ordinary customers like so many others. I wish I knew the whereabouts of Ming. They still owe me a large amount."

"You are a clever man, Mr. Weici. It's a highly sensitive case and there's no point in getting negative publicity for your club because of an official investigation," Yu said, producing the phone transcript. "Now, let me show you something else. The dates and the contents are all underlined in the transcript. The calls are from Xing in the United States. Undeniable evidence. Chief Inspector Chen is coming back with more."

"What's that?" Wei studied the lines in the transcript. "You call that evidence, Officer Yu? You must be kidding. Xing has many little brothers, if that is what 'little boy' means. One of them might have visited the club. As for the calls to my office, for all I know, it could be about the money he owes me."

"You can go on talking like that, Mr. Weici, but then we'll have to move you to our bureau to continue the conversation," Yu said. "It will be reported in newspapers tomorrow, I'll make sure of it. I don't think too many people will come to a place involved in China's number-one corruption case. It's going to be a long and thorough investigation under the Party Discipline Committee."

"Don't think you can bluff me like that. I know your Party Secretary Li Guohua. When he comes to my place, he, too, has to show proper respect to me."

"Calm down, both of you," Old Hunter said, cutting in for the first time. "The club is a nice place. Why can't we talk here? General Manager Weici is a man of the world. He'll understand."

"This is . . ." Weici said, studying the old man for the first time.

"I am an advisor to the bureau." Old Hunter handed over a business card, which presented him as a senior advisor to the City Traffic Control, commonly considered part of the police bureau. "It's a pleasure to meet you."

"Oh, Advisor Gu. I am honored that you are here today," Weici said. "As an old cadre, you have to say something for me. I am a law-abiding businessman. How could I have been involved in the Xing case?"

Advisor was an honorable position, usually filled by high-ranking retired cadres like Comrade Zhao. Weici apparently showed some respect to the title in the business card. But Old Hunter's case was totally different. While serving as temporary head of the City Traffic Control, Chen had created the position for the sake of the "advisor subsidy," which meant more than anything else to the retired cop on a meager pension. Weici couldn't have known that. Yu didn't know about that impressive business card, either.

"There are so many customers here. As a general manager, Mr. Weici may not know whether Ming has come here or not. We have to take that into consideration, Detective Yu," Old Hunter said, squeezing a smile out of all the wrinkles on his face. "It's not easy to run a place with such a golf course. In fact, there's not a single one in the old cadre centers."

"Really!" Weici feigned surprise.

"Yes, I have a passion for golf. Only the membership fee here must be expensive. I don't think I can afford it."

Yu was amazed by the way the old man talked. The part about the membership fee came as an unmistakable hint. But the son had never worked with the father before, so he decided to say nothing.

"It's not that expensive," Weici said with an equally obliging smile, "not unimaginable for an old cadre like you."

"That would be fantastic," Old Hunter said, taking up a cigarette from a shining silver case on the desk. "Oh, Panda. The super premium brand, unavailable on the market. Manufactured only for the top leaders in Beijing."

"Yes, top leaders come to our place too," Weici said, lighting the cigarette for the old man. "Look at those pictures on the walls."

Yu had noticed those pictures upon entering the office. Several politburo members stood with Weici on the green meadow stretching dreamlike toward the horizon. In another picture, a city government leader put his hand on Weici's shoulder like a buddy.

"Oh, has Comrade Zhao Yan visited your club?" Old Hunter said, looking at the pictures. "He is in Shanghai, staying at the Western Suburb Hotel. I'll tell him about your wonderful place."

"Yes, I talked to Comrade Zhao this morning." Yu tried to stage a comeback into the conversation, which had somehow become a golf dialogue between Old Hunter and Weici.

"Here are two VIP cards," Weici said to Old Hunter, taking the cards out of the desk drawer. "Free for three months. All our services included. One for you, and one for Comrade Zhao. You can also bring your friends along with you, like Detective Yu."

"Thank you so much. I'll give it to Comrade Zhao," Old Hunter said after putting the cards into his wallet. "Now let me say something, General

Manager Weici. With so many things on your desk, you may not notice or remember all the details. So how about trying to think again? More closely this time. Perhaps you'll succeed in recalling something."

"You are just wasting your time, Advisor Gu," Yu cut in again. "We'll take him to the bureau, and we'll search every corner of the club. As the proverb goes, *he refuses to drink the wine I offer him, so he has to drink what I order him.*"

"Come, Detective Yu. As another proverb goes, *the mountain does not turn but the road turns, so people will meet one way or another.* You should give him some time to think and check." Old Hunter turned to Weici. "General Manger Weici, I also want to say a word for Officer Yu. He's under a lot of pressure from the Party Discipline Committee. In fact, Comrade Zhao has pushed him again this morning. Comrade Zhao is like Judge Bao in the Song dynasty, always carrying the golden dragon-headed cleaver to behead criminals. The Beijing government is really furious, as you know. Anyone involved with Xing or Ming will be investigated and punished. That's why Comrade Zhao himself has come to Shanghai, sent Chief Inspector Chen to the United States, and signed the authorization for Officer Yu. Officer Yu has to do something."

"I understand all that. I, too, would like to help the government fight corruption. But how can I admit to something I don't know?"

"I'm not saying that you have to admit something you don't know. But try to help us by making an effort—check your computer and talk to your employees. If, hypothetically, you succeed in finding out something about Ming, you would be making a great contribution to our work. In our report to Comrade Zhao, I'll make sure to mention your great help." Old Hunter added after a pause, "And we may not have to touch on the phone call part. Am I right, Officer Yu?"

"I don't think Comrade Zhao has the time to read the transcript line by line," Yu said, "especially without my highlighting those lines."

"Since you have both said so," Weici said slowly, "let me double-check for you."

Weici turned on the computer. With the two cops standing behind him, he keyed in Ming's name and did a name search. Nothing matched there.

"You see, nothing has been found," Weici said.

"He may not have used his real name," Yu said.

"Yes, that's possible. Let me talk to my assistants then." Weici picked up the phone and tried several numbers, asking about the possibility of Ming having come to the club. He seemed to get the same answer. On the fifth or sixth call, however, he appeared to have a different response. Weici rose and said to the two policemen, "Wait here for me."

In about five minutes, Weici came back into the office with an ashen look on his face.

"Officer Yu. I have to apologize. Ming contacted Zhang Boxiong, one of my assistant managers, and has been staying in an unoccupied villa here. He must have bribed Zhang with a large sum. I didn't know anything about it. I have fired Zhang, though I don't think he knew anything about Ming's relationship to Xing, either."

"Of course you didn't know anything about it," Old Hunter echoed. "We appreciate your help."

"Take us to the villa," Yu said.

They were escorted to a free-standing white villa beyond the golf course. A waitress ran up to Weici and whispered something in his ear. He turned to Yu and Old Hunter. "Ming's on the second floor. Here is the key. I'll stay out here. I don't want to see that bastard."

They moved upstairs in silence. Whipping out his gun with one hand, inserting the key with the other, Yu opened the door. In the room, they saw a man in a scarlet silk robe holding a naked girl on a rumpled bed, watching an American sex video, and imitating it. They hadn't heard anything because of the loud moaning and groaning from the TV.

"Who are you?" the man said, his hand still on the thigh of the girl trembling beside him.

"You are Xing Ming, aren't you? We are from the Shanghai Police Bureau. You are under arrest for sleeping with this prostitute."

"No, she's my girlfriend."

"Show me your ID," Old Hunter said to the girl.

The girl, wrapped in a blanket, took it out of a purse on the sofa and said sobbing, "I am a student, but both my parents are laid off. I have to support the family."

Old Hunter glanced at the ID and turned to Ming. "You're having sex with an underage girl. She's only fifteen."

"I didn't know that, officers," Ming stuttered, a broken man. "I don't even know her name."

That should be more than enough. The cops thought it unnecessary to even mention Xing there.

As they marched Ming out, Yu saw Weici waving at them from a distance. He understood. In the car, Little Zhou nodded without asking any questions. He waited for Yu's instruction.

"Where are you going to put him?" Old Hunter asked.

"Where do you suggest?" Yu asked.

"Anywhere but the bureau."

"The Western Suburb Hotel then—under the custody of Comrade Zhao."

"Good idea," Old Hunter agreed. "You know where it is, Little Zhou?"

"I know, though I have never been there."

On the way to the hotel, Yu said to the old man sitting beside him, "I never expected a white face performance like that, Father."

"You know my other nickname, right?" Old Hunter went on, not waiting for an answer: "Suzhou Opera Singer. But you may not know that, for the last five months, I have been enjoying Suzhou opera three or four times a week. What an unbelievable luxury! Guess how? Nowadays, the traditional opera is going totally to rack and ruin. People watch TV and movies and DVDs. In the increasingly fast tempo of this new age, few have the time to enjoy the slow narrative of the traditional Suzhou opera. Most of the Suzhou opera theaters have been turned into nightclubs and actors can perform only in teahouses, like the old days. They make little money, sometimes no more than their bus fare and a bowl of noodles. I'm a regular teahouse visitor, so I am a regular audience member too. It's free."

"I see." Yu knew the old man's alternative nickname hadn't come from his enjoyment of the opera, but from his way of talking as if a character in a opera.

He started up again, more eloquently than usual. "Now for the last few months, it's the *Romance of Three Kingdoms* being performed at the shabby teahouse. I have learned quite a lot from this ancient book of wisdom. As you may not know, those CEOs of large corporations today all read the *Romance of Three Kingdoms* for inspiration in their business operations. For instance, when we talked at the teahouse, I, too, thought of something from the Suzhou opera. Cao Cao suspected Liu Bei was an ambitious rival and kept him under close surveillance. So what could Liu do? He pretended to be a greedy man, asking materialistic favors of Cao. How could such a greedy man have genuine political ambition? As a result, Cao was less on his guard, and Liu was able to get away."

"Now I am beginning to see, Father."

"People have to believe you are vulnerable, and then they themselves will be vulnerable. Weici is a man too familiar with those insatiable red rats in the materialistic world. A lot of them must have asked him for favors just like that. So he took me for granted, believing that he could exchange favors with us and he would get off scot-free. If he believed his cooperation made no difference, why should he give up Ming?" Old Hunter paused, taking out a pack of cigarettes—Flying Horse. "You do not really have the imperial sword, do you? No one knows a son better than his father."

Old Hunter didn't seem ready to stop talking about the *Romance of Three Kingdoms* any time soon. Yu thought the old man was entitled to his moment of triumph.

27

THE ALARM CLOCK FRAGMENTED his dream of a black cat jumping around, almost slipping on the tile roofs in the depth of the night, under the stars, long and chill . . .

Chen got up, made a pot of coffee, and took a quick shower. He had to appear in decent shape, he reflected, smelling the first pleasant aroma. He was going to see her soon, to discuss the delegation's new activities again. He finished the first cup in a few gulps, trying to shake himself out of the fragmented memories of a long night.

He had worked very late the previous night. Reading through the information she gave him, listening to the tape several times, he knew why she had given it to him. With his background knowledge, she hoped that he might be able to get something out of it. There was something going on, he was sure, but he failed to grasp what. Some of the names in Xing's phone calls meant nothing to Chen, except that of "Little Tiger" in an alarming context. So he approached the hotel manager for the use of a computer. He forwarded Yu the phone transcript, and placed a weather phone call to him, believing his partner would get it.

Afterward he lay awake for a long while, thinking. Whether her information could lead to anything, he didn't know. But he supposed that she had gone out of her way for him, and possibly at risk to herself. She might have done so without her boss's permission. On campus, she hadn't said a single word when giving him the large envelope. Instead, she held his hand in hers for a minute. He understood. He read the genuine concern in her eyes. Her eyes so blue, deep, serene, like the Beijing sky in autumn again . . .

Finally he sank into a slumber full of dreams. One of them was a recurring nightmare from his childhood. The black night rubbing its muzzle on the windowpane, licking its tongue into the corners of the moment, he found himself turning into a cat, curling itself in contentment before suddenly jumping out of the attic window, running along the tile roof, fleeing from a faceless enemy. In his then-neighborhood, all the ramshackle houses were perilously connected. He kept leaping from one roof to another. Any minute, he could irrecoverably fall into the abyss, but not yet . . .

The shrill of the cell phone startled him from his recollection of the broken dream. It was Catherine.

"Can you tell me what the Chinese visitors would like to do today?"

"Good question." He did not have an immediate answer. She had a hard time making all the arrangements for the delegation. St. Louis was not a tourist city with many sightseeing alternatives. Shasha could spend another afternoon at the shopping mall, perhaps. She had just received her book contract with a decent advance. As for the others, he had no clue. Then he remembered what Tian had told him about other Chinese delegations in L.A.

"Isn't there a casino boat in the river?"

"Yes, but what about your delegation regulations?"

"As the American host, you can make suggestions. Mark Twain wrote several short stories about sailing on the Mississippi River. So it may have a lot to do with the tradition of American literature."

"I see," she said with a giggle. "It is like a Chinese proverb: *To steal a bell with your ears stuffed*—you simply believe others will not hear the sound."

So she suggested it at breakfast. No one raised any objection, except Peng, who said something more like a question:

"The boat did not move, I noticed. How can a boat be moored all the time?"

"It used to be a real riverboat, all right," she explained. "According to the state law, it's illegal to gamble on land, but legal in the river—as entertainment. As long as it is on a boat, it doesn't matter whether the boat moves or not."

"An excuse," Zhong commented.

"So hypocritical," Bao observed, "typical of American capitalism."

"It's the same everywhere. Gambling is forbidden in China, but the government has recently legalized mahjong," Shasha said. "Everyone knows mahjong is no fun without money put on the table."

Still, no one had any objection. Not even Bao, who might be just as eager to experience the forbidden.

"Well, one place is as good as another," Chen said, understanding it was up to him to say something. "Let's follow the footsteps of Mark Twain. No point staying in the hotel all the time."

"Yes, it's so close," Catherine said.

So around eleven, they got out of the hotel and into a minivan. Chen took his seat in front, behind the driver, and Catherine sat in the seat across the aisle, her hair tied into a plait with a scarlet velvet string. She was wearing a white shirt, a beige blazer of light material, and a matching skirt. Then he noticed she was frowning. Leaning down, she rubbed her bare shapely ankle. He resisted the impulse to do what he had done that evening in the Suzhou garden. He felt her nearness, as if through the memory. Abruptly, his cell phone rang. It was Detective Yu in Shanghai.

"Breakthrough, Chief."

"What?"

"Ming was caught!"

"Really! How?"

"It's a long story. Thanks to the phone record—"

"Where is he now?" Chen knew he had to cut his partner short. It was too sensitive a case to discuss at the moment, with all the delegation members, and Catherine too, sitting in the car.

"I turned him over to Comrade Zhao—"

"Great." Chen understood why his assistant had done so. For someone like Ming, the Shanghai Police Bureau or Party Secretary Li might not be a safe bet. After all, it was a case under the Party Discipline Committee. "I'll call you back. We are going to a riverboat."

This was great, Chen thought. Ming might not be that important to Xing's entire empire, but at least their activities in Shanghai would be exposed, and those red rats could be punished. Some of the evidence thus obtained might help with the eventual deportation of Xing from the U.S.

Also, the investigation of An's case could continue, to which he had made a personal commitment. And it might lead, one way or another, to Little Huang's case.

So he believed that, as a cop, he played a positive role in this important case for his country, even though he had long given up some of the Confucianist ideals regarding an intellectual's responsibilities. Chinese people had been complaining that the government slapped only at the mosquitoes, but not the tigers. This time, however, it was different.

He turned to Catherine. There was no change in her expression. The conversation might not have given her enough clues. He wanted to tell her about the breakthrough in Shanghai, but not in the car. He was not sure about the driver.

Their minivan arrived at the multistoried casino boat moored only two or three minutes' walk from the Arch. At the casino entrance, they were greeted by a chorus of the money dancing and singing out of numerous slot machines, by the neon lights presenting the temptations of fabulous wealth and success. To the Chinese writers, the casino itself was like a surrealistic kingdom in the *Journey to the West,* a classic Chinese novel Chen had read in his childhood.

Bao took a few nervous steps forward and backward before perching himself on a high stool before a slot machine. It seemed as if he were instantly glued onto the stool. He played small, holding a plastic cup in his hand, putting in a quarter a time, and pulling down the handle deliberately, like the conscientious worker he had been in the fifties. Zhong and Peng started walking around like hunters in new, unfamiliar woods, and then vanished like water into sand. Shasha went over to the roulette wheel, watching intently, like a character in the movie adapted from her novel.

Perhaps they were still self-conscious, with all the Chinese regulations in mind, so they did not want to stay in each other's company. And no one wanted Catherine to interpret or explain. So Chen and Catherine were left alone in the first-floor hall, surrounded by the soundtrack of all the coins pouring out of the machines.

"What you gave me was really helpful," he said.

"What did I give you?" she said.

Was she not willing to talk about it? Perhaps it only proved his guess: she had done that for him—in a way she wouldn't like anybody else to know. So he'd better not talk about it.

Shasha wandered back to them with a plastic cup similar to Bao's, with the chips heavier, and different-colored.

"You'd better not try your hand today, boss," Shasha said with a broad grin.

"Why?"

"As an old saying goes, *the one who enjoys the peach blossom luck may not have the money luck.*"

"You are joking again, Shasha."

"Well, try your luck with her," Shasha said. "I am going to try my own somewhere else."

But he believed in his luck for the day, with Detective Yu's call about the great breakthrough. Once more, Gu's advance came in handy. He took his seat at a blackjack table with ten-dollar chips. He dragged Catherine to his side.

"You need to explain the rules for me," he said, thinking he might be able to talk to her about the latest development in the midst of the game.

"It's simple. Nothing but your luck," she said, seating herself beside him.

His proved to be extraordinary. For the first several hands in a row, he drew a twenty or twenty-one. As his luck ebbed a little, the dealer's sank much lower. Chen won even when she suggested he throw in. Soon chips piled up in front of him.

"You're really an experienced hand."

"No, It's the first time."

"First-timer's luck," she said smiling, clapping her hand with his, "from Shanghai."

He found it impossible to talk about things in Shanghai, with the game going on like this and with people standing behind them, watching.

A bunny girl came to his table. Tall, buxom, she looked like anything but a bunny to him. She placed drinks in front of them, and he tossed a chip on her platter—in imitation of an American player. He was too busy picking up his cards and putting down his chips. He lost track of time flowing like the river outside, until a familiar cough startled him. He looked up to see Bao standing beside him, holding an empty plastic cup. An unmistakable sign. Bao had lost all his coins.

"Join me," Chen said, placing a handful of chips in Bao's cup.

"It's a twenty-dollar chip," Catherine said.

"Thank you," Bao said with a weird expression on his face, a mixture of emotions, perhaps. "I may not have your luck. So I think I'll go on playing my small way."

"I don't know how long mine can last," he said, turning toward Catherine, as Bao dragged himself away with a heavier cup. "If anything, you are my luck."

It was true. The breakthrough in Shanghai would have been inconceivable without her help, he contemplated, turning out another ace in his hand. She leaned over and whispered, "He hasn't gotten any more phone calls from L.A."

It was possible that Bao, too, remained in the dark, unaware of the consequence of the information he had given to the L.A. caller. Chen nodded instead of making a response.

Another good hand—eighteen. He staked a couple more chips. The dealer did not show any expression on his face and drew another card—

His cell phone rang. He whisked it out, glancing at the number on the tiny screen. It was from Shanghai. Not from Yu, but from Comrade Zhao. It took him a few seconds before recognizing the number.

"Sorry, I have to take the call outside. It's too noisy in the hall," he said to her. "Keep on playing for me."

He hurried out to the deserted deck. Chinese and Americans must all have been too busy dealing with money, losing or winning.

"How have you called me here, Comrade Zhao?" he said, standing by the rail with its white paint peeling off under his touch. A gull came wheeling over out of nowhere.

"Don't be so alarmed, Chen. I've got your cell number from Detective Yu. It took me several minutes to have it from him. A most capable and loyal assistant."

"I'm sorry, Comrade Zhao. It's not his fault. I told him not to give the number to anybody. I didn't mean to keep it from you—"

"You don't have to explain. I was pleased that Detective Yu delivered Ming to me directly. Excellent job. Now I see why you insisted on his sharing your authorization," Zhao said. "So, our work has come to a successful conclusion!"

"A conclusion?"

"Xing is on his way back to China . . ." Zhao paused, and then went on, "in exchange for Ming flying to the U.S."

"How could that be?"

"A story too long to tell on the phone, Chen. We—some agents—talked to Xing in Los Angeles. They promised him no death penalty for his return and his cooperation with the Chinese government."

"What? Death penalty or not, Xing's finished back in China. A crab in an urn—or worse, in a bamboo steamer. No way for him to get away. He knows that better than anyone else."

"Well, it is all thanks to the arrest of Ming through your information. It's the last straw for Xing. He knows he has no choice." Zhao added, "Besides, he is a filial son, like you, and his mother is so worried about Ming."

"But how could Xing be willing to surrender himself for the sake of his half brother—whom he has never acknowledged in public?"

"Let me put it this way. The arrest of Ming might have been only one of many factors in this complicated case. Through Ming, we got all the necessary criminal evidence of Xing, which would prompt the American government to make the deportation decision. Xing is not dumb. He has no hope for political asylum. Even before Ming's arrest, he tried to flee to another country, but his effort was thwarted by U.S. law enforcement."

"That may be true," Chen said, recalling Xing's interest in selling his L.A. mansion. "So in exchange for Xing's voluntary return, Ming gets away scot-free?"

"I have not had the time to read the detailed report from our agents in L.A. There might be something in it."

"But Ming may have been involved in An's murder, as I have reported to you earlier."

"You don't know for sure, do you? You have nothing to prove her death was related to Ming or Xing. Your bureau will continue to investigate, of course, and the criminals will be punished." Zhao said emphatically, "It is a successful conclusion, Comrade Chief Inspector Chen."

"So that's it—the end of it," he said, trying to gain time to think. Perhaps he should not push Comrade Zhao into saying something definite, irrecoverable. "Our determined effort to push the anticorruption campaign to the end?"

"It is a priority in our effort, to control the damage, as we have discussed. Bringing Xing back to China will make a huge difference. For someone like Xing, long years in a dark cell could be a more severe punishment than a death sentence."

"Comrade Zhao, you must have heard of the death of our interpreter in St. Louis, Little Huang."

"Yes, I have heard of it. But what can you do in another country? You are not there as a police officer. Anything you try to do outside of your delegation status may cause diplomatic troubles. So that's the other reason I have to make this call to you. We believe that the delegation has completed its mission. No need for you and your delegation to stay there any longer. It is the Americans' responsibility to solve the homicide case. They will do their best."

He wondered where Zhao had learned about his other activities here. That, too, could have been a reason for this phone call. Chen decided not to bring up his theory about Huang being a victim of mistaken identity. Things were happening too fast, and were more complicated than he had grasped. Besides, Zhao could easily brush his theory aside for lack of evidence. Those phone records hardly proved anything.

"Anticorruption is a long-term battle, Chen," Zhao went on, "not a matter of an isolated case or two. The Party Discipline Committee is very pleased with your work. Once again, you have proven to be a loyal, resourceful Party cadre in a difficult situation. Indeed, we need young, reliable comrades like you to continue the anticorruption effort in the future."

"Thank you, Comrade Zhao, but—"

"It's a long phone call. We'll talk more upon your return. What about a celebration dinner in my hotel? I know you like good food—the chef here has won the gold award for Sichuan cuisine. The carp in hot broad-bean sauce is a must. I have a bottle of Maotai for you. Remember the two lines by Liu Guo—*Had General Li met with the First Emperor of Han, / he could have easily been a duke*?"

"Yes, I do," he said.

General Li, a legendary figure of the mid-Han dynasty, might have achieved more under another emperor. Liu Guo, a down-and-out Song dynasty poet, spoke about his own frustration through the tragedy of that unlucky general. What the equivalent to a duke in today's official world would be, Chief Inspector Chen had no idea, but he was far from reaching that level yet.

"At your age, I liked the two lines very much. But what happened during those years, you know. Now the time is totally different. A young man like you can and should do something," Zhao concluded. "You will not let me down, I believe."

Closing the phone, Chen remained in confusion, his thoughts muddled and muddy like the waves rolling under his gaze. He had never imagined such a conclusion for China's number-one corruption case.

Perhaps Comrade Zhao had said what could be said, and the rest was unspeakable, or unknown even to the old man.

The Party authorities had planned to punish Xing and all the associated officials, Chen did not doubt that. But the situation had developed out of control, with too many—and at too high positions—involved in the case. So that might have been one of the reasons that the Party Discipline Committee had initially enlisted Chief Inspector Chen, as Yu had guessed. He was part of the show for the Chinese people, while at the same time secret negotiations had been under way with Xing in the States.

Would Xing cooperate by revealing all the secrets? No one could tell. Nor was it that important. After all, the Beijing authorities could have pushed to the end, as declared in the *People's Daily,* with or without Xing's cooperation. Rather, Xing's return was significant more as a sort of successful hushing-over, so the sordid details of the government corruption would never come to be known. So that was it. Some of the red rats might be punished, but selectively, not at the expense of the political legitimacy of the Party. It would be just enough to show people the Beijing government's determination to fight the evil.

And the message for Chief Inspector Chen was unmistakable: the investigation was at an end. He should be satisfied with the conclusion, and with the acknowledgment made by the Party authorities of his work.

But what work? The chief inspector wondered.

What about An?

And for that matter, what about Little Huang?

Had Chen not pursued his investigation the way he had, the two might not have fallen, one of them totally innocent. He could choose to tell himself, of course, that he had no choice, that it was a matter of life and death for him, and for the country too, and that there were different perspectives on everything. As a Party member police officer, he had reasons to be contented with his work, as Zhao had declared.

Still, Chen could not get rid of a haunting sense of guilt. Instead of brooding over it, he tried to think what he could do upon his return to China. An's murderer still had to be caught, though probably not by him. As for the young interpreter, however, the case might never be traced back to those really behind the scene, thousands of miles away, who might be raising their cups in celebration at this moment, behind the high wall of the Forbidden City, where the order for the murder in St. Louis had come from, Chen supposed, rather than from L.A.

A siren resounded over the river. For all the satisfactions expressed by Zhao, his phone call came close to an undeclared suspension of Chen's emperor-special-envoy assignment. It was undeclared, perhaps, because he was still abroad with the delegation. So he'd better go back into the casino hall. It might not matter much if his fellow writers lost some money, but it would be another story, he thought of the diplomatic troubles mentioned by Zhao, if something unpleasant happened to them in the boat.

When so many things are absurd, nothing is really absurd.

To his relief, Chen saw them all gathered in a corner on the first floor, next to Bao, who was still sitting on the stool, pulling the slot machine handle, his cup quite full now. Shasha held a cocktail in her hand. Peng and Zhong kept smoking. They might have lost their pocket money, and they appeared relieved at the sight of Chen. It had been a long phone call from China. Catherine came to him with a check in her hands.

"I waited for you for a long time. I didn't think you were coming back to the table, so I cashed in your chips," she said simply. "It's quite a lot of money. There's no point pushing your luck too far."

It wasn't that much, about fifteen hundred, but she had made the right decision. His luck couldn't last that long.

"Well." He pulled several bills out of his wallet. "Let's make it two thousand and send the money to Little Huang's family—in the name of our delegation."

"Damn it," Shasha said, emptying the money out of her purse. "Only twenty bucks. That's all I have left today."

"We don't have to do that," Bao said, clutching his full cup. "The Beijing authorities will take care of things in the proper way."

"We don't have to do this, and to do that," Chen snapped. "Little Huang died for us—because of us. He was not even a so-called writer like you and me."

28

IT MIGHT BE HIS last day in St. Louis, Chen supposed, stepping into the shabby motel near Jefferson Road. Behind the motel, not too far away, the Arch stood silhouetted against the gray sky, still splendid as always.

He had been told to meet with Feidong, a military attaché from the Chinese Consulate in Chicago. The meeting was arranged more out of formality, though the location of it intrigued Chen. They could have met in the hotel where the delegation stayed.

Feidong conveyed his congratulations to Chen on behalf of the Culture Ministry and the Foreign Ministry. Then basically the same message: in view of the new situation, the delegation would return to China. Speaking as a government representative, Feidong showed proper respect to the chief inspector.

"The leading comrades in Beijing are pleased with your work."

"What work?"

But there was no point arguing with Feidong, or even raising the question. He might not have any clue what work Chen was really engaged with here.

"Well, they are concerned with the safety of the delegation," Feidong went on without directly responding to his question. "If anything else happens, it would be a diplomatic disaster. Then, huge responsibilities."

So the meeting was not merely one of formality. It functioned as double insurance. After Zhao's talk, the message was reiterated more like a warning. Chen had to lead the delegation back. Period.

Chen remained polite, saying little throughout the meeting, because it was a decision he had to accept. There was no point in fighting it.

"Also, there will be no mentioning Comrade Huang's case whatsoever to the Chinese media. The delegation members are not supposed to talk or write about it upon their return."

"Why?"

"It's in the Party's interests."

Of course, anything would be so justified. There was little Chen could do about it. A case might be given to him one minute, and taken away the next. It was a fact he had long known. The final decision was always made in the interests of the Party.

The meeting was shorter than Chen had anticipated. There was hardly anything new to him. He had to be content, he tried to comfort himself, with whatever role was assigned to him—with the appearance that he had played the role successfully. He should not have felt so frustrated. He left the motel and started walking along the deserted street.

A blue jay flushed up, swirling around overhead before it flew away, as if carrying the sun on its back.

Had General Li met with the First Emperor of Han, / he could have easily been a duke. The lines Zhao had quoted in Shanghai came back to mind. In some of his cases, Chief Inspector Chen might not have gone all the way—for one reason or another. This time, he believed he had gone the extra mile, but for what?

A taxi slowed down beside him. An Arabic driver tentatively rolled down the window. Chen got in and gave the hotel name absentmindedly. As the car started out, he realized he was in no hurry to go back. He didn't know how to explain the government's decision to the delegation, though they probably wouldn't make too much of it. It was about time for them to go back.

He didn't have to announce the decision immediately. The delegation was having a meeting with a group of local Chinese writers with a Chinese dinner afterward. They all knew he had a meeting with the embassy people. A meeting no one would try to question. Not even Bao.

So Chen had the late afternoon for himself. He had done what he could, he kept telling himself, and further speculation would not help. Because things were beyond his control. Because he knew his limits. Because it depressed him to think. He did not have to be a cop or a delegation head every minute—at least not toward the end of his last day in the city.

For him, it remained an unfamiliar city, tall buildings looming up along the way like indecipherable signs against the horizon, ebbing to stunted slums before rising up again. He saw a Budweiser billboard of an eagle ceaselessly flapping its neon wings. The brewery had its successful joint ventures in China, its beer so cool and refreshing in Chinese TV commercials, and promoted everywhere by those scantily-clad Bud girls. The company had already made a huge profit in only a few years after its entry into China's market, he had read. He thought of Tian and his ex-Bud-girl wife, whistling softly. Reaching into his breast pocket, he took out the address book, and read out a street name to the driver.

"So that's where you want to go now?" the driver said without looking over his shoulder.

"Yes. Sorry about the change."

"No problem. It's not far away. In University City."

He had not made any plan with Catherine for the evening, for he'd had no clue how long his meeting with the embassy official would last. So he'd told her he would be busy that afternoon, and perhaps that evening too. As most of the local writers at the afternoon meeting were bilingual, her services were not needed. She'd mentioned that instead of staying with them, she might go home.

As the taxi reached the intersection of Delmar and Skinker, he told the driver to stop. Handing the man a twenty-dollar bill, he didn't ask for a receipt, which might reveal his whereabouts. Everybody knew about his "important" meeting this afternoon.

"Let us go," he murmured to himself.

That section of Delmar was lined with bars and restaurants. He strolled past a café. A number of customers sat outside. A young girl was singing with an electric guitar near the entrance, her bare feet beating out the rhythm on the sidewalk, as if in correspondence to what had been already lost in his memory, distantly, with a string and a peg. Next to the neon sign was a secondhand bookstore. He resisted the temptation to step in.

Her apartment building was an old brownstone near the beginning of a quaint side street. One of the second-floor windows was decorated with a spreading cluster of dark green ivy underneath. He thought he recognized it from a picture she had once shown him.

He believed he had learned some things during the trip. Among others, people had to make appointments to visit here. No one simply dropped by, like in Shanghai. It wouldn't do for him to knock on her door like this.

He pulled out his cell phone and called her home number. No one answered. Then he tried her cell phone, which was turned off, unfortunately. It was about four-thirty. She would probably come back soon. He thought he might as well wait awhile here. A nice surprise for her. And he found himself quite contented with the anticipation of it.

For the moment, he didn't want to think about his responsibilities—being a government delegation head or being a chief inspector. Simply being a man waiting for a woman.

He turned into a street corner bar. Instead of sitting outside, he chose a table inside, leaning against the window, keeping her building in sight. It was a small, cozy bar; its walls presented an impressive array of old trophies and posters in a nostalgic statement against time. There was also a stuffed deer head gazing down, forever forlorn. A young waitress in high-heeled slippers came over, blowing out a gum bubble, and put a menu on the table. He wasn't hungry so he had a glass of Chardonnay, and started sipping, watching out. He saw a bald man in shirtsleeves leaning out the window above hers, with a curl of smoke rising peacefully from a pipe.

Raising his glass, he became aware of the other customers there watching him. A Chinese sitting alone in an American bar, he didn't feel comfortable. He wondered whether it was appropriate for him to sit here drinking without an appetizer. The bar was not as hilarious as in the TV show he had watched. No one said anything to him here.

He decided to think over the latest development in the Xing case. Sipping at the wine, he took out a notebook and drew several connected lines across a page. He tried to figure out what had really happened between Xing and the Beijing government.

Apparently, Beijing's agents had been working behind the scenes in the States before Chen's arrival. Xing was a calculating businessman, everything being negotiable. However sordid the bargain, it would be justified as being in the interest of the Party. After all, it was a case concerning the very top, or the very basis, of the Beijing government. Its full consequences would be comprehensible, as Comrade Zhao had suggested, only if viewed from a higher position. That was probably why Zhao had copied out that Tang poem for him.

But if so, why send Chief Inspector Chen to the United States? To get him out of the way for one or two weeks? He didn't think so. It would have been much easier to do that in China, one way or another. Nor did he believe he had been chosen for the delegation on his merit. So here was the heart of the matter. Why all the bother? To the agents working here, the presence of Chen could only prove to be obstructive.

For the first time another possibility occurred to him. He might have been dispatched for a different reason. To attract the attention of the Americans, who had long known about his law enforcement background, and to whom his last-minute delegation appointment must have appeared suspicious. Now it made sense that Party Secretary Li had talked about his investigation at a press conference—so the Americans would learn about it through the Chinese media. Then the agents could work on Xing without being noticed or discovered.

As Detective Yu had guessed from the beginning, it was a show investigation, perhaps never meant to be taken seriously. But Chen had thrown himself headlong into the role, like an earnest yet effective Don Quixote, flourishing his lance, to the annoyance of some people in the Forbidden City. First in China, then on the trip abroad. Literally following Comrade Zhao's talk about a general's free decisions, the chief inspector proved to be a serious threat to the red rats, especially through his exploration into Xing's connection with Little Tiger, leading to the very top. That had triggered the pursuit of his mother in Shanghai, and the attempt against him in St. Louis. Unfortunately, Little Huang fell instead.

Now, as for Xing's return to China, it might be another ironic casualty of misplaced yin and yang. Chen's effort here, while unpleasant to the secret agents, had brought about some surprising results. Through unforeseeable circumstances, Chen and his partners had managed to arrest Ming, which, at least on the surface, appeared to be the last straw for Xing. Chen knew better, though; far more complicated factors had been working behind the scene.

But Chen still had no clue how Xing and his associates had learned that Chen had suspicions about Little Tiger. One possibility pointed to Tian. Not that Tian would have talked to anyone, but Bao and his mysterious L.A. man knew Chen had spent an afternoon with Tian. Still, two friends' unexpected reunion wouldn't have appeared so suspicious. The fact that nothing had happened to Tian spoke for itself. Other than Tian, Catherine was the only one aware of his secret work. He didn't have to consider the possibility. Some of the most crucial information had come from her.

A more likely scenario would be that his phone discussions with Yu had been overheard. After the first few times, they had largely given up their weather terminology. A necessary yet disastrous decision. He had gambled on Yu's home line not being tapped. In one of their discussions, he had mentioned Little Tiger in the context of the Xing . . .

But then these thoughts began depressing him. There would be time enough for him to think, once back in China, about whatever he was going to do or not do, as a cop.

He rose and took a local newspaper from a rack. The waitress came to him again. He had another glass of wine. Reading rather absentmindedly, he noticed three or four grammatical mistakes in one short article. He recalled what American writers had said of his English writing.

You could be a good writer here.

Perhaps he would be able to launch a new career here. The long-faded dream of his college years, of writing whatever he wanted to, and of not worrying about politics and corruption. It wouldn't be a choice, he told himself, made out of any materialistic consideration. It might not be too late—with a wonderful friend staying in the background.

These thoughts had barely come crowding into his mind when he started to drive them out. Even in the confusion of a fleeting moment, he knew he had moved too far from the cherished vision of his college years. Like a green light he had read about long ago, already beyond his reach there and then. Or perhaps like Tian, who, with his booming business in L.A., like it or not, had found a new self with a young wife and a million-dollar mansion. Chen, too, had come to find himself more and more, ironic as it might appear, through those fatal investigations.

Besides, what about the people who had stood by him all the way?

Looking out, he tried to refocus his thoughts on her, which seemed to be the only thing that could possibly cheer him up. With so many gloomy things surrounding him, with the memory of a poet musing at such an evening, with something like a pair of ragged claws scuttling across the floor of the subconscious, however, even those self-indulgent fantasies took on a self-debunking color . . .

He suddenly felt an impulse he had not experienced for a long time. Turning to a blank page in his notebook, he started scribbling—to his surprise, in English, in a quite different strain, almost like a parody.

Shall I go, shall I go
with my Chinese accent, and a roast
Beijing duck, to her home,
when the evening is spreading out
like a gigantic invitation poster
against the clouds of doubt?

I'll go, across the Loop, where
a young girl hums a little air,
her shoulder-length golden hair flowing,

lighting the somber wall, singing.
My necktie asserted by a pin,
my alligator leather shoes shining.
(They will think: "How yellow his skin!")
What will they say—to my quoting
from Shakespeare, Donne, and Hopkins,
In short, I am not sure.
(They will say: "But how strong his accent!")

He took a gulp of his wine, as if smashed with a bizarre combination of rhythm and rhyme—in a language not really his own, and with those lines coming out of nowhere. It appeared doubtful whether they would make their way into a poem, or into anything readable. But he'd better put them down, he knew, while the inexplicable urge still clutched him.

Would it be worthwhile
to bite a Mac with a smile,
to squeeze the difference and all
into a small Ping-Pong ball,
to dream of her white teeth
nibbling at cheddar cheese,
and in a mirror, a dull toad
with a fair swan, when all is told?
Is it her red-painted toenail
that makes me so frail?
Her toes tapping on a bronze
plaque dedicated to Eliot,
in an evening breeze of songs.
Oh am I not an idiot?

Should I explain a Chinese joke
with the help of an English book—
after baseball, chips and dips
and helpless tongue slips,

after deconstructing the character "ai"
into radicals—heart, water, friend and eye,
after the pallid sleepless stress
smoothed by her golden tress
on the rug of an iron tree,
after turning on the TV
without understanding why
those players laugh and cry.
It's impossible to say
what I want to say!
What if she, kicking
off her sandals and trimming
her toenails, should say,
"That is not it at all,
that is not what I meant, at all."
Then how should I begin
to spit out all the butt-ends
of my days and ways
and how shall I pray and pay?

I should be a dragon glazed
along the wall of the praised
Forbidden City. I'm no Li Bai dreaming,
but a damned, chained
monkey gesticulating,
with the name label pinned
on the bosom of a Tang vest.
In short, I am not sure,
walking along a twilight-flooded beach.
I have seen the mermaids dancing
on TV, beyond reach,
beyond reality's pinching.
I don't think that, singing on the sea,
they will shell their tails for me.

He was shocked by the lines rising out of the unlikely moment. In his college years, he had read about surrealist poets writing automatically, as in a trance. He wondered how such a similar experience had befallen him. Perhaps he could think of a number of explanations, but he was not in an analytical mood.

Because he would never be able, he knew, to squeeze the moment into a ball, to start it rolling toward where he would like to go. Not just about what he described in those lines, but more symbolically, like Eliot. No, he was not what he had imagined himself to be—not even in those lines. It was just a moment, and then it was gone.

And it was not a long moment.

He saw a black car pull up in front of her building. A man emerged from the driver's side and opened the passenger door. She stepped out in that black dress with spaghetti straps.

The man did not go in with her, but they hugged outside the door, his hands lingering on her bare shoulders.

A long, passionate hug.

He kissed her on the cheek before moving back into the car. A shining black Jaguar. She stood on the doorstep, watching, waving her hand, until the car rolled out of sight in the growing dusk.

Chen kept watching, spellbound, like sitting in the movies.

She had been busy with the Chinese delegation for days. It was an afternoon when she had a few hours for herself. So of course she had taken care of her personal things.

It was unrealistic to imagine that a young, spirited woman like her would lead a colorless life like his. There should be a man—or men—in her life. Too absurd of him to imagine her shutting herself in after their meeting in Shanghai, as in a Tang dynasty poem—*with the fallen petals in the yard, collected too much to open the door.*

A chance encounter, like in the poem he had once read for her, memorable as the light produced out of their brief meeting, and then they had to move on, along their respective directions. In fact, they had both known it the first time, in China.

So it was this time. He really should be grateful for the unexpected second time. There was no stepping twice into the same river, but it had sort of happened to him. Different, yet nonetheless wonderful.

But for her generous help, he would have got nowhere in his investigation. Or worse, his fate could have been sealed like that of the interpreter.

She was the more realistic one. There was no future of them being together. She knew. So parting like this would be best.

Long after she had gone back into the building, he remained sitting there, against the window. He took his time sipping, after the fashion of a regular customer. The waitress put down another glass for him, and he nodded over those lines, like one really lost.

The window of her room was lit up. He pushed back his chair one or two inches farther from the window. Dimly, he could see her figure silhouetted against a scroll of traditional Chinese landscape paintings hung on the wall.

The sun is setting in the west—
how many times?
Helpless that flowers fall.
Swallows return, seemingly no strangers.

He was about to finish his last glass of wine when she came out, carrying a black plastic trash bag. Now in a white T-shirt and shorts, barefoot, she looked more like a college student. She went into a small lane next to the building. Then, emerging with the trash bag gone, she came to a stop by the mailbox at the foot of the staircase, the doorway framing her against the twilight, her face wistful. He rose from the table. She took out her cell phone.

To his surprise, his phone rang. He glanced at the number shown on the screen. It was from her. No mistake. But for some inexplicable reason, he hesitated to push the talk button.

What would she like to talk to him about? Not about the scene he had witnessed, surely. And what would he say to her?

Then the ringing abruptly stopped.

And she disappeared into the building again. The street stretched in front of the bar, like a tedious argument of ambiguous intent, again leading to an overwhelming question.

Indeed, what could be said by him? A cop who had hardly met his responsibilities, or, to say the least, who was stuck halfway in his work, with two people killed because of him, and their justice apparently beyond hope, with his investigation ordered to stop, which he accepted without a fight. No use denying the fact to himself, he contemplated. The parody of Prufrock threw unexpected light on his spineless self. After all, he was no poet like Eliot, who redeemed himself through writing about those flickering moments. Chen was but a cop beating a pathetic retreat, in spite of all the high sentences from Beijing, and the lines on the notebook did not change that fact. So how could he prove himself worth answering her call? How should he presume—

His phone rang again. He pressed the button in a hurry. "Catherine—"

"No, it's Yu."

"Oh, what's up?"

"Lei's in trouble."

"Lei?"

"Your friend at the *Shanghai Morning*. He called me, saying that you alone can help—to prove that he did nothing wrong that afternoon in the bathhouse. It's urgent, he said, and he insisted that you would understand."

Chen thought he knew why this was happening. Whatever trouble it was for Lei, it was really designed for the chief inspector. A "confession" by Lei would serve to prove Chen's "decadent bourgeois way of life." So those rats were pouncing on him. Lei might be holding on for the moment because he believed in Chen's power to intervene.

"Tell Lei to hold on for one or two days. I'm coming back. And I'll take care of it."

"You are coming back so soon, Chief?"

"Yes. And I'll have a lot to discuss with you." Chen added, thinking,

"Call Comrade Zhao about Lei's trouble. You may tell him I wanted you to make this call."

It might provide some help. Also, Comrade Zhao would explain the Beijing decision to Yu, who had not yet learned anything about the latest development. It could spare Chen the disagreeable task.

"Great. I'll do that right now. Tell you what. Peiqin has been talking about a special dinner for you."

"In celebration?"

"Not exactly. She'll explain. Old Hunter is going to join us too. He's so proud of the part he has played in breaking China's number-one corruption case. And his invention—'red rats'—has gained incredible circulation in the city. He'll bring an urn of Maiden Red he has saved for thirty years."

All that sounded wonderful. He wondered what the occasion could be. Surely it wasn't yet another dinner in honor of his return to Shanghai—in addition to the one in Comrade Zhao's hotel, with his bottle of Maotai, Chen reflected, draining the glass.

But he was still worried about Lei. It came to an ironic circle. He had first heard of the Xing case in the company of Lei, in that bathhouse, and now at the end of the case, Lei was in trouble because of his company. But how could people have learned about that afternoon in the bathhouse? The net around the chief inspector must be a phenomenally large one. Again, it might prove naïve of him to think that Comrade Zhao would step in to help. Then, did he really have a choice?

"One more thing, Chief. Jiang has booked a ticket to Canada. Through a Canadian airline."

"What's the date?"

"Early next week."

That would be before his originally scheduled return, and Jiang could change the date when he got the news that Chen was returning early.

"Hold on, Yu—are you calling from a public phone?"

"Yes, anything else?"

"I'm leaving for China tomorrow. Tomorrow evening, Shanghai time, you move ahead and arrest Jiang and Dong."

"Jiang and Dong—what about the arrest warrant?"

"Remember the authorization for my work as an emperor's special envoy with an imperial sword? Don't worry about a search or arrest warrant. Yu may act on my behalf, that's what Comrade Zhao has agreed too."

"But can we wait until you come back?"

That was a good question. Chen didn't know what would befall him upon his return. He would be relieved of his power as an emperor's special envoy, that much was certain. In a worse scenario, he wouldn't even be able to walk out of the airport as a government delegation head.

"Did you wait until I came back for the raid of the Apricot Blossom Village?"

"I thought—"

"You are a good *go* player. In a *go* game, as you know, you sometimes have to make a win-or-lose strike. I'm not sure I'll have the power to make that strike once I come back."

"Oh, so it's not time for a celebration dinner yet," Yu said. "You don't have to say any more. I'll tell Old Hunter to get ready."

"No, anybody in the special case squad will do, but don't say a word beforehand. Search their homes thoroughly. Keep whatever you find. If people question you, tell them that it's my order—under the Party Discipline Committee. I'll take full responsibility."

"Whatever responsibility, Chief, is mine too."

"Choose a couple of the pictures I gave you—without An's face, if possible, but definitely with Jiang's. Give them to Lei, along with the information about Jiang's Canadian visa. He should know what to do with them."

It was a moment of the fish dying or the net breaking. He had to take action while still in the position to do so. Comrade Zhao had emphasized a successful conclusion for the chief inspector in St. Louis, but it didn't necessarily mean his investigation of those connected to Xing in Shanghai. Thanks to the earlier limelight on Chen and his investigation, and with Lei at his side, he might be able to stir-fry it through the official media too. With the evidence in his hands—Xing's statement at the temple, and then during his phone conversation—Chen should succeed in removing Jiang and Dong from their positions. Somebody would try to intervene, but the news would have spread out. *A canoe is already carved out of the wood.* The Parthian shot by the emperor's special envoy would be seen as justified.

And it could be more than that. With luck, Yu might find more evidence, leading to further developments in the investigation. It might not get Chen too far—he told himself that he had to be realistic—but he would fight every step of the way. From the arrest of Jiang and Dong, Chen would be able, at least, to work his way to the solution of the An case, to which he had pledged himself.

Chief Inspector Chen had always been told to act in the interests of the Party, but for once, an emperor's special envoy for the Party, he believed that he didn't need to wait to be told so.

What was more important, he had been fighting this time, in spite of being blacklisted by some in the Forbidden City, in spite of knowing that his luck, like in the casino boat, was capable of changing at any minute.

And he really should consider himself lucky so far. He was not alone. But for the help from all those people, Yu, Peiqin, Old Hunter, Tian, and of course, Catherine, he would never have pulled through, and because of them, he wasn't going to quit.

Indeed, what more could he possibly have asked for?

In a way, he even had those poets on his side. Poetry could still make something happen. It was through those Prufrock-inspired lines that Chen once more made up his mind to be someone different, someone not always politic, cautious, and meticulous, someone worthy of answering her call, even across mountains and seas . . .

As he walked out of the café, he looked up to her room again. She was reaching out of the open window, looking up to the sky. She did not see him.

He saw a pale moon rising in the sky.

Several lines of Su Dongpo's came back to him in correspondence to the moment.

As people have sorrows and joys,
meeting or parting,

as the moon waxes and wanes
in clear or cloudy skies,
things may never be perfect.
May we all live long,
sharing the same fair moon,
though thousands of miles apart.

Chief Inspector Chen was ready to go back to Shanghai.